The Will of the Empress

TAMORA PIERCE

The Will of the Empress

SCHOLASTIC INC.
New York Toronto London Auckland Sydney
Mexico City New Delhi Hong Kong Buenos Aires

ISBN 0-439-44172-2

12 11 10 9 8 7 6 5 4 3 2 1 6 7 8 9 10 11/0

Printed in the U.S.A. 23

First Scholastic paperback printing, October 2006

The text type was set in Adobe Caslon

Book design by Steve Scott

Dedication

To my intelligent, talented, idealistic, imaginative,
enthusiastic fans, of all ages, of both sexes, of all
religions and races and ethnic backgrounds:
you give me hope for the present and future.
You're the reason why I love to keep doing what I do.
Nobody — but ***nobody*** — has cooler fans than I have.
Thank you so much for taking my books
into your lives.

Calendar

January	Wolf
February	Storm
March	Carp
April	Seed
May	Goose
June	Rose
July	Mead
August	Wort
September	Barley
October	Blood
November	Snow
December	Hearth

Sunsday, Moonsday, Starsday, Earthsday,

Airsday, Firesday, Watersday

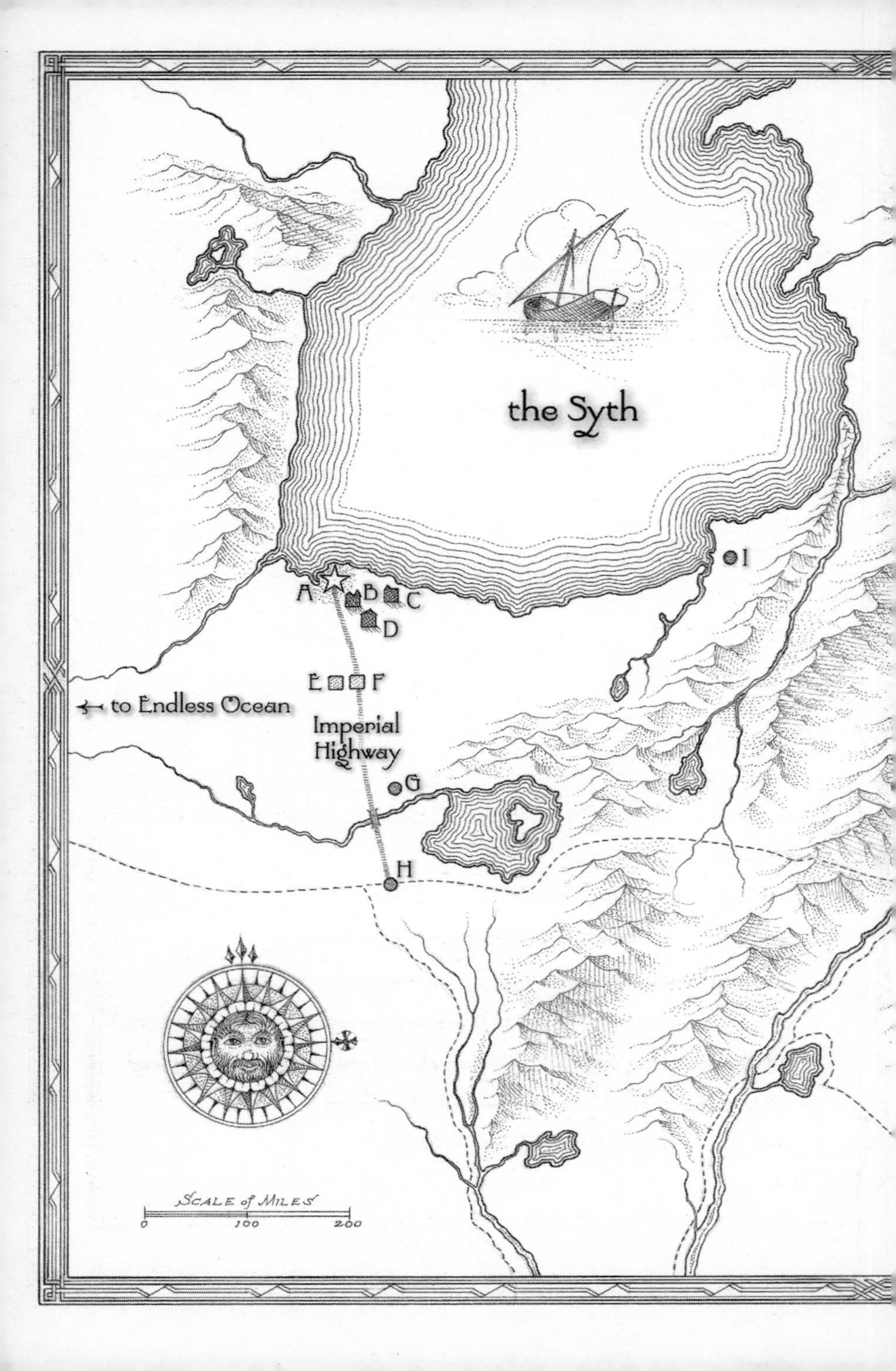
the Syth
A
B
C
D
E
F
to Endless Ocean
Imperial Highway
G
H
I
SCALE of MILES
0
100
200

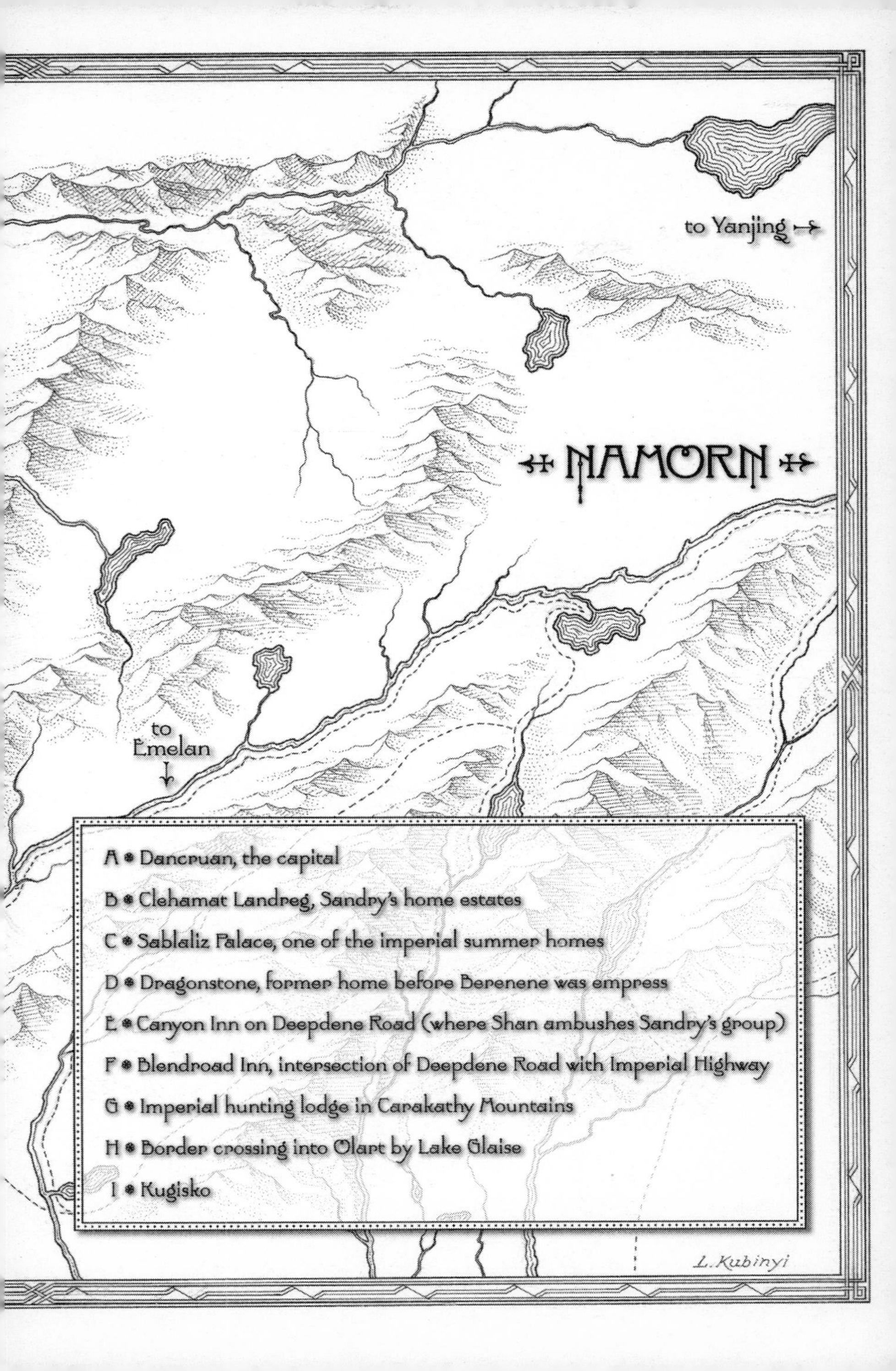

to Yanjing
NAMORN
to Emelan
A • Dancruan, the capital
B • Clehamat Landreg, Sandry's home estates
C • Sablaliz Palace, one of the imperial summer homes
D • Dragonstone, former home before Berenene was empress
E • Canyon Inn on Deepdene Road (where Shan ambushes Sandry's group)
F • Blendroad Inn, intersection of Deepdene Road with Imperial Highway
G • Imperial hunting lodge in Carakathy Mountains
H • Border crossing into Olart by Lake Glaise
I • Kugisko
L. Kubinyi

1

The 12th day of Wort Moon
The year 1041 K.F. (after the Fall of the Kurchal Empire)
In the palace of Duke's Citadel, Summersea, Emelan

Lady Sandrilene fa Toren sat in the room that was her study in her uncle's palace. In her hands she held a thread circle, one that included four lumps spaced equally apart. It was a symbol not just of her first magical working, but of the magical bond she shared with her foster-brother and two foster-sisters, who had been away from home for many months. Today was Sandry's birthday, and she missed them. Once she could have reached out through their connection without even touching the thread, and spoken with them, magic to magic, but not in the last two years. They had traveled far beyond reach, into lands and experiences Sandry couldn't share.

"Daja at least should have been here," she said, and sniffed. "She was supposed to come home a year ago. But no. She wanted to see more of Capchen, and Olart —"

Someone knocked on her door. Sandry hid the circle under a fold of her skirt. "Come in, please," she called, her voice light and courteous.

A footman entered. He carried a parcel wrapped in

oiled cloth and tied with ribbons secured by a large wax seal. "My lady, this has come for you," he said with a bow.

Sandry's mouth trembled. Her hope that the package might be from her brother or sisters evaporated at the sight of its seal. Only Ambros fer Landreg sends packages like this to me, she thought, cross. No gifts or nice, long books and letters from *him.* Only dreary old accounts from my estates in Namorn.

"Please set it here," she ordered, patting her desk. The footman obeyed and left her alone with the parcel.

Other people get to have parties and presents and outings with their friends when they turn sixteen, Sandry reflected unhappily. *I* get another fat package of dry old reports about cherry crops and mule sales from Ambros.

I'm not being fair, she told herself. I know that. I also know I don't *want* to be fair.

Wearily, she gave the thread circle a last check, pressing each lump between her thumb and forefinger. Each one stood for a friend. Each was cool to the touch. The others were too far away for their presence to even register in the circle.

Sandry tucked the thread into the pouch around her neck and hid it under her clothes. She blinked away tears as she thought, I was just fooling myself, hoping they'd be home by now.

She returned her attention to the package. Ambros probably had no idea his tedious reports would arrive today, she reminded herself in her prudent cousin's defense, propping her chin on her hand. And Uncle Vedris and Baron Erdogun gave me presents at breakfast. There's to be a get-together with my Summersea friends tonight. I'm just being petty, sulking over this, too. But really, who wants to go over crop reports and tax documents on her birthday?

With bright, cornflower blue eyes set over a button nose, she stared longingly out of the open windows. Her pale skin still bore the light bronze tint it always picked up in the summer, just as her light brown hair, neatly braided and pinned in a coronet on her head, was gilded with sun streaks. Her cheeks were still girlishly plump, but any touch of youthful shyness those cheeks gave her face was offset by her round and mulish chin. Even at sixteen, Lady Sandrilene fa Toren knew her own mind.

She was dressed simply in a loose blue summer gown of her own weaving, sewing, and design, a gown that would never show a wrinkle or stain, no matter what she had done with her day. Sandry was a thread mage, with the right to practice as an adult. She tolerated no wayward behavior in any cloth in her presence. Her stockings never dared escape their garters, any more than her gowns dared to pick up dirt. Every woven scrap in Duke's Citadel had learned the girl's power since she had come to look after her great-uncle Vedris.

The day's fading, Sandry told herself. I should do *something* before dinner besides pout.

She thrust the bulky package aside.

"Do you know, the only time I ever see you shirk your duty is when Ambros's packages arrive." While Sandry daydreamed, Duke Vedris IV had come to stand in the study's open door. He leaned there, a fleshy-faced, powerfully built man in his mid-fifties, dressed in blue summer cotton of her weaving and stitching. While his clothes were plain and his jewelry simple, there was no denying his aura of power and authority. No one would ever mistake him for a commoner. Neither would they mistake his obvious affection for the great-niece born of his wayward nephew and a wealthy young noblewoman from Namorn.

Sandry blushed. She hated for him to see her at any less than her best. "Uncle, he's so *prosy*," she explained, hearing the dreaded sound of a whine creep into her voice. "He goes on and on about bushels of rye per acre and gross lots of candles until I want to *scream*. Doesn't he understand I don't care?"

Vedris raised his brows. "But you care about the accounts for Duke's Citadel, which are just as thick with minutiae," he pointed out.

"Only so you won't," she retorted. When Vedris smiled, she had to fight a smile of her own. "You know what I mean, Uncle! If I don't stop you from worrying over every little detail, you might fret yourself into a second heart attack. At the rate Ambros goes on, *I'm* the one who will have a heart attack."

"Ah," said the duke. "So you need an altruistic reason to

take an interest, rather than the selfish one that this is your own inheritance from your mother, and your own estates."

Sandry opened her mouth to protest, then closed it. Something about that sounds like he just turned it head over heels on me, she thought. I just can't put my finger on what.

"Very well, then," Vedris continued. "I submit that by looking so conscientiously after your affairs and his own — I know he has properties in his own right — it is quite possible your cousin Ambros courts a heart attack." He straightened. "Just because your Namornese inheritance is in land, and in Namorn, is no reason for you to treat it lightly, my dear." He walked off down the hall.

Sandry put her hands up to cool her cheeks, which were hot with embarrassment. I've never gotten a scolding from him before, she thought with dismay. I don't care for it at all!

She glared at the ribbons on the package of documents. They struggled, then ripped free of the wax seal and flew apart. With a sigh, Sandry grasped the edges of the folded wrapping and began to remove it.

The 18th day of Blood Moon
The year 1041 K.F.
The Anderran/Emelan border

After several side trips following their original journey to Kugisko in Namorn, Dedicate Initiate Frostpine of

Winding Circle temple and his student Daja Kisubo finally crossed back into Emelan. Although it was late in the year, the weather still held fine. The skies were a brilliant blue without a single cloud, the breeze crisp without being cold. Daja sighed happily.

"Another week and we'll be home," she commented, turning her broad, dark face up to the sun. She was a big young woman with glossy brown skin, a wide mouth, and large, perceptive brown eyes. She wore her wiry black hair in masses of long, thin braids wrapped, coiled, and pinned at the back of her head, an elegant style that drew attention to the muscled column of her neck. Her traveling garments were light brown wool with orange patterns, sewn into a tunic and leggings in the style of her native people, the Traders. "I'll be close enough to mind-speak with Sandry any day — well, I could now, but I'd have to strain to do it, and I'd rather wait. She'll have a million questions, I know."

Frostpine grinned. He was brown like Daja, but where her build was solid, his was wiry, his muscles cables that lined his long body. He wore his hair wild around a perfectly bald crown and kept his beard in the same exuberant style. His Fire dedicate's crimson robes were every bit as travel worn as hers. "You can't blame Sandry," he pointed out. "We were supposed to be home the summer before this."

"She'd have questions anyway," Daja said comfortably. Before Sandry had moved to Duke's Citadel, she had shared a house at Winding Circle with Daja and their other foster-brother and foster-sister, Briar and Tris. "She *always* has questions. Well, she's going to have to come to Discipline for answers. I won't spend forever mind-speaking, and once I get back in my own room, I'm not coming out for a week."

Frostpine reined his horse up. "Discipline?"

Daja halted her own mount and turned to smile at her scatterbrained teacher. "Discipline cottage?" she asked, gently reminding him. "My foster-mother Lark? I live there when you're not dragging me everywhere between the Syth and the Pebbled Sea?"

Frostpine ran a big hand through his flyaway hair. "Daja, how old are you?"

She rolled her eyes. "Sixteen," she said even more patiently. "On the thirtieth of Seed Moon, the same day I mark for my birth every year."

"I should have thought of it sooner," he said mournfully. "But I swear, as I get older, the harder it gets to think. . . . Daja, Winding Circle has rules."

She waited, running a finger over the bright piece of brass that wrapped the palm and back of one hand. The metal was as warm and supple as living skin, a remnant of a forest fire, powerful magics, and Daja's ill-fated second Trader staff.

Frostpine said, "You probably know the rule already, at least for most of the temple boarding students. At sixteen, they must take vows, pay for their boarding and classes, or leave. And only those who have not attended temple school as children may attend as paying adults."

"Of course," Daja said. "There's a ceremony, and they give the residents of the dormitories papers to show they've studied at Winding Circle. But that's not for Sandry or Briar or Tris or me. We aren't temple students. We study with some temple dedicates, but not all of our teachers are temple. We live with Lark and Rosethorn at Discipline, not in the dormitories. And we're proper mages. We're — we're different."

Frostpine was shaking his head. "My dear, if you four still needed a firm education, we might be able to make a case, at least until you earned a medallion as the adult mages do," he said quietly. "But the fact is that you have your mage's medallion. As these things are measured, you were considered to be adult mages when you received them, fit to practice and to teach. Of course, you were too young to live on your own then. But now? Unless you are prepared to give your vows to the gods of the Living Circle, you will not be permitted to stay at Discipline."

Daja put her hand on the front of her tunic. Under it, hanging on a cord around her neck, was the gold medallion that proved that the wearer was a true mage, certified by Winding Circle to practice magic as an adult. She, Sandry, Tris, and Briar had agreed not to show it until they were eighteen unless they had to prove they were accredited mages. It was almost unheard-of for one thirteen-year-old to receive it, let alone four. Their teachers had been careful to let them know they had gotten it not only because they were as powerful and controlled as adults. Possession of a medallion also meant they had to answer to the laws and governing mages of Winding Circle and the university at Lightsbridge. "A leash," Briar had described it, "to prove to the law we won't run loose and pee on their bushes." Their teacher Niko had replied that his description was "crude, but accurate." Given that warning, and the fuss people made when they learned she had the medallion, Daja showed it as little as possible.

Frostpine bit his lip, then went on. "I can put you up over my forge for a week or two, but after that they'll make a fuss. You should be able to stay with Lark for a couple of nights, but she does have at least one new student living with her. Perhaps you could go to Sandry's?"

Daja was a smith, with intense bonds to fire, but for all that, she was normally slow to anger. Something in what he had said lit the tiniest of sparks. I don't know if he realizes it sounds like he wants me out of the way, she thought, heat tingling in her cheeks. Or like I can throw myself on my foster-sister's charity. Of course he didn't *mean* it to sound as if he wants me out of the way. Even if we *have* been living in each other's pockets for longer than we'd first expected to. We didn't intend to stay so long in Olart, or Capchen, or Anderran. We didn't plan to spend a whole extra year and a half away after Namorn.

"Daja?" Frostpine asked hesitantly.

I can't look at him, she thought. I don't want to cry. I feel all . . . lost. Funny.

"We should get moving," she said, nudging her horse into motion. The sky remained cloudless, but now the day felt gray. Her eagerness to go back had faded.

"Daja, please talk to me," Frostpine said. "You can stay with me or with Sandry. Frankly, I had expected you would want a house, perhaps even a forge, of your own, since you're of age. Certainly you can afford it. *You* haven't taken vows of poverty."

He's smiling at me — I can hear it in his voice, she thought. I should smile back, not worry him. But I feel empty. Lost, like when the Traders declared me outcast because I was the only survivor of that shipwreck. Why didn't Sandry warn me, all those letters she's been writing? She babbled of the duke's health and something or other Lark wove or she embroidered, but wrote no word of not being able to return to Discipline. Of course not. She has *family*. The duke, and her cousins in Namorn. But me . . . I'm cast out of my home. If I don't have Winding Circle, what do I have?

Briar and Tris will be in the same basket when they come home, Daja realized. They'll be outcasts, too.

I suppose my lady Sandrilene thought we'd be happy to live as poor relatives. She doesn't know what it's like, always being on the edge of homelessness. She'll expect us to be one cozy little family again, only living on her money, until she marries, or His Grace dies. . . . And I'll be left with no home again.

Daja shook her head. It was all a mess, one she didn't want to discuss.

She forced herself to smile at Frostpine. "Where do we stop tonight?" she asked. "Let's worry about the other business when we're closer to Emelan, all right?"

The 26th day of Blood Moon
The year 1041 K.F.
Summersea, Emelan

The first visitor to the house and forge at Number 6 Cheeseman Street was Sandry. Daja could feel her nearness through the magical connection they shared, though Daja's heart had been in such turmoil that she had refused to open that connection to speak to her foster-sister. Now, feeling both apprehensive and angry, she waited for the housemaid to show Sandry into her study.

Sandry thanked the maid and waited for her to leave before she turned on Daja. "I have to learn from your *teacher* that not only have you been in Emelan two weeks, but you went and bought a house of your own?"

Daja scowled at the shorter girl. "Spare me the ballads," she replied. "You knew very well I was close. I could hardly sleep for you bothering me to open my mind."

"Why didn't you let me in? Why didn't you tell me anything?" cried Sandry.

Daja had bottled up her feelings since Frostpine had said that the home she looked forward to was home no longer. During the ride to Winding Circle and her reunion with her foster-mother Lark and her temple friends, Daja had shown a smooth and smiling face. She had quietly found a Summersea house with a smith's forge already attached, then picked out furnishings so she could move in as soon as possible. To everyone — merchants, dedicates, the old smith whose home she had bought, her new servants — she had pretended that setting up her own household was just what she had in mind.

She was tired of pretending. "Tell you that I was being cast out of Winding Circle because I no longer fit?" she asked quietly. "Tell you so you might offer me charity, or so His Grace might offer me charity? How long until *that* charity ran out, and I was left on my own again, Sandry? First I lose my family, then the Traders, then Winding Circle. I need my own place. A home no one can take from me."

Sandry's lips trembled. "So you cast *me* out. You said I was your *saati*." A *saati* was a true friend of the heart, someone who was trusted without reserve. "I thought the friendship of *saatis* lasted forever."

"But first I need to heal. I can't have you picking and prying and worrying inside my mind," Daja said, her face and voice still under control. "I need to tend to myself." Her voice rose slightly. "You didn't even warn me. You've been to Discipline. Did anyone ever say, well, you're sixteen, you can't move back here even if you wish?"

Sandry's chin trembled. "I thought you'd want to live with Uncle and me. I thought we'd *all* be happy to live at Duke's Citadel."

"He's not getting any younger," Daja said cruelly. "One day he'll die and then his heir will kick us out. No, thanks. Now I have it. As long as I have it, Briar and Tris and even you will have a home nobody can make us leave."

Sandry sniffed, then defiantly blew her nose on a handkerchief. "Couldn't *you* throw *us* out?" she demanded angrily.

"No more than I could break that precious thread circle you made when you spun the four of us into one," Daja said. "You know, sometimes I wish that earthquake had never happened. That you'd never had to spin us together to make us stronger. Maybe I wouldn't hurt so much now if I hadn't expected you to know me as well as *I* know me. If I hadn't expected you to know how awful it would feel to lose Discipline cottage!"

"So you punish me by not letting me into your mind. Fine," Sandry retorted. "Sulk. Never mind that you three all left me here —"

"You *said* we should travel!" Daja reminded her. "You *said* we ought to go!"

"You never once stopped to ask if I didn't just say it because you all wanted to go so badly!" Sandry balled her hands into fists. "Not one of you even suggested it wasn't fair that you *all* go. You just said, oh, good, thanks, Sandry old girl, we'll bring you presents from abroad, and off you went. Well, fine! Welcome home, keep your presents, and if you want to talk, you can do it by letter, or in person. You're not the only one who can shut people out, you know!" She turned on her heel to make a grand exit, then hesitated, and turned around again. "And Uncle invites you to supper tomorrow night at six."

Daja blinked, startled at the abrupt turn in the conversation, then nodded.

"Fine!" Sandry cried, and walked out.

Daja rubbed her temples. Welcome home, she thought wearily. Everything's changed, you just upset your sister-*saati*, nothing feels right, welcome home.

The 1st day of Rose Moon, 1042 K.F.
Number 6 Cheeseman Street
Summersea, Emelan

Trisana Chandler's head still ached as she followed the cart that held her luggage down Cheeseman Street. She had spent a hard few days since her return home. Turning her very young student, Glaki, over to Tris's foster-mother Lark for a proper rearing at Winding Circle had been hard. Tris would never admit it, but she was deeply touched by Glaki's tears when she learned that Tris could only visit, not live with, her. It had also hurt to leave her dog, Little Bear, with Glaki and Lark. Tris and Little Bear had been Glaki's family since the child's mother died — it would have been cruel to take away both, and Tris knew it. At least Glaki had adjusted to the loss of Tris's teacher. Niko had interacted with Glaki when necessary, but it was Tris and Little Bear who had played with her, washed her, heard her lessons, and borne the results when Glaki's first magic lessons did not go as planned.

Tris would have found those adjustments hard enough. She had prepared for them all the way home. What she had not prepared for was the effect of a busy harbor city and a busy temple city on her ability to read images carried on the wind. When she had started out to learn it, Tris had been lucky to see any vision for more than a blink of an eye. In the two years of study she had put into it, Tris had only improved the clarity and duration of the images slightly, averaging one or two images per trial. Over the long weeks of her voyage north, constant practice and fewer images to sort through had left Tris open. A flood of far sharper visions assaulted her as their vessel entered Summersea harbor. She had felt the kiss of the ship against the dock while she vomited over the rail. Glaki and the dog had to help her off. Now Tris walked behind the luggage cart, using it as a wind and image barrier, to keep her unhappy stomach from rebelling anymore.

Tris did not look like someone who had already mastered magics that had defeated older, more experienced mages. A short, plump redhead, Tris wore a variety of braids coiled in a heavy silk net pinned at the back of her head. Only two thin braids were allowed to swing free, framing a face that was sharp-featured, long-nosed, and obstinate. Next to her hair, her storm gray eyes were her most attractive feature. Today she hid them behind dark blue tinted spectacles that cut the flood of pictures riding every draft. She was pale-skinned and lightly freckled, dressed for summer in a gray gown and dusty, well-worn boots. On her shoulder rode some kind of glass creature that sat on its hind feet, one delicate forepaw clutching one of her braids.

"Don't hold on so tight," Tris told the creature in a whispered croak. Her throat was raw from constant nausea. It had taken her three days in bed to keep her improved magical skill from making her sick. "They'll love you. Everyone loves you. At least, they'll love you if you don't go around eating their expensive powders and things."

The glass creature unfolded shimmering wings to balance, revealing itself to be a glass dragon. It voiced a chinking sound like the ring of pure crystal.

"No, you hardly ever mean it," replied Tris. While she couldn't exactly understand the creature she had named Chime, they'd had this conversation before. "But you always eat anything that looks like it might color your flames, and then you vomit most of it up."

Though the luggage driver turned the cart through the gate of Number 6, Tris lagged behind, feeling anxious about seeing her sisters again. Just remember all those southern mages who found out I could see a little, or hear a little, on the winds, she reminded herself. How they acted as if I had stolen something from them — as if I *would* steal! How they kept saying I thought myself better than them, when I was trying not to throw up from the headaches. How they started hiding their notes and closing their doors as I came by. Do I want Sandry and Daja to change like that on me? Do I want them deciding I think I'm better than they are, just because I can do a special trick?

It wasn't so bad when I started out, she thought, forcing herself to go through that gate. When people didn't know. But then it got out that time I knew Glaki had fallen and broken her arm. After that they all decided I was going to lord it over them.

She looked at the house. Two young women, one black, one white, were coming toward her. One was in a smith's apron; one was dressed like a noble. Both were wearing smiles as uncertain as the one on Tris's mouth. Tris halted, frowning. For a moment these two were strangers, smooth and polished creatures who moved as if they were sure of themselves. Behind them stood a three-story house with neatly planted garden strips in front, good ironwork around the windows, and sturdy outbuildings to either side. Even the location was expensive.

They look like the world is theirs, she thought bleakly, rocking back on the worn heels of her boots. And isn't it? Daja could afford this house, from all her work in living metal. Sandry's rich. When Briar comes back — if he comes back — he'll be rich, too, from working with miniature trees. I'm the poor one. I'll never belong here like they do.

"I'll be your housekeeper, Daja," she said abruptly. "Not a charity case. I'll earn my keep."

Sandry and Daja looked at each other. Suddenly they — and the look of exasperation they shared — were very familiar.

"Same old Tris," they chorused.

Tris scowled. "I mean it."

Sandry came forward to kiss Tris's cheek. "We know. Oh, dear — you're clammy. And your color's dreadful. Lark wrote you've been ill. Come —" Her blue eyes flew wide open as Chime stood up on Tris's shoulder and made a sound of glass grating on glass.

"Hello, beautiful," said Daja, holding out both hands. "You must be Chime."

The glass dragon glided over to land in Daja's hands.

"Traitor," grumbled Tris. She let Sandry wrap an arm around her shoulders. "Actually, I would feel better for some tea," she admitted.

Daja led the way indoors, cooing admiration of Chime.

The 25th day of Storm Moon, 1043 K.F.
Discipline cottage
Winding Circle temple, Emelan

At first Briar Moss's homecoming was grand. Lark worked her welcoming magic on all of them, erasing lines from Rosethorn's face that Briar had thought would never go away, and making Evvy feel as welcome as if she were Lark's own daughter. Lark barely hesitated on meeting Evvy's strange friend Luvo before she found him the ideal place to sit and watch them all. Briar she saluted, letting him know that he had finally brought them all home safe. At that moment it didn't seem to matter that Tris had left a new student with Lark, or that another student, a fellow so shy he didn't want to share the attic with anyone, lived upstairs. All that mattered to Briar was that he was safe at Discipline, that Little Bear still remembered him, that Rosethorn seemed more like her old self than she'd been since they'd reached the far east. Even the sight of temple habits — Earth green here at Discipline; Fire red, Air yellow, Water blue, novice white on the spiral road — didn't rattle him. This was Emelan, not Gyongxe. Outside the walls he could hear the crash of the sea in the cove and the cry of gulls overhead. Briar was home, and safe.

The first problem came when Rosethorn told him that he could sleep in her room for his few nights at Discipline.

She would stay with Lark for the present. The child Glaki had Briar's old room. There was no question of sharing the attic with the ferociously shy Comas. It felt strange, lying down in Rosethorn's small, neat chamber, but it was only temporary. Since they picked up Sandry's letter when they made port in Hatar, Briar had known that things had changed. It was just as well, he'd thought then. He couldn't live as he did these days in a small temple cottage, under Lark and Rosethorn's far-too-perceptive eyes.

Rosethorn's bed was just not comfortable. It was a dedicate's hard cot, not luxurious by anyone's standard, but Briar was not used to even its mite of softness. With mental apologies to Rosethorn, and a promise to restore the room later, Briar moved the pallet to the floor. That was better, but when had Discipline gotten so noisy? The attic floor creaked — was that fellow up there *rolling* to and fro? Briar couldn't remember if the clock in the Hub tower had ever woken him before. Then he could swear he could hear the dog snoring from Glaki's room.

It was also stuffy. Who could breathe in here?

At last he found his bedroll and crept out the back door, into the garden. It was cold, for Emelan, wintertime around the Pebbled Sea, but Briar's roll was made for Gyongxe winters. It was more than adequate for a night without rain, even in Storm Moon. He laid it out on the garden path and slid between the covers, plants and vines in full slumber all around him. He was asleep the moment he pulled the blankets up around his chin.

He heard the chime of temple bells, summoning Earth temple dedicates to the midnight services that honored their gods. As he fell back into his dreams, flames roared up around him, throwing nightmare shadows on his eyelids. In the distance, triumphant warriors shouted and people shrieked. The wind carried the scent of blood and smoke to his nostrils.

Burning carpets wrapped around him. Briar fought to get free while boulders shot from catapults smashed temple walls to rubble.

Briar gasped and sat up. Sweat poured over his face, stinging in his eyes. He'd ripped his bedroll apart in his struggles, flinging blankets into the winter garden. Shuddering, he gulped in lungfuls of cold air, trying to cleanse his nose and throat of the lingering reek of burning wood and bodies. As his head cleared, he drew up his knees and wrapped his arms around them. Resting his face against his legs, he began to cry.

"It was the bell for services, wasn't it?" Rosethorn was hunkered down close by, a shadow among shadows. She spoke with a trace of a slur.

Briar scrubbed his face on his knees before he looked up. "Bells?" he asked.

Rosethorn had her own share of bad dreams from the last two years. "You slept fine on the ship, with hardly any nightmares. But now you're in temple walls, surrounded by temple sounds, including the calls to midnight service. It started the dreams again. You won't even be able to stay here a few days, will you?"

If she was anyone else, maybe I'd lie, Briar thought. But she was there. She knows. "I jump just seeing all the different color robes," he said wearily. "Doesn't matter that the folk here are different races for the most part. We even use the same kind of incense they did back there." He shrugged. "Evvy will be all right," he said. "Once the stone mages here start teaching her, she'll be busy. And I'll be around." Briar sighed. "So I'll tell her when she gets up. I'll see tomorrow if Daja's got room for me."

Rosethorn got to her feet with a wince and offered Briar a hand. "I doubt that Daja would write to say she has a floor of the house opening onto the garden set aside for you if she didn't mean for you to live there," she said dryly as she helped him to his feet. "And Briar, if the dreams don't stop, you should see a soul-healer about them."

Briar shrugged impatiently and picked up his things. "They're just *dreams*, Rosethorn."

"But you see and hear things sometimes, and smell things that aren't there. You're jumpy and irritable," Rosethorn pointed out.

When Briar glared at her, she shrugged, too. "I'm the same. I don't mean to put it off. Terrible events have long-lasting effects, boy. They can poison our lives."

"I won't let them," Briar said, his voice harsh. "That's one victory the Yanjing emperor *don't* get."

Folding blankets over her arm, Rosethorn looked at him. "There's something I don't understand," she remarked abruptly. "We're having a perfectly clear conversation right now. Before we journeyed east, if I wanted to talk to you, I would have to slip every word in between five or six from the girls in your mind. The four of you were always talking." She tapped her forehead with a finger to indicate what she meant. "Now, all your attention is right here. And another thing. Why weren't they on our doorstep the moment we came home? Tris and Daja are back; Lark said as much. Did you tell them not to come? You aren't the only one who would like to see them, you know."

"I'm not speaking with them," Briar muttered, avoiding her gaze. "Not in my mind. I didn't tell them we're coming, or we're here."

Rosethorn's eyebrows snapped together. "You haven't linked back up with the girls? In Mila's name, why not? They could help you so much better than I can!"

Briar stared at her. Had Rosethorn run mad? "*Help* me? Boo-hoo and wail and drape themselves all over me and treat me as if I was a refugee, more like!" he said tartly. "Want me to *talk* about it, like talking pays for anything, and cuddle me, and cosset me!"

Rosethorn's delicate mouth curled in her familiar sarcastic curve. "Did some imperial Yanjing brute knock you on the head ten or twelve times?" she wanted to know. "That doesn't sound like *our* girls. If you've shut them out for that reason, boy, you took more of a beating than I guessed."

Briar hung his head and ground his teeth. Why does Rosethorn always have to cut through any smoke screen I put up? he asked himself. It's unnatural, the way she knows my mind. He steeled himself to say the truth: "I don't want them in my mind, seeing what I saw. Hearing what I heard, smelling . . . I don't want them knowing the things I did." Sure of Rosethorn's next objection, he quickly added, "And I don't know if I can hide that away from them once they get in. It's everywhere, Rosethorn. All that mess. My head's a charnel house. I have no way of cleaning it up yet."

To his surprise, Rosethorn had no answer to that but to hug him tight, blankets and all. After a moment's hesitation, he hugged her back. With Rosethorn, hugging was all right. She had been in Gyongxe, too.

The 26th day of Storm Moon, 1043 K.F.
Market Street to Number 6 Cheeseman Street
Summersea, Emelan

As a way to build up her defenses against being overwhelmed by sights on the wind, Tris had begun to journey farther afield in her marketing, controlling the drafts that touched her face and the images she chose to inspect. On this day she had offered to go to Rainen Alley to buy Daja's metal polish. It meant she would take Market Street on the way home, spending three blocks on a direct line with the East Gate, able to catch whatever wind came through.

She had barely stepped into that wind when it showered her with pictures. She walked along, discarding or ignoring most as useless, dull, or meaningless, until a solid one gleaming with the silver fire of pure magic brought her to a complete halt.

A young man five feet nine inches tall walked through the slums beyond the East Gate, leading a pack-laden donkey. Atop its more usual burdens the donkey carried boxes with an assortment of *shakkans*, or miniature trees. The young man was a handsome fellow with bronze skin, broad shoulders, and glossy black hair that he wore cropped an inch long. His eyes were gray-green, turning darker green as he returned the admiring glances of the women who passed him by. Those eyes were set over a thin blade of a nose, a sensitive mouth, and a firm chin. He wore a Yanjing-style round-collared coat and leggings in tree green, and rough leather boots with fleece linings. A closer examination revealed what looked like flower tattoos covering his hands. Very close examination showed that the flowers lay under the young man's skin and nails. They also moved, grew, put out leaves, and blossomed.

Tris immediately changed course. If she hurried, she

could have a batch of Briar's favorite spice cookies in the oven when he reached the house.

That night Tris set the dining room table for four. Daja walked in as Tris laid out plates of olives and warm, fresh bread.

"What, no wine?" asked Daja. She was still wet from scrubbing her face and hands after a day at the forge. She carried the tang of hot metal around her like perfume.

Tris raised nearly invisible eyebrows. In here, with more control and fewer drafts, she wore her clear spectacles. "You drink it?" she asked, skeptical. "You never did before."

Daja shrugged. "I just thought, you being all fancy with fresh bread . . ." She peered inside one pitcher, nodded, and poured out cider for herself. "No, you know wine meddles with my magic. But maybe Briar can drink it."

"Maybe time runs backwards," Tris called over her shoulder as she went back into the kitchen. With practiced skill she collected the roasted chicken stuffed with dried fruits, a plate of cheese pastries shaped like small pots, and a bowl of leeks cooked with eggs. The foods had all been among Briar's favorites when the four had lived at Discipline.

It seemed Daja had remembered Briar's fondness for pomegranate juice, since she had filled his cup with that. "Hakkoi pound it, do you want us to roll away from the table?" she asked, amused, as Tris set down the food.

Tris scowled at her. "He's too skinny, if you didn't notice," she said tartly. "What was he eating all this time, leaves?"

"No, there were some grubs, too." Briar leaned against the door, watching Tris. "Daj', what, you're too cheap to hire a cook?"

Tris stuck her tongue out at him — as if she would let a hired cook fix his favorite dishes! — and returned to the kitchen. Going to answer a knock on the door she heard Daja say, "My cook left three days after Tris moved in. I have a kitchen maid who helps during the day, and I'll need to hire a second housemaid. Whom you're under strict orders not to frighten," she called after Tris.

"Not if she does the work right," muttered Tris. She opened the kitchen door to find Sandry, wrapped in an oiled cloak against icy rain. "Why couldn't you come in the front like a civilized person?" Tris asked as she let the other girl in. "And wipe your feet. Don't tell me you walked from Duke's Citadel."

"No, but your manservant's showing my guards where to stable the horses, and this was easier," Sandry replied quietly. She let Tris take her cloak and hat. "Is he here? I thought so, but he's closing me out, just like you and Daja."

"And you're wide open, are you?" Tris asked, hanging the dripping clothes on pegs. "Yes, he's here. And my supper is getting cold."

Sandry turned up her small nose and sniffed the air. "I smell fresh bread," she said happily. "Have you headache tea? I've been reading dull old reports from Namorn all day."

"I'll make you a cup. Go say hello to him," Tris urged.

"How could you be doing reports? No mail comes from Namorn this time of year."

"Uncle suggested it. He thinks it's wise to do a review of the last three or four years all at once, to see what's changed. I know he's right, it's just so tedious."

"I thought it was you," said Daja from the doorway. "Didn't you come here to say hello to our boy, not talk about reports?"

Sandry looked past her and saw Briar. "Oh, you're so *thin*," she said mournfully, and walked past Daja with her arms held out.

Tris poured the tea water, noticing that her hand on the grip of the pot trembled. It's all wrong, she told herself. We should be in Discipline, with the kitchen and the table all in one room, and Lark and Rosethorn . . . Stop it! she ordered herself tartly. She put down the teapot and slid her fingers behind her spectacles to wipe away tears. When she could see again, Daja had taken charge of the teapot.

"Things change," Daja said softly. "We change with them. We sail before the wind. We become adults. As adults, we keep our minds and our secrets hidden, and our wounds. It's safer."

2

The 29th day of Carp Moon, 1043 K.F.
Number 6 Cheeseman Street
Summersea, Emelan

Duke Vedris, riding into the courtyard followed by his guards, was dismounting when he heard Daja's familiar voice raised in a bellow. "*Tris!* That little flying glass monster of yours just stole fish roe pearls!"

A moment later the duke heard Briar shout, "Tris! Tell this creature it cannot roost in my *shakkans*! Lakik's teeth, I'd have her guts for string if she had guts!"

From the top of the house, booming on a mad swirl of wind, they heard Tris yell, "I'm *meditating* up here!"

The duke looked at the sergeant of his guard. "Did you know that the magical rune for discord is the combination of the rune for house and two runes for mage?"

The woman grinned. "I wonder what it would be for a house with three mages?"

"Number 6 Cheeseman Street," murmured one of the other guards.

The shutters on a third-floor window slammed open,

and a red head poked out. "Mila's blessings! One moment, Your Grace!" Tris called. The shutters closed with a snap.

"Your Grace is lucky," said the guard who had just spoken. "That one likes you. It could be so much worse for us all if she didn't."

The duke frowned briefly at the man. "Tris is sharp-tempered, it's true, but she is a good friend to those in need."

The man bowed his head. "Yes, Your Grace."

Within minutes a manservant had taken charge of the guards and the horses and Tris had settled the duke in the sitting room. "I'd like to speak with the three of you, if I may?" asked Vedris when she had served him tea. "I know you're busy, but I have a rather large favor to ask."

Tris curtsied, blushing slightly. "Of course, Your Grace," she said. "The others are on their way. They just need to tidy up."

He smiled at her. He had long known that the younger Tris had admired him, as a young girl would admire a polished older man who talked of books with her. From the color on her cheeks it seemed that some of her old feeling still remained. "Did you summon them from here?" he asked. "Sandry told me you had all closed your connections to one another."

Tris's blush deepened. "I sent the maid. We're not who we were, Your Grace," she explained. "Would you like it if Sandry walked freely in your mind, among all the things you have been and done?"

"Shurri Firesword, I would not!" The very thought gave Vedris gooseflesh.

"They say travel gives you a world of experiences." Briar came in, still drying his hands. "Well, I have plenty of experiences I wouldn't share with my worst enemy."

Vedris raised his eyebrows. "Not even with the girls, who understand you best?" he asked mildly.

Briar grinned. "*Particularly* not with the girls."

"I know about the cookmaid," Tris muttered. "You're lucky she's too silly to think you're serious."

"What are you worried about?" snapped Briar. "I make sure any girl I go walking with knows I'm not serious."

"Walking?" asked Daja. She entered the room and kissed the duke on the cheek before she looked at Briar and raised an eyebrow. "Is that what you call it?"

Vedris saw that all three of the young mages frowned, despite their jokes. The discord Sandry had told him about still continued, it seemed. "Please spare me what *any* of you call it," Vedris said delicately. At the sound of his voice, they all looked at him. Briar grinned and shrugged, taking a chair. Daja followed suit, while Tris poured out tea for the others.

As she did so, Chime sailed into the room on wide-spread wings. She dropped the bag of tiny, fish roe pearls in Daja's lap — one pearl floated in her glass body where a real creature's stomach would be — and continued on to settle gracefully on the duke's shoulder. Emitting the musical glass croon that was her purr, Chime rested her head against Vedris's cheek.

"Like any beautiful creature, you live for worship," he said affectionately as he stroked her neck with one finger. They had met on Tris's first visit to Duke's Citadel after her return home. Vedris never tired of looking at Chime. "I brought you something that will agree with you much better than pearls." Reaching into his belt purse, he brought out a small packet of parchment and opened it on his silk-clad knee. A small pile of gold dust lay inside it.

"You spoil her, Your Grace," Tris said as Chime walked once around the duke's neck, purring, before she walked down his chest to the offered treat. Neatly she began to eat the gold dust as if it were grain. Despite their earlier anger with her, Daja and Briar watched, fascinated, as the dust flowed in a ribbon down Chime's clear gullet.

Once Chime had finished, she flew to the window seat and curled up on a cushion to nap. Tris settled next to her.

Vedris folded up the empty parchment, satisfied that the interlude with Chime had relaxed these three prickly young adults. "I understand that I am about to ask a great deal. I am certain that you three have had your fill of travel. However, I have been presented with a . . . situation. You are aware that Sandrilene inherited considerable estates from her mother in the empire of Namorn."

"One of her mother's cousins administers them for her," said Tris.

"And she's a *clehame* — what they call a countess — from her mother's inheritance there," added Daja. "The women inherit titles on their own in Namorn."

"But even without all that, she's still awful rich." Briar was watching vines move around the deep scars on one of his palms. "From all the investing and things she does here."

"Yes, but she has neglected the Namornese side of her affairs. In part the fault is mine," confessed the duke. "We have tried to play down Sandrilene's financial situation, your teachers and I. Her magical abilities seemed more important at first. You know what the world is like. Heiresses are normally pawns, unable to live their own lives or to make their own decisions. It is not a life that Sandrilene would enjoy. Here, we have protected her from that.

"But in protecting her, we also kept her from doing her duty to those for whom she is responsible in Namorn," Vedris continued. "The people on her lands, who farm them and reap the profits for her to live on. Her cousin Ambros has looked after her interests for all of these years, managing them as well as his own lands. I know that it was wrong to encourage Sandrilene to stay here when she has responsibilities elsewhere. Berenene, the empress of Namorn, is also a kinswoman of Sandrilene's. She has expressed . . . displeasure that I made no effort to force Sandrilene to go to her Namornese family."

Briar tapped a flower on one knuckle, turning it from

yellow to blue. "Your Grace, her displeasure — was it military, or money?"

Vedris chuckled. "I have truly missed you three. It is so agreeable to be understood. The threats have been financial. If Sandrilene were to remain in Emelan much longer, Namorn might find other sources of saffron and copper. Certain goods that pass through Emelan would be more highly taxed in Namorn. Those who pay those taxes would be told it would cost less to ship their goods through other countries. Debts owed to banks in Emelan would be repaid more slowly, or frozen. Last year, interest paid on Emelan's loans to the Namornese empire never reached our banks. Her Imperial Majesty has indicated to me that there are ways to make our friendly relations even *less* friendly."

Briar leaned over and spat in the empty hearth. "Imperial language," he said, his voice quiet but savage. "Imperial double-talk. They speak pretty and sharpen their knives. The Yanjing emperor is just as bad."

"Then he and the empress must have a wonderful time together," remarked Daja casually. "They've been at war off and on for eight years."

"It is the language of diplomacy," said the duke. "I use it myself."

"I'll venture a guess," said Daja, tugging her lower lip. "Sandry found out about the blackmail."

Nodding, the duke said, "My seneschal let it slip.

Sandrilene was quite outraged. She insists on making that visit to Namorn, to satisfy the imperial request so that Emelan — that our people — are no longer way inconvenienced on her account." Vedris leaned forward, bracing his elbows on his knees. Here comes the difficult part, particularly in light of what I heard on my arrival, he thought. "My next step is troublesome. If I send guards, it would be perceived as an insult. As a suggestion that I do not trust Sandrilene's relatives to care for her, that I fear for her safety within the empire. A very few guards would not be taken as an insult, but they would be too few to help her, should she need help."

He stopped to sip his tea and sample one of the pistachio crescent cookies, biding his time. They would guess what he wanted, but they would also want him to say it aloud. They wouldn't want to seem childishly eager or interested in front of each other. Inwardly, the duke sighed. He liked them all, and hated to see them unhappy. Daja's homecoming had been a bitter experience, and remained so. Tris had run into the kind of professional jealousy that adults found hard to deal with. Both girls had confided a little to him in their Citadel visits, even if they could not talk about those things with Sandry. He had not spoken much with Briar, but he had with Rosethorn. He had also seen that same haunted look of Briar's in the eyes of countless soldiers and sailors who had survived battle. Vedris hoped that if he could persuade all three of them to help with his plan, it might heal some of their wounds. The difficulty was that they had never been easy to persuade.

"I would be easier in my mind if one, or two, or even all three of you were to go with Sandry," he admitted. "Empress Berenene has great mages at her command, but they are all academic mages, drawing their power from themselves and channeling it through learned rites and spells. In my experience, academic mages underestimate ambient mages like you, who draw your power from your surroundings."

Briar snorted. "You bet they do," he muttered scornfully.

The duke continued. "They will not expect you to be formidable guards for her. Moreover, you three have lived with more facets of the adult world than Sandrilene has. Daja, I understand that you may feel you have not completely made this place your home, and I shall not hold it against you, should you refuse me. Tris, I know you have plans to attend Lightsbridge next spring —"

"Lightsbridge!" chorused Briar and Daja. The university at Lightsbridge was the rival school of magecraft to Winding Circle. It was a citadel of learning, particularly for academic mages, as Winding Circle tended to specialize in ambient ones. Apparently, thought Vedris, Tris had not shared her plans with her housemates.

"You've got your mage medallion," added Briar. "You don't need Lightsbridge!"

Tris scowled. "I do if I need a license to practice

plain street magic," she informed him. "Talismans, charms, potions — that kind of thing. Don't you understand how much people *resent* us for having medallions? People don't even usually have a license at eighteen, let alone a medallion. Well, I mean to study at Lightsbridge under another name, an *ordinary* name, so I can get an *ordinary* license, so I can earn my living as an *ordinary* mage!"

"You're going to lie about who you are?" asked Daja, shocked.

"Niko's set it up for me," Tris said shortly, naming her teacher. "I'm going to do it, and that's final. Unless . . ." She looked at Vedris uncertainly.

"After this summer you will be free again to do as you please," the duke reassured her. "Either Sandrilene will return home, or . . ." He looked at his hands. He did not want to speak the possibility aloud, but he owed his young friends honesty. "Sandrilene may feel that her duty requires her to remain in Namorn. In that case, I hope you would feel yourselves under no further obligation, and return to your own lives." He looked at Briar. "I am *most* reluctant to ask you, of course. You have come home so recently. I will understand if you refuse. But — forgive me for saying it — Empress Berenene is a famed amateur gardener. With your own reputation having spread in the time you have been away, I suspect she will be quick to admit you above all to her inner circle."

"Does Sandry speak Namornese?" Daja wanted to know.

Vedris felt hope stir in his chest. "I suspect it is quite rusty. I know Ambros fer Landreg's reports are in Namornese, so she reads it well."

Daja nodded. "But I speak it." She smoothed one hand over the metal that coated the other. "You're really worried, aren't you, Your Grace?"

"I know that Sandrilene is capable of extraordinary feats. And they will think the less of her because her magic works through thread," Vedris replied. "But she is only one mage, and there are ways to deal with mages. She is extraordinarily wealthy in Namorn — I don't believe you know to what extent. Heiresses are always in great demand. Empress Berenene is a powerful woman who has made it clear that she thinks Sandrilene belongs in her court. Few people tell Her Imperial Majesty no."

Briar smirked. "Sandry will. Sandry tells everyone no, sooner or later."

Daja grinned; Tris smiled.

Vedris put down his teacup. "I know you will need time to consider it."

Tris stared into the distance. "At least Daja and I should go. Two of us will be harder to distract than one."

Briar made a face. "You need me, too," he said. "In case all those hot-blooded Namornese noblemen make you girls addled."

"I have yet to be *addled* by any man, Briar Moss," said

Daja. "Believe me, a few have tried. Dazed a little, but only because they reminded me of you. I had hoped you were one of a kind."

"You'll come?" asked Tris, startled.

"You aren't the only one who owes His Grace," Briar informed her. He looked at the duke. "Sir, even if Sandry weren't our sister, you helped us along a lot, the four years we lived at Discipline. It would be an honor to ease your mind."

The duke sighed with relief. He hadn't been sure all of them would be willing, particularly not when they were at odds. "Getting to Namorn will be easy," he said. "Third Caravan Saralan is here, and will leave for Namorn on the tenth day of Seed Moon. Their guards will protect you on the road. I will cover all of your expenses, and I consider myself to be deeply in your debt." He smiled at them. "Thank you. I feel more comfortable with this than I have felt since Sandrilene told me she would go."

The next morning Sandry arrived with her guards and a cart piled with bolts of cloth. Since Tris had gone to do the marketing and Daja was at Winding Circle, the maid fetched Briar.

Briar took one look at Sandry and knew trouble was in the air. Sandry's bright blue eyes sparkled dangerously, and little red flags of temper marked her cheeks. "We thought you'd be *happy* to have us along, you wanting togetherness and all, so what's put pins in your noble rump?" he asked, jamming his hands into his pockets. "And what's this for? Tents? Or you think we're too poor to have clothes?"

Sandry glared at him. "I doubt you have court clothes from cloth and stitching that I have done," replied Sandry. "And I refuse to answer your other, *vulgar* question."

As the house's manservant carried in the first load of cloth, Briar rolled his eyes. "I've been vulgar for years and it never bothered you. If you think I'll put off getting my trees ready for Rosethorn to look after so you can stick pins in *me*, think again. I don't have time for fittings." He turned and went into the house, back to his workroom. He knew Sandry would follow. When she wanted a fight, nothing stopped her from getting it.

While he waited he busied himself with his *shakkans*, preparing them for the trip to Winding Circle. They grumbled as he checked their leaves, branches, and soil before he set them in their traveling baskets once more. Like Briar, they had looked forward to staying in one place for a while.

"You'll like it so well with Rosethorn, you won't even remember me," he told them with a gentleness he rarely showed to people these days. "And *she* won't take you anywhere anytime soon."

"Then why agree to come, if you didn't want to?" Sandry demanded from the doorway. She carried a sewing basket in one hand.

Briar didn't look at her. "Because His Grace asked me to."

"Oh!" From the sound of her voice, Sandry had just gotten angrier. "So if my uncle asked you to reopen our old connection, you'd do it for *him,* but not for us."

Briar closed his eyes, drawing serenity from the very old miniature apple tree under his fingers. Had she been so childish before? "His Grace would never ask something so foolish of us."

"Foolish!"

Briar turned so he could glare at Sandry. He didn't want his irritation flooding into his tree. "Look here. It's one thing to be all happy and friendly and romping in each other's minds when you're little, Sandry. Kids think of kid things, and we *were* kids, for all we were powerful enough and well-taught enough to get our mage medallions." In his upset he'd slid back to his native street slang, using the word for a young goat to mean a child. "We kept our minds neat and clean and orderly for our magic and it was easy, because we were *kids.* We're not kids now. We can control our power because we're stronger, and that's nice, because our minds are messy adult minds!"

"You mean *your* mind is messy," Sandry retorted, crimson with fury. "You, all well-traveled to distant lands, with your mysterious war and your Yanjing emperor, while you left silly me at home to stay a child!"

Briar took a step forward to glare down into her face. I also forgot how gods-curst aggravating she can be, always poking at a fellow's sore spots! he thought. "Why does it always have to be so witless *personal* with you?" he demanded.

Sandry braced her fists on her hips and rose up on the balls of her feet to lessen the five inches of difference in their heights. "Personal? Personal is what I've had while my brother and sisters raced all over the world, in case you've forgotten, Master Big Britches!"

Briar gaped at her, astonished. "You said you didn't mind!"

Sandry glared up into his eyes. "I *had* to say that, idiot. You were going if I liked it or no. All I could do was salvage my pride!"

Now Briar's temper came to a boil. "That bleating noble's pride, so much more meaningful than the kind us ground-grubbers get —"

Sandry retorted, "Better than your stiff-rumped street-boy fecklessness that makes fun of anything serious!" She thrust out one hand and shoved him on the chest. Briar rocked back on his heels and grabbed her wrist.

"Well." Daja stood in the door, arms crossed over her chest. "I can see this will be a *splendid* trip."

Embarrassed, Briar turned back to his plants. Sandry shoved out of the room past Daja.

After a long silence, Daja asked, "Does this mean you're not going?"

Briar, who could feel a hot blush swamp his face from the tip of his nose to the backs of his ears, shook his head.

When he heard no sounds that meant Daja had left his workroom, he mumbled, "Girls. Always getting their skirts in an uproar over a lump in the mattress."

"But you feel better for yelling at her," Daja suggested, her voice very dry.

Briar shrugged. He kept his back to Daja so she wouldn't see the slow smile that spread across his lips. It *was* good to see that Sandry still had some spice in her.

After a long moment, he heard the sounds of Daja's retreat from his workroom. "Tell her I'm not wearing fussy embroidery or pointed shoes!" he yelled over his shoulder.

"Tell him I'm putting hoods with the faces sewn shut on all his tunics!" Sandry yelled from somewhere inside the house.

"Tell each other yourselves!" called Daja from somewhere between them.

Briar grinned. For a moment it felt like it had in the old days, back at Discipline cottage. Daja's house had felt like home.

The 17th day of Seed Moon, 1043 K.F.
The Erynwhit River
Southwestern Gansar

Briar was smugly pleased to find that, unlike most non-Traders who rode under the protection of Trader caravans, the four were not kept to a separate camp, guarded by the Traders but shut out of Trader conversations and Trader campfires. He tried not to smirk at the non-Traders when he passed their lonely fires. The four would have been forced to join them if not for Daja. Though she had once been a Trader outcast, the same powerful act of magic that had left her with living metal on one hand had also redeemed her name with all Traders, and made her and her friends known and respected by her people. Now Daja carried an ebony staff, its brass cap engraved and inlaid with the symbols of her life's story, like any Trader's staff. Now she could do business with Traders, eat with them, talk with them, and travel with them, as could her brother and sisters.

"Those fires look awful lonesome," Briar confided to Tris their first night on the road.

She was not fooled. "Stop gloating," she replied.

The people of Third Caravan Saralan soon found there was much of interest about Briar and the girls. The children and quite a few adults were entranced by Chime. They took every free moment to feed the glass dragon and collect the flame- or puddle-shaped bits of glass that Chime produced afterward. The yellow-clad and veiled mimanders — mages — were drawn to the depth and power of the magic that filled the 152-year-old miniature pine *shakkan* that was Briar's companion. They consulted Briar about the magic that could be worked with *shakkans*, while the Trader negotiators began the slow process of bargaining for a long-term contract to buy the trees Briar was prepared to sell. The Traders even negotiated an exchange with Sandry: her embroidery on their own clothes in trade for a chance to examine weaving and embroidery done only within the rare Trader cities. This was the work of very old and very young Traders, who were exempt from the custom that forbade their people from making things. Sandry jumped at the chance: Rarely did a non-Trader so much as glimpse the work, let alone get the time for a close look at it.

Briar, Sandry, and Daja soon found something they could agree on in that first week: Tris had grown very odd. She seemed to flinch each time a fresh breeze blew through the camps and the caravans. Briar thought she would drive him mad, changing the location of her bedroll several times each night. He slept lightly, trying to avoid dreams of fire and blood. Tris woke him when she moved. While Tris didn't drive others to growl "pesky, jagging, maukie girl" as Briar did, it was almost as if by trying to be quiet and disturb no one, Tris disturbed everyone.

"I left Winding Circle so I could sleep!" he cried their fourth night on the road. "Not so's I could be jumping every other minute thinking we're under attack when it's just you missing your feather bed!"

"That's why we ride with the caravan, so their *guards* watch in case of attack," she replied with heavy and weary sarcasm. "Anyway, since when are you such a cursed light sleeper? The time was that we had to dump buckets of water on you to get you to crack an eyelid."

"People change," snarled Briar. "You didn't used to squeak at every least little thing." I'm not going to say I can't even trust Trader guards to know when trouble comes, he thought, moving his bedroll as far from hers as he could manage. Anyone can be taken by surprise. *Anyone*. You'd think she'd know that, at her age.

It's enough to make a person stuff her in a baggage wagon, thought Daja gloomily as she cleaned her teeth on their seventh morning out. Today they were to reach the river Erynwhit, which marked the border of Emelan and Gansar. Daja was wondering how she was going to put up with Tris's behavior all the way to Namorn. She agreed with Briar, particularly since last night Tris had been sleeping, or moving, near Daja's bedroll.

"Why don't you see if you can ride in a wagon?" she demanded when Tris twitched one time too many over breakfast. "So you won't have to keep the rest of us awake all night while you look for a soft spot, or worry about the wicked breeze drying your cheeks all day."

Tris replied with a cold look that, in earlier years, made Daja want to put her in a keg and nail the top on. It was a look that froze the person who had dared to speak to Tris. We shamed it out of her when she lived with us, thought Daja, glaring back at her sister. I guess she fell into her old, bad ways after we weren't around. "In the civilized world, people answer other people back," she told the redhead.

"Daja, it's too early," moaned Sandry. She had stayed up late, working on her Namornese with the Traders. For once, Daja saw, Sandry wasn't her bouncy morning self.

"Certainly too early for those of us who couldn't get a whole night's sleep in the first place," growled Briar as the Traders began to pack the wagons up.

The caravan, even the sleepy four, pulled together and took the slowly descending road before the sun cleared the eastern mountains. Soon they descended to the flat canyon floor the Erynwhit had carved between towering cliff walls. The river spread before them. It was a lazy flat expanse no more than a hundred yards wide and barely three feet deep even at this time of year, when snowmelt should have swollen it enough to cover the whole canyon floor. The ride leader told Daja that, twenty years earlier, this road had been impassable in springtime, until some lord or other built a dam far upstream.

Thanks, whoever you were, she told the unnamed noble silently. Without your dam and this crossing we'd have to ride a hundred miles to the bridge at Lake Bostidan.

On moved the caravan, herd animals, riders, and the first of the wagon groups. Daja was about to enter the water when she saw that Tris had halted her mare in midstream. The mare turned and twisted, fighting Tris's too-tight grip on the reins.

Daja ground her teeth, then rode over. *"Ease up on your horse's mouth,"* Daja growled. "You're hurting her, you'll make her hard-mouthed, wrenching her about that way —"

Tris pulled the horse's head around in an abrupt turn, kicking the mare into a gallop while still in the water. Daja stood in the stirrups to yell, "We taught you how to ride, Oti log it, Trader tax you! A hard-mouthed horse earns less on resale!"

Tris didn't seem to hear. She galloped her little mare onto a hillock where the road entered the water and drew her to a halt. There, she rose in her stirrups, facing upriver.

Why is she taking her spectacles off? wondered Daja, as vexed with Tris as she had been in years. She looks completely demented, and she's blind without them — *now* what?!

Tris ripped off the net that confined her braids, and turned the mare. Setting the horse galloping straight for the river, she grabbed a handful of air and placed it in front of her mouth. "Get 'em across!" she yelled. She had done some trick: Her voice boomed in the canyon. "For your lives, get them across! Move!"

The caravan leaders and the head mimander started to ride back to Tris.

"There is no storm, no flood," cried the mimander. "You frighten our people —"

Tris stood in her saddle, her gray eyes wild. The ties flew from the thin braids that framed her face. They came undone, laddered with lightning bolts that crawled to her forehead and back over her head. "Are you *deaf*?" she bellowed. "I didn't ask for a vote! *Move them!*" She thrust an arm out. Lightning ran down to fill her palm. It dripped to the ground. Wagon drivers whipped their beasts, wanting to put the river between them and Tris. Herds fled, splashing among the wagons and the riders.

Chime shot into the air. Lightning rose to cling to the dragon, outlining her graceful figure. Down she swooped, harrying the Traders' dogs and sheep, driving them into the river and keeping them from fleeing downstream. Briar and Sandry charged back into the water, followed by Traders, making sure people rode across instead of fleeing along the river's length.

I'll kill Tris when everyone's safely out, thought Daja, keeping the column tight on the upriver side. For causing such a fuss, for frightening everyone, and why? The mimander said there's no flash flood coming. His *specialty* is weather with water — the ride leader told me so when we left Summersea!

She glanced at Tris. The redhead screeched, "Not fast enough!" at the mimander and the caravan leaders. Two long, heavy braids popped free of their ties. These did not crawl with lightning, like the rest of Tris's braids. They *were* lightning.

She dragged fistfuls of blazing power from each and

squeezed them through the gaps between her fingers, creating about seven strips of lightning in each hand. *"Move!"* she screamed, and hurled them in the caravan's wake. Lightning cracked like whips over the heads of horses and mules. It lashed close enough to one herd of sheep to singe wool and to leave scorch marks on the side of a nearby wagon. Daja saw Tris drag on it to keep it from touching the water. Thank the gods for that, she realized. One strike in the water and we all might cook.

Three lightning strips flew at the mimander, the caravan leaders, even Daja herself, nipping at the rumps of their horses. Thunder boomed in the canyon, startling the herds into a run. Animals, Traders, and non-Traders alike decided they'd had enough. They, Sandry, and Briar fled across the river with Tris behind them, just in back of the last wagons.

"Keep going!" Tris screamed, her voice hoarse. Now she used her lightning to goad the caravan's rear and its front, scaring the horses and the oxen who pulled the wagons until they rushed up the inclining road. The end of the caravan was a scant twenty feet above the canyon floor when a rumbling sound made the cooler-headed riders stop.

Rocks pattered down the cliffs that overlooked the road. Bits of the ledge that overlooked the canyon floor crumbled away from its edge. In the distance they could hear a dull roar.

This time, Tris, clinging to her horse's mane, didn't need to speak. Everyone scrambled to move higher on the steep road. They were sixty feet above the riverbed when a wall of tree- and stone-studded water snarled down the canyon to swamp the river flats. It ripped boulders from the ford, ground the road away, and plowed on down into the canyon again. Had they been just a little slower, the savage torrent would have swept them up and carried the remains far downstream.

"But there was no rain, no snowfall, higher in the mountains." That lone voice belonged to the mimander. Daja did not look at his veiled eyes, out of consideration for his shame. Trader mimanders studied one aspect of magic all their lives. They chose their specialty when they were young, and risked their lives to learn all they could about winds, or the fall of water from the skies, or avalanches, or storms at sea.

How humiliating, she thought. It must look like he missed this coming, even after years of study. He knows this caravan puts its life in his hands.

And how humiliating, to yell at your sister because she doesn't have time to save over two hundred people and explain herself, too.

Briar looked at the swirling mess below. He blinked. For a moment the trees were bodies: gaudily dressed men, women and children who were missing limbs or heads, their wounds streaking the brown water red. They were joined by the bloated corpses of yaks, goats, even birds, and by the corpses of soldiers. The stench of the rotting dead swamped him.

Not here, he thought, closing his eyes and clenching his teeth. Gansar, not Gyongxe. Peacetime, not war. Not here.

When he opened his eyes, he saw the remains of trees and the bulk of stones. Only the stench of death continued to haunt his nose.

He forced himself to study *this* flood, the one that was real right now. Already it was clawing at the earthen walls on the far side of the river flats. "You ask me, I think the dam broke upriver, master mimander," he commented. "It was too old, maybe, or it needed fixing, or something, but some of those rocks look like dressed stone. It wasn't your fault if that's so. A dam break isn't weather."

Tris, limp along her mare's neck, nodded briefly.

Daja was looking very sheepish, he saw. She rode over to Tris. "I'm sorry," Briar heard her mutter. "I should have —"

"Trusted me?" Tris's reply was muffled, but it clearly stung Daja. "Remembered it's my favorite thing in all the world to act like a crazy person before strangers, and it would have been nice if my sisters and brother had said, 'Oh, she's peculiar, but she's usually peculiar for a reason'? Go away, Daja. I don't feel like blushing and accepting your kind apology just now, thanks all the same."

Daja drew herself up. "All that traveling and all those conferences, and they never taught you how to be gracious."

"You want Sandry for that. She's up ahead. Leave me be."

Briar rode over and touched Daja on the arm. He jerked his head, a sign for her to come aside with him. When she did, he whispered, "Remember? She gets all worked up, and she snaps at the first nice voice she hears. She was probably scared witless. I'll put on the heavy gloves and gentle her some." He winked and rode back to Tris, getting her attention by poking her in the arm. "Hey, Coppercurls, nice fireworks," he said, keeping his voice light. She looked like one of the warrior dedicates right after battle: exhausted, but still not quite sure it was safe to stop fighting. Briar had learned to handle them carefully when they were in that state. "Maybe you ought to do like Chime and eat something so the lighting will come out of you in colors."

Tris replied with a suggestion that Briar knew would be physically impossible. He grinned. Offering Tris his canteen, he said, "Have some water, and don't spit it back in my face."

As Tris obeyed, Briar looked at Daja and shrugged.

Daja smiled reluctantly. That's right, Daja thought. Tris gets really frightened, and then she bites the heads off of people. I had forgotten.

I wonder what else I've forgotten — about Tris. About Sandry, and Briar.

I hope I remember really, really fast.

Sandry was livid. Had she been less aware of what she owed to the people around her, she would have shaken Tris until her teeth rattled. Furious as she was, she still remembered one of her uncle's most often-repeated lessons: "Never express anger with a friend or a subordinate in public,"

Vedris always said. "They might forgive a private expression of anger or a deserved scolding, but they never forget a public humiliation. It is the surest way to destroy a friendship and to create enemies."

The caravan found a wide cove off the road where they could halt to collect themselves and calm the children and the animals. Sandry then went to give Tris a piece of her mind. The mimander beat her there. He had backed Tris up against a tall stone by the road, his yellow-robed body shielding her from onlookers. Sandry moved to the side of the stone to eavesdrop.

"The world does not appreciate such stunts," the man told Tris softly but fiercely. "Do you know the harm you could do with such dangerous magic? What if a wagon had rolled, or if animals had fallen? When you scry a thing, you announce it immediately — you do *not* stage a panic in mid-river! I mean to file a complaint with Winding Circle —"

"They will tell you your complaint has no merit." Tris's voice was low and cold. "I did not scry this. As soon as I knew it was coming, I told everyone with the ears to hear. Forgive me if I did not consult you. There *was no time.*"

"What am I supposed to believe, *kaq*?" demanded the mimander. He'd used the most insulting term for a non-Trader there was. "Did you see it on the wind, like some fabled mage of old? I suppose you — a child! — expect me to believe that!"

"Go away. Tell your bookkeeper goddess you'd rather

question the debt you owe me for your life than consider ways to repay me!" snapped Tris. "On second thought, don't bother! There's no coin small enough I'd consider worth-while exchange for your life!"

Sandry smothered a gasp and pressed herself into a crevice behind the rock that hid her. Is she *mad*? Sandry wondered, horrified. If she were a Trader he'd have to kill her for so many insults! She said he was questioning his gods for letting him live. Then she told him not to bother repaying her — a Trader, not to repay! — and then she told him his life isn't worth anything!

Finally the mimander replied, his voice shaking. "I expect no better of a *kaq*."

He walked away.

Sandry's temper blazed again. Tris not only orders us around like the Queen of Everything, but she insults our hosts! I have to remind her she used to have manners!

She yanked herself out of her crevice, shook her riding breeches clean of the leaf-litter that had collected there, took a deep breath, and walked around the rock. Tris had left it, to sit on a fallen tree next to the spring nearby. She patiently held one side of her snood, Chime the other, as her braids twined around each other, forming a snug ball. There was no way to tell now which had carried lightning and which had been lightning. Even the two thin braids that framed her face were neatly done up and tied again.

Sandry halted in front of her. "Never have I given you

the right to order me around. Neither have Briar or Daja. And we have certainly not given you the right to throw *lightning* at us." Despite her resolve to be firm, her voice quivered.

Tris's eyes flicked to Sandry dangerously, though Tris's hold on the snood remained steady as her braids moved and wriggled to fit themselves inside. "Pardon me for not kissing your hand and saying pretty please, since that's what you're used to these days," she replied, acid dripping in her voice. "Had I known I would offend, *Clehame*" — she turned Sandry's Namornese title into an insult — "I would have let everyone die so I wouldn't inconvenience you."

"I know you are ever so much more clever and educated than the rest of us, but it's not as if we are dolts. We *did* get our medallions at the same time as you. We have something between our ears besides hummus! And if the bond between us were open, there would have been no need for such antics!" replied Sandry, losing her temper in spite of herself.

Tris let go of the snood. With a flap of her wings, Chime leaped on top of her head to keep it in place. If either girl had not been in a rage, they might have thought it funny.

"Did it occur to you that you might not like what is in my head now?" demanded Tris. She hurriedly grabbed a fistful of hairpins and began to pin her net in place. "Or do you think I'll be easier to control once you're behind my eyes, Your Ladyship?"

Sandry's eyes filled with unexpected tears. She felt as if Tris had slapped her. "Do you really think that of me?"

"I don't know what I think," growled Tris, taking off her spectacles. "Go away, will you? I have the most vile headache. I just want to be alone." Chime took flight off of Tris's head.

"With pleasure," Sandry replied with all the dignity she had left. "At the rate you're going, you'll be a caravan of one, just as alone as you please."

"I cannot believe you, my lady." Unknown to the two girls, the caravan's leader had come over. "She has saved all of our lives with fearsome magic, she is pale and sweating — and you choose to quarrel with her?" To Tris, the woman said, "My wagon is cushioned, with heavy drapes to close out the light, and there is cool mint tea. Will you rest your head there? Briar says he has a headache medicine that may help you."

Sandry turned and fled. If anything, she felt even smaller than she had when Tris had accused her of wanting to control her. Why didn't I notice she was ill? she wondered. And why is she being so mean to the three of us? She was that way to strangers when we lived together, but not us. Unless . . . of course. We're strangers.

She stopped, her back to the caravan. Reaching into the small pouch that always hung around her neck, she brought out the thread with its four equally spaced lumps. Sandry turned it around in her fingers, handling each lump, feeling each familiar bit of magic. Maybe we were this cord once, but for now it's only a symbol, she thought wearily. A symbol of four children. Now we're four adults who have become strangers. I have to get used to that. I have to get used to it, and think of ways to make us stop being strangers once and for all.

She sighed, and returned the thread circle to its pouch. And how will I do that? I have no notion in the least.

3

The 27th day of Goose Moon, 1043 K.F.
Twelve miles outside Dancruan,
Capital of the Namorn Empire

If Chime had not seen a magpie in the meadow and given chase — she had developed a furious dislike of the vivid black-and-white birds on their way north — the four would have quietly entered Dancruan as part of Third Caravan Saralan. Their arrival would have followed the structure of diplomatic propriety. They would have been introduced to the court as so many others were introduced, as part of the summer flow of guests from abroad. Instead, not long after the caravan emerged from the shelter of Mollyno Forest, the magpie flew at Chime and smacked the glass dragon with its wings, plainly outraged by Chime's very existence. Chime voiced a scraped-glass shriek of rage and gave chase over a nearby meadow.

"Tris!" yelled Briar. "Do something!"

"She'll be back," replied Tris calmly. She turned a page in the book she was reading as she rode.

The sun inched higher in the sky, with no sign of Chime. Sandry finally sighed and found Saralan's ride leader. "You'd best go on ahead," she told him. "I know you have ships to meet at the docks today. Business is business."

"I don't like it," said Daja behind her. "It's not what's due to your consequence, entering Dancruan with just us for company."

Sandry giggled. "As if I cared about such things!"

"You should," the ride leader told her soberly. "You will find they care about it very much at the imperial court." He raised his staff and galloped to the front of the caravan, voicing the long, trilling cry that was the signal to move out. Everyone who had gotten down from horses or wagons to stretch their legs took their places once more. The caravan rolled on without their four guests: Traders kept their good-byes short, to avoid the appearance of owing anything to those they left behind. Sandry had always liked that philosophy, but then, the nursemaid who had practically raised her had also been a Trader. Now she and her friends waved their farewells to their companions.

As the last wagons and herds left them behind, Sandry felt a weight fall from her slender shoulders. While she had enjoyed riding with the caravan, she was glad to be rid of the witnesses to the squabbles that had continued all the way here. Now, with the Traders out of earshot and the other three silent, she heard actual quiet. Only birdsong and the whiffle of the wind passing over acres of meadow grass met her ears. Mages were accustomed to time alone. That had been scarce on the long trip north.

Enjoy it while it lasts, she told herself, filling her mind with the jingle of bridles and the shush of moving air. Once we get to Dancruan, things are bound to be noisy. Music, politics, gossip. It's bad enough when Uncle receives his nobles. I hear my cousin's court is much larger and, unlike Uncle, she holds her court all year round.

She turned her horse in order to look at her brother and sisters, wondering yet again how they would fare — how *she* would fare — in a sophisticated place like the imperial palace. Briar had unsaddled his horse and flopped onto the meadow grass, his bronze face turned up to the sun. He had even taken his *shakkan* from its traveling basket and set it on the ground, more like a pet than a plant. All the grass around him was in motion, straining to touch him or the *shakkan* without blocking the sun that fell on their two new friends.

He isn't frowning, thought Sandry, amazed. I don't think I've seen him without a hint of a scowl since he came home. When he's like this, if he weren't my brother, I'd even find him handsome. Certainly the Trader girls seemed to think so!

When someone blew a horn in the distance, Briar stirred to glare at Tris. "You *know* where your monster is. Will you kindly get her back here?"

Sandry looked at Tris, who had remained in her saddle to read. The redhead turned a fresh page of her book and did not reply.

Briar sighed his exasperation. "We could be eating midday by now."

"I was enjoying the quiet," Sandry remarked mournfully. She looked at Daja. "Weren't you enjoying the quiet?"

Daja, who had dismounted to practice combat moves with her Trader's staff, brought the long ebony weapon up to the rest position, exhaled, then looked up at Sandry. "I'm staying out of this one. So should you," she advised Sandry. "Otherwise, they'll start a quarrel with us when they get bored of fighting with each other."

"I'm not quarreling," Tris said mildly. "I'm reading."

"Girls," Briar said with disgust. "Aggrimentatious, argufying —"

"Is it that you learned too many languages, and so you must mangle the ones you have?" Sandry asked, curious.

Tris closed her book with a snap and freed a braid from the coil at the back of her head. "Chime's coming. She's being chased by riders," she said, thrusting her book into her tunic pocket. "Nobles. There are falconers far behind them. I suppose they were hunting." She scowled. "Right now they're hunting Chime."

Daja walked over to stand next to Sandry, leaning on her staff. "The wind's blowing toward us. Tris could just be hearing them," she remarked. "Except how would she know about the falconers? I think she's *seeing* things on the wind, these days."

Sandry looked at Tris. The breeze came out of the north, making Tris's braids stream back from her face. "Don't be silly," replied Sandry. "Even her teacher can't do *that*, and Niko's one of the greatest sight mages in the world. Most of the mages who try to see things on the wind go mad."

"But now and then, one has to succeed," Daja murmured. "Otherwise there wouldn't be stories of those who can do it."

"Stop gabbing and *move*," ordered Briar. He saddled his horse and Daja's with a speed none of the girls could match. "You want whoever is coming to catch you on the ground?" He swung himself into his saddle and took a cloth-wrapped ball from the pocket of his open jacket. Just to vex him, Daja spun her staff lazily around in her hand until it rested on one of her shoulders. Only after she had carefully holstered the length of wood did she gracefully mount her horse.

Over the nearest rise in the ground came Chime, the sun glinting in darts of light from her wings. Seeing them, she voiced her grating alarm screech and sped up. Shooting past Tris, she stopped herself by tangling her claws in the back of the redhead's tunic. Tris made not a sound, her eyes on the hill as Chime hid behind her.

Like Tris, Sandry focused on the crest in the ground and the party of riders who surged over it. She was quick to note that their hunting clothes and horses' tack alike were edged in gold and silver embroidery, the work of countless hands. They were accompanied by guardsmen, business-like warriors in leather jerkins sewn with metal plates, worn over full-sleeved red shirts and baggy pants. The guards wore round armor caps and held crossbows on their laps.

"Is this your witch-thing, peasants?" demanded a big, handsome young man as the hunting party came within shouting distance. "It ruined our sport! Drove off every grouse and wood pigeon for miles!"

Daja asked her friends, "Did he say 'peasants'?"

Briar looked over his shoulder at her. "He definitely said 'peasants.'"

"Someone needs spectacles." Tris pushed her own spectacles higher on her nose.

Sandry crossed mental fingers. For the first time since they had reunited, they sounded as they once had at Discipline cottage.

A woman rode forward, past the man who had shouted at them. Four of the guards and another richly dressed man who glinted a magical silver trotted their horses to catch up with her. Briar whistled in soft admiration for the woman. Sandry couldn't blame him. The lady was a splendid creature who wore her russet hair curled, coiled, and pinned under a bronze velvet cap in an artless tumble. It framed an ivory-skinned face, large brown eyes, an intriguing mouth over a square and stubborn chin, and a small, slight slip of a nose. Her clothing hugged a very shapely figure.

Eyeing the lady's bronze velvet high-necked coat and wide breeches, Sandry felt a pinch in the place where she kept her pride in the clothes she made and wore. Lark warned me I'd get a dreadful case of style envy at the Namornese court, she told herself with the tiniest of sighs. There's just something to this lady's garments that gives them the, the *sauciest* look. And what I wouldn't give for a nice, close look at those lapel and seam embroideries! I can see a few magical signs to ward off injury and enemies, but I *think* there are others, ones I don't recognize.

Remembering her manners, Sandry met the lady's amused eyes once more. This time she realized there was something familiar about that beautiful face. Among her family heirlooms Sandry had portraits, including those of her mother's parents. This woman looked very much like Sandry's grandmother. Belatedly the young woman realized who she must be. Blushing deeply, Sandry dismounted to curtsy deeply to her cousin Berenene dor Ocmore, empress of Namorn. Briar was next to dismount, followed by Tris and Daja. As Tris curtsied, Briar and Daja bowed, as befitted a young man in breeches and a Trader in leggings.

Berenene rode forward until her mount stood a yard from Sandry. "Look at me, child," she said in a voice like warm music.

Sandry obeyed. From the way the empress's horse shifted, the woman was startled, though that beautiful face showed not one drop of surprise. "Qunoc bless us," Berenene whispered, naming the west Namornese goddess of crops.

"Lady Sandrilene fa Toren? You are the image of your mother."

Sandry would have argued — her mother had not possessed a button of a nose — but arguing and empresses did not mix. "I'm honored, Your Imperial Majesty."

The empress looked their company over. A slight crease appeared between her perfectly arched brows; the tucked corners of her mouth deepened. "But where is your entourage? Your guardsmen, your ladies-in-waiting? Do not tell me you came all the way from Emelan with just these few persons." She looked at Tris and Daja. "Unless these young women are your ladies?" Her tone made it clear she believed they were nothing of the sort.

"These are my foster-sisters, Your Imperial Majesty," Sandry replied, still deep in her curtsy. Tris's was beginning to wobble. "And Briar is my foster-brother. We traveled with Third Caravan Saralan —"

The empress cut her off. "Traders? Where are they now?"

"We sent them ahead," Sandry replied. "We needed to rest, and they had a ship to catch."

The empress leaned forward, resting her arm on her saddle horn. "All of you, please rise, before the redheaded foster-sister falls over," she commanded. Tris blushed a deep plum color as she rose. Daja and Briar straightened.

"You brought your foster family," the empress said, her brown eyes dancing. "What are their names, if you please?"

"Forgive me, Your Imperial Majesty," replied Sandry, her voice even. I'd bet every stitch I have on she already knows quite well who everyone is, she thought. *"Ravvikki"*— Namornese for a young woman —"Trisana Chandler." Tris curtsied again. "*Ravvikki* Daja Kisubo." Daja bowed. Using the word for a young man, Sandry continued, "*Ravvotki* Briar Moss." Before they had entered Namorn, they had agreed that they were not going to claim the title of mage unless a crisis arose. By then they had all been thoroughly sick of explaining how they could be accredited mages at eighteen.

"Welcome to my empire," said Berenene with a gracious nod. To Sandry she added, "My dear, two sisters and a brother, however devoted, are not sufficient protection for a maiden of your wealth and position. Men of few principles might see your unguarded state as the chance to capture a wealthy young bride."

Sandry noticed Briar's tiny smirk and the sudden, bored droop of Tris's eyes. Only Daja's face had the perfect, polite expression that told onlookers nothing of her true thoughts. Daja and I should have spent the trip teaching them a diplomat's facial expressions as well as Namornese, Sandry thought, vexed. It would be impossible not to guess that Briar and Tris thought they were a match for would-be kidnappers, something that would never cross the mind of an ordinary young man or woman.

Stop fussing, Sandry ordered herself. I know very well my cousin has had spies on me for years, and she is aware we're all mages.

Now that the empress's riders had stopped chasing her, Chime decided it was safe to move. She wriggled out from under Tris's loose riding tunic and up to the redhead's shoulder.

Instantly Berenene's companion, the one who was not in uniform, moved in front of the empress, one hand up. The silver fire of magic flared from his palm to wrap around Berenene like a shimmering cocoon.

"He's good," Briar muttered to Daja out of the corner of his mouth. "I thought you said her boss mage was some old woman named Ladyhammer."

"Do you see any old women riding with this crowd if they don't have to?" Daja inquired.

Chime ignored the magic. She rose to her hindquarters on Tris's shoulder, one paw clutching Tris's hair for balance, surveying the Namornese curiously.

Chime, you show-off, thought Sandry with affection. "That's Chime, Your Imperial Majesty," she told Berenene. "She's a curiosity that Tris *found* in the far south."

"Curious indeed," said the mage who still guarded the empress. His dark eyes had been amused when they first rode up, but they were steady and serious now. "It's not an illusion, or an animated poppet. It looks like glass, or perhaps moving ice."

"Tris," Sandry said, a hint for the redhead to explain.

Tris sighed. "She's mage made. A new mage, one who started out as a glassblower, had an accident. It turned out to be Chime."

"I don't believe the imperial glassmaker, *Viynain*"— the Namornese word for a male mage —"Warder, has ever made anything of the kind," the empress remarked. "If he could, he would have done so for me. My dear Quenaill, if the creature had meant harm to us, surely it would have attacked by now. I can hardly see my cousin Sandrilene, who has been gone for so long. My dear, allow me to present the great mage Quenaill Shieldsman. Doubtless you have heard of him at Winding Circle."

Sandry nodded graciously to indicate that she had indeed heard the name, but the truth was that she remembered little else. Their teachers were forever talking about great mages, so the names did stick after a time. Apart from her own specialties, Sandry had very little interest in the practice of magic by the better known professionals. She was far more curious about the latest fashions and weaving patterns by those who excelled in those fields.

The mage Quenaill shifted his mount so Berenene had a clear view of the four, but he remained on his guard. As he lowered his hand, his protective magic vanished into his body.

"Now I'm *really* impressed," Briar murmured to Daja. "I couldn't do it that fast."

"You don't do shields at all," Daja whispered in reply.

"But if I did, I wouldn't be that fast," Briar said.

Sandry sighed. "It is a long story about Chime, Your Imperial Majesty," she said, pretending she couldn't hear the soft dialogue to her left. "I am sorry that your hunting was interrupted."

"At least I know you are here at last. And you are expected in Dancruan," Berenene replied. Even while Quenaill had rushed to protect her, she had not moved as she casually leaned on her saddle horn. "For weeks, Ambros fer Landreg has spoken of little but preparing the town house for you."

"The caravan will let the *saghad* know we are on our way, thank you," Sandry replied, using Ambros's Namornese title.

Berenene smiled. "You will need to rest, no doubt, after your long journey. You may call on me the day after tomorrow — shall we say, at ten in the Hall of Roses? It is more intimate than is the throne room. And of course your . . . friends are invited to attend with you. In fact, I insist on it." Her brown eyes caught and held Sandry's blue ones. She nodded, smiled, then turned her horse. Quenaill and the guards followed her with the ease of a well-oiled clock. She slowed when they came abreast of the first of her companions, the handsome young man who had yelled at the four earlier, and extended her hand. Without hesitation the man got his horse moving so that he could catch and kiss the hand, riding up on Berenene's free side. Once he was level with her, she leaned closer and caressed his cheek, then urged her horse into a gallop. Quenaill and the man kept up with her as if they had read her mind, while the rest of her court and her guards spurred their own horses into motion. The group followed Berenene as if they were one creature at the end of her leash.

Only after the hunting party had ridden out of view beyond the ridge did Briar say, "Did you notice that none of her friends so much as twitched when Chime came out? They were all boiling when they came chasing our glass friend over that ridge, but once Her Empressness was talking to us, they sat there like so many well-trained dogs. They didn't even show fang at Chime."

"I hope you're more diplomatic than this when we get to court," Daja told him. "Nobles dislike being compared to dogs."

"Whether they dislike it or no, I'll name them for what they are, and I'll be ready for them," Briar snapped. "Don't you go letting the pretty clothes fool you, Daja. If you'd ever been hunted by a pack of nobles, you wouldn't be so nice about what you call them."

The reminder was like an itch Sandry couldn't scratch. I'm getting so tired of this! she thought. "More experiences you've had that you won't explain, Briar," she said irritably. "Talk about something pleasant or don't talk." She swung herself into her mare's saddle.

Briar took a drink of water before he said thoughtfully, "There were some uncommonly pretty ladies with that pack, Her Imperialness not the least of them. I look forward to time spent in *their* company."

"You're disgusting," said Tris, beckoning to Chime. The dragon rubbed her head against Tris's and slid down to the girl's lap.

"Can I help it I like the ladies?" Briar demanded, needling her with innocence on his face. "There are so many delightful ones in the world, each beautiful in her own way. Even you, Coppercurls."

"Briar!" cried his sisters.

"I didn't mean that I'd gratify her with my attention," Briar said impatiently. "Kissing one of you would be like kissing Rosethorn."

Daja chuckled. "Kissing Rosethorn would be safer than kissing Tris," she pointed out. "Mildly, anyway. Minutely."

"Cursed right," Tris said. "*I'm* not kissing anyone. *I'm* going to Lightsbridge."

"You won't be safe there," replied Daja as she mounted her horse once more. "Frostpine and I went to the university after we left Namorn. I think kissing's all those students think about. Well . . . that, and drinking. And throwing up."

"I'll bet the mage students don't drink that much," Briar said as he swung back into his saddle. "Elsewise, Lightsbridge would prob'ly be a smoking hole in the ground." He shuddered along with the three girls. None of them had liked their first attempts at drinking, or cleaning up the wreckage of the abandoned barn they had chosen to do it in.

"Well," Sandry remarked as Tris mounted her horse,

"we may not want to drink, but in just twelve more miles, we can unpack and laze in hot Namornese baths."

All of them groaned with longing as they took to the road once more. Daja had described the Namornese baths with such eloquence that, after weeks of travel, the four could hardly wait to give them a try.

Sandry listened to them with the tiniest of smiles. So who we were together before, it's not entirely gone, she thought. A common threat, and we're closer than ever. And we all want hot baths.

It's a start.

Berenene, empress of Namorn, allowed her maids to take away her hunting dress and let Rizu, her Mistress of the Wardrobe, replace it with clothes more suitable for afternoon wear. Once her hair was set in order again, she told Rizu and the maids to tidy up and left her bedchamber for her most private workroom.

It was small compared with her other rooms, its walls lined with bookshelves and maps. The chairs, particularly her own, were designed for comfort. The desk met Berenene's exact requirements, its drawers and furnishings within her reach. Beside it was a window that looked out onto any part of the palace she wished it to, needing only the proper word to change what it showed her. At the moment it was filled with views of her favorite gardens. Berenene loved springtime. Winters in Dancruan, or anywhere else on the shores of the vast lake called the Syth, were long and iron hard. She bore them with the help of her precious greenhouses, but she reveled in the arrival of spring and the wild growth outdoors.

A leather folder sat on her desk. She sat in her cushioned chair and kissed the lock that kept its contents safe. The lock, like so many of the men at the court, responded eagerly to her lips. It popped open.

Inside were sheets of parchment, condensed notes of reports that she had been assembling for more than seventeen years. Its contents dealt with all things that touched on her young cousin Sandrilene. The girl had been foremost in her mind since the mages of the Living Circle communications chain had sent word that she was on her way from Emelan. Now that Berenene had actual faces to put with the notes — the sketches and portraits her spies had made were well enough, but she trusted her own judgment most — she wanted to review the file one last time.

She lifted a painting on vellum. It was a very good portrait of Sandry, all things considered. She's added more curves since my agent in Emelan painted her, Berenene mused, but the likeness is nearly perfect, right down to her posture and expression — I didn't really need Sandry's resemblance to her mother to tell me who she was.

Berenene skimmed the written notes until she reached the all-important summary.

The lady Sandrilene appeared to be a stitch witch on her arrival at Winding Circle temple. Following the earthquake in which she and her friends were trapped, they linked their magics together somehow. All of their powers, including hers, increased by magnitudes. Since that time she has woven magic like thread, created healing bandages and clothing that disguises the wearer, and turned her opponents' garments against their wearers. At thirteen she was granted her mage's credential by the governing council at Winding Circle, an honor normally reserved for those at least twenty years of age or older. At fourteen, she took over the running of her paternal great-uncle Vedris of Emelan's household and lands. Vedris is known to respect her advice in matters such as trade, magecraft, and diplomacy. At present she seems to be at odds with her Winding Circle friends. They do not appear to act in magical concert as they did before the other three departed on journeys with their teachers. Should they reforge that old link, there is no way to estimate what works of magic they might create. Certainly they will be able to communicate over distance once again: The limit of that distance was once judged to be approximately a few hundred miles.

Duke Vedris of Emelan will not be complacent if his great-niece is forced to act against her will. There is open speculation in Emelan that he intends, as is his right under that country's laws of succession, to name Lady Sandrilene as his heir over the sons of his own blood. It is believed that his older son Gospard will acquiesce, though his younger son Franzen will not. There is no confirmation of these rumors; no changes of the duke's will have been filed. If His Grace learned she had been imperiled in any way, he poses no military threat, but he is a major threat to southern trade. With his allies there he could well cut off the trade in gems and spices. Her Imperial Majesty also has a number of bank accounts in Emelan that would be at risk.

Lady Sandrilene is an extraordinary girl. Although she possesses her mage's credential, she does not flaunt it. She is aware of her lineage and quick to assert the rights of her noble birth if she feels that she is not respected. The lady has a temper. She has engaged in flirtations in the last year — one with a temple novice, two with the sons of noble families in Emelan — but they have been flirtations only. The lady does not appear to be interested in marriage at present.

The empress set the papers aside, tapping her chin with a perfectly manicured finger. "Why couldn't the richest heiress in all Namorn have been a noble little sheep?" she asked the empty air.

She took up the next portrait: that of Briar Moss, as he called himself. Ah, yes, she thought, amused. She had seen the way his eyes lingered on her curves once he had relaxed a little. The young gallant. More importantly to me, the green mage. He may be only eighteen, but he is definitely male, and I can handle men. And that *shakkan* on one of the packhorses — that must be the one the spies wrote about, the one he began with. What a beauty it is! If that's a sample of his art, then I must entice him into my service. A talented young man, coming from poverty as my reports say he does . . . I will pay him a fortune to tend my *shakkans* and oversee my other gardens. He'll wonder how he could ever have lived anywhere else, by the time I've done with him!

She set aside the notes about Briar. She knew what she needed to do as far as he was concerned.

The third portrait was of Daja Kisubo, the dark-skinned young woman who was clothed Trader-style. Cast out from the Traders, yet carrying a staff and dressing like one, Berenene thought. And they've made her wealthy. Not all outcasts are so fortunate. I wonder if that metal piece on her hand hurts? I know she makes incredible things with the excess from it: a living metal leg; gloves that enable someone to handle fire without getting burned; a living metal tree that blooms copper roses.

She glanced at her notes.

Daja Kisubo has excellent connections in Namorn. She has close ties to House Bancanor in Kugisko, and thus to the Goldsmiths' Guild and its network of banks throughout the empire. From the work that she and her teacher did while in Kugisko, she has alliances with the Mages' Society of Kugisko and the present head of the Smiths' Guild for all Namorn. Politically, at least, she is as powerful as Lady Sandrilene in Namorn.

These mages! sniffed Berenene as she set the notes aside. Isn't it bad enough they support one another, without meddling in non-mage politics? The allegiance of the Kisubo girl would gain me friends among the smiths and the mages, which is always useful . . . The Traders might not involve themselves in my politics on her behalf, but the living metal trade would come here. Then the taxes on the sales of those living metal toys would enter *my* coffers, not Vedris's.

She was an outcast once. Outcasts always respond well to offers of position, if I can find no better inducement for our young smith.

The last portrait was that of the redhead, Trisana Chandler, the fourth member of Sandry's little family. Berenene drummed her fingers on her desk, frowning slightly. Trisana was the unknown quantity among Sandry's companions. Some of the stories about this girl that her spies had sent on were simply outlandish. Still, there was that glass dragon — made by an imperial subject and the nephew of the present Imperial Glassmaker. The boy had been promising before an accident on the shores of the Syth had nearly killed him. They had sent him away, believing he was useless to the family. Berenene remembered it well.

Then word came from so far south, it's barely on my

maps that his skill is better than ever — he's making glass that lives — and this girl Trisana had something to do with it, Berenene thought. A merchant's daughter, allied to my cousin and these other two, the student of the great mage Niklaren Goldeye. A loner. A puzzle.

The notes read:

What is provable about her is that she is a weather witch of some skill, can manipulate winds, and has been able to earn sums by calling rain, finding water for farmers and towns, and supplying winds to ships. She invests what she earns, has added to her savings, and is respected by her bankers in Emelan.

Other tales are unconfirmed: Emelan — she destroyed an entire pirate fleet with lightning. Tharios — she can scry the wind. Ninver, Capchen — she caused it to hail indoors, created windstorms in her parents' home, made her father sink into the ground when he punished her. Winding Circle temple — she may have put a temporary halt to the change of tides.

Berenene smiled and closed the folder. It must have embarrassed my agents so, to pass on such wild tales. But they did it, which is what they were ordered to do. I will make sure they are duly rewarded. Whatever else, the presence of a girl who can cause such rumors would give my enemies something to think about.

The empress nodded. The notes had confirmed the conclusion she had already reached: Each of these four young people would be an asset to the empire, and well worth any trouble it might take to convince them to stay. My court and I will put out our best efforts, Berenene told herself, closing the folder and locking it once more. They'll be so enraptured with us and with Dancruan, they won't even remember there *is* an Emelan.

4

It's one thing to know Sandry is wealthy, thought Daja when the gates opened and guards bowed them into the courtyard of the Landreg town house. *I'm* wealthy, after all. So's Briar, for all he keeps it to himself. And it's even one thing to know Sandry's a noble, a *clehame.* I always thought I could handle it. Now — I'm not sure I can handle this.

"This" was the sprawling marble pile that was the Landreg home in the capital. Two-thirds of it wasn't even in use at present. Sandry's mother's family — whose title passed to daughters and sons — had not lived there in years; her cousin Ambros's family seldom stayed there. "This" was also what looked to Daja like a small army of servants and men-at-arms, tricked out in matching liveries, lined up on the house's steps and in the courtyard, bowing or curtsying as Sandry walked past. "This" was gilding on the edges of the furniture inside; hardwood floors polished like glass; tapestries glinting with gold and silver thread; branches of candles hung with crystal drops. Even the rooms prepared for the other mages seemed like suites for royalty, with heavy brocade drapes and plush, intricate carpets. The baths assigned for the use of Sandry and her guests were luxurious works of porcelain, marble, and crystal.

If Daja hadn't been so overwhelmed herself, the sight of Tris mincing her way through such elegance like an offended cat might have given her a bad case of the giggles. Tris had never liked a display of wealth, Daja remembered now. She approved of spending money only on books and the tools with which to work magic.

That first evening at supper, watching Tris handle her gilded cutlery as if it were red-hot, Briar said abruptly, "Why'd you ask for a room all the way at the top of the house? Some poor girl has to go climbing up all those stairs to get you to come down and eat. If you were on the same floor as Sandry and Daja, or on the ground floor with me —"

Tris glared at him. "I like it higher up, if it's all the same," she said flatly. Then she charged the subject. "Sandry, I thought your cousin, Lord — *Saghad* — Ambros was going to be here to meet you. To start showing you around your holdings and so forth."

Sandry looked up from the note she was reading. "He was, but this says there was a minor emergency on the estate that he had to attend to. He says he'll be back soon, and apologizes that things aren't in better order. I have a reprieve from the account books."

Briar snorted. "What's his notion of 'better order'—

perfection? This place is spotless." He eyed his sorrel and spinach soup. "Now, here's an odd combination of plants."

"I warned you about Namornese cooking," Daja said. "It takes getting used to, but I love it."

"Anyway, didn't you tell the Traders you actually drank tea with yak butter in Gyongxe?" asked Tris, trying the soup. "I wouldn't talk about odd food, if I were you."

"It was really cold, and the fat helped," Briar said. He tried the soup, frowned, and tried another spoonful. When the maid was finally able to take his bowl, it was empty. She leaned over a little farther than necessary to remove the spoon he had used, earning herself a grin and a wink from Briar.

"Don't you start," Sandry told him when the maid had left the room. "I don't want you bothering the servants here."

"I already talked to the housekeeper," murmured Tris.

"I don't *bother* them," Briar said lazily, his eyes glinting through his lashes. "But if they appreciate my attention, I'm hardly going to hurt their feelings."

"Did you used to be this way?" demanded Sandry, glaring at him. "I don't remember you being this way."

"They say you travel to gain experience," Briar said, and yawned. "That's what I did."

Daja was relieved when a footman brought in a plate of trout cooked in wine and began to serve it. It feels so strange to be talking about experience — sex — with them, she realized. I don't see why Briar keeps plunging in. I tried the kissing, and the petting, that time in Gansar, and that other time in Anderran. It just felt . . . awkward. That one boy smelled of sweat, and the other one had chapped lips. But Briar *likes* it. Lark and Rosethorn like it. Frostpine likes it. I wonder if Tris . . .

She sneaked a look at Tris. The redhead had a book in her lap and was reading it between bites.

Perhaps not, with Tris, Daja thought. You'd have to get her attention first, and she'd probably hit you with a book. She looked up and met Sandry's dancing blue eyes. Sandry had noticed that Tris was reading at the table, too.

Daja grinned. At least some things are still familiar, she thought. And at least Sandry is still Sandry, whether she lives in a marble pile or no.

They spent the next day apart, indulging in their own interests and business. While they had been able to get away from each other within the confines of the caravan, they had still been kept to the company of their fellow travelers. For Tris and Briar, accustomed to long hours of solitude, it had been something of a trial. Daja, used to working with those who shared her forge, and Sandry, surrounded by her uncle's staff and household, still welcomed the chance to brace themselves for their presentation at court.

All of them explored the open parts of the rambling house, its gardens, and some of the High Street shops that lay beyond its gates. Briar went as far up the hill as the beginning of the palace walls before he ambled back to Landreg House in time for lunch. In the breezes that flicked over the Landreg walls Tris caught a glimpse of him as he inspected both the vines adorning the walls of some of the other noble town houses and the faces and figures of the women he passed.

Tris frowned and closed her eyes until that puff of air had blown past her. She had requested an upper room of the house to get glimpses of the city, maybe even of activity on the Syth, not of Briar doing the things that Briar normally did these days.

"And that goes double for him smuggling a girl into his room last night," she told Chime, who sat on the balcony rail beside Tris, grooming a rear paw with her tongue. "Do you know what the housekeeper told me? She said her girls are careful about baby-making, and none of them are fool enough to fall in love with a mage. I hope she's still so even-minded about it by the time we leave!"

Chime looked up at Tris, making an anxious clink. Tris sighed. "Oh, I know he plays fair and doesn't promise anything he doesn't mean. Rosethorn would have made sure of that. I just wish it was more to him than, just, just *play.* It *ought* to mean more, don't you think?"

When Chime did not answer, Tris looked at her and smiled reluctantly. "You haven't the least idea of what I mean, have you? And silly me, for asking you such questions!" She picked up Chime and turned to stare into the wind from the Syth again. The empress and her court were out riding on a beach to the northwest — the wind carried her images of

Berenene's unforgettable, laughing face and those of her courtiers: Quenaill the mage, the angry huntsman of a day ago, a buxom young woman with glossy brown ringlets, a blond man with eyes like turquoises, and other men and women in their twenties and early thirties, attractive and vivacious. They rode well, managing their horses in hard sand and soft, laughing silently and chattering. Any shreds of talk came too far behind the images for Tris to bother with.

They're as pretty as a flower bed, she thought, running her fingers over Chime's wings. I don't belong with people like that. I don't belong in a house like *this.* How can I do any good for His Grace here? I'm just a merchant's daughter in clothes my rich friend made for me. I doubt it will come to lightning and cyclones with *this* crowd — more like powder puffs at fifty paces. What possible danger can they offer that I could protect her from?

She turned abruptly and took Chime inside.

Sometime after midnight Briar roused to the sound of horses arriving in the courtyard behind the stable. Curious, and hungry, he pulled breeches on over his nightshirt and went to the kitchen. Sure enough the cook Wenoura was there, a robe over her own nightdress, setting a teapot to boil. She was on good terms with Briar already: He always made an effort to get to know the cook. Without hesitation she ordered him to put out glasses and saucers, since he knew where they were, and take down three plates from a cupboard. Briar obeyed as she bustled around the huge kitchen, producing a slab of cheese, a pot of preserves, a loaf of dark bread, and a ham.

As Wenoura sliced the ham, a footman opened a rear door, letting in a disheveled man. Briar moved back into the shadows for a quiet look as the footman helped the new arrival to remove his gloves and mud-splashed hat. He had already removed his boots and outer coat in the mud room. Fellow must have ridden here in a hurry, to get mud on his hat, Briar realized.

"They're to see the empress in the morning, *Saghad*," the first footman said.

"That's to be expected," replied the new man in a quiet, precise voice. "Though you'd think she'd be allowed a week or so to rest before the court nonsense begins."

The cook, now slicing bread, looked at Briar in the shadows, then shrugged. She wasn't about to say there was a stranger present.

The newcomer worked kinks out of his neck. He wore a blue indoor coat and tan pants, crushed from time in the saddle. Broad-shouldered and wiry, he was about three inches taller than Briar. Like Tris, he wore brass-rimmed spectacles, and his eyes were bright blue behind them. His heavy gold hair was cropped just below his ears. It framed a fair-skinned face mildly scarred from some childhood pox, with a long, straight mouth and a long, straight nose. He had Sandry's eyes and determined chin. "Wenoura, you're a lifesaver," he told the cook as she set food on the long kitchen table. "I didn't stop for supper."

"I'll heat a soup if you like, *Saghad* Ambros," she replied, glancing again at Briar.

Briar took the hint. "*Saghad* Ambros, hello," he said, stepping out into the light to greet Sandry's cousin. "I'm Briar Moss. I think *Clehame* Sandrilene told you she would bring friends." As the older man struggled to rise, Briar grinned. "Please don't stand. I'm not the kind of person people get up for. And I'd never put myself between a man and his supper."

Ambros looked quizzically at Briar. "I hear you've caused people to stand quite precipitously, *Viynain* Moss," Ambros said dryly. "But I appreciate the permission. My legs still feel as if I'm in the saddle."

"You've heard of me?" Briar asked, settling on the bench across the table from Ambros. "I'm sure it was most of it lies. I'm a reformed character these days."

Ambros chewed and swallowed his mouthful before he said, "My cousin only wrote me that you are a very fine plant mage and her foster-brother," he replied quietly. "Are you a reformed plant mage or a reformed foster-brother?"

Briar was about to straighten him out when he glimpsed the wry glint in Ambros's eyes. Well, well — a Bag with a sense of humor, he thought, using his old street slang term for a rich person. "Reformed from everything," he said, as straight-faced as Ambros.

The cook snorted.

"I am," insisted Briar in his most earnest tone of voice. "My approach to the ladies is strictly worshipful. I celebrate our mutual devotion to Qunoc. It's a great deal of work, but I don't begrudge it in the least."

"Well, if you fertilize any of the fields you till, I hope you will fertilize the mothers' purses as well," Ambros said. "A man should take responsibility for what he sows."

"Responsibility is my middle name," Briar told him, earnestly. "Droughtwort is my other middle name." The droughtwort herb rendered any man who ate it sterile for days. Briar was determined not to sire any children who might be left parent-less if something happened to their mothers.

Ambros raised pale brows at Briar. "So thoughtful," he remarked. "*How* old are you?"

"We think eighteen," Sandry announced from the doorway. "Even Briar isn't sure. Cousin, I didn't expect you to come tonight, or I would have stayed up to greet you." She came forward with her hands outstretched, her robe and nightdress billowing around her slender form.

Ambros almost toppled his bench as he scrambled to his feet. "*Clehame* Sandrilene," he said as he took her hands in his. Bowing, he touched her fingertips to his forehead.

"Don't be silly, Cousin," Sandry said, kissing both of his cheeks as he straightened. "With all you have done for me over the years, it's I who should be touching *your* fingertips."

"The honor is mine," Ambros said, kissing her cheeks

in return. "I have the correct frame of mind for the work, and your people are not shirkers."

Briar filched a slice of bread and began to eat it in bits, watching as Sandry coaxed her formal cousin back to his place and his meal. How did she know he'd come here? wondered Briar. Her rooms are on the other side of the house. She was yawning when she went to bed.

He rubbed his eyes as if he were sleepy, when in fact he was adjusting his mind for the trick of seeing finer magics. He could not avoid seeing plain workings, like the kitchen spells to preserve foods and spices and discourage fire. Those were common to any house that could afford them. It took discipline, practice, and skill to view the more subtle handling of magic that he and his sisters had learned in recent years. Once he thought he had the trick of it, he looked at Sandry.

For a moment, he saw it: a spider-thin web of silver that spread around her body, vanishing into the walls, ceiling, and floor all around her. A blink, and the web vision was gone. Briar arched his eyebrows.

You've been lazy, he scolded himself, taking some cheese. Time was you could do that and have it last. *You'd* better practice, my lad. Maybe you've been chasing girls and letting your skills go, but with an empress and her great mages to watch, you'd best brush up fast.

It was funny, but the teacher-voice in his head always managed to sound like Rosethorn.

Briar leaned back, eating his cheese. Sandry's not

snoozing at the reins, he thought, listening as Sandry and Ambros went through the polite dance of a first noble meeting, as if they weren't wearing bedclothes and rumpled garments. She's thrown a web throughout the house, with her at the middle. If anyone who touches it doesn't belong, she'll know.

Without interrupting Ambros and Sandry, Briar got to his feet and returned to his room. How long had it been since he'd meditated? He was going to start tonight.

Sandry noticed that Ambros's eyes followed Briar when he left. When Ambros looked at her again, she said, "I saw you'd introduced yourselves."

"He's very handsome," Ambros replied, his eyes guarded.

Sandry giggled. "I'm sorry, Cousin, but if you knew how ridiculous that is," she explained. "You're not alone, of course. People have said it about Briar and all of us girls at one time or another. But believe me, nothing could be further from the truth. It really would be like courting a brother or a sister."

Ambros smiled crookedly. "Forgive me for falling into common error, then," he apologized. "But you should brace yourself, because you will certainly hear it enough at court."

Sandry shrugged. "The court may gossip as it likes," she said, propping her chin on her hands. "It's of no consequence to me. If I meant to stay, I would take an interest, but I don't."

That made her cousin sit back and frown at her. "You don't mean to stay?"

"I told you in my last letter that I would be going home in the fall," replied Sandry. "You *did* get my letter?"

Ambros rested his knife and fork on his now-empty plate and sipped his glass of tea. "Yes, but . . ."

Sandry waited. He seemed just like his letters: dry and fussy, methodical and precise. She knew he never made overblown promises about the wealth from a harvest or a new mine. If anything, he would tell her to expect less than the funds that usually arrived. If something concerned him, she was prepared to pay attention.

Finally he said, "The empress believes you will change your mind. She is certain of it."

Sandry smiled. Is *that* all? she thought. "I'll explain," she promised, patting her new-met cousin's hand. "I hardly ever say things I don't mean. Once she gets to know me, she'll understand that."

"Would staying here be so bad?" he asked. "You have hardworking tenants who would adore you, and lands that require the touch of their rightful mistress. True, we have some malcontents, but they are everywhere. We could easily double our mule breeding if you were to grant us the monies to do so. And grain dealers need a hand on the rein. I caught Holab trying to short-weight us on barley twice last year. If you don't watch them every second . . ." He caught himself and smiled. "I'm sorry. My wife says I will talk estate affairs until people's ears fall off if I'm not stopped."

"But why should I take your place, when you know and

love the holdings so much?" Sandry asked. "You know every inch of the ground, and my mother hardly ever even visited. You know those people by name, and you look after them. My uncle Vedris needs me. What will I have to do here? Be a butterfly while you continue to do all the work?"

"You will have a husband to take care of such things," Ambros replied steadily. "The empress wishes you to be an ornament of the court. No doubt you'll be given a place there, Mistress of the Imperial Purse, or chief lady-in-waiting —"

"With maids who are far better informed than I am about palace ways to do things," Sandry told him. "I will be bored silly. And you know the saying, 'A bored mage is trouble waiting to unfold.' As for marriage . . . The man I marry would have to be very unusual, Cousin. I doubt I will meet him at court."

Ambros sighed, then covered a yawn. "Forgive me," he apologized.

Sandry got to her feet; Ambros did the same. "Forgive *me* for keeping you from your bed when you're obviously worn out," she said. "Don't let me keep you up a moment longer. Will you be coming to the palace with us tomorrow?"

The older man smiled thinly. "Her Imperial Majesty does not invite me to intimate court occasions," he explained. "She once informed my wife that I was as dry as a stick and not nearly so interesting."

"Then she doesn't know you at all," Sandry replied firmly. She dipped a polite curtsy. "Good night, Cousin."

Ambros put a hand on her shoulder. *"Clehame —"*

"Sandry," she told him. "Just Sandry. Lady Sandry, if we're in public, I suppose. But Sandry the rest of the time."

"Sandry," Ambros said, his eyes direct, "the empress can be quite determined."

Sandry smiled brightly at him. "She seems very reasonable. I'm certain that, when the time comes, I won't have to insist."

5

The 29th day of Goose Moon, 1043 K.F.
The Hall of Roses, the imperial palace
Dancruan, Namorn

The next morning, Daja watched her friends as the four of them waited in an outer chamber to be announced to the empress. Sandry busied herself with a last inspection of their clothes, tugging a fold here, smoothing a pleat there — simply fussing, because the clothes adjusted themselves. When she reached for Briar's round tunic collar, he thrust her hands away. "Enough," he told Sandry firmly. "We look *fine.* Besides, she already saw us in our travel clothes. This fancy dress ought to be good enough."

"Things are different here," replied Sandry. "Did you see the way that footman looked down his nose at us? We're not at all fashionable here, and appearances matter more. I don't want these popinjays sneering at us."

"Well, things may be different, but *we're* the same," retorted Briar, preening in front of a mirror set there for just that purpose. "We're still mages, and the only folk that should concern us are mages."

Daja had to admit, he looked quite trim in his pale green tunic and trousers. Even the moving flower and vine tattoos on his hands seemed to want to match his clothes. Their leaves were the pale green of spring, the tiny blossoms white and yellow and pink, with only the occasional blue rose or black creeper. Still, he needed to remember that not everyone would agree with him. In Trader-talk she told Briar, "Don't talk nonsense. These people matter to Sandry, so they should matter to you."

Briar glared at her. When Daja returned his gaze with her own calm one, he rolled his eyes and shook his head. "They're only mattering to me for the summer, and then I'll have nothing more to do with them," he replied, also in Trader-talk. "I've had my fill of nobles."

"Unless they want to buy something from you," murmured Tris in Trader-talk.

Briar grinned like a wolf, showing all his teeth. "Unless they want to buy," he said amiably. "Then they're my new, temporary best friends."

The gilded doors to the Hall of Roses swept open, propelled by the footman who had guided them to the waiting room. He bowed low to Sandry, and indicated they could enter the room beyond.

Sandry gave him her brightest smile and swept by him, a confection of airy pink and white clothes and silver embroidery. Briar followed Sandry. Tris, respectable in a sleeveless peacock blue gown over a white undergown with full sleeves and tight cuffs, pressed a coin into the footman's hand as she passed him, accepting his murmured blessing with a nod. She had spent long hours on the road with Daja discussing the proper amounts for tips in Namorn. Daja, dressed in Trader-style in a coppery brown tunic and leggings, carrying her staff, accompanied Tris into the larger hall.

"*Clehame* Sandrilene fa Toren," announced a herald. "*Viynain* Briar Moss. *Viymeses* Daja Kisubo and Trisana Chandler."

Daja, Briar, and Tris exchanged a quick grimace. Someone at court had decided to ignore the plainer titles of *Ravvotki* and *Ravvikki* they had used when they first met the empress and openly address them as mages. Reluctantly Daja reached inside her tunic and fished out the snake-like living metal string on which she kept her mage's medallion. Briar took out his, dangling from a green silk cord, and Tris hers, hung on black silk. Quickly, as they approached the empress, they arranged the medallions properly on their chests. Daja knew that Sandry wouldn't bother. Sandry understood that showing her medallion would not change how anyone saw her.

Producing their medallions had an instant effect on Sandry's companions, however. Daja felt her back straighten. She saw it happen with Briar and Tris, too. We *are* eighteen, after all. We're allowed to wear the medallions in public, Daja realized. And maybe having them in the open is actually . . . helpful. We're not Sandry's lowborn foster family, or that's not the most important thing about us. We are accredited mages from Winding Circle, which doesn't grant the medallion to just anybody. We have reputations. We are people to be reckoned with.

As they walked toward Berenene, Daja saw that the sight of medallions on the chests of Sandry's companions also had an effect on some of the other mages who were present. They were obviously not happy to see young people wearing that credential. Even Quenaill, the great mage who stood close to the empress, smiled crookedly as he bowed in greeting.

We earned it fairly and properly, thought Daja with a smile that gave away nothing of what went on behind her eyes. And if you don't play nicely with us, we'll even show you how.

To make herself forget jealous mages, she surveyed the room as if she would have to describe it in an exercise for one of her former teachers. Roses figured on wall hangings, damask chair cushions, and on the silk drapes framing long glass windows that also served as doors to the outside. Large Yanjing enameled vases filled with fresh-cut blossoms stood everywhere, so the room was filled with their scent. Like exotic flowers themselves the elegant courtiers sat or stood in small groups, talking quietly as they watched the newcomers. Daja couldn't help but notice that a number of them were attractive men in their twenties and thirties. While the women also were attractive, they fit more of a range of ages, from some in their twenties to one in her sixties who stood just behind the empress herself. The guards along the wall were also good-looking young men, with the hard look of professional soldiers. The Traders had said gossip claimed the guard was the source of those of the empress's lovers who were not noblemen.

Daja also saw that everyone, however intense their private conversations, kept one eye on Berenene. The empress had made herself the focus of the room. She draped herself elegantly, supporting her upper body so that it curved like a swan's neck, drawing the eye from her shoulders to her tiny waist. Today she wore a dusty-rose-colored open robe over a cream undergown. A veil of sheer, cream-tinted silk caressed her coiled and pinned hair. Dangling locks hung down around her face, hinting that she may have just come from bed.

The air is saturated with longing here, thought Daja, watching the glances of the men, the empress's smiles, and the movement of the noblewomen's hands. It's not just the men — the women want to be her, or have her power over men. It's all for Berenene, and she *wills* it to be that way.

They came to a halt before the sofa. Sandry sank into a full curtsy. Tris, with a few wobbles, followed suit. Briar and Daja bowed as deeply as they had when they first met Berenene, in respect for her power and her position.

"Oh, please, let's have none of that formal business here!" said the empress gaily. "Sandrilene, you look simply *lovely.* May I steal your seamstress?"

Offered the empress's hand, Sandry took it with an impish smile. "I am my own seamstress, Imperial Majesty," she said, her blue eyes dancing. "Otherwise I just fuss over other people's work and redo their seams. So much better doing it myself and having it done right."

Daja heard the quiet murmur behind them. Sandry heard it as well, because she went on to say, her voice slightly raised, "I *am* a stitch witch, after all."

"The reports of your skills hardly describe a humble stitch witch." The sixty-year-old woman who stood behind the empress wore a medallion of her own. Daja and the others didn't need it to mark the woman out as a mage: Power blazed from her in their magical vision, power as great as that shown by any of their main teachers at Winding Circle. Despite her power as a mage and her obvious position of trust, she was dressed simply in a white undergown and a black sleeveless overgown. Apart from jet earrings and her medallion, her only ornaments were the black embroideries on the white linen of her gown.

"*Viymese* Ishabal, forgive me," said Berenene, though her eyes were on the four, watching their reactions. "Cousin, *Viymeses*, *Viynain*, may I present to you the chief of my court mages, *Viymese* Ishabal Ladyhammer. Ishabal, my dear, my cousin *Clehame* Sandrilene fa Toren and her foster family, *Viymese* Daja Kisubo of Kugiskan fame —" Daja looked down, embarrassed. She had done a few very noisy, messy things in Kugisko. Berenene's chief mage would surely know exactly what they had been, and how foolishly Daja had behaved for things to get so messy. Berenene continued: "*Viymese* Trisana Chandler." Tris bobbed another curtsy without taking her eyes from Ishabal. The empress smiled and added, "And *Viynain* Briar Moss." Her eyes caressed Briar as he bowed.

For a moment Daja considered sending the thought *Now he's going to be insufferable for weeks* to the other two girls, but she stopped herself. If I start, they'll want to stay in contact all the time, until they stop wanting to, and they shut me out, she told herself. No contact is better.

"It's an honor to meet you, *Viymese* Ladyhammer," replied Sandry with courtesy. "Your fame extends well beyond Emelan. I remember Mother talking about you."

"I told her not to go snooping in my workroom," the mage said graciously. "Your mother was always one to learn the hard way." Ishabal Ladyhammer was silver-haired, with deep-set dark eyes and a straight nose. Her mouth was elegantly curved and unpainted: In fact, she wore no makeup at all, unlike other women at court. "Your fame, too, has come to us," she said, looking at each of the four. "It will be interesting to speak with you. I know of no other mages who received their credential so young."

"It was as much to keep a leash on us as to say we could practice magic, *Viymese*," Briar said casually. "We're just kids still, at heart."

"That would be frightening," Ishabal replied, her voice

and eyes calm. "A 'kid' such as you claim to be would not have been able to destroy the home of a noble Chammuran family in the course of a few hours' time, and without wrecking the city around it."

Briar shrugged. "I had help. And the place was old."

"Are you all so modest?" inquired Berenene.

Daja had watched the empress as the others had spoken. Those large brown eyes were busy, checking each face for a reaction. I bet she doesn't miss much, thought Daja. No more than I would, in her shoes.

To be a woman on the throne of the largest empire north of the Pebbled Sea and east of Yanjing was no easy task. Keeping control over famously hotheaded nobles seemed too much like work to Daja. Namornese nobles were notorious for their love of fighting — if not for the empire, then among themselves. Since taking the throne at the age of sixteen, Berenene had kept her nobles busy with wars and grand progresses of the empire that wrung out the purses of her subjects. Now that the empire was stalled at the Yanjing empire's Sea of Grass in the east, and the Endless Sea in the west, Berenene was probably worried about how else to keep her people occupied.

Send them to the new lands, across the Endless, Daja thought with a mental shrug. That ought to keep them busy. Let them conquer the savages over there, if they can. The explorers who report to Winding Circle have said the native peoples in the new places have their own powerful magics, rooted in their soil. Let the Namornese try to beat them, if they need something to do.

While Daja had mused, Sandry had been explaining that the four of them weren't modest, just aware of how little they actually knew. "Having a credential just means you realize how much you have yet to learn," she explained gracefully. "Really, the Initiate Council at Winding Circle gave us the medallion as much to make sure we would have to answer to them as to acknowledge we had achieved a certain amount of control over our power."

Daja's attention was caught by movement at a side door. A woman in her early twenties entered the room, bearing a large, silk-wrapped package that shimmered with magical silver cobwebs. The woman's green silk overdress and amber linen underdress were stitched to outline the ripe curves of her body. Her mouth was as richly full as her figure, her dark eyes large and long-lashed. She wore her curling brown hair loose around her shoulders, covering it with an amber gauze veil held in place with jeweled pins. When she saw that Daja was looking at her, she smiled. Her eyes were filled with so much merriment that Daja simply had to smile back. Who is she? the girl wondered. She has to be the most beautiful woman of the empress's court.

"Ah, Rizuka," said the empress, smiling brightly at the new arrival. "Is that the Yanjing emperor's gift?"

The woman came over to the sofa and curtsied elegantly, despite the package in her arms. "Imperial Majesty, it is,"

Rizuka answered. Her voice was light and musical. "Forgive me for taking so long to bring it, but I knew you would not need me earlier, and I had the mending to finish."

The empress laughed. "You know me too well, my dear. *Clehame* Sandrilene fa Toren, *Viymeses* Daja Kisubo and Trisana Chandler, *Viynain* Briar Moss, allow me to present my Wardrobe Mistress, *Bidisa* Rizuka fa Dalach. Not only does Rizu ensure that my attendants and I do not go clothed in rags, but she oversees the liveries for all the palace staff."

Rizu curtsied as the four returned her greeting. *Bidisa*, thought Sandry. Baroness, in Emelan.

"Sandrilene, my dear, I asked Rizu to bring this for your inspection," Berenene continued graciously. "I received this gift from the emperor of Yanjing, and I am simply at a loss. Of course I must send him a gift of like value, but, to be frank, none of us have seen cloth of this sort before. I would hope you might give us your expert opinion."

"I'd be happy to, Cousin," Sandry replied. "Though how unusual can it be, that you haven't seen it before?"

Cradling the package on one arm, Rizu undid the silk tie that closed it and pushed the wrapper back. It revealed a bolt of cloth that reflected light in an array of colors, from red-violet to crimson. Daja, Tris, and Briar also drew closer to look.

They're impressed, Sandry thought. So they should be. Those threads are one color of silk wrapped around another, leaving bits of the original color to peek through. And those threads are twined, two shades of violet so close together that you can't call them by different names, but they still add two colors to the weave. While the embroideries — Mila bless me, but they look like they were done by ants, they're so small.

She held out her hand to touch the cloth and stopped, her palm an inch away from it. Her instincts shrieked for her to keep the silk away from her skin.

"Hmm," Sandry murmured.

Reaching through a side slit in her outer robe into one of her pockets, she found the dirty, mineral- and root-laced lump of crystal that was her night-light. Despite the materials trapped inside it, the crystal gave off a clear, steady light that made it easier to see the individual twists and turns of thread in the cloth.

Three layers, she thought, viewing the material closely. The bottom layer, crimson silk wrapped in bloodred silk. The outer layer is the two violet threads twined together. There's a cloth-of-gold thread in the outer layer, too. It shapes half the embroideries. But the second layer, *that's* the odd one. The smaller embroideries are tucked in there, out of sight, and the cloth doesn't want me to look at them. As if I could be stopped!

Sandry pulled a thread of her power from her inner magical core and used it to draw a circle with the index finger of her free hand just over the cloth's surface. Then she smoothed the fire until it was a round disk. She released that into the cloth.

Invisible tiny pincers, like beetle claws, sank into her magic.

Immediately she yanked free and retrieved her power. That's so shocking! she thought, distressed and angry, seeing the full shape of what had been done in this cloth. All that careful stitchery done on this, embedding the signs and making them inert. They won't even start to work until the person who wears this cloth scratches or cuts herself. Then the signs come alive to release a speck of rot here and there, until her blood's poisoned. It must have taken his mages *months* to do it, not to mention the time spent on just the right threads and embroideries to hold the spell. I hear there's been famine in Yanjing, and he's got his people wasting time and money on *this*? What kind of an emperor lets his people suffer while he sends something like this to Dancruan?!

She looked up and met her cousin's brown eyes. They flickered with mirth.

Ah, thought Sandry, returning her crystal to its pocket as she straightened. My cousin Berenene knows it's dangerous, and she's testing me. Probably *Viymese* Ladyhammer already told her about the magic on the cloth. That's why Berenene's Lady Rizu left the wrapping on it, and why she doesn't let the silk touch her anywhere.

"What do you think, Cousin?" the empress wanted to know. "It's so lovely, I don't want to fritter it away. I should use it for something special, but I can't think of what."

Two tests, Sandry told herself. The first to see if I would find the magic. The second to see how clever I am politically. If I tell her to send it back, she knows I'm silly enough not to know, or care, that I'd be insulting the emperor of Yanjing, who's her most powerful neighbor and sometimes enemy. The same thing is true if I tell her to destroy it, or lock it away. Besides, some poor servant might want to look at the pretty thing, and end up dying for mere curiosity. What does she think I do for Uncle, write up his party invitations?

Sandry thought fast as she tied the wrapping closed around the deadly cloth once more. "Imperial Majesty, this is too splendid a gift to waste on anyone who can't appreciate the craft that went into it," she said at last. She smiled at Rizu before she looked at Berenene again. "We westerners lack the subtlety to appreciate the artistry in this. But do you know, I am virtually certain the Yanjing ambassador is someone of culture and wit. And he — it's a he?" Rizu and Ishabal both nodded. "I'll bet the ambassador misses Yanjing," Sandry continued. "A noble from their realm . . . well, he's probably the best person in Namorn to appreciate this cloth. I am certain he would be deeply grateful if Your Imperial Majesty would grant him this piece of his homeland as a sign of affection." Sandry didn't have her old connection to her friends, but she didn't need it to feel them relax around her. They, too, had sensed that something about the cloth was very wrong.

Berenene laughed and clapped her hands as Ishabal nodded to Sandry. "Wonderful, Cousin! You have solved our dilemma most delightfully. Rizu, see it done right away." As Rizu left them with the cloth, the empress told a young man who hovered nearby, "Jak, you silly boy, stop pretending you aren't interested. *Clehame* Sandrilene fa Toren, may I present *Saghad* Jakuben fer Pennun? Jak is one of my dearest young friends. He's also your neighbor, near your estates outside the town of Kilcoin."

Sandry knew she had passed the test. She smiled and extended her hand to a very attractive young man. Big, broad-shouldered, with crow's-wing black hair and bright chestnut eyes, he was delightfully handsome, with an infectious smile. He kissed her fingertips. "Hello, fair neighbor," he said in an engaging, boyish voice. "If you ever wish to borrow a cup of honey, I will be glad to oblige, though a creature as sweet as you will probably never run out."

"I know what that is," Sandry retorted, having heard variations on this theme since she had moved into her uncle Vedris's home. "That's flattery. Don't do it again, please."

Jak pouted and looked at the empress. "Great lady, *you* said I did flattery well."

"You did before today," Berenene told him with a catlike smile. "I fear our cousin has bowled you over and made you clumsy."

"But I can't admit to it," protested Jak. "She'll just say I'm flattering again."

Sandry giggled and retrieved her hand since Jak had yet to let go of it. "Don't admit to it," she advised. "You've almost returned to my good graces."

As if responding to an invisible signal, others moved in to be introduced, including more handsome young men who had paid attention to Jak's greeting and avoided his mistake. Everyone also greeted Daja, Briar, and Tris. Berenene watched them all with the amusement of an aunt supervising beloved nieces and nephews. When the noblemen began to argue over who would bring Sandry tea and who could fetch her a plate of delicacies to nibble on, Sandry curled her lips in a wry smile. If only Uncle could see me now, she thought. Not that he'd have much use for these pretty courtiers. When Uncle sees a strong young man idling about, he puts him to work. And only think, a week ago I was riding in the mountains, wishing I could sew my sisters' and brother's mouths shut to stop them from arguing!

As Jak brought her tea, Berenene ordered Quenaill to fetch Sandry a chair. Once Sandry took her seat with a word of thanks, Finlach fer Hurich offered her a plate of tiny dumplings, fresh strawberries, and marzipan roses. Redheaded, with a handsome face composed entirely of carved angles, he rivaled Jak for looks. As he and Jak hovered around Sandry, she noticed that they glanced frequently toward Berenene. She was about to demand that they decide who they wanted to talk to when she saw the mage Ishabal and another older woman whispering together and looking in her direction.

It hit her like fireworks: These are my cousin's choices, Sandry realized. She's picked Jak and Finlack as the ones she wants to court and marry the heiress if they can. Uncle warned me she'd try this. If I wed a Namornese nobleman, I stop taking my income to Emelan. My wealth stays here.

Sandry veiled her eyes with her lashes as she bit into an early strawberry. So the summer's game of snare-the-heiress begins, she thought cynically. It will be interesting to see how they try to do it, especially now that they know I don't care for flattery.

She sighed. I hope they're entertaining, at least. Otherwise I'm going to be very bored until it's time to go home.

After an hour of further mingling, Berenene proclaimed it was too fine a day to spend indoors. She invited her court and her guests outside to view her gardens. Immediately Rizu went to a pair of doubled-glass doors that opened onto a marble terrace. When she struggled with the latch, Daja went to help her.

Rizu smiled at her through the curls that had escaped her veil. "These old things are always stiff this early in the year," she said. "I told the servants to oil them yesterday, but it was a bit cold last night."

Daja reached into the latch with her power and warmed

the oil in its parts. The latch turned. The doors swung outward. "You just have to know how to talk to locks," she told Rizu.

"So I see," the young woman replied, and laughed. "Obviously I need to learn a new language. My goodness . . ." She looked at Daja's brass-wrapped hand. "Is that jewelry?"

"Not exactly," Daja replied. She offered the hand for Rizu's inspection and turned it over so the other woman could see the brass on her palm. As Rizu inspected her hand, Daja felt warmth start under her skin where Rizu touched her. It fizzed up into her arm, making Daja feel both odd and pleased at the same time.

"Does it hurt?" asked Rizu, awed, when she saw the metal was sealed to Daja's flesh.

Daja shook her head. "It's part of me. And it's a long story."

"I'd love to hear it," said Rizu, walking onto the terrace. "If you don't mind telling it?"

Daja smiled and tucked her hands in her tunic pockets, falling in step with Rizu as the nobles surged out into the morning sun. "Well, if you insist."

Tris drew back as the courtiers streamed outside. Let them go walk and flirt and gossip about people I don't know, she thought, meaning the nobles, not her friends. If I wanted to be bored, I'd have tried embroidery. She smiled. And Sandry would scold me for saying it's boring, she added.

The truth was that the breezes surrounding the palace at ground level drowned her in images and voices trapped in its air currents and drafts. They were the gleanings from the hundreds of people who walked and worked on the grounds. Tris could block out most of the voices, but it was harder to keep bits and pieces of pictures from assaulting her eyes, and Sandry had forbidden her to wear her colored lenses on the day she was to be officially presented at court.

I need spectacles that block the images without looking odd, Tris told herself. Or I need to tell Sandry that I don't care how strange I look.

Or . . . there are advantages to staying indoors, she thought. This is a new place. Better still, this is a new wealthy household, which means more books. I doubt the empress will even notice I'm gone, she told herself. She's so busy watching Sandry, I'll bet she has eyes for little else. I wonder where Her Imperialness keeps her library?

Briar drifted through the crowd of nobles, getting to know who was who, particularly among the women. He didn't go all out with any one female, not today. You've got all summer to spend in this human garden, he told himself, when the urge to single out a particular beauty caught him up. And some of these flowers are well worth the effort to cultivate. You don't want to race around clipping them like a greedy robber.

A few male mages drifted his way to get acquainted. They accompanied their greetings with a subtle pressure to see if Briar was weak or unprepared, a magical touch like a too-strong handshake. It was a popular game with insecure mages, particularly men, and Briar withstood it without pressing back. He ended the conversation and moved away from the pressure as soon as was polite. Why do they waste their time like this? Briar wondered for perhaps the thousandth time since he had begun his mage studies. They aren't competing with me, or me with them, so why bother? None of my teachers ever tried that nonsense.

"Stop that," he finally told the last mage crossly. "I'm not going to yelp like a puppy and I'm not knocking you over, either. Stop wasting my time and yours. Grow up."

Quenaill was within earshot. He came over, waving off the man who had begun to turn red over Briar's remarks. "You'd better hope Her Imperial Majesty doesn't catch you at such tricks with her guests, particularly not with a garden mage," he advised the nobleman. As the older mage left, Quenaill smiled quizzically down at Briar. He was a hand taller, the tallest man at court. "You think it's a waste of time?" Quenaill asked. "Not a way to gauge the potential threat of a stranger?"

Briar dug his hands into his trouser pockets. "Why?" he asked reasonably. "I'd be an awful bleat-brain to try anything here, where even the pathways are shaped for protection."

"You don't want others to respect you?" asked Quenaill. He had the look in his eye of a man who has stumbled across some strange new breed of animal.

"What do I care if they respect me or no?" asked Briar. "If I want them to learn that, I won't use a silly game to teach it. I save my power for *business.*"

"Well, my business is the protection of Her Imperial Majesty," Quenaill reminded him.

"And mine isn't anything that might mean her harm," Briar replied. "You obviously know that already. I'm a nice safe little green mage, all bestrewn with flowers and weeds and things."

Quenaill covered the beginnings of a smile with his hand. When he lowered it, his mouth under control again, he said, "Little plant-strewn green mages aren't safe, not when they wear a medallion at eighteen. I was considered a prodigy, and I was twenty-one when I got mine."

Briar shrugged. "That's hardly *my* fault. Maybe your teachers held off because they were worried about you respecting them — and maybe mine already knew I respected them for anything that truly mattered."

Quenaill began to chuckle. Once he caught his breath, he told Briar, "All right. I give up. You win — such tests of power *are* pointless in the real world. But if you think any of these wolves won't try to show how much better than you they are, in magic or in combat, you're in for a rude awakening."

Briar brushed off the idea as if it were a fly. "Just because they want to dance doesn't mean I'll do the steps," he replied. He and Quenaill fell into step together as the court wandered down into the park that surrounded the palace. "So where did you study?" he asked as they followed the lords and ladies.

They had a decent chat before one of the ladies claimed Quenaill's attention. Briar wandered on by himself, inspecting the wealth of plants that ornamented the paths. The sight of a pool drew him down to the water's edge to see the green lily leaves that covered its surface. Buds stood up from the water on long stems, still too tightly furled to betray the color of the blossoms within.

He heard the rustle of silk behind him. Without looking around, Briar muttered, "Aliput lilies! How did she get Aliput lilies to grow so far north?" He let his power wash away from him, over the pond's surface, but he detected only the tiniest whispers of magic in the edges and along the bottom, in charms to keep away rot and insects.

"It wasn't easy," Berenene replied, amused. Briar turned his head; she stood just a foot from him, with the court spread behind her like a gaudy cape. "I shelter them in the greenhouses all winter, in pools with just enough warmth to keep them alive. I have to do that for all the temperate land plants. They don't last ten minutes in one good blast from the Syth in November. The first year I was empress, I lost a fortune in water lilies because I left them out in October."

She sighed, a rueful curl to her slender mouth. "My father forbade me to import any plants whatsoever. He told me he would not waste good Namornese coin on garden frippery. That first year I was empress, I feared he was right, and that it was a fool's idea to spend all that money for something that went black with frost burn instantly and never recovered."

Briar looked up into her large brown eyes, interested. This was a side to her that he had not expected. True, the imperial gardens were one of the wonders of Namorn, but he thought that was the work of imperial gardeners. He had no idea that the empress herself took an interest beyond having the fame of them. "But you tried again," he said.

"By then I'd had three assassination attempts on my life, and a peasant rising that took five thousand troops to put down," she said, staring into the distance. "I thought that if running the empire was going to be so treacherous, I owed myself something to remind me that there was *some* good in being empress." She smiled at him. "I have papyrus plants growing in the next pond," she said. "Would you like to see?"

Briar hurriedly got to his feet. "I'm your man, Imperial Majesty."

She looked at him. "Are you indeed?" she asked with an impish smile. "Then you may offer me your arm." Briar did so with his most elegant bow. She rested a white hand accented with rings on his forearm and pointed to one of the paths. "That way."

The courtiers parted before them as they climbed to the next path, then fell into place behind. Briar looked at his companion, still trying to puzzle out how he felt about the discovery that this powerful woman liked plants. "So do you oversee all these gardens, Imperial Majesty?" he inquired.

Berenene put her head back and laughed. Briar's eyes traveled along the line her lovely throat made. They should do statues of her as Mila of the Grain, he thought. Or the local earth goddess, Qunoc. I'm surprised all these lovesick puppy courtiers haven't put them up all over the country. He glanced back. The lovesick puppies glared at him.

"I would not have the time to oversee each and every garden here, let alone at my different homes," Berenene told Briar. "And so many of them are displays of imperial power. They're impersonal. But I do have spots that are all mine, with gardeners I trust if my duties keep me away, and I have my greenhouses. There's always time in the winter to get my hands dirty. Here we go."

They walked out of the shelter of the trees into bright sunlight, an open part of the grounds that would draw sun all day long. Here stretched the long pond bordered by tall papyruses. It was bordered by a wooden walkway. Berenene led Briar up onto it. "I hate to lose good shoes in the mud," she explained, "and we have to keep the edges boggy for the reeds. Do you know what those are?" She pointed through a break in the greenery at the pond's edge.

Briar whistled. "Pygmy water lilies," he said, recognizing the small white blossoms among the spreading leaves. "Nice."

"I tried to crossbreed them," the empress said, leaning her elbows on the rail that overlooked the pond. "I wanted a red variety. I've had no luck, so far. But *you* might."

"It would take longer than I plan to stay," Briar told her, watching a father duck patrol the water near a stand of reeds. I'll bet he's got a lady friend with eggs hidden there, he thought. To the likes of him this expensive little stretch of water is just a nesting-place.

"It's a pity," replied Berenene. "I think between us we would create gardens the whole world might envy. But if your mind is settled, I would not try to change it."

A glint of light on the far side of the long pond caught Briar's eye. "Imperial Majesty, I think you might change any fellow's mind, if you chose to," he said gallantly, but absently. "What's over there?"

"My greenhouses. Would you care to see them? Or would you think I was trying to tantalize you?" Berenene inquired wickedly.

Briar looked into her eyes and swallowed hard. If Rosethorn was here, she'd say this was way too much woman for me, he thought. And maybe she'd even be right.

Berenene gave him a long, slow smile. "Come." She took his arm once more as they set off down the wooden walkway. The hammer of many shoes on the planks made the empress turn and scowl. "You all have my leave to remain here," she said sharply. "We're going to the greenhouses, and you know I can't let any of you in." To Briar, she said, "The last time I went there with three — *three*, mind! — of my courtiers, one of them knocked over a palm and one broke a shelf of clay pots. They're all grace on the dance floor or battlefield, but not in a greenhouse."

Briar looked back, met the smoldering eyes of a number of young nobles, and grinned.

6

Once the empress and Briar vanished into the long greenhouses, servants appeared with ground cloths to spread on the grass. The nobles occupied benches or cloths in the sun to await Berenene's return. Small groups wandered through a complex of flower gardens nearby, while Rizu invited Daja to sit with her and some of Berenene's other ladies-in-waiting. Sandry, unwatched for a moment, stepped back under a shady tree. She looked on as Jak, Finlach, and other men who had eyed Berenene as they hovered around Sandry formed a clump of watchers. Their eyes were fixed on the greenhouses as they muttered to one another.

"Silly *amdain*," a man said near her right shoulder.

Sandry glanced back and up. She had seen him in the crowd, the hunter who had been so angry with Chime. He was a tall man even not on horseback, with glossy dark blond hair, direct brown eyes, and a clever mouth. It was a face that was made for smiling, which he was doing at that very moment. "Why do you say that?" she asked, knowing *amdain* meant fool in Namornese.

"Her Imperial Majesty sets her pretty boys to courting you, and the moment she isn't here to make them hop, they start sulking about her and ignoring you. In their shoes, I wouldn't grumble about her walking off with your friend." He stood loosely, his green coat open, his hands in the pockets of his baggy black trousers. "I'd be making certain you remembered my name when you went home tonight."

Sandry raised her chin. "If you were present earlier, you'd know I don't care for flattery."

He grinned down at her. "What flattery? I'm talking common sense. Here you are, all the way from Emelan. You have to be more interesting than most of my friends, who know nothing but the roads between their lands and the imperial palaces."

Sandry covered a giggle. He wasn't as obviously handsome as redheaded Finlach or swarthy Jak, but he was good-looking in a friendly, approachable way. I wonder if his nose got that flat bit in the middle when someone hit it? she asked herself. "Forgive me," she said with a smile of her own. "You must think I'm dreadfully conceited."

"No, but you must feel like bait at the moment," he told her. He offered her a large hand. "I'm Pershan fer Roth. Shan."

Sandry let him take her hand. "Sandrilene fa Toren. Sandry." His grip was warm, strong, and nicely brief, after so many men had already tried to make a romance of a handclasp. "Let's see," she murmured, looking at him. "Are you a *cleham? Bidis? Saghad? Giath?*" The last title was equal to that of duke.

"No, no, no, and no. My father's the *giath*, my older brother the heir. I'm just Shan," he said with a scapegrace grin. "I'm Master of the Hunt. In other words, I tell the servants what to do, and they make all the arrangements."

"It doesn't sound as if you enjoy the post," Sandry remarked.

"It beats crop management for my father and brother. Here I've little to do except inspect the hunting gear and animals from time to time, scout new places to hunt, flirt with pretty girls, distract their mothers and chaperones for my friends, and make Her Imperial Majesty laugh. The life of a younger son at the empress's personal court."

"Are there many of you here?" asked Sandry. "I would think most couldn't afford the life."

"Oh, Her Imperial Majesty gives us posts with salaries that help us survive," Shan replied with a casual shrug. "She likes handsome men, and she'd be the first to tell you those of us who depend on her for a living are very devoted to her interests. We had better be."

"What did you mean before, she set her pretty boys on me?" Sandry asked. She had figured it out, but she wondered what this outspoken man would say.

Shan dug his hands in his pockets. "You're not very good at playing the empty-headed noble," he informed her. "Of course you know our mistress would prefer that you and your fortune be confined strictly to Namorn from now on."

Sandry had suspected as much, and hoped he would report her answer to her cousin. "That's not up to her, or to Jak or Fin or anybody. I make my own choices."

Shan grinned at her. "Very fiery," he said with approval. "She's had people oppose her before, you know. It never quite worked out as they wished it to. The will of the empress is not easily ignored."

She sniffed in disdain. Then something made her add, "Besides, I'd never marry any man who's so obviously in love with someone else, like they are. Isn't my cousin a bit old for them?"

"Being imperial inspires a great deal of passion," her companion replied. "Money inspires more passion still. I'm surprised you don't know that, being a *viymese* and educated and all. I hear you mage students run wild at the temple and mage schools."

Sandry fiddled with a button and ordered herself not to blush at the sudden turn in the conversation. "I dislike passion, and I was much too young for it at Winding Circle," she said firmly, watching the courtiers mingle like so many butterflies. "If your friends try it on me, they'll only be disappointed."

Shan studied her for a moment, long enough that Sandry felt the weight of his attention on her. She looked up into his puzzled face.

"You really think you can defy her," he remarked slowly. "You really think you'll beat her. Sandry, *nobody* beats Her Imperial Majesty. Not in the long run. She's as beautiful and as treacherous as the Syth, and at least the Syth is limited just to weather. If I were you, I'd do the wise thing and accept one of her pets. Jak's a good sort. Not particularly clever, but easygoing and cheerful. Once you're married, the empress will move on to some other game and you can go where you please, as long as you produce an heir."

Here it was again, the ghost in the corner of her life, the one she had been sick of years ago. She had escaped it at Winding Circle, only to run into it again the moment she returned to noble society. She hated it. Why do people insist on seeing me as a doll dressed up in wedding clothes? she thought, furious. I'm a person with skills and friends and worth of my own beyond my fortune in lands and money. Beyond being an heiress! And to be told I'm not just a wedding doll, but one that will fold up the moment Berenene frowns at me — it's just too much!

"You must think I have the will of a jelly," she told Shan tartly. "That I'm one of those sweet noble girls who does as she's told."

"If you're not, I'd advise you give it a try just this once," Shan told her gravely. "Berenene is implacable. And I'd warn your friend, *Viynain* Briar, if I were you. None of us would dare to raise a hand or even to criticize Her Imperial Highness, but him? Jak's too good a soul to think it, but I wouldn't put it past Quenaill or someone else to arrange an accident for Briar, to keep him from ousting anyone she favors. I wouldn't even be surprised if Fin bundled him up and dropped him off a cliff some night, *viynain* or no. His uncle is a *viynain* with a soft spot for Fin, and he's head of the Mages' Society of all Namorn."

"Why do you care?" demanded Sandry. "Why should you care what happens to us?"

Shan chuckled. "Because I want to marry you myself, *and* stay on the good side of your magical friends," he said teasingly. "It would be a shame to have a bride who weeps for her friends all the time."

Sandry frowned, but a smile kept tugging her mouth. It was hard to take Shan seriously.

Shan's grin broadened. "See? You like me already. I'm housebroken, well-trained, not so handsome that all the other wives will be flinging themselves at me. . . ."

Sandry laughed outright. "Are you always silly?" she asked when she caught her breath.

"Always," Shan told her. "It's part of my charm. Did I mention I'm charming?"

"Just tell me you're not serious about marrying me," replied Sandry. "Truly, I mean to return to the south when autumn comes."

"But you'll break Jak's and Fin's hearts," protested Shan.

Sandry giggled again.

"You watch. Berenene will find out that they didn't court you in her absence and the fun will begin." Shan scratched his jaw. "No, she doesn't care for it when people don't hop to. They'll have to do something really desperate, like, oh, rescue you from a rampaging bear or something."

"I'll remember to be wary of bears, then," Sandry replied solemnly. "Do many of them get inside the palace walls?"

Shan leaned back against the tree behind them. "I have a feeling the population is about to increase." His face was sober and earnest, but his eyes danced. "Bear importation will be the newest fashion. We can hold hunts through the palace galleries. Everyone will buy new wardrobes, and the grand prize winner will carry you off over his saddle."

Sandry sighed. "I think I'd prefer to marry one of the bears."

"No, you wouldn't," Shan told her earnestly. "My father is one, and he's gone through three wives. Is it true that your friend Daja walks through burning buildings?"

"Ask her yourself," Sandry replied impetuously, holding out her hand. "Come. I'll introduce you." As he wrapped a very large palm around hers, she felt an agreeable ripple of gooseflesh course along her arms.

Rizu and her circle of friends sat or reclined on the grass in a loose arrangement with Daja at their center, joking and laughing together. When Sandry approached with Shan, the Namornese ladies greeted him happily and made room for him and Sandry.

"Oh, sure," said Shan as he took a space between Rizu and Sandry. "Now that I come to you with another woman, you'll happily let me join you." To Sandry, he said, "Would you believe half of these ladies have broken my heart?"

Rizu slapped his broad shoulder. "Tell us you didn't enjoy it." To Sandry, she said, "Be careful of this one. A few jokes with him and you're in a secluded little nook with his hands where they shouldn't be!"

"Pershan fer Roth, this is my friend, Daja Kisubo," Sandry said, introducing them. Deliberately testing them and him, she added, "Daja, Shan says it's the empress's will that I marry one of those young men who hovered around me in the Hall of Roses." From the cynical smiles of the courtiers, she saw that Shan had told her the truth, and that the empress's plan was common knowledge.

Daja clasped Shan's hand, smiling. "I hope the empress has some years to wait for that marriage," she said lazily, turning her face up to the sun. "Sandry's made up her mind to go home before the mountain passes close. She's just here to inspect her estates and return to Emelan. Unless your bucks mean to chase her to the border?"

The young ladies around them cried aloud at this, protesting that Sandry would never see the best of Dancruan if she didn't stay for at least one winter's social season.

"Then she wouldn't have to worry about going home," Rizu announced with a broad smile. "She'd be frozen to this place!"

Once inside the main greenhouse, Briar expected the empress to drift along, pointing out this sight and that, attended by bowing gardeners. And I'd've been dead wrong, he thought.

It was true, the gardeners in sight had looked up when the door closed behind the lady and her guest, but they immediately returned to their work when they saw who had come in. Next, the empress had opened a drawer in a table that stood against the outside wall and pulled out a worn pair of gardener's gloves, which she then tugged onto her hands. Briar watched as she briskly walked over to tables that held pots and boxes of flowering plants.

"Most of these are for gifts," she explained to Briar, inspecting potted lilies for mites on the undersides of their leaves. "The guild heads, ambassadors, and my fellow monarchs claim to prize what comes from my garden, so from time to time I gratify them with a plant. Coleus is always popular. The leaf colors go very well with the colors favored by those who live in east Namorn and Yanjing, and it brings cheer during wintertime. The same with cyclamen." She caressed samples of each with gentle fingers, pinching off a wilted leaf here and there. "My goodness. What on *earth* . . ."

Briar sighed. The greenhouse plants had noted his presence. At first the ones closest to him began to move, bending toward him or turning their flowers toward him as if he were the sun. As he watched, the more distant plants began to shift as if they could crane to see him. They reached out with leaves like hands, wanting his touch and his influence. "Sorry," he told the empress, thinking to the plants, Stop that! Before you get me in trouble!

The plants began to bristle, turning sharp edges outward and stretching out thorns if they had them. If anyone tries to trouble you, they will soon learn you have friends, their quivering stems seemed to say. They will learn the world can be filled with green enemies.

Now, enough! Briar told them impatiently. Is that how you would treat this nice lady, who gives you rich earth and water and helps her people keep the itching things from your leaves and roots? It's because of her that you sit warm in here when the cold wind makes your house rattle. She saves you, her and her friends, from the white death of snow and ice. She ties you with cloth when you get too heavy for your stems, and she gives you good things to eat. It's her that gives the others their instructions to look after you and care for you, too.

One after another, the plants that surrounded them shifted the surfaces of their leaves and the positions of their stems. Flowers turned their open faces toward the empress, who watched them all without giving away her feelings.

She smells like us sometimes, said the roses and gardenias. She is quick with the clippers and the fork. She has touched each of us, often. She handles us gently.

"It's all right," Briar said gruffly. "They just needed reminding of who they owe this soft living to." He suddenly remembered to whom he spoke. "Your Imperial Majesty." He glared at the plants within his view. "They didn't mean to distress you. They like you."

"I'm grateful, *Viynain*," Berenene replied. "This is the first time I ever had to wonder what might happen to someone they dislike. Actually, I had no idea they had thoughts or feelings."

"Not like we know them, Majesty," Briar explained. "Your Imperial Majesty" was just too much of a mouthful to use each time he spoke to her. "They don't have brains, exactly, but their bodies remember things like who waters 'em, who clips 'em, and so on. They just were so excited, feeling me come in, they forgot themselves a bit." Now calm down! he ordered them silently. Act like I'm just another person! He glared at the vine that had reached out to twine around one of his hands and insert its tendrils up his baggy sleeve.

The vine released him and returned to the trellis it had adorned before Briar had come into the greenhouse. Berenene watched it go. "I take it this happens to you fairly often," she commented wryly.

"Only till they get used to me being around," replied

Briar. "They're like kids — children," he explained. "They get all worked up, and they need time to calm down. You should see them around my teacher, Rosethorn. They can't not touch her when she's by. It's like she's the sun, except then the moss and funguses would stay clear of her, and they don't. Are those potted palms?" He wandered over to the stand of large, tree-like plants, hoping to distract her from thinking about plants on the move. In his travels he had discovered that some people reacted oddly to it. Stopping next to the nearest one, he ran an appreciative hand over its trunk.

"It's vanity, I know," said the empress. "But it's so satisfying, knowing I have a bit of southern warmth when winter shrieks down off the Syth."

Briar smiled. "Winters are always hard if you like seeing green things about you," he admitted. "I tried to get my teacher to visit Dedicate Crane's greenhouse — he was my other plant teacher, back at Winding Circle — but she's old-fashioned. She growls how plants are supposed to have their own season, then surrounds herself with potted plants all winter long. She just can't get the tropicals to thrive in her workshop."

"I've read Crane's book, you know," Berenene said, leading him farther back into the greenhouse. As they walked, the gardeners continued to work. When the empress moved inside the palace she was followed and preceded by bows and curtsies. Idly, Briar wondered, How long do you s'pose it took her to break her gardeners of the habit?

There was a wave of motion here, but it was directed at Briar, and it came from the plants. He called some of his power up and let it trickle away in the tiniest of threads, running to every plant and tree in the building. He did the same in the next greenhouse, and the next, and the next. The empress had a complex of them, each closed by its own doors and connected to its neighbors by wooden halls.

"The things you learn," Berenene said as she led the way into yet another greenhouse. "Mites. I had two greenhouses that connected, and the treacherous little *nalizes* got into everything. Once again I had to start from scratch. That's the problem with gardening. One mistake will do more than just teach you. It can wipe you out." She stood back and smiled. "I understand you have an interest in *shakkans*, Briar Moss. Would you care to grant your opinion of mine?"

He had seen bigger collections in the imperial palace in Yanjing, but nowhere else. This greenhouse had been divided in half with glass and yet another door. In one half, miniature trees and the gear to care for them were arranged with an eye to the light that filled the greenhouse. A number of the step-like shelves on Briar's left were empty, but the marks that water, earth, and light left on the unstained wood indicated that upward of twenty plants were missing. "Your pines?" Briar asked, nodding toward the empty spots.

Berenene favored him with a warm smile. "Exactly so. When I think they have a chance, I bring them onto my windows and terraces. I tend to be more cautious with the ones that are not evergreens. It's not unknown for the Syth to blow in a night's frost even this late in the spring."

Looking around, Briar saw a miniature forest of Quoy maples, each perfectly set in its large, flat tray. He was drawn to it like iron to a lodestone. The emperor of Yanjing would wilt to have something like this, Briar thought as he touched the miniature leaves with gentle fingers. He can't grow maples at all, let alone a forest arrangement. The trees nearly purred under his touch, welcoming the gentle trickle of his green magic as it flowed along their stems. From there, Briar found several shapes of rhododendrons, all blooming beautifully. A step away he found miniature apple trees in bloom. He moved from dish to dish, tree to tree, noting which had been wired to follow a particular shape, which trees displayed new grafts, which were very old and which were only made to look old. He lost all track of time and his companion as he inspected each and every plant. All were lovingly tended and in the best of health.

When he looked up, Berenene was gone. Briar frowned. How long did I pay her no mind? Did I vex her, ignoring her like that, and she went stomping off? he wondered. She seemed to understand a fellow might get caught up, but it's hard to tell what way empresses will jump.

Then he saw spring green motion through the blurred glass of the divider. She had gone into the other half of the greenhouse. He followed her, passing through the glass door and closing it in his wake. This side of the building was hot and damp, as hot as the jungles of southern Yanjing. It was an entirely different world, filled with wildly gorgeous, complex flowers. There were as many different containers for them as there were colors and shapes of flower, ranging from pots to stick holders and slabs of cork. The empress handled the blooms very carefully, inspecting them for problems, shifting them if she felt the light was too strong.

There were rolls of muslin at the inside top of the peaked roof, each with a cord that dangled to within arm's reach at the center of the room. Briar noted small, ship-like cleats on the metal strips between panes of glass.

Curtains, he guessed. In case she thinks the light's too strong in one part of the room, she can pull down the curtains and secure the cord so the muslin's close to the glass. And when she says so, they roll them up again.

He knew instinctively that she was the only gardener in charge of this room, though she might have helpers to do the basic work when she could not. But these flowers bloomed with good care, and her face glowed with happiness as she tended them. Even more than the *shakkan* house, this was her place to be happy.

"Did you see all you wished?" she asked without looking at him. "Are they not splendid?"

"The emperor of Yanjing would perish of envy if he knew," Briar assured her. "Even his collection isn't as good as yours."

"I should send him something he does not have, then," murmured Berenene, moving on to the next plant. "As my thanks for his delightful gift of cloth. What do you think of my orchids?"

Briar jammed his hands in his pockets. He didn't entirely approve of orchids. "Parasites," he said, one gardener to another.

The empress chuckled. "They are not. They don't destroy, and real parasites do. Not that I object to parasites outside my garden," she said knowingly. "I am surrounded by them, all as gaudy and pretty as my orchids. That's what courtiers are, you know."

Briar shrugged. "Turn 'em loose and let them do something worthwhile," he suggested, going over to eye a pot of striped orchids. They moved uneasily, sensing his disapproval.

"Ah, but what I think is worthwhile for my nobles and what they feel is worthwhile are so often different things," Berenene explained. In the light her creamy skin was luminous. "The problem with nobles is that they never have enough. They always want more. They would get into mischief without my eye on them, and some of that mischief would be directed at me. I would rather keep them in my palatial hothouse, where I can prune them quickly if they show signs of plotting."

"Seems to me they'd plot more if you kept 'em too close," Briar said, "but I'm not as good with people as I am plants." He scowled at the striped orchids, which had begun to tremble. "Stop that," he commanded them. "I won't hurt you, now I know you aren't really parasites. Here." He stretched a hand out to them and gently touched their stems, sending calm into their veins. "I'd never hurt you." Thinking of pruning, he added, "Not unless it was good for you."

Berenene shook her head as she carefully watered a series of boat orchids. "Now *I* do not understand why you talk to them, and why you might allow them to speak to you. I love them because they are so beautifully silent."

"Ouch." Briar winced. "I suppose then that you've got the worst job in the world, with folk yattering at you all day."

The empress laughed. "I've grown accustomed. As long as I have my refuges here, I shall do well." She looked up at the sun and sighed. "I suppose I've left them unwatched long enough. It's nearly midday, and they get cranky when they are not fed." She caressed a blazing pink tree of life orchid. "Like my beauties, only my nobles are noisier by far. Well, I have my beauties among them, too, to console me." She removed her gloves and put them away, then left the orchids and walked over to Briar.

"Like that Jakuben, and Finlach?" he asked, following her out through the *shakkans.*

"Ah, them I am willing to share," replied Berenene. "Here. This will be quicker." They left through a side door in the wooden corridor, one that opened onto a flagstone path through the open gardens. "It's my hope that one of my lovely lads will convince my dear cousin Sandry to remain in Namorn."

You'll need more to convince her than she'll get from those cockawhoops. Briar thought it, but he did not say it. And it's not my place to tell her Sandry has a will of steel and a mind of her own. Berenene will have to learn that by herself. For the sake of her plants, I hope the lesson doesn't sting too bad.

Out on the grass, Daja and her companions continued to wait as the palace clocks chimed the passage of one hour, then two. Watching those around her, Daja decided it was like being among turtles. Everyone basked in the sun, contentment on their face. Even the men who joined them, like Jak and Quenaill, did it.

"Is this a northern thing?" Sandry asked after the clock marked the second hour, adjusting the seam in one woman's gown with her magic. "You come out to bake like buns on a tray?"

"Wait till *you* survive a Dancruan winter," advised the

black-haired and black-eyed Caidlene fa Sarajane, a lady-in-waiting. "Then you'll love the sun, too."

"But it's terrible for your skin," Sandry pointed out. "You'll get all leathery in time."

"We have lotions and creams and balms for our skin," said Rizu, leaning her head back so the sun gilded her face. "And winter is much too long. We'll risk it."

Daja looked around. "I thought I saw older people inside, but no one here is older than thirty," she remarked.

Their companions chuckled.

"We're supposed to keep up with her," Rizu explained, smiling. "Mornings, you never know if she'll take it into her head to go riding —"

"Or hunting," said Jak, who sat cross-legged on Sandry's other side. "Or to the beach," he continued dreamily, "or to market . . ."

"The older ones rejoin us later in the day if there's nothing else going on," Rizu said. "Today Her Imperial Majesty wanted those closer in age to Lady Sandrilene to meet her, and she didn't want it formal."

"The Hall of Roses is for fun." Caidlene plaited grass stems to make a bracelet. She had already outfitted half of their group with them. "The Hall of the Sun is for the full court and more private ceremonies, and the Hall of Swords is for audiences, elegant receptions, and the like."

"So it's like a code to life at court," commented Sandry.

"If you know where people are, you have a good idea of what's going on."

Daja smiled. "Writing a guidebook for us, Sandry?" she asked. "Or for you?"

Sandry made a rude noise in reply.

"What's going on is that our empress took your friend into the greenhouses, where she won't allow most of us," grumbled Quenaill, his hazel eyes smoky.

"Speak for yourself," Rizu said. "She lets some of her ladies come in."

"Well, their friend Briar is hardly a lady," Jak pointed out. "And he'd better mind his manners with Her Imperial Majesty."

Sandry and Daja exchanged a smile. Nobody makes Briar mind his manners but Rosethorn, thought Daja, knowing that Sandry thought the same thing. And Briar's not such a fool as to offend the empress, no matter what these court fluff-heads think. "He's a green mage," she said aloud, choosing the diplomatic comment. "If she's got a problem with bugs or something, she'll want his advice. Does she keep *shakkans*?"

"Dozens," replied Jak. "They're her second favorites, after her precious orchids."

"Well, then, there you are," Daja said. Movement tickled her skin: Rizu was curiously tracing the outline of the metal on the back of her hand. It made Daja shiver. She smiled shyly at Rizu and continued: "Briar's made himself rich on fashioning *shakkans.* She probably wanted his advice. They're tricky creatures."

"They've been in there a long time for him just to inspect some runty trees," grumbled Quenaill. "I saw how he looked at her."

Rizu laughed outright. "Quen, you silly creature, only think how insulted she would be if he *hadn't*!" she teased, nudging Quenaill with her foot. "When she goes to two hours of effort to dress every morning, men had *better* look at her!"

"Women, too, eh, Rizu?" snapped Fin.

Now all of the women laughed. "Next you'll be jealous of the sun and the moon for looking at her," said one of Rizu's friends with a wicked smile. "And her mirror."

"Her bath," suggested Caidlene, her eyes sparkling. "He'll break into the imperial chambers some night —"

"When she's not there," Shan interrupted. "Never break into her chambers when she's there. The last fellow who tried is nothing but a greasy spot."

"He thought she would like a pretend kidnapping, for the sake of romance," murmured Rizu in Daja's ear. "She didn't. Only a dunderhead would have thought she'd like it."

"*Anyway,*" Caidlene said, glaring at Rizu and Shan for interrupting, "Fin will burst into her chambers and attack her bathtub. Then our new friend the smith mage here . . ."

She winked at Daja. "She'll turn Fin into a bathtub so he can embrace Her Imperial Majesty at long last."

"And he'll get soap in his mouth," joked Shan. "His borscht will never taste the same."

"Tubs don't eat soup," replied another man with a grin. "They're always being emptied."

Fin grimaced. "Don't listen," he told Sandry. "Do you believe these are my friends?"

Daja watched Sandry giggle and wave his remark away. It seems she likes a bit of flattery, whatever she might say, Daja thought. Though if any of them think that Sandry might mistake flattery for true affection, they will be in for a sad awakening. She's too levelheaded for that. Or she always was.

Sandry glanced at Daja and smiled crookedly.

She still is, Daja told herself with satisfaction.

Shan draped his grass bracelet over one of Sandry's ears. She laughed and took it off, then threw it, discus-like, to Daja. Within a moment, grass bracelets flew through the air as their group reached and grabbed, everyone trying to collect the most.

"Ah-hah," Shan said, getting to his feet. It was a long look from the ground to the top of his head, Daja noticed. Now the other courtiers were rising to their feet. In the distance they could see the empress and Briar emerge from behind the greenhouses, Berenene on the young man's arm.

As most of the court surged forward, Daja kept Rizu back. "They aren't, well, *courting* Her Imperial Majesty, are they?" she asked quietly. "She's old enough to be their mother — or at least, mother to some of them."

Rizu flashed her lovely smile. "Well, it's the fashion, for everyone to be in love with her. She makes sure of that," she replied, her voice as soft as Daja's. "If they're hanging on her every word, she says, they stay out of trouble. Besides, if she makes one of them her favorite, like some in the court, they can make their fortunes on offices like that of Chancellor of the Imperial Purse and Governor of the Imperial Granaries."

"Would she marry any of them?" Daja inquired, awed.

"Hardly!" Rizu said, amused. "Give a husband governance over her? No one but Her Imperial Majesty even knows who fathered her three daughters." She tugged at an eardrop, smiling wistfully. "Being a woman with power in Namorn is nearly impossible. She's managed it by never letting us take her for granted. She can ride all day, dance all night, and then wants to know why your work isn't done the next morning — *hers* is. She has spies and mages by the barge load, and she pays close attention to them. Men have tried to get control over her, and failed. Nowadays, they don't even try. But that's her." Rizu shook her head. "She's one of a kind."

Tris was absorbed in a history of the Namornese empire when she realized it was stuffy in the small library she had settled in. Putting her book aside, she got to her feet and went to open a shuttered window. Leaning out, she smelled lightning mixed with water. In the distance she could feel a rapidly climbing build of wind. A storm! she thought, excited. And with so much water-smell to it, I bet it's on the lake. I wonder if I can get a look — it's worth the image-headache, to see a storm on the legendary Syth.

Her student Keth had described the lake's storms to her so eloquently that Tris would even forego reading to watch one. She placed her book where she had found it, closed the shutters, and went in search of a view. Turning a hall corner, she nearly ran into the chief mage, Ishabal Ladyhammer.

"I'm sorry, *Viymese*," Tris said. "I wasn't looking."

Ishabal smiled. "In any case, I was looking for you, *Viymese* Chandler. Her Imperial Majesty and the court are sitting down to afternoon refreshments, and would like you to join them."

"Must I?" Tris asked, pleading in spite of herself. "I think you've got a nasty storm brewing in that oversized pond of yours, and I'd love to take a look at it. I've heard so much about them."

Ishabal chuckled. "Our weather mages predict no storms for today."

Tris straightened. It had been a long time since anyone had doubted her word on the weather. "Are they always right?" she asked coolly.

Ishabal raised black brows that made an odd contrast

with her silver hair. "No weather mage is *always* right," she replied in a tone that said this was a fact of nature.

"With normal weather, that's untampered with?" Tris shrugged. "Suit yourself. I'll come to these refreshments of yours once I've had a look at the Syth, if you'll direct me to the outer wall."

Ishabal covered a smile with one well-groomed hand. "I shall do better. I shall take you there myself." She stopped a passing footman with a snap of the fingers and murmured something to him. As he hastened back the way she had come, Ishabal pointed to another hallway. "This way." She led Tris down through the axis of the palace, into a wide room. It held an enclosed staircase that led onto the inner wall that surrounded the palace. From there they took an enclosed bridge to the outer wall that followed High Street on one side of the palace, and the cliffs on the other three sides.

"Don't you like walking in the open air?" Tris asked on the bridge to the outer wall. "Why enclose your stairs and bridges?" She wasn't exactly complaining. She could no longer simply let the open air pour over her at will, though sometimes she risked headaches and bewilderment in the open wind just because she missed it so much.

Ishabal smiled ruefully. "Why? The god Sythuthan will turn your breath into a frozen diamond necklace at winter's height," she replied. "We dare not walk outside up here at that season — these stairs and bridges are the closest we get. Fortunately, at that time the god himself, and the lake, are defense enough. No one has to die on guard on this open part of the wall." They stepped through the doors on the far side of the bridge. Here was a walkway broad enough that three people could ride abreast on it easily. The whole of the Syth stretched out four hundred feet below at the foot of the crenellated wall. The young woman and the old walked some two hundred feet along the top, the wind pulling at their hair and gowns, until Tris halted in one of the crenels, or stone notches. She pointed to the gray mass of storm clouds some ten miles offshore.

"I spoke out of foolish national pride," Ishabal said, leaning against the merlon at the side of the crenel. "The god Sythuthan is a notorious trickster with a nasty habit of hurling storms at us with no warning to our mages."

Tris bit her lip. The wind showed her a sharp image of a distant scene that was just a blurred dot to her normal vision.

"I hope all the fishing fleet got back to shore," Ishabal remarked worriedly. "The storms are infamous for the speed in which they appear."

"They're trying," murmured Tris. The image of the fleet tore out of her hold. She closed her eyes and did a trick with her mind, shifting the shape of her eyes and of the power she slid in front of them. Carefully she removed her spectacles and tucked them into a pocket inside her overgown, then opened her eyes. Now she could see across the miles without being forced to rely on a windblown image. A small fishing fleet struggled to turn and race for the shore, caught in a crosswind that left it becalmed.

Ishabal's hands were moving in the air. Suddenly everything in front of the wall ripped, and Tris's view was ablaze with silver fire. "Ow!" she cried, clapping her hands to her watering eyes. "What did you *do*! That *hurt*!"

Ishabal, who had turned the air before them into an immense scrying-glass that showed them the fleet in exact detail, asked, "Hurt? What do you mean? Why do you hold your eyes — child, what did you do?"

Tris yanked a handkerchief out from under the neckline of her undergown. "What I *normally* do, *prathmun* bless it!" A blessing from the outcast *prathmun* of Tharios was no blessing at all. Tris wiped her eyes and changed her magic until her vision was normal, then returned her spectacles to their proper place on her long nose.

Ishabal clasped her hands before her as she watched the fleet struggle to move again. "If you may correct your vision as you like, why do you wear spectacles?" she inquired, her voice distant.

"Because I like them," Tris grumbled. "Because I have better things to do with my magic than fix my vision when ordinary glass will do."

"Isha, what is this?" The empress, along with her court,

Sandry, Daja, and Briar, had come to join them. "Your messenger said *Viymese* Trisana predicted a storm on the Syth."

"And more, Imperial Majesty." With a wave of the hand, Ishabal spread the zone of air along the walkway so the entire group could see the drama that unfolded miles away.

"Are you going to do something, *Viymese* Ladyhammer?" asked Tris, mindful of her manners now that they had company.

"This is not an area in which I have expertise, *Viymese* Chandler," Ishabal replied. To Berenene, she said, "They won't be able to escape in time, Imperial Majesty."

"We'll see about that," Tris said. She hated making a scene. More than anything she wished the court would go back to its refreshments, but she was in no position to give orders. Those fishing crews were running out of time. She drew an east wind braid from the net at the back of her head and undid it, unraveling half. Berenene and Ishabal were forced to step back as wind roared around Tris, stirring dust and grit on the walkway. Tris turned up her smiling face into the air current as the wind tugged at her. Carefully, stretching out both arms, she pushed her wind out over the wall and through Ishabal's spell.

Once it was in the open air in front of the cliff, Tris clung to lengths of the wind like reins, letting her magic stream through them into the billowing air. For a moment her grip on the wind shuddered as the air tossed, confused.

Why was it starting in the south, it seemed to ask, if it was an east wind?

"Because I need you to go north first, then east," Tris whispered to it. "Now, go. I'll tug when you're to take your rightful path. You have sails to fill and boats to send home."

That satisfied her wind. It liked to fill sails. North it went, Tris keeping a light tension on her airy reins. She moved both into her right hand, then searched her head to find a braid with a hurricane's force bound up in it. Unraveling only a third of it, she thrust its power north, straight at the onrushing storm. The lesser hurricane raced ahead of her east wind, spreading as it flowed high over the masts of the fishing fleet. Tris gave it a fresh shove north, then tugged on the east wind's reins. The wind found its natural path at last, slowly, as Tris dragged on its reins, until it struck the limp boats' sails with a strong punch. The sails filled to the cheers of the court, watching through Ishabal's spell. The fishing boats scudded through the rough lake water, headed for the shore.

Tris ignored the fleet. She had released the east wind. All of her will was fixed on that quick-moving storm and its battle with her lesser hurricane, as the force she had turned loose fought to keep the storm from advancing. Sweat trickled down her round cheeks. Making even part of a hurricane obey was hard work, particularly when its biggest need was not to halt a storm, but to join in and help it along.

They don't want me anymore, her east wind seemed to say. Now what?

Tris risked a glance at the fishing fleet. They had made harbor safely and were furling their sails as the ships drifted toward their docks.

"Thank you," Tris murmured. She released her east wind, setting it free of any future claims. She could always braid up another. "Now for the interesting part."

She let one end of her small hurricane feed into the storm. It plunged in gleefully. The storm, though, was another matter. If I let it loose, with my bit of hurricane in it, there's no telling what other fleets or even villages it'll destroy, she told herself. And I knew I couldn't hook it with anything weaker than a piece of hurricane. Oh, curse it all. I'll have to take the whole thing back in before it does any harm.

She took a deep breath, wishing she had a moment to pray. Quickly the hurricane struck sparks that turned to lightning as it wove itself among the thunderheads. Tris leaned on a stone merlon, letting it hold her on the wall, then reached with her magic to grip the hurricane's tail. Sweating, she dragged on it with all of her strength, drawing it toward her as Sandry might draw a fine thread from a mass of wool.

Once Tris had brought that storm thread to her, she jammed the end into a coin from her pocket. Once it was secure, she twirled it until the thread of storm began to spin. All storms were drawn to spin, as Tris knew very well: The trick was in keeping them controlled, not allowing them to break free to become a cyclone or full-sized hurricane. Around the wind spun, dragging the storm into the funnel that ended in her thread. Out stretched the storm-parts woven in with her bit of hurricane, twirling under Tris's magical grip. She kept the air moving, shaping it as a fine web so that its natural strength could never overwhelm her once it reached her. If she had looked up, she would have seen the long funnel of cloud that stretched from the storm to her, narrowing until it became her thread.

On and on she spun, making the thread into a ball of yarn, a skill she drew from part of Sandry's magic still mingled with hers. Finally she had turned the entire storm into a ball the size of her hand. She broke it free of the coin, then attached the ball to her partially unraveled hurricane braid. Eager to get out of her hold, the storm sprang into her braid, feeding itself into the many hairs as if it raced along a thousand streets. Once it was absorbed, Tris tied off the braid with a special ribbon that would hold no matter what, and tucked it back into the net with the other braids. Into her pocket went the coin.

She swayed. Hands grabbed her and helped her sit in a crenel. Tris looked up.

It was Briar who had helped her sit as the court stared at her. Sandry came over with a handkerchief to wipe the sweat from Tris's face. Daja grinned as she leaned on her staff, watching. Ishabal looked thoughtful, as did the empress herself.

Tris lurched to her feet to curtsy, Briar holding her by her elbow. She looked at her brother, her eyes pleading. She didn't want to have to explain, not to these well-dressed strangers. Better still, she didn't want to talk at all, not until she got all those storm powers inside her calmed down.

Briar winked at her and turned to the empress, though he continued to brace Tris. "So, Your Imperial Majesty," he said cheerfully. "Might we go back to those refreshments? She'll be fine once she's got some food in her."

7

The refreshments had been set on a terrace tucked out of the wind. Most of the courtiers filled their plates from long tables laden with food. Two of the empress's ladies brought selections to her and her companions, who included Sandry and her friends. The black-haired Jak maneuvered himself into a seat on Sandry's right, while the redheaded Finlach — Fin, he had told Sandry to call him — sat on Sandry's other side.

While pretending to listen to Jak's talk of northern hunting, Sandry kept an eye on Tris, who had taken longer to walk to the terrace after juggling storms. She had obviously meant to sit with Daja and her new friends, but then she balked when some young women flinched away from her. Apparently they were unnerved by Tris's magical working up on the wall — never mind that it saved lives! thought Sandry.

Seeing their reaction, Tris turned to lean on the terrace rail as if that was what she had intended all along. Sandry was about to go offer Tris a seat when Briar, who had helped Tris to walk, stepped in. He turned her around and lifted her up to sit on the wide, flat rail, then went to get food for the redhead. While he did that, Quenaill sat beside Tris, smiling at the scowling girl. Ishabal stopped to speak with the two of them, touching Tris on the shoulder before she moved on to sit with the empress.

So even here, mages stick together, Sandry thought with satisfaction as Briar brought a full plate to Tris. *That's* good to know.

She returned her attention to Jak just in time to say, "Oh, but I don't care for hunting very much." Jak's handsome face fell. Sandry smiled at him. "Did you want me to lie about liking it?" she asked meekly.

"I ask only that you make me miserable," he replied, and let his shoulders sag.

Sandry took a second look at him. Was that a *joke*? "I'm not amused," she said in warning.

"I didn't think you would be," Jak said with a sigh. "The words just slipped from my mouth on the wings of truth."

Sandry deepened her scowl. That's the problem with growing up with Briar, she thought irritably. It makes you inclined to like every jokester who comes along. "That was just plain bad," she said tartly.

"I know," he replied, still in that mournful tone. "I can't help but lose ground with you."

After most of the dishes were cleared, servants brought around one last series of treats: strawberries, cheeses, sweet and salty biscuits, and marzipan candies shaped to form the Landreg family crest, a compliment to Sandry. She shook her head over them, bowed from her seat to the empress, and took a few. Servants carried the tables away as the palace clocks began to chime the hour.

Sandry took a deep breath. The previous night, after Briar had gone to bed, Ambros had persuaded her not to put off visiting the lands of her inheritance any longer. Sandry had agreed: She had come to see her lands, after all, not to socialize. She had not mentioned it to Berenene all day, but time was passing. It's midafternoon, she thought. If we're to leave early for Landreg tomorrow, it's time to go back to the town house and pack. And it's time to say, oh, Cousin Berenene, so nice to stop by for a day, but after I've ignored my obligations for years, I've promised Ambros I'd actually attend to them, so we're going away again for a couple of weeks.

Her rebellious self muttered, And so much for you parading all these would-be husbands for me! Maybe now you'll realize *I'm not interested!*

She nibbled her lip. Sometimes the only approach is the direct one, she told herself. It's not like Berenene can say she herself hasn't been telling me to mind my lands. Excusing herself to Jak and Fin, Sandry went over to the cluster of nobles that had formed around the empress. They noticed her and turned, opening the path between Sandry and Berenene.

"Sandry, we've been discussing some entertainments for you," Berenene said with a smile. "Of course, there are parties, but which do you prefer for daytime: picnics, hunting, rides?"

Sandry dipped a curtsy. "Forgive me, Cousin, but I must beg your indulgence and ask you to reconsider your plans," she said quietly. "I have promised my cousin Ambros that I would inspect my home estates as soon as I had recovered from our journey here. My friends and I will be leaving for Landreg tomorrow morning."

Briar, Daja, and Tris, who were nearby, traded looks. This was news to them.

The tiniest of frowns knit the empress's chestnut eyebrows.

"I do apologize," Sandry continued, "but I really had no chance to mention it earlier. If I don't go soon, it will be a slap in the face to my cousin, who has worked so long and hard in my interest, as well as to my tenants and servants. You yourself, Imperial Majesty, have told me that I have neglected my estates. To come to Namorn after so many years away, and not tend to my obligations immediately . . . I know you would not like me to further shirk my duty."

For a very long moment no one spoke or moved. They're afraid, Sandry realized, listening for clues from the people around her. They're afraid of Berenene when she loses her temper. I'd better keep that in mind. She's all sweetness now, but that's not how she's remained the sole ruler of Namorn for twenty-odd years.

"What can I say?" asked Berenene with a gentle shrug. "Duty is duty. I can hardly reproach you for making the visit I urged you to make in my own letters. But please, return to us soon, dearest cousin. We have weeks of delights to share. And of course we hope that your friends share in them, too. I certainly would like to avail myself of *Viynain* Briar's expertise in my gardens."

She extended a soft, ivory hand. Sandry kissed it and curtsied deep, hearing Tris's skirts rustle and Daja's and Briar's tunics whisper as they bid their own farewells.

"I know!" said Berenene, a broad smile on her lips. "We shall send some of our young people with you, to guard you and entertain you. Jak, Fin, um . . ." She bit her lower lip in thought, then added, "Rizu and Caidlene. I can surely spare the four of you. Yes, even Rizu," she told the smiling maid. Berenene waved off any protests Sandry was about to utter. "I insist. They will be agreeable company for you. Caidlene is a cousin by marriage of Ambros fer Landreg — I'm certain he will not object. They will meet you tomorrow morning."

"Your Imperial Majesty, I mean to leave at dawn," argued Sandry. Wonderful! she thought. There's no way I can refuse without being thought rude, and now I have two of her husband-candidates to pester me! Illogically she wondered, Why didn't she add that nice Shan? She continued aloud, "We'll have guards, and Cousin Ambros to guide us —"

"Then you certainly need livelier people for your party," Berenene interrupted. "*Saghad* Landreg is a wonderful man, but . . . sober. And my young people will be there at dawn." She looked at each of the four nobles she had named. "Will you not, my pets?"

What can any of them say? wondered Sandry as the men bowed and the two ladies curtsied. And what can I say? If I kick up any more of a fuss, she *will* get angry. There's no sense in picking a fight this early in the summer. Aloud, she said, "Cousin, you are too generous. Of course I will welcome your friends."

A footman guided them to a courtyard where hostlers stood with the horses, talking with Shan. He, too, held a horse's reins, a glossy black stallion's. When he saw them, he grinned. "I thought I'd accompany you home, so you wouldn't get lost." Since they had only two miles of High Street to ride, this was clearly a joke. "I wish I could go with you, but we have hunts scheduled for a delegation from Olart and one of the empress's cousins from Lairan. It would be nice to get home for a visit." When Sandry raised her eyebrows in a question, Shan explained, "My parents' estate is only ten miles south of Landreg."

"She can't spare you even for a visit home?" Sandry asked as a hostler helped her mount. "She's sparing Rizu, and Rizu is in charge of her clothes."

Shan chuckled as the others swung into their own saddles. "She could spare us all if she chose — the servants take over if we're needed for social duty, after all. But she likes us to have the illusion we're useful." He mounted his horse and maneuvered the stallion so that when their group rode out of the courtyard, he fell into place on Sandry's right. Daja rode on her left, leaving Tris and Briar in the rear.

"Besides," Shan continued as they passed the first set of inner gates, "most of what I have I owe to Her Imperial Majesty. The least I can do is lend a hand. That cousin from Lairan can be an imperial-sized pain."

"We'll be back before you know it," Sandry told him shyly. "All ready for whatever my cousin throws at us." She turned in the saddle to point to Briar and Tris. "Daja you know, but I don't believe I introduced you to my other friends, Briar Moss and Trisana Chandler."

"Pershan fer Roth," Shan called back with a nod. "Shan. I know I saw *Viynain* Briar with Her Imperial Majesty, but I don't recall seeing *Viymese* Trisana before midday."

They clattered through the last set of gates in the outermost wall, where the guards came to attention as Sandry rode by. Their party rode down to where the broad palace street met High Street. By now it was bustling with traffic of all kinds, traffic that made it a point not to linger in front of the road to the palace. The guards there kept a sharp eye on it all.

"Are all of my cousin's troops so very attentive to their duties?" Sandry asked Shan when they were out of earshot.

"She likes to keep them sharp, so she rotates in some of the frontier units every three months or so," he explained. "They still have their edge from fending off border raids and the odd rebellion, and they get easier duty, so they're grateful. Kidnap attempts aren't unheard of, so it's nice to know the gatekeepers are on their toes."

"Kidnapping?" asked Daja, obviously skeptical. "In the *palace*?"

"Near the palace. It's a west Namorn tradition, in a way," explained Shan. "See, the custom is —"

A lean, wild-eyed white man dressed in a ragged green robe over even more ragged clothes lunged in front of them, almost under the feet of Sandry's horse. She drew up hard to save him a kicking, while Shan dragged his infuriated stallion's head away from the man's outstretched arms.

"Game pieces, game pieces," the stranger cried, grabbing the bridle of Sandry's mount. "See the pretty game pieces, the ladies and the mages, two in one, a nice long game of capture the pieces." He had bright, dark eyes, and dark, wiry hair that looked as if it had been cut with a cleaver. "Who will play the game, and who will keep the lady trophy? You, huntmaster, a pretty heiress for your mantelpiece? Best two out of three? Best man wins? So many games to play!"

Daja couldn't believe her eyes. "Wait!" she called as Shan dismounted. From the look on the nobleman's face, she didn't think he meant to send the scarecrow along with a coin and a kind word. "It's all right!"

"It is not!" barked Shan. "He mocks a member of the imperial family —"

"No," Daja said impatiently. "I'm pretty sure I know him, and he's just addled." She guided her horse around Sandry until she had a clear look at the man. "Do I look like a game piece to you?" she demanded. "Take a good look. I was dressed a little differently, the last time we met."

The man stared up at her, wide-eyed, then covered his gaping mouth with bony hands.

Daja sighed. Trader guide me, it's him. The last time I saw him, I was about to walk back into a burning building, and he'd just helped me get a clutch of crazy people out of it. "Is that the robe I gave you?" she asked him.

He nodded, hands still covering his mouth.

Daja looked at the rest of their group. "Go on. I'll look after my friend, here."

"You *know* this man?" demanded Shan, startled.

Daja smiled, though she hadn't taken her eyes from her crazy helper. "We met when I lived in Kugisko," she replied. "We did rescue work together in a big fire." She looked at the others. They still remained motionless, staring at her. "We'll be along. Shoo. You're frightening him."

"Not as bad as he frightened us," grumbled Briar. Sandry looked at Shan and nodded. With a grimace the nobleman swung back into his saddle and rode with her, Briar, and Tris on down High Street. All around them the foot traffic that had come to a halt resumed, though they kept well away from Daja and her new companion.

Daja swung out of the saddle and waited until her friends were out of earshot, holding her mount's reins in her metal-plated hand. "Sandry is the empress's cousin," she told her companion softly when the others could no longer hear. "You're lucky that Shan didn't cut you in two with his sword."

"I know she's the cousin, but she's a game piece, you're all game pieces, and the great lady thinks she knows the rules to play with you. She doesn't, she doesn't at all, and I went to see you in Kugisko but the servants made me leave because you were ill." He spoke quickly, but his voice was crisp and his eyes were clear and direct.

I don't understand what *exactly* he's trying to say, but I know a genuine warning when I hear it, she thought. She looked him over. He's ragged and dirty, but his nails aren't bitten down, and he's only trembling a little. "They never did tell me your name," she remarked.

"Zhegorz. I had a last name once but my family doesn't like me to use it, because they say I don't belong to it like they do so I never even remember it now it's been so long —"

Daja cut him off by resting her hand on his arm. "When did you eat last?" she asked. Cupping his elbow in her free hand, she steered him down a narrow side street, away from the gawkers and any spies who might report his ravings to the crown. Her horse followed calmly when she tugged on his reins. "And where in Hakkoi's name have you been sleeping?"

"Beach caves," he replied, watching everything but the street in front of them. Daja braced him when he nearly tripped over a mound of horse droppings, and maneuvered him past hazards after that. "Sand's good for scrubbing clothes, and there's a stream, but I had to come because of the game pieces —"

"You can tell me about the pieces later, Zhegorz. When did you eat?"

He shrugged. Daja had the peculiar notion that if she looked into his eyes she would see comets and whirling stars where common sense ought to be. With a sigh, she pulled him around the corner onto Kylea Street, where she found a strawberry vendor's cart. She grabbed a woven reed basket filled with strawberries and flipped a silver argib coin to the vendor who sold them, then thrust the basket at Zhegorz. "Eat those," she ordered. She had to spend the next several minutes showing him how to remove the leafy crown after he ate one strawberry whole. He was silent as he worked his way through the basket, popping fruit after fruit into his mouth.

He's starving, thought Daja as she continued to steer

him along the back way to the town house. The Namornese gods are cruel, to make someone like him mad. For all his raving, he's got a good heart. Most crazy people would have run off on their own in that fire, or never even offered to help. Not that he offered, but he did as I told him when I ordered him to. And he didn't want me to walk back into the burning hospital. That was sweet.

The servants' gate at Landreg House was open. Gently, Daja guided Zhegorz inside and turned her mount over to a hostler who came for it. Then she looked at her charge. "If I put you in a hot tub in the bathhouse, will you stay there?" she asked him.

Zhegorz ran a quivering hand over his chopped hair, his eyes scuttling back and forth. "Is the tub hot or the water hot?" he asked. "Specifics, what's to be heated and what's not —"

Daja interrupted him again. "I *forbid* you to talk crazy," she told him sternly. "Not here. Here you will talk like a normal human being or say nothing, one or the other."

"What's normal?" the man asked. He rubbed his long, bumpy nose. His thin lips trembled.

Daja frowned at him. "I don't know. You're older than me — you think of something. But don't frighten the servants, all right? I'm going to put you in the bathhouse to wash up, and I'm going to see about fresh clothes. You *stay* in the bathhouse until I come for you, understand?"

"Do I shave?" Zhegorz asked. He was hollow-cheeked and stubbly. Daja shuddered to think of him with a sharp blade. Someone had shaved him recently enough that his salt-and-pepper beard was only stubble now. "Some other time," she said, grateful not to deal with that on top of everything else. She led him into the bathhouse and waited as he undressed behind a screen, wrapped a towel around his waist, then climbed into a tub full of steaming water. The servants kept the baths ready at this time of day for anyone who might come in.

"Stay," she ordered as he leaned back against the side of the tub. He nodded, thin lips tightly closed. It seemed he had chosen silence of the alternatives she had given him. Daja could accept that. Off she went in search of clothes and something more for him to eat.

Shan left Sandry and the rest of her party at the town house gate with a bow, a smile, and a cheerful good-bye. Briar and Tris nodded, but otherwise said nothing as they surrendered their mounts to the stable hands and followed Sandry into the house.

"I believe Daja will be bringing a, a guest of some sort," Sandry told the head footman. "See that they have whatever they need, and please tell Daja she will find me in the book room." I can't *wait* to hear what that was about! she thought.

She then found the ground floor book room. She wanted nothing more than to sit and put her feet up on a hassock — attendance on an empress involved a great deal of standing, even when one was privileged enough to be allowed to sit in her presence now and then. She was just relaxing when she realized that Briar and Tris, instead of going to their rooms, had come in behind her and shut the door. They both stood there, Briar with his arms crossed over his chest, Tris with her fists propped on her hips.

"What?" demanded Sandry as they glared at her. "What did I do?"

"Did it occur to you that perhaps we might like to be consulted on yet another long ride?" demanded Tris.

Briar added, his voice mockingly proper, "Thanks ever so for asking, *Clehame* Sandry. Our lives are yours to arrange like you arrange embroidery silks. We have no minds — or rumps — of our own to help us decide if we want a day-long journey so soon."

"I asked you, didn't I?" demanded Sandry, startled. "I was sure I asked you. I told Cousin Ambros."

"You did not," snapped Tris. "You *told* us, like you'd *tell* 'Cousin Ambros.' In front of the empress and her court, so it's not like we could discuss it with you."

"Well, you could have said something before now," replied Sandry with a shrug. "My lands *are* the main reason I came."

"Tell you in front of the court, or the servants, or the empress?" Briar demanded. "Is all this royalness making you soft in the head?"

Sandry tightened her lips. "No one would have known if you'd spoken to me the way we *used* to talk to each other," she said mulishly. "*Silently.* Remember? No one to eavesdrop, *ever.* Now stop complaining. If you want to stay here, I'll go on to my estates with Ambros by myself."

"And have the imperial friends who're coming along report back that we gave them the cold shoulder?" asked Briar. "Maybe *you* don't have to worry about them getting us in trouble, but we aren't highborn. We're vulnerable."

"You're just being disagreeable," Sandry told them both. "I'll say you both got sick, will that silence you?"

"You treating us like equals instead of servants — *that* will silence us," Tris replied. "You didn't act like this back at Winding Circle. Either we're your household or your family. Make up your mind."

Sandry's mouth quivered. I'm homesick, she realized, distressed. I'm homesick, and I don't want them to scold me anymore. "Oh, leave me alone!" she cried, wanting them out of the room before she actually began to cry. "I didn't ask for you to come! It was Uncle's idea — I just wanted to make him easy in his mind! How was I to know you two had gotten all, all prideful and arrogant?" She fumbled in her pocket for a handkerchief.

"*We're* prideful and arrogant?" demanded Briar, shocked. "Who's issuing orders around here, *Clehame*?"

"Oh, splendid. Tears. *That* solves ever so much," snarled Tris. She flung the door open and stamped out of the room.

Briar followed her out after he allowed himself one parting shot, "See you at dawn, *my fine lady.*"

Sandry managed to wait for the door to close behind them before her eyes overflowed. I didn't feel so blue on the road, she thought, tears spilling over her cheeks. There was too much to do, and we had the Traders with us. But this court, with its standing and sitting and curtsying and sitting and bowing and standing and walking and gossiping and curtsying . . . Uncle *never* makes anyone carry on like that! We bow or curtsy when we see him, and that's that for the day. And I never, *ever* felt like I was surrounded by envious people in Emelan, not like I do here. Everyone wants what I have, and I just want to go home!

Her soft mouth hardened. And Briar and Tris can just go and do as they like. Obviously we had something wonderful as children that we can't have now we're grown. I was a fool to think we could, and now I have more important things to worry about.

Tris climbed up the flights of stairs to her room and proceeded to shed the clothes she had worn to court as Chime fluttered around her in welcome. All of them had decided Chime was too excitable for their first day at court. Although her mind knew that Sandry had woven all kinds of protections against stains, wrinkles, and mishaps into the fine cloth and seams, Tris could never be as comfortable in her dress-up clothes as she could her other garments. Now she tugged on a linen shift and a blue cotton gown with a sigh of relief. Her court shoes came off to be replaced by leather slippers.

Comfortable at last, with Chime on her shoulder, Tris was on her way downstairs again when she nearly ran into Ambros fer Landreg. "Excuse me, *Saghad*," she said, curtsying for what felt like the hundredth time that day. They had been introduced briefly over breakfast that morning.

"*Viymese* Trisana," he said, with a bow. "Did you enjoy your visit to the palace?"

As much as I'd enjoy a rat pasty, she thought, but she did not say it. "Please, it's just Tris. I'm not much for titles as a rule."

"Then you must call me Ambros," he said in his quiet way. "You are Sandry's sister, after all, which makes us kin of some kind. At least we are better than acquaintances, or should be."

Tris smiled at him, appreciating that tiny hint of a joke. She liked this man; she had thought she might. Everything she had heard of him from the duke and from Sandry had spoken well of him. Sandry called him prosy and picky all the way here, but in her shoes, I'd want someone meticulous and careful looking after my affairs, Tris thought. Someone I could trust to check everything.

She realized she had a piece of information that he might want. "I'm afraid there are going to be a few more of us visiting Landreg than you had expected," she explained. "Her Imperial Majesty invited four of her courtiers to bear us company, and I think — I'm not sure — Daja met a friend she means to invite to stay for a while." It had been interesting to see Daja go all protective over someone as unendearing as a crazed beggar in the street.

Ambros grimaced. "I had anticipated the noble company," he admitted. "Her Imperial Majesty won't want Sandry to forget the attractions of life at court if it can be helped. I am grateful we have only four extra nobles. I half-expected Her Imperial Majesty herself to come to call."

"Shan fer Roth mentioned something about a cousin from Lairan coming to visit the palace," Tris offered.

"Ah. That would explain it. Thank you for the warning, though, *Viy* — Tris." Ambros smiled at her. "You'll find Landreg can house all manner of guests. My family is already there." He bowed and headed on up to his rooms, while Tris continued down to the kitchen.

Wenoura, the cook, looked at her from where she chopped onions and gave a leopard's grin. "Someone I can trust to chop without dismembering herself," she said. She and Tris had gotten acquainted the day before, when Tris had needed something to do with her hands. "Aprons are on those hooks. I sent the maids out to shop and they aren't back. Take over for me while I warm soup for that one." She jerked her head toward the table at the end of the room.

Daja sat there with her friend. Her face might as well have "don't ask" written on it in light, Tris thought, helping herself to an apron. Chime unwrapped herself from Tris's neck and glided down to the floor to curl up under the worktable. Onions had no charm for the glass dragon. As Tris tied the apron over her dress, she yanked a thread of breeze from the back door to carry the scent of the onions away before they reached her sensitive nose. She yanked a second, fatter thread of air from the front of the house past Daja so that she could eavesdrop on what she said to the bony man. Only when those bits of business were taken care of did she begin to cut up the peeled onions that awaited her attention.

"Zhegorz, why are you here?" Daja asked the man as he drank from a heavy mug. "I thought you'd still be in Kugisko —"

"Locked up," said the man — Zhegorz, Tris repeated to herself — when Daja fumbled her words. "I got out of the hospital. I told them I was cured. I acted cured. I can do that. They didn't have the kitchen witch look at me. She always knows the truth, see, and she would have told them. Maybe she smells it on me, I don't know, but I pretended to be like them for a whole week. The locked wing was crowded and there were more like me waiting so they asked me questions and gave me an argib and new clothes and let me out."

"That green robe you were wearing isn't new," Daja said as Wenoura set a pot of soup to heat on one of the small stoves. "That's the robe you wore when you helped me get the others out during the fire. It's still got scorch marks on it."

"I told them it was my lucky charm," Zhegorz replied. "It *is* my lucky charm. I wore it and even though I knew the governor saw me at the fire and I knew his torturers would come for me, I pretended to be like the outside people and fled Kugisko, and it worked. So the robe is lucky because the torturers didn't get me. I truly *was* better outside the city, in the grasslands, or they're grasslands when there's no snow. But it's hard to eat grass and I'm no hunter, so I go back to the cities and towns and I leave those places when the voices get to be too much but I have to eat." He hung his head. "I made my way here alone with my, my . . ." He sighed, his bony shoulders slumped. "Madness."

Wenoura rolled her eyes at Tris, who had finished the onions and started on the parsnips. It was getting stuffy in the kitchen. The cook went to a set of shutters and opened them.

"But there are voices, don't you hear them?" asked Zhegorz suddenly.

Tris freed her string of breeze now that she was finished with the onions, letting it mingle with the larger one. The maids had returned, their voices blurring Daja's and Zhegorz's. One of them took over on chopping.

"Well, the maids are back," Daja told him. Tris removed her apron and hung it up, then went to wash her hands near where the pair sat so she could hear.

"No!" Zhegorz cried. "Voices everywhere in the cities and towns, voices in the air, talking of love and fighting and money and families and —"

Daja trapped his hands in hers, holding his eyes with her own. *"Calm down,"* she told him sternly. "You're safe."

Tris dried her hands with a frown.

"But sometimes the voices and visions, though I haven't seen so many visions, sometimes they have secrets and if you let them slip, husbands and fathers and soldiers come for you with knives!" protested Zhegorz. He trembled from top to toe. "They hunt for you and they hurt you to see how you know their scheming, so nowhere is safe — even when it's just the blacksmith meeting his best friend's wife in a barn, they hurt you because they think you spy!"

Tris went over and closed the open window.

"It's *hot* in here!" Wenoura protested. "We need fresh air!"

Tris turned to look at Zhegorz. He had gone silent, white-faced under his stubble. Daja released him so he could cover his face with his hands. He was still trembling.

Tris opened just one of the shutters this time, the half that wouldn't let air blow directly toward Daja's table. Neither Daja nor Zhegorz seemed to notice, though the cook and maids sighed their relief. The kitchen *was* heating up.

Tris went over and plumped herself down next to Zhegorz. "Where are you from?"

He flinched from her.

"Stop scowling at him," ordered Daja, frowning at the redhead. "You'd frighten a Trader's dozen of crazy people with that frown. Zhegorz is my friend, and I won't have you scaring him."

"She's not scaring me, I don't think," muttered Zhegorz.

"Well, you should be scared," Daja told him stoutly. "Most sensible people are." She forestalled his protest by raising her brassy hand. "You're sensible enough, even if you are crazy."

"If he is, maybe he has reason to be," Tris said, closing her eyes. "How old are you, Zhegorz?"

He blinked, his thin mouth trembling. "I . . . don't know," he said at last. "One emperor and two empresses . . ."

"Forty-five, maybe fifty," Wenoura said behind Tris. "Were you too little to remember the old emperor's death?"

Zhegorz shook his head, appearing to search his memory.

I don't envy him the task, Tris thought, watching him count on his fingers. No doubt it's under layers and layers of magical potions and treatments and being locked up. It wasn't readily apparent to her daily vision, but that could mean simply that if he did have power, as she suspected, he'd tried to bury it. Deep inside herself she worked a change over her vision, closing her eyes before she brought it up to them. For the second time that day she placed a layer of magic over her eyes, though this was very different from the one she had used to see the fishing fleet. Once she felt her eyes begin to sting — they didn't like this trick, not in the least — she opened them.

Normally she saw magics, including traces, as silver. This particular spell, one she had learned not long before her return to Emelan, showed her different magics in different colors. From this perspective, Zhegorz was coated with patch on patch of power, different spells from different mages. He'd been given all kinds of healing potions for his madness, ordinary healings for illnesses, broken bones, and decayed teeth, and a number of truth spells for the secrets he wasn't supposed to know. Threaded around and through them, almost vanishing under her gaze before it emerged in its full strength, or part strength, was a bright gold thread that belonged to Zhegorz himself.

Tris got up and walked around the table, eyeing him from every angle. The man was an insane patchwork doll of all the spells that had been worked on him since —"When did they first say you were mad?" she asked him.

He would not look at her. "Fifteen," he mumbled. "For my birthday they sent me to Yorgiry's House, because I talked to the voices. I went home sometimes after, but I always got worse. They began to leave baskets of food and clothes at the garden gate, but they'd lock the gate. They wouldn't come out until I was gone. That happened two or three times. Then one time the healers let me out and my family wasn't there anymore. They had sold the house and moved away. I think I was twenty." He looked at Daja. "The old emperor died around my fifteenth birthday. All of us who were mad got new black coats to wear for mourning."

"He's fifty-two or thereabouts, then," Wenoura said. "By that count." She turned: The maids had all stopped what they were doing to listen. "I don't see supper magicking itself onto the table," she said sharply. "Get back to work, you lazy drudges. We've supper and breakfast to fix and food for them and the nobles to eat on the road tomorrow while you gape like a field full of cows!"

Zhegorz looked at Daja, trembling. "You're going away?"

Daja looked at Tris, who frowned at Zhegorz as she pulled on her lower lip. I remember *that* look, Daja thought. Just because we aren't in each other's minds doesn't mean I don't know what she's thinking right now. And she won't say another word until all her thoughts are lined up. She thinks he has magic. She's thought it since she opened only one shutter. And it must be strange magic, or she'd have told him outright. Or there's something peculiar in it.

Just because Tris isn't talking doesn't mean *I* can't, she told herself. "Yes, but it's all right." She reached over and closed her hands around Zhegorz's trembling fingers again. "Yes, we're going away, but you aren't to worry, because you'll be with us. It means you'll be out of the city — it's worse in the cities, you said?"

Both Zhegorz and Tris nodded.

"You'll be with us. Zhegorz, you know my magic's a little — odd, right?" Daja asked.

Zhegorz nodded. Tris stopped pulling her lip and began to chew on the end of one of her thin lightning braids, lost in thought.

Doesn't that *hurt*? wondered Daja, watching in awe as the redhead nibbled her source of sparks. To Zhegorz, Daja said, "Well, hers is, too, and so are the magics of the lady who owns this house and our brother." She spoke under the clatter as the maids and Wenoura got to work. "And the thing with having odd magic is that you are more inclined to spot it in somebody else. My friend here — her name is Tris — she's already figured out you hear voices because she hears them, too, on the winds."

Zhegorz yanked around to stare up at Tris. "You hear them, too?" he asked in wonderment.

"For years," Daja said when Tris only nodded. "So part of what's wrong with you is that you never learned a way to manage what you hear, or even that the problem was magic all along. We don't know about the visions"— Daja glanced at Tris, who shook her head —"though *maybe* they're on the winds?"

Tris shrugged.

"Well, she'll figure it out, I suppose, and you'll stay with us while she works on it."

Chime had endured enough of the maids and cook who now bustled around her napping place. She wriggled out between their legs and took flight, to land on the table in front of Zhegorz. The man flinched away and knocked the bench over to land on his back.

"That's just Chime," said Tris, reaching down a hand. "She's all right. She's a living glass dragon. They're not very common."

Daja snorted: In her dry way, Tris had made a joke. Zhegorz stared up at Tris, then cautiously took the offered hand. As she helped him to his feet, he said in a voice filled with wonder, "Are all of you decked in marvels? Are all of you as mad as she is?" He pointed to Daja with his free hand. "She walked into a burning building that was collapsing. And before she did it, she saved my life and the lives of others who were as mad as me. Madder."

"Collapsing buildings?" Tris asked Daja. She released Zhegorz to put the bench upright again. Gingerly the man sat to peer at Chime, who had decided to charm. As she wove her way around and between his hands and arms, chiming, Daja looked away from Tris.

"A man I knew, supposedly a friend, was setting fires," she mumbled. "It's not something I like to discuss."

"She burned him up," Zhegorz said, smoothing reverent fingers over Chime's surface. "Her and other fire folk who were present at the execution. The governor was furious." He looked at Daja. "It was quicker than letting him burn slow. And he broke the law."

Wenoura handed Tris a bowl of hot soup and a spoon. The redhead set them down in front of Zhegorz. She didn't appear to see the single tear that escaped Daja's eye before Daja blotted it away. Daja could still remember that cold afternoon and that roaring pillar of flame. Knowing she and the other fire mages had saved Bennat Ladradrun an agonizing death hadn't soothed the pain of his betrayal.

"Hush," Tris was telling Zhegorz. "Some things you can't fix by making excuses for them."

And how did you learn that? Daja wondered. Or is it something you just never forgot, after you killed all those pirates?

Tris looked around. "I should ask the housekeeper if there's a guest room that can be made up for you."

"I'll take him." Briar strolled in, hands in his pockets. They hadn't seen him arrive. "The servants can put a cot in my room. You'll want me close by anyway, old fellow. If you get the horrors, I have drops that will help."

"Putting him in a room on the downwind side of the house will help even more," Tris replied. "I think part of his problem now is he's had too many such drops."

"Sleeping drops, with no magic in them, then," Briar said. He sat next to Zhegorz and offered a hand. "Briar Moss. These two are my mates." Not everyone knew this was slang for close friends, so he added, "My sisters."

Gingerly, Zhegorz offered his own hand. "I can tell," he said, his voice soft.

Briar clasped his hand, then let go and glared at Tris. "You know, I don't go around feeding everybody magic the first time they sneeze," he said belligerently. "It's not good for them. You get used to it, and it stops helping. You'd be a lackwit not to know that."

"Not wanting to butt in or anything," said one of the maids with a wink at Briar, "but shouldn't you be asking my lady before you go bringing in . . ." She rethought the word she was about to use and supplied, "Guests?"

Briar, Daja, and Tris all exchanged glances. Daja could see they felt just as she did. They were bewildered at the thought of *having* to ask such a thing of one of them.

"But I had a house and it didn't bother us then," she said.

"You're different," Briar and Tris said together. They looked at each other and smiled wryly.

"Then it shouldn't be different here." Sandry emerged from the shadows by the door into the kitchen. "Don't I get to meet our new guest?"

Zhegorz lunged to his feet so fast that he ended up knocking the bench over again. He and Briar went sprawling onto their backs. Sandry helped Briar to his feet as Tris assisted Zhegorz again. Chime rose onto her hindquarters and made a crisp series of splintering glass noises at Sandry. It sounded rather like a scolding. Sandry almost dropped Briar on his rump again when she clapped both hands over her mouth to cover her giggle. He staggered to stay on his feet, then grabbed the bench and set it back up.

Sandry looked at them, waved for the maids and the cook to stop curtsying, and said quietly, "I'm still me, you know. And you were very right to scold me. I didn't think to ask you."

Tris propped her fists on her hips. "It's just as well now," she said, eyeing Zhegorz. "He'll need someplace quieter than this to stay until we can sort him out."

Zhegorz blinked down at his stout protectress. Standing, he was five inches taller than Tris. He should have more of a presence, thought Tris. He's a grown man, after all, older almost than the four of us together. But maybe it's that he's spent so much of his life running and hiding from things, and being locked up. Maybe inside he's not that much older than fifteen.

"I'll make sure you have a room, and somewhere we must have spare clothing," Sandry assured Zhegorz softly. "Will you mind a day's ride tomorrow?"

The man's eyes shuttled from Sandry to Briar, to Daja, then to Tris. "You won't want to adopt me when all your secrets come popping out of my mouth," he warned them, rubbing a temple. "It always happens."

Briar clapped Zhegorz on the back. "Well, if it happens, and I doubt it, we'll make sure you've got a pack full of clothes and food, at least."

"We're not going to get rid of you," Daja said, glaring at Briar. "We blurt people's secrets all the time. You'll be safer with us."

"It's settled, then. Come on, Zhegorz," said Briar companionably.

As he led their new comrade off, Sandry looked at Tris. "Will we be able to help him?" she asked.

Tris was looking at the chewed end of one braid. "At least enough to get him back to Winding Circle," she murmured. "I think he'll have to go there in the end."

"But you're going to be nice, right?" Daja asked. "You're going to be gentle with him, because he's all broken to pieces inside."

"When am I not nice?" demanded Tris with a scowl.

That reduced Daja and Sandry to laughter. Each time they met Tris's glaring gray eyes, a fresh surge of laughter began. Finally Tris herself began to smile crookedly. "Well, nice by my standards, anyway. Treat me right, or I'll make sure you get rained on all the way to Landreg in the morning."

Briar had difficulty getting to sleep that night. Bedding down alone — alone in the bed, Zhegorz had a cot in the dressing room not fifty feet away — was a strange new experience for him of late. He hadn't deliberately set out to ensure there was always someone warm and cuddly to share his blankets with, but it was an agreeable coincidence. It helped that he was so friendly, and the ladies were so friendly in return. He certainly could tell none of them, or worse, tell his sisters, that he had a horror of sleeping alone. Admitting that to anyone would force him to admit there was something wrong with him.

He lay awake for over an hour, listening to the small noises that Zhegorz made, settling into his mattress, then falling to sleep. The crazy man buzzed in place of snoring. It was a soothing kind of noise, hardly crazy at all. When Briar finally realized what it was, it soon lulled him to sleep.

He ran through a series of rock-sided canyons, all of them stripped of vegetation. He reached every way around him with his magic, seeking even a blade of grass to keep him company, but the ground here was bare and dry, a desert high above the forests and plains of all the world. He kept looking for a way out of the canyons, but all he saw was smooth rock walls, innocent of cracks or ledges.

Behind him Briar heard the thud of Yanjingyi war drums, a loud, flat thump echoed by thousands of marching feet. The sound had followed him into the stone corridors, driving him like game in the dark. Now came the thin, shrill blast of the Yanjing emperor's battle trumpets, and the frightful first roars of the black powder called boom dust. They were blowing up the stone canyons . . .

. . . which turned into the twisting hallways of the First Temple of the Living Circle, jammed with dedicates, fleeing the attacking Yanjingyi army. Briar fought against their rushing tide, trying to find Rosethorn and Evvy, his student. Where were they? Evvy was small, yet — she could have been trampled in this chaos! He screamed her name, but it was lost in the cries of the frightened civilians who had taken shelter in the temple.

Everything went dark. Suddenly Briar was crawling over heaps of loose and wet bodies, feeling his way, shuddering. He knew he was crawling on the bodies of the dead. He reached out and felt a dying flare of green magic, plant magic. Screaming, he clutched the dying Rosethorn to his chest.

"... know it's a bad idea to wake a dreamer, but it didn't sound like you're enjoying yourself and if I can't get you to wake I'll have to get one of the *Viymeses*, though perhaps —"

Briar grabbed Zhegorz's skinny arm and sat up, glaring into the older man's eyes. He could see them clearly: Zhegorz had managed to light a candle. "Don't you *dare*," Briar ordered softly. "They're not to know you caught me bleatin' like a kid, you got me, daftie? Elsewise I'll plant a bit of green on your lip that will grow your teeth shut, you got me?"

Zhegorz blinked at him, his odd blue-gray eyes bright. "I don't think that's possible," he replied. "I don't believe it would cling."

"It's got stickers on it, and they sink in the cracks." Realizing the man had no intention of telling on him, Briar released Zhegorz's arm. "It's only a dream."

Zhegorz sat cross-legged at the foot of the bed. "So you'll give me drops for *my* dreams, but not yours?"

Briar rubbed his aching head. "Just what I need — a daftie that makes sense," he grumbled. "Besides, your dreams is bleating, and mine is real. Except for some bits. And those might have been real."

"But *Viymese* Tris thinks some of mine are real, too," Zhegorz pointed out in a reasonable tone.

"*Viymese* Tris thinks too much, and she yatters about it too much," Briar grumbled. "You'd best learn that right off."

"If I learn it, will you take the drops?" asked Zhegorz.

Briar stared at him, baffled and confused, then began to chuckle. "Crazy you may be, but when you get an idea in your head, you stick to it," he said when Zhegorz raised an eyebrow. "How about I just make us both some sleepy tea instead? We'll be all right with a cup of that in our bellies."

The tea sent Zhegorz back to bed, at least. Briar had known it would have no other effect on him than to calm him down. Instead he pulled his chair up to his work desk and put his hands around the base of his *shakkan*, letting the tree's centuries of calm banish the last shivers from the dreams that had made him so reluctant to sleep alone anymore. Looking at it, he realized that while he'd been occupied with preparing for court, the *shakkan* had slyly put out a handful of new buds.

"Nice," he said with a grim smile. "But you still don't get to keep them."

When the maid came to wake them before dawn, she found Briar asleep with his head on his desk, one arm around his *shakkan.* Tiny clippings from the tree lay next to its tray from its late night trimming.

8

The 30th day of Goose Moon, 1043 K.F.
Landreg House, Dancruan, to
Clehamat Landreg (Landreg Estate), Namorn

Rizu, Jak, Fin, and Caidlene arrived with the dawn, just as the hostlers were bringing out horses for Sandry and her escorts. They all greeted one another sleepily. No one was inclined to conversation at that hour. Zhegorz, who had shown a tendency to talk rapidly in bursts the night before, huddled silently in the patched coat they had found for him. He rolled his eyes at the sleepy-eyed cob who had been saddled for his use, but once he was on the sturdy gelding's back, he seemed to do well enough.

Ambros, pulling on his riding gloves, frowned as he looked at their scarecrow. "How shall we explain him?" Sandry's cousin wanted to know. "You can't just go around adding strangers to your entourage without questions being asked, Cousin, particularly not when you came to us without a single guardsman or maid."

Sandry looked crisp in her blossom pink riding tunic and wide-legged breeches, but her brain had yet to catch up. "Ambros, how can you even think of such a thing at this hour?" she demanded, and yawned.

He gazed up at her as she sat on her mare, his blue eyes frosty. "Because there are going to be at least two spies outside the gates, and more on the way," he added. "Young women in Namorn do not enjoy the license they appear to do in the south, Cousin. There are good reasons for that."

Jak leaned drowsily on his saddle horn. "Can't we just let the spies guess and decide when we're awake?" he asked.

Ambros glared at him, his mouth tight.

"I think we're probably supposed to be spies, too," said Caidlene, who had been lively enough the afternoon before. "Which is silly, because we'd have to be awake to be spies." She sipped from a flask that steamed in the chilly spring air. "Tea, anyone?"

"He's my secretary, *all right*?" demanded Sandry, out of patience with it all. "I didn't realize what a complicated social life I should be leading in Namorn, so I had to hire a Namornese secretary, Cousin — will that satisfy you? May we get on with our lives?"

Ambros snorted and mounted his gelding. Zhegorz looked around at his traveling companions and their guards. "Secretary? I don't even have pens, or ink, or —"

Briar leaned over and slapped him on the shoulder. "I'll set you up in style," he reassured Zhegorz. "You'll be a king of secretaries."

As a pair of guards opened the gates, their company formed up in pairs to ride through. Leading the way with Ambros, Sandry heard Zhegorz complain, "I'm not sure I even know how to *write.*"

And here I thought Tris was the one who was always bringing home strays, thought Sandry, shaking her head as they rode onto High Street. Now she's got Daja and Briar and me doing it, too. She glanced sidelong at Ambros, whose long mouth was tight. She couldn't help it: Her own lips twitched. I would love to hear Ambros explain how I can have a social secretary who can't write.

Just as Tris had vaguely warned them the day before, rain began to fall as the servants closed the house gates behind them. Ambros halted their party, looking at Sandry as Rizu moaned and Caidlene sneezed.

Sandry turned in the saddle. "Tris?" she asked.

Tris, who already had a book in one hand, looked up, startled. Sandry indicated that water was falling from the sky — though surely even Tris would notice when her book got wet! she thought.

The redhead glared up at the clouds. Though Sandry saw or felt nothing, the soft rain parted, streaming to either side of their company, just as if they were protected by a glass shield. Tris looked around, making sure that everyone, including their guards and packhorses, was included under her protection. Then she raised her eyebrows to silently ask, All right?

That's our Tris, thought Sandry, resigned to her sister's eccentricities. She nodded and turned to Ambros, who stared at Tris, unnerved. Sandry nudged him with a booted foot. Remembering where he was, Ambros set his horse in motion, though his eyes followed the curve of the rain as it rolled away over his head. The others followed, though the guards and the courtiers visibly hesitated.

Sandry caught up to Ambros. I hope he learns to take odd magics in stride, she thought. He'll be seeing them all summer, and they aren't all going to be nice, quiet ones like redirecting the rain.

Given the early hour, there was very little traffic on the streets around the palace. They found more as they wound down into the commercial parts of town. There the big wagons that supplied the city came in to unload their burdens of produce, meat, eggs, and cheese. Their party slowed still more approaching the gates, and on the roads that led from them. Once they had traveled some miles from the city, however, the traffic thinned. They made very good time overall. Sandry wondered at the amount of room they were always given on the road, until she realized that anyone who had the time to notice that invisible shield over their heads moved as far from their party as they could while still remaining on the road.

At midmorning they halted at a good-sized inn where Ambros was recognized and given prompt service. The riders dismounted for hot tea and fresh-baked rolls, while the hostlers rubbed the horses down. Once they were back in the saddle, everyone was awake and feeling more cheerful, despite the gloomy weather. Caidlene took Sandry's place next to Ambros, talking about court news and about Ambros's four lively children. Jak rode with Sandry, pointing out landmarks. Fin and Briar rode together, talking about horses. With Tris absorbed in her book and Zhegorz inclined to huddle between the packhorses and the rest of their guards, Rizu and Daja soon fell into conversation. Rizu had an endless fund of court stories. It wasn't long before Daja realized many of the stories were also cautionary tales about different figures at court, particularly the empress. The picture Rizu drew of Berenene was one of a woman who was determined to have her way.

"Are you afraid of her?" Daja demanded as they reined in at a second inn. It was well past midday by then. Everyone was starved. "You sound like everyone fears and loves her at the same time."

"Because they do," Rizu explained. "She is a great ruler. Like most great rulers, what she wants, she will have."

Sandry, dismounting nearby, heard this. "But that must be dreadful for her character," she remarked. "No one can have everything they want. It gives rise to overconfidence, and arrogance."

Daja looked at Sandry's round chin, which was set at its most mulish angle. "I don't think she'll appreciate a lesson from us," she warned, letting a hostler take her horse. "I'd as soon not have to leave in a hurry, thank you. It's a long way to any border."

"I don't care to leave places in a hurry, either," Briar said as he followed the ladies into the inn. "One of these days I won't be fast enough on my feet."

A woman bustled forward to guide them to tables. "Remember old *Saghad* Gurkoy?" Ambros asked as they took seats in a private room. "Beggared, him and his entire family." His blue eyes glinted as he looked at Fin. "Your father was the empress's chosen beneficiary in that matter."

Fin shrugged. "If you want to try to stand between her and what she wants, *Saghad* fer Landreg, I will wish you well. I promise to burn incense in the temple of your choice when you're gone," he informed Ambros, who was not at all offended. "She was going to do as she willed. And if it pleased her after that to give what she had taken to my father, well, she *really* didn't like it when Gurkoy told her no, either."

"No one is all-powerful," insisted Sandry.

"Maybe, but you'd be surprised how much damage can be done by someone who thinks he is," Briar said bitterly as maids put mushroom and noodle soup and herring salad in front of them.

"What on earth *happened* to you?" demanded Tris, glaring at Briar. "You've done nothing but hint since you came home. Either tell us outright or stop hinting!"

Briar glared at her. "What do you care? You don't bother with what's real — only with what's in books."

The Namornese were good at pretending they hadn't heard an outburst from one of their companions. They must have a lot of family dinners like this, thought Sandry. Or maybe even imperial ones.

The rain continued as they took the road again, still mostly dry under Tris's shield. Now the courtiers were truly awake. Soon everyone but Zhegorz and the guards were playing silly games like "I See" and "Fifteen Questions." The group continued word games as Ambros led them off the main road at last onto a smaller, well-kept road paved in stone like the main highway to keep wagons from making ruts.

After another hour, Briar demanded, "So when do we get to these precious lands of yours?"

Ambros looked back at him with a smile. "You are *on* Clehamat Landreg," he told Briar. "The extended estate, at least. Grazing and farming lands. We've been riding over them since we left the highway."

Briar looked at Sandry. "You never said."

"I didn't remember," she answered. "The last time I was here was ten years ago. All I remember was that I was bored to tears. Nobody would play with me."

At last they reached a stone wall that stretched as far as the eye could see. Another road led through a framed stone opening in it. This new route was stone-paved as well, but only the center was as well-kept as the roads they had followed to get this far. Stones were missing from the edges, and stones in the roadway were cracked and broken. As Ambros turned onto it he called back, "Now we are on the Landreg lands that are part of the main estate."

It was another hour before they saw more than isolated houses, or fields green with the spring's planting. Eventually they came upon a massive herd of cows at the graze, then shepherds and goatherds with their flocks. They passed apple and pear orchards that already showed small green knobs that would become fruit, and cherry orchards where the fruit was starting to turn orangey red. At one point Briar reined up and squinted at a distant field where glossy brown animals grazed.

"That's a lot of mules," he said to no one in particular.

Ambros replied, "It's only one herd. The entire Landreg family is famed for the mules we breed and sell."

"It's been a family specialty for more than two hundred years," Sandry added with pride.

Briar, Tris, and Daja exchanged glances. It was Daja who grinned and said it aloud: "That certainly explains more than it doesn't."

"I am not listening to you," Sandry told them loftily as the courtiers laughed. "Do you notice that I am not listening to you?" she continued. "Mark it well. I ignore you."

"And I feel ignored," said Briar, rejoining them. "I am so ignored and unheard that I know it won't matter if I say, Why does it not surprise me, that the Landregs breed mules?"

When they came to a river spanned by a bridge, Ambros

led their party onto a small, muddy, rutted track that bore away from the bridge. Sandry drew her mount up. "Wait a moment," she called, frowning and confused. "I remember this bridge. We ride over that and we come to the village not long after, and the castle after that."

Ambros turned his mount. "In better times we would," he said heavily, something like shame weighing down his shoulders. "But the bridge is not safe. It's old, and it's needed work for some time, replacements on the roadbed and the supports. Then two years ago we had heavy flooding that weakened the supports more. It's not safe. We must ride six miles downstream to the ford."

Sandry didn't like the sound of that. "I don't understand. This is the main castle road. Why hasn't it been repaired?"

Fin said, "Are those ripe cherries over there? It's early, but I want to see. I'm a bear for cherries." He rode toward an orchard nearby, passing out from under Tris's shield and into the rain. Without a word, the other three courtiers followed him. The group's men-at-arms drew back out of earshot. Zhegorz fidgeted, obviously not knowing what to do, while Briar and Daja exchanged glances. What's going on here? Briar seemed to ask Daja with his eyes. Her shrug said, I have no idea. Tris hadn't seemed to be paying attention, but she closed her book, holding her place with a finger.

Ambros rode back to Sandry's side. "Forgive me. I didn't know what else to do," he said, his cheeks slowly turning red. "I'd put off doing the work, that was first. And then we had so much flood damage everywhere that year, and late that summer the taxes went up. I could not repair the bridge, pay the taxes, and send you the usual amount. Your mother's written orders are clear. She, and then you, must receive that exact sum every year, without fail."

Sandry tightened her fingers on her reins. I knew Mother's instructions for our income, she told herself, ashamed. I *knew* she didn't leave any room for the steward to exercise his judgment. But I thought he would, anyway. I thought . . .

She suddenly remembered those columns of dry, boring numbers: the ever-increasing tax sums, the estimated costs of the flood damages, and the profits from the estates. If she had done all of the additions, gone over the accounts entry by entry, she would have seen that there wasn't enough money for everything.

"I thought we could manage the bridge repair last year," Ambros continued, his quiet voice strained, "but Her Imperial Majesty raised the taxes again, to cover fighting on the Lairan border. Again, it was a matter of repairing the bridge or sending what we are ordered to send to you. Our obligation to you comes first."

"What of the taxes?" demanded Sandry, her voice trembling. "You paid them."

Ambros looked surprised that she had even asked. "The taxes must be paid. I went to moneylenders last year. This year, the gods willing, I should be able to pay it back if I raise the mill taxes and the wool taxes on the tenants."

Sandry leaned closer to him. "You should have *told* me," she said fiercely. "Not relied on me to refigure all of your accounts." She could feel her cheeks blush hot with shame. "You should have said the problem in so many words! I have more than enough money for my needs. I could have foregone the payments both years and never even noticed!"

Slowly, as if he feared to anger her, Ambros said, "Your mother, *Clehame* Amiliane, was most clear in her wishes. Those monies are *always* due to the *clehame*, whether the year is a good one or not. And I did not know you well enough at all to ask. I *still* don't know you that well." Very softly he added, "Cousin Sandry, the penalty for a steward who shorts his master — or mistress — is the lopping off of the thieving hand. Not only that, but I would lose the lands I hold in my own right. My family and I would be penniless."

"I would *never* insist on such a thing!" cried Sandry.

Daja glanced back at the courtiers. If they had heard, they did not so much as turn around in their saddles.

Ambros rubbed his head wearily. "*Clehame* —"

"Sandry!" she snapped.

Meeting her eyes steadily, Ambros said, "*Clehame*, imperial spies are everywhere. The imperial courts are all too happy to uphold such matters on their own, particularly if there is a chance they may confiscate lands for the crown.

It is how Her Imperial Majesty grants titles and incomes to her favorites."

Taking a breath to argue, Sandry thought the better of it and let the breath go. "Let's just ride on," she said, feeling weary in her bones. I should have paid attention. I should have fixed this years ago. Thanks, Mother. You've shamed us both. And I have shamed myself. "Tomorrow, if it is safe, Ambros? Please start work on that bridge at once. Repay the moneylenders all that you owe. Don't send me anything for the next three years. I'll write a note to that effect, and have it witnessed."

This time she led the way down the muddy track to the ford, emerging from Tris's shield to get wet. Briar turned. The moment he put two fingers in his mouth, Tris plugged her ears. Zhegorz and Daja both yelped in pain as Briar sounded the piercing whistle that he had once used to summon the dog who had stayed at Winding Circle. The courtiers heard, turned their mounts, and trotted back to the main group, the guards falling in behind.

As Daja swore at him in Trader-talk, Briar grinned at Tris. "You remembered. How sweet."

She shrugged. "It's not a sound I'm likely to forget. Besides, that's how I could get Little Bear to come to me when he and I traveled together." She tucked her book in a saddlebag so he couldn't see her face. "It kept me in mind of you while I was away."

Briar rode over to elbow her. "You just reminded yourself

how quiet it was without me to pester you when you were away," he said, joking, actually touched. "You ain't foolin' me."

She actually grinned at him.

In time they crossed at the ford and returned to the road on the other side of the unsafe bridge. Fifteen minutes after that, they crested a slight rise to find a good-sized village below them on both sides of the road. It boasted a mill, an inn, a smithy, a bakery, and a temple, in addition to housing for nearly five hundred families — a large place, as villages went. On the far side of the village and the river that powered the mill rose the high ground that supported the castle. From here they could see the outer, curtain wall, built of granite blocks. Behind that wall they could see four towers and the upper part of the wall that connected them.

"Landreg Castle," said Ambros as they rode down toward the village. "Home estate of the *clehams* and *clehames* of Landreg for four hundred years." As they followed him, the rain, which had slackened, began to fall harder. Tris sighed and raised her shield again just as someone in the village began to ring the temple bell. People came out of their houses to stand on either side of the road. Others ran in from outer buildings and nearby fields.

Sandry checked her mare, then caught up with Ambros. "Cousin, what are they doing? The villagers?"

Ambros looked at her with the tiniest of frowns, as if a bright pupil had given a bad answer to a question. "You are the *clehame*," he said gently. "It is their duty to greet you on your return."

"How did they know she was coming?" asked Briar.

Ambros raised his pale brows. "I sent a rider ahead yesterday, of course," he explained. "It's my duty to send advance word of the *clehame*'s return."

Sandry's mare fidgeted: The young woman had too tight a grip on the reins, dragging the bit against the tender corners of her horse's mouth. "Sorry, pet," Sandry murmured, leaning forward to caress the mare's sodden neck. She eased her grip. Without looking at Ambros, she said softly, "I didn't want this, Cousin. I *don't* want it. Please ask them to go about their business."

"Bad idea," said Jak. Sandry looked back at him. The dark-haired nobleman shrugged. "It is," he insisted. "They have to show proper recognition of their sovereign lord. You can't let them start thinking *casually* of us, Lady Sandry. Peasants should always know to whom they owe respect."

"I don't need ceremonies for respect," snapped Sandry, growing cross. Her cheeks were red again as they passed between the outlying groups of villagers; she could feel it like banners telling the world she wanted to crawl under a rock. As she rode by, the men bowed and the women curtsied, keeping their eyes down. "And it's not me they should be bowing to," she insisted quietly, feeling like the world's biggest lie. "It's my cousin here. He's the one who works for their good. Do they do this for *you*?" she demanded of Ambros.

"They bow, if they're about when I pass, but I'm not the *clehame*," Ambros told her, keeping his voice low so the villagers would not hear. "You don't understand, Cousin. We have a way of life in Namorn. The commoners tend the land, the artisans make things, the merchants sell them, and the nobles fight and govern. Everyone knows his place. We know the rules that reinforce those places. These are your lands; these people are your servants. If you try to change the rituals for the way in which we live, you undermine all order, not just your small corner of it."

"He's right," said Fin. "Trust me, if they didn't pay you proper respect —"

Rizu cut him off. "Lady Sandry, custom isn't just enforced by the landholders. Rebellion in one village is seen as a threat to all nobility. They would have imperial lawkeepers here in a few days, and then they'd pay with one life in ten."

"On my own lands?" whispered Sandry, appalled.

"Lords have been ill, or slow in mind, or absent," Ambros replied, his voice soft. "Order must be kept."

"I can't tell them not to do that again?" Sandry wanted to know.

"Only if you want to weed the cabbage patch," joked Fin. Caidlene poked him in the ribs with a sharp elbow.

"Well, that's what we call 'em at home," the young nobleman protested. "Cabbage heads. All rooted in dirt, without a noble thought anywhere."

Weed the cabbage patch, thought Sandry, horrified. Kill peasants.

She looked at the villagers, trying to glimpse their faces. It took her a few moments to realize that while the rain was falling heavily, the people on the ground were not getting wetter. She looked up. The space covered by Tris's magical umbrella had spread. It was so big, she couldn't see the edges, only the flow of water overhead, as if the village were covered by a sheet of glass. She's still reading, thought Sandry, looking back at Tris. She can hold off all this rain, and still keep reading.

A smile twitched the corners of Sandry's mouth. She thought, Somebody's been practicing.

They crossed the river, passed through the fringe of houses on the far side, then began the climb up the hill to the castle. Halfway up, they heard the rattle of a great chain. The portcullis that covered the open gate was being raised. The drawbridge was already down, bridging a moat too wide for a horse to jump. On top of the wall, men-at-arms in mail and helmets stood at every notch, watching her. One of them, standing directly over the gate, raised a trumpet to his lips and blew it. As Sandry and Ambros rode first over the drawbridge, golden notes rang out in the sodden air.

Inside they found the outer bailey, where many of the

industries that supported the castle household were placed. Everywhere men and women dropped what they did to line up along the curved road that led to the gate to the inner bailey. As their group passed, they bowed or curtsied.

Uncle Vedris would never allow them to waste time at work on this nonsense, Sandry thought, outraged, though she hid her true feelings to nod and smile at those who lined the road. He'd jump on you quick enough if he thought you were disrespectful, but he didn't need all this, this *stupid* ceremony to prove it. I'm *so* glad he can't see me now.

As they clattered through the inner gate, Sandry's jaws began to hurt. She was actually grinding her teeth in frustration. With an effort she made herself relax, working her jaw to loosen the tight muscles. She glanced back at the others and saw something that made her grin. Little Chime sat on Tris's saddle horn, wings unfurled, chin held high. The glass dragon obviously thought all of this celebration was for her.

And so it is, Sandry thought with a grin. It's not for me — it's for her.

With that idea in mind, she was able to smile more naturally at the men-at-arms who waited by the inner gate, and to nod at the groups of people who stood inside, in the court in front of the main castle. Her smile widened as four little girls, their ages ranging from five to twelve, broke free of the servants to race toward Ambros, shrieking, "Papa! Papa!"

He laughed and dismounted, kneeling in the mud so he

could hug all four at once. "You'd think I'd been gone for years instead of a few days," he chided, his eyes glowing with pleasure. "What is your cousin supposed to think of such hoydens?"

Sandry dismounted before someone could help her to do it. "She thinks they are delightful," she said, walking over to stand beside Ambros. "She thinks their father is blessed to have such lovely girls."

"Their father is," said Ambros, getting to his feet. "Girls, this is your cousin, *Clehame* Sandrilene fa Toren."

Reminded of their manners, the girls all curtsied to Sandry. The one who looked to be about ten thrust a bouquet of slightly wilted flowers at Sandry. "I picked them myself," she said.

"And I thank you," Sandry replied, accepting them. "I love to get flowers after a long ride."

"Good, because doubtless they were picked in your own garden," Ambros said, an arm around the oldest girl's shoulders. "And chances are, they were picked when someone should have been at her lessons."

"But Papa, I was *finished*," protested the flower-bearer. "I *was*!"

Ambros had just finished introducing his daughters when a tall woman, her hair more silvery than blond at an early age, came forward, still wiping her hands on a small cloth. "And this is the most beautiful flower in the castle gardens," said Ambros, his face alight. "*Clehame* Sandrilene fa Toren, may I present my lady wife, *Saghada* Ealaga fa Landreg."

Sandry and Ealaga curtsied to each other gravely. Then the lady smiled at Sandry. "You and your companions must be dying for a hot bath," Ealaga suggested. "A dreadful day to ride — you couldn't have waited for better weather?" she asked her husband as hostlers rushed forward to help the riders dismount and to take the horses' reins.

"I wished our cousin to have time to thoroughly review the state of things here before she must return for Midsummer," Ambros explained. "The will of our empress is that *Clehame* Sandry bear her company for most of the season. As you can see, my dear, she sent four of her young courtiers to bear the *clehame* and her friends company until it was time to return."

"Wonderful," said Ealaga with a smile. "Rizu, you're always welcome, and Ambros, you ought to remember Caidy is my mother's own great-niece. And Jak and Fin I know quite well." To Sandry, she explained, "He's always *positive* we are spinning wildly out of control, when he is prepared for everything. Really, what can you do with such a man?"

Sandry laughed. "It seems as if you married him." There was something about Ealaga that reminded her very much of Lark, one of the four's foster-mothers. To Sandry, it was enough to make her relax.

* * *

"You're not supposed to be here," a thin, short woman informed Tris as the redhead was putting her book in a saddlebag. "Servants around to the side entrance, my lord should have told you. We need you to tell us which luggage belongs to the *Clehame*."

Tris looked down her long nose at the speaker. "I've been demoted, seemingly," she answered, her voice extra dry. "From traveling companion to maid. Do I *look* like a maid to you?"

The woman brushed her own russet brown dress and embroidered apron with one hand. Tris looked down and realized that a sensible navy riding tunic and breeches so wide they might be skirts could resemble a servant's clothes.

"Ah. Well, I'm not," she said. "Sandry doesn't have a maid."

The woman's eyebrows went up; her jaw dropped. "No *maid*?" she asked, appalled. "But how does she dress?"

Tris bit her lip to stop herself from saying, "One piece of clothing at a time." Instead, she rethought her answer, then said, "The *clehame* is accustomed to looking after herself."

"But that's indecent!" whispered the woman. "Who presses her gowns? Who stitches up any rents in her clothes?"

"She does it," Tris replied, unbuckling her saddlebags with a glare for the hostler who had come to do the chore. Slinging the bags over her shoulder, Tris told the woman, "No one mentioned your *clehame* is a stitch witch? Trust me, if you handled her clothes, you'd only mess them up. They never wrinkle or tear." Helpfully, enjoying the sheer bafflement on the proper servant's face, Tris added, "She weaves her own cloth, you see."

A blunt-fingered hand rested lightly on Tris's sleeve. "*Viymese* Tris, I just wanted to thank you for keeping us dry in all the wet today," Rizu said. Her large, dark eyes danced with amusement. "I've never known anyone, *Viymese* or *Viynain,* who could hold protection like that and still read."

"Viymese!" exclaimed the servant woman. Her voice squeaked a little on the last syllable. "Forgive me, *Viymese,* I didn't mean to, to intrude. . . . I must assign a maid to the *clehame,* and to yourself, of course, and —"

"*Viymese* Daja and I don't require maids," Tris said, pointing to Daja, who was grinning at Rizu. "And I think you'll find *Clehame* Sandry will only be grumpy if you give her one." The woman must be a housekeeper. "Surely you have someone who would be happy to attend *Saghada* Rizuka fa Dalach and *Saghada* Caidlene fa Sarajane."

The servant dipped a rushed curtsy and scuttled away. "You looked like you needed rescuing," Rizu commented, smiling. "Servants get more wedded to the social order than nobles do, I think."

"Licking the boot that rests on their necks," grumbled Tris, her eyes still on the fleeing servant.

"Oh, no, we dare not rest it someplace that they might not like," protested Rizu, mock-serious. "They retaliate so deviously. Before I learned better, I found all my hose tied in one big knot, and the maid who was assigned to me had gone home to care for a sick parent. I went six months with hose that fell down because they were stretched all out of shape. Mother said that *truly* noble people didn't hit their maids with a brush, and made me wear the hose until they were worn out. I missed two birthday cakes that year because I was out tying up my hose, *again*."

Tris smiled, but her eyes rested on Zhegorz. He started twitching again while we rode through the village, she thought. He's hearing things still, even behind these walls. Castle gossip, I expect. Tris had gotten so good at ignoring voices on the wind that she had to concentrate to hear them clearly. She did so now, registering a bit of kitchen gossip, almost drowned out by the clang of pans and a shriek of dismay over burned oatcakes. Here someone scolded a dairy maid for dozing off over the churn; here hostlers commented to one another about the new horses they had to care for. It was all commonplace, but Zhegorz flinched as if each sentence were a dart sticking in his flesh.

Making up her mind, Tris excused herself to Rizu and went in search of the housekeeper. Daja caught up Tris. "It's my crazy man, isn't it?" she demanded. "You've been watching him like a hawk all day, even when you pretend you're reading. You're certain he's got what you have, aren't you? Hearing things?"

A blast of wind threw an image over both outer walls

into Tris's eyes: A cow struggled in a bog. Three men tied ropes to her so they could haul the wallowing beast out of danger. Tris whipped her head around in time to see Zhegorz. He stood just downwind of her. "Maybe that, and maybe more," she said. "Look, will you steer him over by the wall, out of any breezes? I'll see about getting a room for him."

"He stays with me." The girls turned. Briar stood behind them, his hands in his pockets. "You looked at the insides of his wrists, either of you? He stays with someone, and unless you want people talking about your reputations from here to the north shore of the Syth, it's got to be with me."

"What's wrong with his wrists?" Daja wanted to know.

Tris marched over to Zhegorz, who faced into the wind that blew from the cow, his pale eyes wide and fixed. Tris seized his wrists and turned them so she could see the insides. Broad stripes of scar tissue, some old and silver-beige, others recent and reddish-purple, streaked the flesh between his palms and the insides of his elbows.

Zhegorz blinked, trying to see past the vision on the air to the person who handled him so abruptly. Tris yanked him around, turning him until the breeze struck his back, not his eyes. "Briar's right. You stay with him, Zhegorz. No more of *this* nonsense," she said, stabbing a finger into one of the scars. Zhegorz flinched. "Listen to me." She still didn't want the others knowing of her latest skill, but she needed to reach this man, to convince him that his visions weren't the product of madness.

Too bad he didn't have Niko to tell him that madness is a lot more interesting than rescuing cows, she thought as she dragged Zhegorz into a corner of the yard, away from Briar and Daja. "I see things on the wind, understand?" she asked quietly. She stood with her back to her brother and sister to keep them from reading her lips. "Pictures from places the wind passed over. A moment ago we both saw a cow trapped in mud, and three men trying to free her." Zhegorz gasped and tried to tug free. Tris hung on to his arm with both hands. "Stop it!" she ordered. "You're not mad. You're a *seer,* with sounds and with seeing, only nobody ever found you out because they were too busy thinking you were mad. Now you have to sort yourself out. You have to decide what part's magic — are you listening? — what part's understandable nerves from thinking you were out of your mind, and what part's had so much healers' magic applied that it's muddled everything else about you. I know what you saw because I *learned* how to see like that. But you never learned it, did you? It was there, from the time you were just a bit younger than me, only the magic sniffers missed it, or your family never even gave you a chance to *show* you were in your right mind." She talked fast, trying to get as much sense as she could fit into his ears, past his years of flight, hospitals, medicines, and terror. Slowly, bit by tiny bit, she felt the tight, wiry muscles under her hands loosen, until Zhegorz no longer fought her grip.

"Real?" he whispered, his voice cracking.

"As real as such things get," Tris told him. "Keep the seeing things part between you and me for now. Briar and Daja already guessed that you can hear like I can, but they don't know about me seeing things."

"Why not?" Zhegorz asked simply. "They love you."

Tris sighed, troubled. "Because the chances of someone learning to see on the winds are tiny. They'll think I think I'm better than they are." Seeing the man's frown, Tris grimaced. "They gave me a hard time all the way here about going to university," she explained. "And other mages — when they found out I could do it, when so many fail . . . they decided I was prideful, and conceited. I don't want Briar and Daja and Sandry to be that way with me. And Briar already said having a credential from Winding Circle isn't good enough for me. This would just make it worse. You know how family gets, once you turn different."

Zhegorz nodded. "Maybe you're too sensitive," he suggested.

Tris stared at him, flabbergasted, then began to laugh. "Look who says so!"

Slowly, as if he weren't quite sure of how to go about it, Zhegorz smiled.

Everyone felt better after hot baths and clean clothes. Best of all, Ealaga was too wise to subject them to a formal banquet after a day's travel. Instead, they took their suppers in a small, informal dining room rather than in the great main hall with its dais, hangings, musicians' gallery, and massive fireplace. That treat was reserved for the next night.

For that night's meal the courtiers provided light talk, jokes, and news for the company. Rizu managed to coax a funny story about learning to skate in Kugisko from Daja, while Jak flirted and teased Sandry until she laughingly talked about Duke Vedris and some of the mishaps her student Pasco had gotten into. In the withdrawing room after supper the servants brought wine, tea, and fruit juice for them all, as well as cheeses and biscuits. Chime enchanted them with her flights in the air, candles and firelight throwing brightly colored flashes from her glassy body. When the travelers began to show weariness, Ealaga instructed the maids to show them to their rooms.

Sandry was asleep the moment she crawled under the blankets. She didn't know how long she stayed that way before someone grabbed her hand. She sat bolt upright, ready to launch a fistful of power against her attacker's clothes, and opened her eyes to darkness.

Dark! she thought, horrified. Someone's grabbing me and it's dark, where's my light, my lamp!

Then she saw a nimbus of light around the darkness over her. The person who had woken her stood between her and the chunk of crystal that was her protection against ever being left to wake in the dark. Sandry pushed the person back a step, allowing more light to flow over the intruder's shoulder. A woman of thirty or so stood beside Sandry. Her face ran with tears. She continued to hang on to one of Sandry's hands as if her life depended on it.

"*Clehame*, I beg you, don't call for the servants!" the woman begged softly. "Please, I mean you no harm, I swear it on my mother's name!"

"You silly creature!" the girl snapped, trying to tug free. "I don't have to call the servants — didn't they tell you I'm a mage? I might have hurt you! Especially when you got between me and the light, for Mila's sake."

The woman refused to let go of her. "Please, *Clehame*, I don't know if they said you were a mage, but it wouldn't make any difference. I would be better off killed by magic than live on as I live now!"

Sandry pushed herself upright until she could lean over and grab the crystal with her free hand. Holding it, she brought the light closer to her captor's features. The woman flinched back from it, but her grip on Sandry's hand did not ease, and her haggard dark eyes never left Sandry's face.

The stranger looked as if she'd been lovely as a girl, and had not yet lost all trace of her looks. Her hair was light brown and coarse, tumbling out of its pins. Her nose looked as if it had been broken once, and deep lines bracketed her nose and wide mouth. She wore a coarse white undergown and practical dark overgown, short-sleeved and calf-length to reveal the embroideries underneath. The clothing was good in its weave and stitching, the embroideries well-done. With her power Sandry could tell the cloth and embroideries were well-made. Her guest may have been a peasant, but she was not poor.

"How did you get in here?" Sandry demanded. "The castle gates are closed."

"I came in this afternoon, with a shipment of flour," her visitor replied. "I smuggled myself up here. I hid in one of the wardrobes so I would not be sent home before the gates closed for the night."

"Then why not reveal yourself while I was *awake*?"

The woman hung her head. "I have slept badly all week, fretting over this," she confessed. "It was warm in there, and there were folded comforters under me. I . . . fell asleep," she confessed. "Truly, I did not mean to frighten you, but I had to speak to you before, before anyone comes to find me." She was rumpled enough to have spent hours folded up in a wardrobe.

"I don't know what you think to accomplish by this invasion," Sandry told her sternly. "I'm only here for a short time."

"But you can help me!" the older woman whispered, her grip so tight that Sandry's fingers began to ache. "You're the only one who can. If you don't, I will die by my own hand, I swear it!"

Sandry scowled. "I really don't approve of drama, *Ravvi* — at least tell me your name."

"Gudruny, *Clehame*," the woman whispered, her head

bowed. "I will not give you my married name, because I never wanted it and wish to be rid of it through your mercy."

Sandry shook her head with a sigh. "I don't see how I can help you there," she told Gudruny. "But in any case, let me put on a robe and slippers, and let's get some real light in here. You can tell me all about it. Now please let go, before my fingers break."

If anything, Gudruny's hold tightened. "Swear it on your ancient name," she begged. "Swear to me by all the gods you will not call for the guards."

"I *swear.* Though, really, my word as a noble should be enough!" From the way Gudruny's eyes scuttled to the side, she didn't share Sandry's opinion of a noble's word. Sandry shook her head, then asked, "May I now have my hand?"

Gudruny released it as if it had turned into a hot coal. Sandry massaged her aching fingers, then started to get up. Gudruny leaped to her feet and fetched Sandry's robe, helping her into it while Sandry thrust her feet into her slippers. Before Sandry could move, Gudruny knelt before the fire, poking the embers into flame and adding fresh wood. Even though it was spring, the air was chilly.

Sandry lit a taper from the flames, and with it lit the wicks on a branch of candles. She had to be desperate, to do this, she thought, remembering the way her Namornese companions had spoken of dealing with the peasants who didn't pay nobles the proper respect. I doubt they'd be very kind to someone who crept into a noble's bedroom. The least I can do is hear her out, and make certain she comes to no harm. Once they had decent light, she nodded to one of the two chairs that framed the hearth. "Seat yourself. Should I ring for tea?" When Gudruny half-leaped to her feet from the chair, Sandry grimaced. "Very well, no tea. Please stop leaping about like that." As Gudruny settled back, Sandry took the other seat. "Now," she said, folding her hands in her lap. "Tell me what brings you up here. A direct tale, if you please. I've been riding all day, and I want some rest."

Gudruny looked down. "Ten years gone I was considered quite the beauty," she said, her voice soft. "All the lads were courting me, whether they had prospects or no, and even though I had no fortune of my own. And I was vain, I admit. I teased and I flirted. Then Halmar began to call." She swallowed hard and added, "Halmar Iarun. He was in his twenties, and I in my teens. He is the miller, like his father, and he's done well as miller. He said he'd had his fun, and it was time for him to be setting up his nursery, and he'd decided I would do." Gudruny sighed. "I would *do,*" she repeated. "As if he had a field of choices, and I met most of his requirements. Oh, I was angered. I sent him off with a host of insults, and went back to my flirtations."

Tears trickled down her cheeks. "One day my mother sent me out to gather mushrooms for supper. I went to the woods three miles from here, where I knew there were edulis mushrooms — my favorites. I was gathering them when

Halmar came for me. He ran me down on horseback, caught me, and took me to a shepherd's hut up in the hills. There he kept me, according to the custom." Gudruny's lips trembled. Sandry found a handkerchief in the pocket of the robe and passed it over.

"He did not strike me, not then," Gudruny whispered. "He said he wanted me to love him. He said I would love him and agree to marry him, or I would never see my parents again. He tied me up while he was gone, and he came back to me each night, to feed me and to tell me how much I was missed, until . . . until I signed the marriage contract. A priest took our marriage vows, or rather, Halmar's vows, since they didn't need mine. I am his wife now, and the mother of our two children."

Sandry listened to this astonishing tale in silence, fury rising up from her belly until so much of it was collected in her throat that she could hardly breathe. "You married a man who would do that to you?" she demanded after Gudruny had been silent for at least a moment. "You live in the house of a man who would treat you that way?" She jumped to her feet to cry, "Where is your pride? How could you bear him children? How could you share his bed?"

Gudruny looked at her as if Sandry had just started to speak Old Kurchali. "I had no choice," she whispered, her lips trembling. "He would have kept me there forever. Other men do worse to make women sign the marriage contract. And once it is signed, the wife has no rights. Most marriages are not made with a contract for that reason. But in west Namorn . . ." She shrugged, her bony shoulders dimpling the cloth of her gowns.

Sandry stared at Gudruny, her hands clenched on the back of the chair. "But you can run away," she pointed out.

"And with a contract he can ask anyone to give me back," snapped Gudruny. "The only way a woman can be freed of the contract would be if she petitioned her liege lord to set it aside."

"Then why didn't you?" Sandry wanted to know. "Cousin Ambros is a fair man. How could you not go to him?"

"Because he is not the liege lord here," whispered Gudruny. "Your mother rode by me, twice, when I tried to ask her years ago. Now I come to you. Please, *Clehame.* I will do anything you ask, if you will but free me of him."

Sandry realized she was trying to shrink away from Gudruny. Surely she had not just said that about her mother. Sandry had known for years that her mother was a pleasure-seeker, a pretty woman who cared only about her husband, her daughter, and having fun. She had never considered that those things might make her mother a very bad noble-woman. "What about your own family?" Sandry wanted to know. "Surely they protested. Didn't they search for you while he had you captive?"

"My family was just my parents," replied Gudruny. "My sisters had married away from Landreg, and I had no brothers. People in the village searched for me, but . . . there are signs a man leaves, to show he has taken a woman for a horse's rump wedding. That's what we country folk call it. Mostly it is a harmless way to get past an overbearing family, or to avoid waiting to wed, or to add spice to a runaway marriage. He told them that I'd decided he must court me, and they believed him. I had made enough mothers angry, toying with their sons. They were glad to think I would marry this way." She thrust a hank of hair back with a trembling hand and looked curiously at Sandry. "You truly did not know of this custom? To kidnap a woman, or pretend to, and hold her in a secret place until she escapes, or is rescued, or signs the contract and is wed?"

"I've never encountered anything like it before," Sandry replied grimly. "Gudruny, if you are lying to me . . ."

Gudruny slid to her knees. "The custom comes to us from old Haidheltac." She named the seed country from which the Namornese empire had sprung. "You might even inquire of the empress, if you dared. It was done to her twice, but she escaped both times before she could be forced to sign the contract. The punishment visited on her captors, once she was free, made all men think twice about trying such things with her."

"But wouldn't she react the same if it happened to other women?" demanded Sandry, feeling as if the safe and level earth were swinging wildly under her feet.

Gudruny wiped her eyes again as tears spilled down her cheeks once more. "She said, when a noblewoman came to her, that any woman foolish enough to be caught was a caged bird by nature, and must content herself with a keeper."

Sandry shivered. That sounds like Berenene, she thought unhappily. It would be like her, to despise other women because they didn't manage to escape like she did. "Well, there's nothing we can do right now with the gates closed for the night," she told Gudruny. "In the morning I will set this right for you, Gudruny." She bit her lip, to stop it from trembling with shame. When she felt she could speak without her voice betraying her, she said very quietly, "I beg your forgiveness for . . . my family. For our not doing our duty by you. You deserved better." She cleared her throat, quickly wiped her cheeks, then said more briskly, "There's a trundle bed under mine. You can stretch out there, at least."

Gudruny pulled out the trundle as Sandry banked the fire again. "What of your children?" Sandry asked once she had climbed back into bed. "What happens to them?"

Gudruny smiled wanly as she sat on the trundle. "They will remain with me," she said, turning to blow out the candles. "The children belong to the mother, as they do everywhere." She took off her shoes by the glow from Sandry's crystal, and crawled under the blankets of the trundle bed, which had been made up for the maid Sandry didn't have. "The father may pay — must pay — for their keeping, but the children are the mother's. That is something the empress approves. I will get to keep my children, since she has decreed that the only bloodlines the law need concern itself with are the mother's."

"Of course," murmured Sandry, her eyes sliding closed. "So the fathers of her own daughters cannot claim the throne in their name. I'll have to hear testimony," she murmured. "Hear what those who know you have to say. After so much has been done wrong here, I must be sure to do right."

If Gudruny answered, Sandry did not hear. She was fast asleep.

9

The 1st day of Rose Moon, 1043 K.F.
Clehamat Landreg to
Pofkim Village, Namorn

Daja woke to shouting. A glance at the bolted shutters showed bits of pale morning light creeping through the cracks in the wood. She went to her chamber door and opened it.

"— rot you, I know she slithered in somehow!" came a muffled roar from the ground floor below. "She was gone all night! Gudruny, I know you're here! You'd best pray, because when I — take your hands off me, oaf!"

Frowning, Daja pulled a robe over her nightshirt and went out to the gallery around the main hall to see what was going on. Footmen struggled with a wiry commoner whose face was full of rage. It was the commoner who yelled for someone named Gudruny.

Across the gallery the courtiers ventured from their rooms, looking as if they could use a few more hours in bed. Briar emerged from his chamber, saying back over his shoulder, "Stay here, Zhegorz. Some *kaq* has his underclothes in a twist." He came to stand beside Daja, taking in the scene below.

A third door on their side of the gallery slammed open with a crack that drew everyone's attention. Tris surged to the gallery rail, robe and nightgown flying in a wind that rattled all of her braids, released from their coil for the night. Seeing her red, sharp-nosed face, framed by moving lightning bolts, the people downstairs went still. Tris gripped Chime with both hands as the glass dragon screeched with distress, shimmering with lightning of her own.

"Quiet," Tris ordered Chime. To Daja's surprise, Chime obeyed. To the people downstairs, Tris said, "This is not what I expected in a nobleman's house. Who are you, and how *dare* you wake us?"

Now Ambros and Ealaga emerged from their rooms. From the look of them they had started to dress before the fuss broke out.

"Do you stand between a man and his lawful wife, it is *you* who are in the wrong, *Viymese* or no!" shouted the troublemaker. "My wife sneaked in here last night, telling all manner of lies, I don't doubt, and I will have her back!"

"A missing wife does not grant you an excuse to disrupt others' households in this coarse manner, Halmar Iarun," Ambros said coldly, leaning on the gallery rail. "Where is your respect for the *clehame*? She is here at last, and this is the welcome you give her?"

Sandry marched from her room, towing a rumpled woman with coarse, brownish-blond hair. "If this is Halmar Iarun, then I am glad he is here," she announced flatly. "You, down there — you are the man who kidnapped this woman and forced her to sign a marriage contract ten years ago?"

"Uh-oh," muttered Briar. "She's all on Her Nobleness already."

"It's too early," grumbled Daja. Briar was right. All three of them had seen that stubborn jut of Sandry's chin and the blaze of her eyes before. In this mood, Sandry was capable of facing armies armed only with her noble blood.

"I am her wedded husband under law," barked Halmar. "Halmar Iarun, miller."

"Down, cur!" barked one of the footmen, kicking Halmar's legs from under him. The man thudded to his knees. "The *clehame* can have you beaten for your lack of due respect!"

Halmar bowed his head.

"Are you finished?" Sandry demanded, her eyes on the footman.

He looked at her, swallowed hard, and went down on one knee to her, all without releasing his grip on Halmar's arm. His companion, still holding the miller's other arm, slowly went to one knee as well. Every other servant in the lower hall did the same.

Briar looked at Daja and rolled his eyes.

"Poppycock," muttered Tris.

Sandry glanced at them, frowned, then looked down

at Halmar again. "I have news for you as your liege lord, Halmar Iarun. Your wife Gudruny has asked me for her freedom, as is her right under law?" Sandry glanced at Ambros, who nodded. "Well," continued Sandry, "I decree that she is now free of you. Your marriage is at an end. You will pay for the care of your children by her. That is *my* right under the law. And shame to you, for using such a disgusting trick to marry her!"

"She was lucky to get me!" Halmar cried, trying to drag free of the men who gripped his arms. "Her family didn't have a hole-less garment to their names, did she tell you that? Holding up her nose at the likes of me when everyone knew she hadn't a copper of dowry. I did her a favor to marry her. I'll provide for my children — I'm no *naliz,* to let my own blood go hungry! But she'll see not an argib from me in back wages, or whatever you womenfolk cook up between you —"

"Another word," said Ambros, his voice pure ice, "and I will have you flogged at the village stocks, for disrespect to nobles, one stripe for each of us." Halmar looked up at the faces that stared down at him from the gallery.

As far as he knows, we're all noble, and he'll be sleeping on his belly for a month if he doesn't bite his tongue, thought Daja coolly. Ambros should know the only way to douse a fire like that is drown it in a tempering bath. Ice water would silence him fastest. A plunge in the Syth, maybe.

"Get him out of my sight," ordered Sandry.

The footmen rose, hauling the man with them. They bowed deep, forcing Halmar to bow with him, then half-marched, half-dragged him from view.

Ambros looked across the stairwell at Sandry. "You should still have Halmar flogged for disrespect," he said quietly, his voice carrying perfectly to everyone in the gallery and the main hall below. "We don't encourage the lower classes to speak so to the nobility here."

Sandry flapped a hand as if she brushed away a fly. "Either I'm so important that the squeaks of a beetle like him aren't worth my attention, or I'm not important, which means I can't hire his former wife as my maid and her children as my pages. Which is it, do you suppose, Cousin?"

"I thought you didn't need a maid," Tris reminded Sandry, her voice flat. Her lightnings were just beginning to fade.

Gudruny looked at Sandry. "You don't? Lady, I do not wish to be a burden — I can get sewing work in the city. I never meant to be a charge on you —"

"Hush," Sandry told her gently. She glared at Tris and said, "It's been made clear to me that it's very strange for me not to have a maid. Gudruny will add to my consequence. All right? Does that suit you?"

"Don't bite *my* head off," retorted Tris as Chime climbed up to her shoulder. "Did they deliver your consequence in the middle of the night? I didn't hear it arrive."

"They smuggled it in with the morning bread," commented Briar. "They didn't want us getting in the way of her consequence."

Sandry propped her hands on her hips and glared at him. *"Enough."*

"Yes, *Clehame*," said Briar. He bowed and returned to his room.

"Yes, *Clehame*," added Tris. She bobbed a curtsy and retreated to her own chamber with Chime.

Sandry looked at Daja, clearly upset, and opened her mouth, but Daja shook her head. Let them calm down. They always listen better after breakfast, she thought, though she didn't use their magical tie. She knew that Sandry would understand without that.

"Well, I know what Her Imperial Majesty would say," volunteered Jak. Unlike the others, he looked fresh and ready for the day as he leaned on the gallery rail, grinning with amusement. "She'd say a *clehame*'s word is law, whether she means consequence or the marriage of one of her servants. Particularly when the *clehame*'s of imperial blood. You're a spitfire in the morning, aren't you, Lady Sandry? The poor sod who marries you may not be ready for so much hot pepper in his bed."

Sandry stuck her tongue out at him.

She's forgotten that newly arrived consequence already, observed Daja.

Gudruny sank to the floor, weeping. "Enough," Sandry

told her kindly. "It seems you weren't lying, which is really just as well, if you're to work for me." She looked over at Ambros. "Would you send a few men-at-arms with *Ravvi* Gudruny, to help her pack and to bring her children here?"

Ealaga looked at her husband. "You said things would be different with the *clehame* at home," she remarked with a twinkle in her eye. "I see now you weren't joking. Perhaps you should order that the catapults be inspected, in case she wants to practice with those later." She turned and vanished into her room.

Rizu laughed from her position across the stairwell. "Where's the fun in that?" she asked Daja. "Get dressed. You and Caidy can go riding with me."

As Daja nodded her agreement, Jak offered, "I'll ride."

"Not me," grumbled Fin. "I'm going back to bed."

Ambros continued to watch Sandry. "I was not her overlord," he said cautiously. "I could stop him from beating her, but that was all I could do."

"Please don't rub my nose in it, Cousin," Sandry replied gloomily, urging Gudruny to her feet. "I'm already feeling guilty." Of the woman at her side, she asked, "You petitioned my mother twice?" She led Gudruny back into her rooms.

Daja sighed. "I'd hoped to sleep late," she said to no one in particular.

"Give me an hour?" Daja asked Rizu. The young woman nodded and returned to her chambers, while Daja went back to get dressed. Once clothed, she checked on Sandry.

Her friend stood in her personal sitting room, staring bleakly through an open window. Sounds of rummaging came from the bedroom. It seemed as if Sandry's new maid had gone straight to work. "Was it all that dire?" asked Daja, curious. "It had to be solved first thing in the morning?"

Sandry grimaced. "You mean I should have done it with more ceremony? Probably. But Halmar rushed in first thing, remember? I think Cousin Ambros would have stopped me if I were in the wrong. You didn't see her, Daja. She hid in here to talk to me." She gave a tiny smile. "Well, then she fell asleep and woke me in the middle of the night. He kidnapped her, and he forced her to sign a marriage contract. She could only be free of it if my mother — or I — decreed it." She returned to her watch over the view outside her window. "Daja, my mother didn't only refuse to hear her. She, she *ignored* Gudruny. She ignored the whole thing and left Gudruny with a man who forced her. I didn't think my mother was like that."

"Like what?" asked Daja. "Like a noble?"

"Uncaring," whispered Sandry. "Oh, I know she was flighty. So was Papa. They were like children, in a way. They used their money to travel and have fun all the time, never asking where it came from or what they owed to the people who provided it. They were wrong in that, very wrong. If I've learned nothing else these last three years, I've learned that much." She turned and went to sit in the chair next to Daja's. "And yet — I don't want to be responsible here. I don't want to stay here. My home is with Uncle, and the three of you. But won't I be selfish if I insist on going away again? Won't I be turning my back on these people?" She bowed her head and covered her face with her hands.

Daja stroked her friend's hair. Sometimes she has too good a heart, Daja thought. I had forgotten that. "It depends on how you do it," she said gently. "I just don't think you should be deciding all this on a bad night's sleep and an ugly scene first thing in the morning. You need to eat something. And you'd best tell the housekeeper to make provision for your new maid and her children."

Sandry winced. "You're right. Will you keep Gudruny company while I go?"

Before Daja could say, "I think you're supposed to have the housekeeper come to *you*," Sandry was out the door. Looking into the bedroom, Daja saw that Gudruny was staring out at her. She walked over to the woman. "I don't think we've been introduced," Daja said. "I'm her sister, Daja Kisubo. There's another sister and a brother. You saw them outside, maybe, the redhead and the young man with the short black hair. We're all mages. Real mages. With a medallion." She lifted hers from under her robe and watched Gudruny's face as the woman looked at it. She wanted Gudruny to understand her perfectly. "If you try to take advantage of Sandry, that would be sad. We really won't like it. People usually wish they'd just left the four of us alone after they've experienced us as unhappy."

Gudruny was trembling. "I didn't know about her family. I thought she was an only child. And no one mentioned mages, either. I didn't ask her to give me work." She licked her lips. "Though it would keep me safe from Halmar taking revenge. And my parents will never forgive me for losing Halmar's income for our family. I don't know why she was so generous, but I hope you'll understand if I don't run away screaming. I have nowhere to go." She met Daja's eyes squarely, though she gulped when she did it.

Daja had to grin. "Ah. The Sandry effect." She held up a hand. "No, I don't expect you to know what I mean. You just reminded me that when we four lived together — at Winding Circle temple in Emelan for four years — now and then we'd find people who looked flattened, dismayed, and happy. Then we always knew Sandry was nearby. Once she decides to make your life better, look out! It's easier to throw yourself off a cliff than it is to keep her from sweeping you up when she's in that mood." She changed the subject abruptly and offered her hand. "Daja Kisubo. Was Halmar really as pinheaded as he was talking out there?"

Gudruny sighed and sat on Sandry's bed. "Halmar was never denied anything by his family — he was the only male child. And he taught me not to deny him anything once we were married." She smoothed her crushed skirts. "When he beat me I sought help from *Saghad* Ambros and got it. But . . . I never knew Halmar's moods. He would punch the wall next to my head, and throw things at me or our children. He would lecture me for hours into the night, until I'd agree to anything just so he would let me sleep. I was always shaking, never sure what the children or I might fail at next." She tried to smile, but couldn't quite manage it. "I don't believe I've had a night's sleep in ten years." Gudruny looked up at Daja. "So what kind of mage is the *clehame*?"

Daja went over to Sandry's workbasket. "First rule: Don't touch this or anything in it, ever, all right? Even if you need scissors, or needle and thread, get them elsewhere. It may look like a sewing basket, but it's her mage's kit."

Gudruny looked at the basket, then at Daja. "I may only be a miller's wife, or a miller's onetime wife, but that doesn't make it right to mock me, *Viymese*," she said with injured dignity.

Daja rolled her eyes. "I don't mock, not when it comes to magic," she retorted. "Sandry is a mage with weaving, spinning, sewing. Even her pins have magic in them. You don't know what they'll do if you use them. Make sure your children understand it, too. Briar thought once he could give his hands a little tattoo with vegetable dyes — he has plant magic — and Sandry's needles. Now he has plants made of ink that grow and move under his skin."

Gudruny's lips moved in a silent prayer. Feeling she had made her point, Daja asked, "You have two children?"

"Yes," Gudruny admitted. "My boy is seven, my daughter ten. I'll be certain they know — they are good children, and they mind me. But I have never heard of a mage whose kit is a sewing basket."

"You've heard of stitch witches, though. Where do you think they keep their mage kits?" Daja opened the shutters, letting the morning breeze into the room. "Did you see the redhead?"

"Her hair was sparkling," whispered Gudruny. "Actually, it looked like . . ." She hesitated, as if afraid to name what she had seen.

"Lightning," Daja said for her. "That's because it was. Tris's mage kit is her hair — her braids. She keeps different magics in each and every braid, but the lightning is hard to keep in one place, particularly when she's out of sorts."

The sitting room door opened, and Sandry returned. "Well, that's that. Apparently there are other rooms off these for the maid the housekeeper *expected* me to have. I don't believe I've ever been made to feel so, so *ramshackle* in my life by someone who was so terribly polite. She even managed to scold me for not making her come up here. I wasn't aware I had to answer to my own housekeeper!"

"You're frightening your new maid," Daja said gently. *Sandry* ought to be throwing off lightnings right now, she thought.

Sandry looked at Gudruny. "Oh, cat dirt," she said wearily. "Gudruny, don't mind me. I'm cross, but it's nothing to do with you. I'm glad you've met Daja. And Cousin Ambros says the men-at-arms are ready whenever you are. You can go get your children and your belongings when you wish."

The woman looked from Daja to Sandry and back again. "I have a thousand things to say, and none of them make sense. You will never regret this day, *Clehame.*" She grabbed Sandry's hand, kissed it, and fled.

Sandry looked at Daja. "What did you talk about?"

"I just started to tell her the less complicated things. You *did* say you didn't want a maid, you know," Daja remarked, leaning against the wall.

Sandry wrinkled her nose. "What else could I do? He looked like the vindictive sort. And maybe now servants will stop carping at me over my lack of a maid."

Daja came over and kissed her cheek. "Ah. You did it just to silence the servants," she said. Inside, through her magic, she added, *But you still have a heart bigger than all Emelan.*

Sandry smiled, her lips trembling. *If this morning's work brought one of my sisters back into my heart, then this whole trip was worth it*, she replied through their now open magical connection.

Aloud, Daja teased, "At least until the next time Chime gets into your workbasket." She heard brisk footsteps and Rizu's and Caidy's voices outside. "Some of us are going riding," she told Sandry. "Want to come?"

Sandry grimaced. "Ealaga wants to give me the inner-castle tour, then Ambros will show me the outer castle. I get to spend my afternoon looking at maps and account books." She sighed and slumped into a chair. "I shouldn't complain. I've been reaping the benefits of these estates like mad for years. It's only right that I learn the state they are in. And maybe I should have seen to it before this."

"Another day," Daja promised, feeling sorry for her. "I leave you to your tours."

Skipping breakfast, Daja dressed quickly and hurried out to the stableyard. Rizu and Caidy were already in the saddle and nibbling on sweet rolls. An hostler came forward with Daja's saddled and bridled gelding. She mounted and steadied the animal, wishing she had thought to wheedle a snack from the cook on her way out.

Rizu offered her a steaming roll. She had a pouch full of them. "One thing about riding with the empress," she explained, "you learn the quickest ways to get hold of breakfast before you ride off at sunrise."

"Actually, Her Imperial Majesty would think the day was half over at this point," said Caidy, looking east. "We tend to sort ourselves into two groups over time: the ones who couldn't sleep past dawn even if we wanted to, and the ones like Fin, who sleep in every chance they get."

"Will you look at this?" Rizu asked. "Here we are, three females, all mounted up and ready to ride. If Jak and Briar don't get out here soon, I say we should leave these lazy men behind *and* eat all the rolls."

"Jak was complaining just last week that women always

keep him waiting," Caidy explained. "He's *never* going to hear the end of this."

"End of what?" Jak sauntered into the stableyard, a sausage roll in one gloved hand. A hostler led his mount over to him.

"You're late," Rizu said.

"You're still here, so how can I be late? And here comes Briar." Jak pointed to a side door.

"We were all here and ready to go," Rizu informed Jak as Briar accepted the reins of his horse.

"Isn't *Clehame* Sandrilene coming?" Jak wanted to know. "I thought I'd be needed to save her from ferocious goats and the like."

"Those goats should look for someone to save them from *her*," Briar told the young nobleman. "Haven't you been paying attention?"

"She has to do responsible things," Rizu informed Jak. "Unless you want to hold account books for her to read, I'd mount up."

Jak shuddered as he followed her suggestion. "That's what I have older brothers for," he said, patting his bay's glossy neck. "Responsible things." He looked at Briar. "Race you to the river bridge," he said quickly, and urged his mount into a gallop.

"Coming through!" Briar yelled, setting his own horse to a trot. He pulled himself up into the mare's saddle as she moved, effortlessly swinging his leg over her back. Caidy laughed and galloped alongside Briar as they raced for the first gate.

Rizu sighed. "Children," she said. "Overgrown children, the lot of them." She and Daja followed the racers at a more leisurely pace. "Let's hope all of the gates are open, or this will be a short race." She winked at Daja.

Daja looked down, feeling her cheeks grow warm. She wished she had long, curling lashes like Rizu's. They made everything she did look flirtatious.

For the next two days, Sandry's companions amused themselves while Sandry acquainted herself with her ancient family home and its management at the hands of Ambros and his father. After that the group ranged farther afield with Ambros on rides to introduce Sandry to her many acres and those who worked them. They lost Briar for a day when he got to talking with the man in charge of the river tolls and crossings. All it took was the mention of particularly tough, long waterweeds that fouled oars and rudders to sidetrack Briar from his flirtation with Caidy. She pouted for two days and reserved her smiles for Jak, until Briar produced a small bottle of lily-of-the-valley perfume, made so that one drop would leave her smelling hauntingly of the flowers. That gift returned him to her good graces.

Daja, too, enjoyed the rides, partly because they took her to the villages that lay on Sandry's vast holdings. Those villages had smiths, men and women who were more than happy to talk with, and to trade tips with, another smith. After time spent in the nobles' glittering company, Daja needed the solidity of the forge and those who worked in them. She always felt excited among the nobles, as if she stood on the brink of some great discovery. It was wonderful, but exhausting. Metal brought her back to earth.

Tris never accompanied them. She was too busy working with Zhegorz, teaching him ways to shut out the things he saw and heard, being more patient with Daja's jittery friend than Daja believed Tris could ever be. Something she learned on her travels gentled her a bit, Daja thought one night over supper, watching Tris rest a hand on Zhegorz's shoulder as he stared into the hearth fire. If she doesn't think anyone's watching her, she can actually be *kind.* Tris. Who would have thought it?

Sandry thought she would go mad with Ambros's dry recounting of grain yields, mule sales, and tax records, but she had to admire his work. In those immense account books she could trace the progress he and his father had made with her holdings. His father had done well, but he had spent as little as possible to maintain buildings and roads and to handle the payments for those who worked the land. He saved every copper in order to send quarterly payments to Sandry's mother and then to Sandry.

When the writing in the books changed to Ambros's tiny, spiked handwriting, she saw that he had made loans and collected interest, then used that money to invest in crop management and exports. He had used *those* profits to make improvements to the estates, increasing production and creating a wider variety of goods to send to market. The problem was the one that she had observed in Emelan, the increase of taxes on the estates.

Sandry was poring over tax records one sunny afternoon a week after their arrival when Tris came to ask her permission to take Gudruny's children and Zhegorz up into the watchtower. "The guards refuse to let us go without permission from you or Ambros or Ealaga," she said drily, leaning over Sandry's shoulder. "What are these?"

"Imperial taxes. You know, maybe the guards won't believe you," Sandry remarked, picking up her shoulder wrap. A tiny hope, that perhaps Tris would reopen their connection as Daja had, surged in her heart. Sandry immediately crushed it. Tris was too wary, and too preoccupied with Zhegorz. Her chances were better with Briar for now. "I should go along so they'll know you have my permission for certain. Where are Ambros and Ealaga, anyway?"

Tris did not reply. Instead, she frowned, running a finger down a column of numbers.

Sandry waited, then nudged the redhead. "Tris? I asked you something, sister dear. Tris?" When this didn't produce a response, Sandry poked Tris hard.

Tris scowled at her. "They aren't in the castle, all right?"

Sandry pointed at the book. "What's so interesting? Don't say Ambros is witching the sums, because I won't believe you."

Tris snorted. "And I'm the Queen of the Battle Islands. No, it's not Ambros. Don't you see? There are more entries as you get older — more taxes, and more of them coming directly from the throne. First you were taxed four times a year; then six; then there's a double tax in this year. . . . He's as mule-headed as you, your cousin."

Sandry blinked at Tris. "You should be a prophetess, you're so cryptic," she complained. "Just say what it is right out, Tris."

Tris rolled her eyes. "She was trying to drain his purse for some reason. Probably so he wouldn't be able to send you this exact sum each year, because that's the only amount that remains the same. He's been scrambling, cutting other spending, but that amount remains the same, even during the last three years when he's had to cut everything else to the bone. And here's this year. One levy of imperial taxes, when last year there were three already. I'll bet he never said a word to you, did he?"

He sent me the tax records, so I could see for myself, thought Sandry, ashamed. *She* knew why this year's record was so different. She had sent word north via mages that she was coming to Namorn in late spring.

"The instant she knew I was coming, she stopped taking so many taxes out of these lands," Sandry whispered.

"Why didn't he say anything to me? I just assumed he was coping with it all."

"It was a point of pride for him." They turned. Ealaga stood in the doorway. "He felt that you would believe he had mismanaged things, if he could not make your payment. I begged him to let you know the people here were being forced to pay for your absence, but . . ." She shrugged. "He is yet another Landreg mule."

"Landreg House breeds very fine mules!" cried Sandry, her family pride stung.

"Yes," Ealaga replied drily, her gaze direct. "I believe it is because the breeders share a few traits in common with them."

Sandry heard a squeak that might have been a smothered laugh from Tris. She turned to glare at her sister, then remembered something she had seen in the books. She seized the volume that held the previous year's accounts and leafed through it hurriedly, this time noting many expenditures where lines had been drawn through to show they had not been made. She stopped at the one that had puzzled her. Through the line drawn over it she read the words "masonry/stones/tiles — Pofkim repairs." She carried the heavy book over to Ealaga and showed the Pofkim line to her. "What should this have been?" she asked.

Ealaga sighed. "You haven't seen Pofkim yet. It's on the northwest border, in the foothills. Flooding two years ago ruined some of the houses and made others unstable. It also changed the water. They could only sink one new well when they need three. They're all right . . . We help as we can, but . . ."

"He felt he had to make the payments to me, and the empress raised taxes to get me here. I don't understand that," Sandry complained. "How would that get me to come?"

"The landholder may appeal to the imperial courts for tax relief," Ealaga replied steadily. "Only the landholder. The Namornese crown has a long and proud history of trying to keep its nobles on a short leash."

"So Sandry asks for relief, and then she can go home to Emelan," suggested Tris.

"They can only ask for relief from a specific tax," Ealaga replied. "Once Sandry is gone, Her Imperial Majesty will simply impose new ones."

Sandry stared at her, her mouth agape. "But . . . I could never go home," she whispered. "She'd keep me here, even knowing I hated it." She scowled suddenly, a white-hot fire burning inside her chest. I *hate* bullies, she thought furiously, and Berenene is a bully of the first degree. So she's going to *make* me stay here? I think not! Even if I have to beggar myself to cover her stupid taxes, I will. She will not punish my people ever again, and she will not make me obey!

She took a deep breath and let it out. If Tris had gotten that angry in my shoes, every thread in this room would have knotted right up, Sandry thought with pride. But

I have control over my temper. "I would like to ride to Pofkim tomorrow and review its situation for myself," she told Ealaga loftily, holding her chin high. "Will you make the proper arrangements, please?"

Ealaga curtsied. If there was a mild reproof in her eyes, Sandry ignored it. I answer to no one but Uncle, she thought stubbornly. It's time *all* these Namornese learned that. To Tris, she said, "I believe I will join you and the others on the watchtower."

Tris propped her fists on her hips. "Not if you're going to act the countess with them," she said flatly. "I've just got Zhegorz calm enough to go out among people at all, and the way Gudruny's been telling her kids about your generosity, and how splendid you've been, they'll bolt and run the minute they see your nose in the air."

Ealaga quietly left the room as Sandry lowered her nose to glare at Tris. "I am not acting the countess!" she said tartly. "And *you* should talk!"

"I mean it," retorted Tris. "Act like a decent person or you can't come."

Sandry met her friend's stormy glare and quickly realized how ridiculous she was making herself. "I *am* a decent person," she said mildly. "Tris, you don't understand. I'm going mad with all these games people play to get me to do what they want. 'Fit only to be waited on and to be married,' remember? It's what that woman said to me all those years ago? Well, all these curst Namornese think I'm fit for is to be sold off to the highest bidder, like some prize . . . mule."

"I suppose I'm supposed to be sympathetic now," replied Tris at her most unsympathetic.

Sandry had to laugh. "No," she said, linking her arm through one of Tris's. "You're supposed to take your sister and fellow mage student to say hello to your friends."

"Good," Tris said, towing Sandry toward the door. "Because I'm not in a sympathetic mood."

Sandry made a face when Gudruny opened the shutters the next morning to reveal a gray and drizzly dawn. After her request at supper the night before, Ambros had sent word to Pofkim that their *clehame* was coming for a visit in the morning.

It seemed she would be visiting with a smaller group than usual. Even early morning riders like Rizu and Daja chose to return to bed when they saw the dripping skies. "Yes, Tris can keep us dry," Daja told Sandry with a yawn, "but there will be mud, and inspecting, and people bowing and curtsying, and the only time that's bearable is when it's a nice day. Have fun." She twiddled her fingers at Sandry and Tris in farewell.

The guardsmen who had been assigned that morning to accompany the girls and Ambros had never been treated to one of Tris's rain protections before. For some time they rode under her invisible shield in silence, with frequent glances overhead at the rain that streamed away from three feet above.

"It's quite safe," Sandry told them, trying to make them feel better. "She can do it over an entire Trader caravan and still read without losing control over it."

Tris, crimson-cheeked, shot a glare at Sandry and continued to read. Ambros finally drifted over to Sandry's side. "I'd get sick to my stomach doing that," he told Sandry in a murmur. "I can't read in carriages or ships, for that matter."

"I think if Tris got sick she wouldn't even notice," Sandry replied. "Look at Chime." The glass dragon flew in and out of Tris's magical shield as if it were no barrier at all, sprinkling rain droplets all over the members of their small group. "*She's* having fun," Sandry added with a grin. She looked at Ambros. His blue eyes followed the little dragon. Chime gleamed rainbow colors in the morning's subdued light. She spun and twirled as if she were a giddy child at play. There was a smile on Ambros's lips and a glow in his eyes.

He's not such a dry stick after all, thought Sandry, startled. You just have to catch him being human.

Suddenly she felt better about this man who so often reminded her of her obligations. She had been seeing him as a taskmaster. Maybe if I tried treating him as family, he might warm up to me, she thought. She fiddled with an amber eardrop, then asked him, "Did you know my mother's father at all?"

He was willing to talk of their relatives, and proved himself to be a good storyteller. Sandry was laughing as they rode over one last ridge and down into the valley that cushioned the village of Pofkim. Startled by what lay before her, she reined up. Now she understood why flooding had hurt the place so badly. It was all bunched in the smallest of hollows, huddled on either side of a narrow, brisk river that churned in its channel in the ground. "Were they mad, to build it here?" she asked her cousin.

Ambros shook his head. "You can't see them, but the clay pits are in the hills on the far side of the river. They need to be close to the water to transport the clay. They can't get enough of it out by horseback to make it worth the expense, but people in Dancruan are eager to line up at the wharves to bid on loads. They make very good pottery with it in the city. And goats and mules find plenty to graze here, but the footing's too steep for cows and the growth too scanty for sheep."

Sandry looked the village over. Now she saw the flood marks on the lone bridge over the river and on the walls of the buildings. Here and there were houses that had collapsed in on themselves. The outside walls of several homes were braced with wooden poles.

"If the wells are bad here, how can they put down new ones that won't be bad, either?" she asked.

"The one well they've been able to sink is higher up.

They built a makeshift aqueduct to carry the water to the village, but a good wind knocks it over. With money they can sink new wells up where the water is good, and build stone channels to bring it to the village." Ambros sighed. "I'd wanted to do that this year, but . . ."

Sandry scowled. Was there no end to the repairs her family's lands required? "Sell the emeralds my mother left to me, if we haven't the cash," she said briskly. "They aren't bound to the inheritance. I can sell them, if I like. If you can't get more than enough money for them to fix all this, you aren't the bargainer I take you for, Cousin."

"Are you sure?" he asked as they entered the outskirts of the village. "Won't you want them to wear, or to pass on?"

"The need is *here.* And I'm not much of a one for jewelry," Sandry replied as people came out of their homes.

"Oh, splendid," she heard Tris murmur. "The bowing and scraping begins."

Sandry sighed windily and glared at the other girl. "Let loose a lightning bolt or two," she snapped. "*That* should put a stop to it, if you dislike it that much."

"Instead, they'll fall on their faces in the mud," Ambros said drily. "Somehow that doesn't seem like an improvement."

Sandry shook her head — Ambros has been listening to my brother and sisters too much! she thought, half-amused — and dismounted from her mare. One of her guards also dismounted and took her mount's reins. Once that was taken care of, Sandry looked at a small boy. He was doing his best to bow, though the result seemed shaky. "How do you do?" she greeted him. "Are you the Speaker for this village?" The Namornese called the chiefs of their villages Speakers.

The boy sneaked a grin at her, then shook his head. A little girl standing behind him said, "You aren't stuck-up. They said you would be."

"Maghen!" cried her mother. She swept the little girl behind her and curtsied low. The curls that escaped her headcloth trembled. "*Clehame*, forgive her, she's always speaking her mind, even when it will earn her a *spanking*. . . ." She gave an extra tug to the child's arm.

Sandry lifted the mother up. "I'm glad there's someone who will speak to me directly, *Ravvi*," she replied softly. "Maghen? Is that you back there, or some very wiggly skirts?"

The girl poked her head out from behind her mother. "It's me," she said frankly.

"Do I seem stuck-up to you?" Sandry wanted to know. "*Ravvi*, please, I'm not offended. Let her come say hello."

"She has a way with people," Sandry heard Ambros murmur to Tris. "I wish I did."

"You show them you care about them by looking after their welfare," she heard Tris reply. "Do you believe her when she says put whatever funds you need into help for your tenants? Because she means it. She won't ask you later what you've done with her emeralds. When she gives her word, you may trust it."

Whenever she makes me truly cross, I have to remember she says things like this, thought Sandry as she acknowledged Maghen's curtsy. I still wish she hadn't closed herself off from me, but I'm so glad she came!

10

The village Speaker soon arrived, trailing a few bewildered goats. Tris stepped back, out of the way of the dance of manners required when Namornese commoners met the noble whose lands they worked. Once the greetings were done, Sandry asked to see the homes and wells damaged by floods in earlier years. Tris watched it all with Chime on her shoulder, her book safely tucked in a saddlebag. Since the dragon was clear unless she'd fed recently, most of the villagers couldn't see her until they were close to Tris. One bold girl reached out to touch the small creature, and only looked around when Chime began to purr. When her eyes met Tris's, the girl jerked her hand away with a gasp of alarm.

Tris made herself smile in what she hoped was a friendly way. Looking at the trembling smile on the girl's lips, she told herself, I think it worked.

After that first experiment with the village girl, she got to keep on performing her social smile. The children — those who didn't have to return immediately to work at the tasks of daily living — came to meet Chime. While she held the dragon so her new admirers could touch her more easily, Tris shifted until her nose was pointed into the rainy day breeze.

Someone upwind is making soap, she thought as she sorted through scents. And that's butter in the churn. Oh! Household privies and animal manure, she thought grimly. Really, these people should learn to clean up more if they don't want their water going bad. I'd better let Sandry know they need to collect their manure, before it starts leaking into their well water.

She smiled happily. There's wet spring earth. I *love* the smell of wet dirt. And here's the river under all of it.

She frowned. The river was young and ferocious, clawing at the banks. Tris didn't know a great deal about bridges, but she did understand rivers. Left to its own devices, this one was probably digging the banks away from the piers that supported the bridge.

Handing Chime over to the girl who'd touched her first, Tris left their tour and ambled over to the steep banks near the bridge. Closing her eyes, she let her power spill down the earthen sides. They were awkwardly held in place with a patchwork of boulders, bricks, smaller stones, and even planks of wood. She felt the swirling and thrusting river as it tugged the man-made walls, trying to pry them apart. They needed to be strengthened without disturbing the bridge, or they would collapse into the river, clogging it.

Tris took a breath and sent threads of magic down into the ground as Sandry might set the warp threads on a loom, reaching deep into the clay soil. Stones of every size peppered the ground underneath her and under the far riverbank, more than enough to shape solid rock walls. The problem, of course, was that they were scattered throughout the ground, separated by the dense earth.

Tris grinned, her pale eyes sparkling. This is a wonderfully knotty problem, she thought. The trick is to warm the ground just enough to make it easy to mold, then to start shaking it just enough to move the stones as I want them — and just enough that the villagers don't panic and run from the earthquake. Her fingers danced through her layers of braids, seeking out the ones she had used to trap earth tremors and those in which she had braided the heat of molten lava. They were heavy braids bound with black silk thread in special knots to contain the forces in them.

She sat down on the muddy earth with a plop, settling into the most comfortable cross-legged seat she knew. Carefully she began to undo the knots on her braids, sorting through the spells that would release their power for her guidance. Control is the thing, and patience, she told herself over and over, concentrating. They won't know I did a thing.

"Oh, good, it's one of her rainy-day gowns. Tris! Tris!" Someone — Sandry — shook Tris by the shoulder. Tris stirred. "Tris, you've been here for half the day. You're scaring the nice people! You've scared me, and Chime, and Ambros doesn't look that well, either!"

Tris blinked. Getting the earth to calm down once she was finished had been the hardest part of the whole thing. She had forgotten how tiring it was to force what was left of the power of the tremors and the volcanoes back into their proper braids. Weakly she fumbled to tie them up.

"What?" she demanded irritably, squinting up at her sister. "I wasn't bothering anybody. I was just sitting here." The rain had finally stopped.

"She made the ground *ripple,*" said someone very young. "It all shivered and rumbled and twitched, and nobody dared go on the bridge."

Tris turned her head on her *very* stiff neck. The speaker was the girl child Maghen. Of all the people who stood and stared at her, Ambros and their guards included, only Sandry and Maghen had dared to come within reaching distance of Tris.

"I was repairing the walls on the banks," she explained to the child. "Otherwise they were about to drop into the river." She looked up at Sandry, her gray eyes glinting. "Or would you rather I'd have let them alone until they collapsed and you *had* no river?"

Sandry smiled at her. "You'll feel better once you've eaten something," she said practically. "And I didn't make your boots. They'll be scraping mud off them for a week." She offered Tris her hand.

Tris took it, and fought her body — it had been in one position for much too long — to get to her feet. The mud seemed far deeper than it had been when she sat down. As she struggled and lurched, worried that she would pull Sandry into the clayey soup, she looked at herself. From her waist down she was coated in mud.

Maghen saw Tris's self-inspection. "You sank," she explained. "The ground went soft and you sank, and you didn't even move. Oooh," she whispered as Sandry and Tris brushed at Tris's skirts. The mud slid off as if the cloth were made of glass.

Tris grinned at Maghen. "When Sandry makes a dress for a rainy day, she makes sure no one will have to wash it twelve times to get it clean," she told the child. "Really, she's very useful to have around, even if she *is* a *clehame*."

Sandry elbowed Tris in the ribs. "Shake that mud off your stockings, too, while you're at it," she ordered.

Tris obeyed.

"Come see," begged Maghen. "Look what happened." She towed Tris closer to the river's edge. On both sides, a hundred yards upstream of the bridge and roughly the same length downstream, the riverbanks were secured by solid stone walls. Closer examination showed them to be made of thousands of pieces of rock, large and small, fitted tightly together into barriers a foot thick. Tris bent down to look under the bridge. The walls continued under it, supporting and filling in the spaces around the piers. The riverbanks would stay put for a few decades, at least.

"Not bad for a day's work," she told Maghen, and trudged back to Sandry and Ambros. The man had procured sausage rolls, which he offered to her. Tris took two — she was ravenous — and ate quickly and neatly as the guards mustered the nerve to bring forward their horses. When she was done, she shook hands solemnly with Maghen and waited for Sandry to mount up.

"I'll make sure the villagers thank you before we return to the capital," Ambros murmured to Tris. "They're just . . . unsettled. The ground quivered and growled for hours."

"I didn't mean to unsettle anybody," Tris grumbled as she swung herself into the saddle. "I just didn't want you to have to pay to repair the riverbanks along with everything else." She smiled crookedly. "Sandry might actually have to sell rubies, or something."

As Ambros mounted his horse, Sandry looked back at Tris. "Donkey dung," she said. "I was so hoping to sell the rubies Papa bought Mama. I prefer garnets, you know. They have a much more pleasing color."

Chime glided over to them from wherever she had been as they set their horses forward, waving good-bye to the villagers. Ambros shook his head and continued to shake it. "I've never known anyone like either of you," he said, befuddled. "Not a noblewoman who didn't prize expensive stones, nor a young woman who could stir up the earth like a stew-pot and say, 'Oh, by the way, I've just saved you a hundred gold argibs in riverbank shoring.' Not to mention the lives of the few who always manage to fall into the river and die during the work."

"Then you've led a sheltered life," Tris informed him.

Sandry patted Ambros on the arm. "We lived in a very rowdy household," she added sympathetically. "You should be glad we didn't live here, with all the mistakes we made."

"But you . . . ," Ambros said, looking at Tris.

Tris slapped her mount's withers lightly with the reins, sending the horse into a trot ahead of the group. I hate it when they go on and on about the things I can do, she thought irritably. Why can't Ambros just let it drop?

It'll be different when I get an academic mage's license at Lightsbridge, she told herself. Then I can just do all the work mages are expected to do: charms and spells and potions and things. The trouble with the Winding Circle medallion is that when I show it I have to explain about weather magic — a Lightsbridge license won't require that. People won't fuss at me for being odd. I can live a normal life.

As she crested the ridge, the wind brought an unexpected metallic tang to Tris's nose. When she straightened to get a better whiff of it, the scent was gone. She drew her mare up and raised a hand to signal the others to slow down.

"What's wrong?" demanded Ambros.

The wind shifted. Tris no longer smelled whatever it was. Slowly she lowered her hand.

"Maybe nothing," Sandry replied to her cousin. "Maybe trouble coming."

"Maybe one of those villagers slipped off to warn someone we'd be coming this way — bandits or the like," one of their guards suggested. When Ambros frowned at him, the man shrugged. "Sorry, my lord, but we couldn't watch everyone. There's no word the Pofkim folk have any dealings with outlaws, but you never know."

On they went, the guards with hands on their weapons, riding around Sandry and Ambros in a loose circle. Tris refused to retreat into their ranks. After seeing her work with the riverbanks, none of the guards insisted that she move inside their protection.

They had gone two miles when a spurt of wind showed Tris metal plates sewn to leather and shoved the tang of sweat, oil, and iron into her sensitive nose. She sneezed and reined up. Twenty men trotted out from behind a stone outcrop at the bend of the road and rode wide to encircle them. Some guards tracked them with their bows, sighting on first one, then another rider. Ambros and the remaining guards drew their swords.

Three of the newcomers halted directly in front of their party. One of them was an older man, gray with age and red-nosed from too much drinking, though his seat in the saddle was assured and his gaze clear. Another was a redheaded man in his thirties who wore a gaudy blue tunic over his armor. He grinned at them, but there was nothing friendly about the double-headed ax in one of his hands. The third man was barely older than Sandry and Tris themselves. He wore a metal cuirass and held a bared sword in his trembling grip.

"Good day to you, *Saghad* fer Landreg," the redheaded man said casually.

Ambros looked as if he'd bitten into a lemon. "*Bidis* fer Holm. *Saghad* fer Haugh." He directed the glare that went with the *Saghad* title at the oldest newcomer. For the youngest of them, Ambros spared only a sniff of disdain. He spoke to Sandry, though his eyes never left the men in front of them. "Behold the least savory of the so-called nobles who haunt your borders in search of easy pickings. *Saghad* Yeskoy fer Haugh is uncle to *Bidis* Dymytur fer Holm and father to that young sprig of a rotten family tree."

"Ah, but Dymytur is your eternal slave, fair *Clehame*," the redheaded man said, bowing mockingly in the saddle. "Now, which of you wenches would that be? Please tell me it's not the fat one, Ambros. Fat redheads always spell trouble in our family — look at my mother. I suppose I could cut this one back on her feed, get her a little less padded."

Tris sighed and leaned on her saddlehorn. "I wouldn't touch you to kick you," she told him rudely, her brain working rapidly. Ambros must think I'm worn out from the river, she thought. Oh, dear. I suppose a little surprise won't hurt him. He really ought to know that Sandry isn't a helpless maiden. Now seems as good a time as any for him to learn.

"You're going to try that thing, aren't you?" demanded Sandry, her eyes blazing. "You're going to try and kidnap me and force me to sign a marriage contract so you'll get my wealth and lands."

"Oh, not *try*, dearest, wealthy *Clehame*," Dymytur assured Sandry. "We're going to do it. Your party has eight swords, and we have twenty."

"Isn't that just like a bully," Sandry replied shortly. "You think you have a sword, so you don't have any vulnerabilities. Out of my way!" she ordered the guards.

They hesitated long enough to infuriate Sandry. Before she could shout at them, Tris said, "Do as she says, please."

The guards flinched at the sound of her voice. When they looked at Sandry and met her glare, they reluctantly kneed their horses to either side to open a passage for her. Ambros lunged forward to grab Sandry's rein and missed. "Are you Emelanese mad?" he demanded coldly, his cheeks flushed.

"No, we aren't," Tris told him quietly. "We know precisely what we're doing."

Sandry rode forward until her mount stood between those of two guards.

"I'm not going with these people," Sandry replied, her blue eyes fixed on her would-be kidnappers. "I can't abide men who don't dress properly."

Tris saw the billow of silver fire that passed from Sandry to strike the three nobles in front of them. It spread to their followers, jumping from man to man, until it formed a ring that passed through them all. For a moment it seemed as if nothing had happened. The only sound was the wind over the grasslands around them.

Then a man yelped. He wore a leather and metal plate jerkin over his heavy tunic. Now the tunic collapsed into pieces, squirmed out from under the leather, and fell to the ground. Another man in Tris's view grunted as his breeches fell apart at the seams and wriggled off. The tunic under the youngest noble's breastplate also went to pieces and crawled away, while the cloak tied around his neck disintegrated into a heap of threads. Yeskoy hitched his chin, as if trying to adjust the shirt under his armor. Instead, a cloud of threads trickled from his sleeves and the hem of his armor, like milkweed down.

"Maybe if you had women you didn't treat as slaves, your clothes would hold up better," Sandry continued, her hands white-knuckled on the reins. "Oh, but look. Your leather workers don't do very well, either."

Now the stitches on the leather tunics gave way, as did the stitching that secured each metal scale to the leather beneath it. Leather breeches came apart at the seams; boots fell to the ground in pieces.

"I doubt their saddlers like them, either, *Clehame*," remarked one of the guards.

All the stitchery in the saddles, tack, and saddle blankets was unraveling. Men slid to the ground, reins in their hands, stumbling as they landed in piles of leather and cloth. Their belts gave way as Sandry's thread magic called to the stitches that held the buckles in place. Leather-wrapped weapon hilts came apart in their owners' fists. By the time Sandry was done, twenty naked men surrounded them. Only a few still held the better-made swords. Even the binding that secured the double-headed ax to its haft came apart, leaving Dymytur to scrabble for the sheathed sword that lay among his belongings. The horses fled, unnerved by the feel of things coming apart on their sensitive backs.

"I'd surrender if I were you," yet another of Sandry's guards advised. "She's been nice. She hasn't asked the redhead to look after you. The redhead isn't at all nice."

"I've been working on it," complained Tris.

Ambros looked at the ring of naked men. "Do you know, I would have thought that, for a mission to kidnap a young girl, you'd all be better . . . equipped."

"That's why we needed her, curse you!" snarled Yeskoy. "A plumply dowered heiress — do you think one of the imperial pretty boys will serve you any better, *Viymese Clehame*?" Although he was covering his private parts, he still managed to look fierce. "You'd best get it into your head, magic or no, you'll be married soon enough. You won't hold your nose so high when you've a belly full of brats and you're locked up in someone's country castle while he prances for the empress!"

Tris looked at Sandry. "What do you say? There's hail coming in the next storm. I could hasten it along, bring the hail down here. By the time I'm done, they'll look like they've been kicked by elephants."

Sandry leaned forward. "I will *never* marry in Namorn, willing or no," she said, her voice low and ferocious. "Never, never, never. Get out of my sight, before I tell my friend to send for that hail."

Dymytur hesitated, his eyes still on Sandry. His uncle snarled wordlessly and dragged him back, away from Sandry's group.

"The empress has mages, too!" Dymytur shouted, enraged. "Great mages who will tie up your power in a wee bow, so you'll marry whoever she pleases as she commands. Then you'll see about your never-never-never!"

He turned and ran for the nearby woods, his kin and his warriors following at a stumbling trot. Sandry spat on the ground in disgust, and kneed her mare forward down the road. After a moment's hesitation, Ambros and their guards followed. Tris remained behind for a moment, undoing one of her wind braids. She drew out a fistful of its power, held it on her palm while she gave it a quick stir with a finger, then turned it loose. It circled the area in a powerful blast, strewing leather and cloth all over the wide fields around the road. Only then did she follow the others.

* * *

Sandry fumed in silence all the way back to the castle. How dare these people? she asked herself silently, over and over. How *dare* they? What gives them the right to assume they may tell me how I am to live? They don't know *me*. They don't even *care* to know me. They look at me and all they see is a womb and moneybags.

"Do people do this with *your* daughters?" she demanded sharply of Ambros after they had ridden several miles.

Her cousin cleared his throat. "Only a fraction of women are at risk. If a woman is already bound by marriage contract, like most of the young ladies at court, she is considered untouchable. There are women and girls who are related to families or individuals considered too powerful to offend, like Daja's friends in Kugisko, the Bancanors and the Voskajos. The rest of us keep our daughters close to home in their maiden years."

"And it's considered safe to offend *my* family?" Sandry asked, her voice cutting.

"The head of *your* family is the empress," Ambros murmured. "And the empress wants you to remain here."

Sandry suggested what the empress could do about it in words she had learned from Briar.

Ambrose flinched and shook his head. "It was folly of me to let us come out with less than two squads of men, but we needed every free hand for the plowing. I thought we would be safe enough inside our borders. Holm and Haugh must be desperate, to strike at you here." He frowned. "And someone from Pofkim must have been in their pay, to let them know of our visit."

"Or someone at the castle got the word out when you announced this jaunt last night," Tris said, matter-of-factly.

Sandry glared at her.

"What?" demanded Tris. "I'm not saying you shouldn't venture outside your precious walls. It isn't as if we didn't handle the whole mess with no bloodshed. Though I don't see why you didn't arrest the nobles, at least," she told Ambros. "It *was* highway robbery, in a manner of speaking."

"I wanted to get Sandry home," Ambros said. "We'd have had our work cut out for us, to round them up and hold them, even without their weapons. And, well, there is the matter of the unspoken law."

"What unspoken law?" Sandry wanted to know.

Ambros sighed and scratched his head. If he hadn't been such a dignified man, Sandry would have described his look as sheepish. "The one of runaway marriages," he said reluctantly at last. "No magistrate will penalize a man who kidnaps an unmarried woman for the purposes of marriage. Or if they do, it's a fine, and one so tiny that it's insulting. The only exception is if someone is killed during the kidnapping. Then the man must die."

"Mila of the Grain, of course we must punish him if he kills someone, but kidnapping?" cried Sandry. "A mere bit of manly folly! I'm sure if he apologizes to the woman and gives her flowers, she'll come to thank him!"

Wincing, Ambros continued in his dry way: "The custom's from the old empire, the one west of the Syth. Those we've conquered since have chosen to, well, honor it."

"That's barbaric!" snapped the girl.

All around them the guards from Landreg bristled.

"It *is*!" Sandry insisted, swiveling to look at them. "Around the Pebbled Sea, women control their own lives, within limits. No one can force us to marry against our will!"

"Actually, they can, but they have to be sneakier about it," remarked Tris, watching the clouds overhead. "Contracts, and bride prices. Telling the girl it's for the good of the family, that sort of thing."

"It's not right, the Namornese custom is barbaric, and I won't be forced to marry anyone!" Sandry snapped. "Anyone who tries to force me will learn a sharp lesson!"

"Any would-be kidnapper with chain mail would still be wearing it even after you were done with your spell," Ambros observed. "And if they know what you can do, they'll be sure to prepare ahead of time."

"I am not helpless deadweight," Sandry whispered, her eyes blazing. "I am no victim, no pawn, no weakling."

Tris sighed as they trotted onto the road that would take them to the castle gate. "No weakling against the imperial mages? Ishabal is a great mage. So's Quenaill. Do you even know if you could face down great mages, if one was trying to kidnap you?"

"If you three weren't fighting what we used to be, I wouldn't think twice about it!" cried Sandry, furious. "But no, you fear I'll discover something naughty in your minds. Or silly. Or ugly. It's like the three of you went off to have your adventures and then you come home and blame *me* because we're all different! I want us to be what we were, and all you care about is that travel broadened you!" To her disgust she realized she was weeping as she shouted her resentments. "Forgive me for wanting my family back!" Before she disgraced herself even further, she kicked her horse into a gallop and pelted headlong up the hill to Landreg Castle.

On their return Sandry retreated to her rooms. As they waited for the bell to call them to the dining hall, it was left to Tris to tell Briar and Daja what had happened that day.

Daja nodded when Tris told them about Sandry's last outburst. "She mentioned that to me, back home," she admitted.

"But she said when we left she didn't mind," Briar complained. They had gathered in his chambers, watching as he put together a blemish cure for Ambros's oldest daughter. He spoke to his sisters as if he were doing nothing else, but his hands were sure as he added a drop of this and two drops of that to the contents of a small bowl. "She told us to stop being silly and grab the chance when it was offered."

"What else could she say?" Daja wanted to know. "If you've forgotten, she hates to distress people."

"That wasn't apparent today," Tris murmured, watching the flames in Briar's hearth. "She left those kidnappers in plenty of distress. And she certainly gave *us* the rough edge of her tongue, coming back. I can't recall ever seeing her angry enough to yell."

"She hates being treated like a *thing*," Daja reminded them. "She always hated it when people looked at her and saw a noble girl, not a human being. And she's been running Duke's Citadel since a few months after we were all gone. It must be hard, going from mistress of a castle and adviser to a nation's ruler to someone who's supposed to go where she's bid and do as she's told."

"If she doesn't like it, let her sign it over to Ambros," Briar suggested, wiping off the slender reeds he used as droppers. "Sign it all over and go home."

"I think it's a matter of pride," Tris remarked slowly. "She hates being treated like a noble, except when she wants to act like one. Like today. She was happy enough with the villagers and everything. It was when those idiots tried to make her into a prize that she got all on her dignity. If she gives up these estates now, it will be like she's been forced to surrender what's rightly hers out of fear."

"She'll think she's shirking," added Daja. "She already thinks it, with all the things that didn't get done because they had to pay so much out to her, and because of people like Gudruny."

"No, it's not that she's afraid to shirk, though Lakik knows she hates that," Briar told them, pouring his cure into a small glass bottle. "She's got the bit between her teeth now. It's how she always gets, when someone says she has to do anything she thinks challenges her rights. Remember when I stole my *shakkan* and Crane and his people were chasing me?" He reached out and stroked the tree, which he kept nearby whenever he was working. "There she was, all of ten and no bigger than an itch, standing in front of the house and telling Crane and his students she *forbade* them to come onto her ground." He shook his head with an admiring grin. "Nothing between her and them but a flimsy old wooden fence and gate, and there she was, telling them they weren't allowed to pass."

Daja chuckled. "Or the time she said she wanted me to sit at table with her, and the other nobles balked, and she pulled rank on them. She was that strong-willed even eight years ago."

"Then she must hate all this," said a soft voice from the doorway. The door had been open, but they had thought everyone else had gone downstairs. Now Rizu leaned against the frame, her arms crossed over her full bosom. Her large, dark eyes were filled with pity. "Noble girls don't usually get to dictate the terms of their lives in the empire. I was wondering how she'd come by the regal manner. I suppose it was losing her parents that made her grow up so fast?"

The three looked at one another. Tris shrugged, then Briar, indicating Daja could decide what to tell the older woman. Briar thought it would be all right to trust Rizu a little. He'd noticed she listened more than she gossiped, and she hardly ever said a hurtful word. Briar liked her, for all that he felt she was unavailable to the likes of him. Since she was always friendly, he knew it wasn't that she had problems with his being a commoner or a mage. He just wasn't her type. That was fine with Briar. Caidy, with her sly eyes and her habit of touching his arm, or his shoulder, or his chest, was far more intriguing.

"Well, her parents traveled a great deal, you know that," Daja replied to Rizu's question. "She was with adults more than children, and her parents could be a little . . ."

"Distracted," Briar supplied, writing down instructions for the use of his blemish cure.

"That," agreed Daja. "And once Niko, who found us four, once he saw we had magic, we were spending more time among adults, and with each other. Then there was the earthquake, and the pirates."

"Forest fire," added Tris softly. "Plague. His Grace's heart attack."

"And getting caught up in murders, and having a student to teach, and handling a kind of magic most of us can't even see," Briar explained. "It rearranges the way you look at the world."

"I should think so!" said Rizu, awed. "You've led such adventurous lives!" She leaned her curly head against the door frame. "All this must make her feel like a bird in a cage, then," she commented. "Maybe the three of you feel that way, too?"

Briar grinned as Tris chuckled and Daja shrugged. "We don't like cages," Briar replied for all three of them. "We tend to stay away from them while we can."

"You're lucky you're not noble, then," said Rizu, a shadow passing over her face. "We're supposed to think our cages are open air."

The supper bell chimed at last. Daja was the first to get up and leave the room. As she passed Rizu, she linked her arm through the woman's, drawing her along with her. "Come away with us, then," she offered casually. "Live without cages."

Rizu threw her head back to laugh. The light gilded the line from her chin down to her bosom. Daja looked at that gilding, and away, feeling heat rise in her cheeks.

They sent up a tray of food from supper when Sandry refused to come downstairs. She poked at it with her fork, far too angry to eat. She kept trying to sort out her feelings, but they continued to tangle. How can I feel selfish for yelling at my friend, proud because I finally *said* something, humiliated at the idea that I might be carried off a prize sheep, frustrated because I hadn't unraveled those disgusting kidnappers all the way, ashamed of myself for sulking, *and* homesick? she asked herself, stacking vegetables on top of meat for entertainment's sake. All at once?

I hate it here, she decided, pushing away from the table. I hate how you never know what people are really thinking. I hate being a prize sheep.

Someone tapped on her door. "Come in," she called, thinking that Gudruny had come to collect the tray.

Fin opened the door and stepped into the room. "We missed you at supper, Lady Sandry," he said. "Ambros told us what happened."

Oh, dear, thought Sandry as he came over to kneel by her chair. He's going to try to court me.

Fin caught her hand. "Forgive me that I wasn't there to protect you," he said, his blue eyes blazing. "I should have been. I'd have sent those dogs on their way before they could set so much as a wrinkle of worry on your brow. I'll do it now, if you ask it. Ambros can give me a couple of squads and I'll find those curs and bring them back for your judgment."

"That's very good of you, though I am certain they are long gone by now," Sandry replied gently. "But truly, I needed no defenders. I *can* take care of myself, Fin. And Cousin Ambros needs the men for plowing."

"Plowing, over your honor and safety? I knew Ambros was little better than a bookkeeper, but what an insult! And you shouldn't have to defend yourself!" he protested. "You are a gentle creature who must not be touched by sordidness like that! From now on, I'm your devoted servant. My sword is at your command. And if any more hedge-knights distress you, I'll make sure they get a lesson they'll remember for what's left of their lives." He kissed Sandry's hand fervently. "Unlike them, I care only for your happiness."

Sandry couldn't help it. Her mouth curled with disdain. "And my moneybags?"

Fin kissed her hand again. "Don't interest me in the least," he assured her. "You don't see something precious and beautiful and consider its cost — or, at least, a true nobleman does not. Leave that for the merchants, and the Traders. Those of us of rank know what real value is."

She got rid of him finally, after two hand kisses and more fervent promises of protection. He waited until after dark to offer to go recapture those men, Sandry thought dismally as she wiped her hand with her cloth napkin. Oh, I'm not being fair. He's been fidgeting ever since we came — no doubt he *wants* to go kidnapper-chasing.

Briefly she remembered Dymytur's furious, red face as the man had shouted at her. For an instant she fought the urge to call Fin back and to order Ambros to give him enough men to capture Dymytur and his uncle. It was harder than she had expected to resist the temptation.

Humiliation again, Sandry thought glumly. I *hate*

uncomfortable emotions. They're so . . . Her stomach cramped. Sandry wrapped her arms around her waist and thought, Uncomfortable.

She had managed a spoonful of stewed apples when someone else knocked on her door. "Come in," she said, thinking this must be Gudruny.

Jak entered, a smile in his brown eyes and on his handsome lips.

Mila of the Grain, have mercy on me, thought Sandry as she gave Jak her most polite, chilly smile.

"I came to see how you did," he said easily, digging his hands into the pockets of his light indoor coat. "I missed you at supper." Sandry had noticed that, in the jockeying at mealtimes, Jak had most often gotten himself into the chair next to Sandry, being smoother and more adept at distracting others than Fin. "Ambros told us what happened," Jak continued. "You should write to Her Imperial Majesty."

"I thought she was contemptuous of women who got taken, since she managed to escape when it happened to her," replied Sandry.

"Well, she'll approve of you taking care of the matter yourself, but it's not just that. May I sit?"

His eyes were so open and friendly that she caught herself gesturing to a chair before she'd really considered it. Jak dragged the chair over beside hers and sat, leaning forward to brace his arms on his knees.

"You *are* all right, then?" he asked. "No aftermath jitters, no fiery wish for revenge now that you've had time to reflect?"

Sandry smiled. "None at all. Such men are their own worst enemy."

"You certainly deserve better," Jak replied. "A man of culture and refinement. Someone who can make you laugh."

"But I don't want to be married," Sandry pointed out reasonably. "I'm happy being single."

"But think of the freedom you'd have as a married woman!" protested Jak. "You can ride wherever you like — within limits, of course. There's crime everywhere. But on your own lands you'd be safe. You'd have your lord's purse to draw on, his lands and castles and jewels to add to your own, an important place at court . . . what?" he demanded as Sandry gave way to giggles. "Why are you laughing?"

"Because I'm not interested in any of those things, Jak," she explained when she could speak. "I know other girls are, but I have all I need when it comes to wealth, and if I were as poor as a Mire mouse, I would be able to earn my way with my loom and my needles. With Uncle Vedris I *am* important at court. You're sweet, truly you are, but you don't know me in the least."

Jak looked down. "And I suppose that gardener, that boy, does?" he asked quietly.

"Briar?" Sandry cried, shocked. "You think I prefer — please! He's my brother!"

"I hadn't noted the family resemblance," Jak said.

"Well, it's there," Sandry replied. "I would no more kiss Briar than . . . oh, please! It's just too grotesque to even think about!"

Jak grinned at her. "Well, that's a relief, at least." He must have heard the genuine disgust in Sandry's voice. "Look, just forget what I said," he continued. "We can still be friends?"

"Yes, of course," Sandry told him, offering her hand. Jak clasped it with a smile, then left her alone.

He's sweet, she thought. If I wanted a husband . . .

Suddenly she saw Shan's face in her mind's eye: the easy smile, the wicked twinkle in his eyes, the firm, smiling mouth.

Nonsense, she told herself strictly. "I don't want a husband. *Any* husband." She said it aloud, in the hope that it would sound more real that way.

She shook her head with a sigh and put all of the dinner things back on the tray. She opened the door, then fetched the tray and set it in the hall. With that chore taken care of, she closed and locked her bedroom door. Gudruny and her children had their own door to their bedroom, which meant Sandry could have a good night's sleep without one more interruption, from anyone. I'll write to Uncle and set a date for my return home, she told herself, taking out paper and pen. After that, I know I'll sleep well.

11

The 4th day of Rose Moon, 1043 K.F.
Sablaliz Palace to
Clehamat Landreg, Namorn

Three days later, at the Sablaliz Palace, just twenty miles from the Landreg estates, Ishabal Ladyhammer found the empress in her morning room, watching the sun rise. Berenene, wearing only a light nightgown and a frothy lace wrap, read over reports as she ate a light breakfast. Her cup of the fashionable drink called chocolate cooled as she read and reread one report in particular, drumming the fingers of her free hand on the table. She only looked up from her reading when the door opened and Ishabal, dressed for the day, came in with a sheaf of papers in her hand.

"Have you seen the reports from *Clehamat* Landreg?" Berenene wanted to know. "Shall I ring for more chocolate?"

"You know that I cannot abide the stuff, Imperial Majesty," replied Ishabal. At Berenene's nod she slid into the seat across from the empress. "I have already breakfasted. And yes, I have read the reports from Landreg. They are fascinating."

"Fascinating, my foot," Berenene said crisply. "I want

fer Holm and fer Haugh to know I am displeased. If they haven't learned that no one may nibble the apples in *my* garden until I have had my taste, they must be made to understand it."

"Fer Holm and fer Haugh are ruined, Imperial Majesty," Ishabal said gently. "Ruined men are desperate."

"Can you believe it?" Berenene asked, shaking the papers that she held. "She undid their clothes. And then she undid everything else they had with stitches in it. That had better not happen to me, Ishabal."

"Charms against such magics are easy enough to make," said the mage. "Surely these men have been punished enough. The heiress escaped. How could we improve upon such humiliation as she gave them? They were forced to run naked to Pofkim, where the good people sent them on their way with pitchforks and laughter."

Berenene looked at her chief counselor from under raised brows. "My empire, my garden. They tried to take what is mine," she repeated patiently. "The laughter of villagers is not punishment enough for poaching my property. I prefer the sight of such bold and brawny fellows on their knees before me, thank you all the same."

She glanced at the report again. "I am also disappointed at the lack of information about my cousin's new 'secretary.' Really, the girl might have chosen him to infuriate me. First she is accosted by a madman — whose life Daja saved back in Kugisko. Then she hires this Zhegorz, as her secretary — or so our spies tell us. Except that her secretary spends his hours magically protected by Trisana and Briar, so our spies know nothing of what they are doing. Zhegorz spends precious little time writing, certainly. And now I am told that we have no history of the man before Daja met him in Kugisko, because the hospital where he was locked up burned to the ground, including its records! All we know is that he came to Dancruan sometime last summer and that he lived on begging and charity. Oh, yes, and that all who knew him swore he was mad — those who were not mad themselves!" She dropped the papers on her table. "I can't justify taking agents off important security work to concentrate on someone appearing to be a madman in need of magical help, but there's no denying it, Isha." Berenene drummed well-manicured nails on the tablecloth. "I dislike mysteries, and peculiarities are like an itch I cannot scratch."

"Here is something to divert your mind," said Ishabal, handing over a piece of paper. "My investigator mage just returned from an inspection of the new river walls at Pofkim."

Berenene snatched the paper and read it over twice. "He says the walls are solid all along their length," she murmured. "Under the bridge as well, and solid around the timbers and piers, as if they were poured mortar made of stone. The villagers say the ground shook and produced these stones for *hours*? Impossible." She looked at Ishabal and raised her eyebrows. "It *is* impossible." It was half a statement, half a question.

The great mage helped herself to bliny filled with jam. "I trust my mage. The girl did it. She managed a storm in the Syth, she made the ground produce a multitude of stones and pack them into walls along the riverbank, without disturbing the bridge. I find her . . . intriguing." She tucked a strand of silvery hair behind her ear. "She would be a very useful addition to Your Imperial Majesty's mages, if she chose to join us."

Berenene flapped a hand, as if she was not particularly interested. "Then she is your concern, not mine. Recruit her. Offer her plenty of money. These merchants' spawn always grasp quickest for wealth. Offer her whatever amount you think is just. Certainly she sounds useful. . . ." Her voice trailed off, indicating her lack of interest in the subject. "Do you know, I am disappointed in Jak and Fin," she told Ishabal. "Staying abed while Sandry goes riding with a tiny escort — really! I don't care if they had caught pneumonia, the girl will never be convinced of their devotion if they are not constantly at her side. They would have looked so brave, shaking their swords at fer Holm. Honestly, Isha, these men! If we didn't hold their coats for them, how would they ever manage?" She tugged a bellpull.

Almost instantly a maid popped into the room. That was one of the things Berenene liked about this seacoast palace: It didn't take forever for servants to respond to a summons.

It should also prove less intimidating to visitors such as her young cousin, for example, than the palace in Dancruan. She had brought her court here yesterday, to enjoy the sea air, she had said. In truth, she had brought them here to continue her siege of Sandrilene.

"Have word sent for my attendants to have their horses saddled," she informed the maid. "We're going to pay a visit to Landreg."

The maid bobbed a curtsy and left at a run.

Berenene saw that Ishabal was watching her. "I miss my cousin," the empress said innocently. "She must be tiring of account books and prosy Ambros. And she's had three days of close confinement to the castle and the village, to keep her from would-be kidnappers. She'll be eager for imperial entertainment. There is safety for tender young heiresses in a large group such as ours. Besides, I haven't seen Ealaga in months."

"If you were a bit kinder to Ealaga's husband . . .," murmured Ishabal.

"He knew he thwarted me when he refused to tell Sandry they were short of money and required her presence," Berenene said tartly. "Besides, he *is* prosy. A fine steward for the girl's lands, but dull." She inspected her nails. "Perhaps, when Sandry has given over her lands to her *husband's* direction, I may speak to Ambros about the Imperial Stewardship. If he does with the realms as he's done with her property, we shall prosper. Though I'll make *you* do all the talking with him, Isha." She got to her feet in a rustle of light silk. "Will you ride with us? You'll have a chance to talk with *Viymese* Tris."

The mage smiled. "You will have Quenaill to protect you, Majesty. And I will be here, making charms to defend your men against the power of a stitch witch, should things come to force. I do hope for all our sakes that they will not. The more I consider what Lady Sandry did to her kidnappers, the more I am concerned about what she may do elsewhere, if her hand is forced. Have you forgotten the prodigies that were reported of these four young people?"

The empress leaned against the wall. "They did prodigies in concert with their teachers, in a time when they shared a mutual tie," she said patiently. "I have also not forgotten the reports of their behavior since their reunion in Summersea, Isha. No two of them have worked in magical concert since then. They've had plenty of chances to do so on their way to us or while they've been here. Instead they quarrel. Their bond is shattered. Without it they are lone mages. You and Quenaill would not be the highest-paid mages in the empire if you could not find a way to best any lone mage."

"What if you force them to reunite?" demanded Isha stubbornly. "I have some experience of young people, remember."

"Your children and grandchildren? They are well-behaved mice. I happen to understand high-spirited youngsters," replied Berenene. "They are always very proud and very certain that their errors are the blackest crimes known in the world. These four are no different. You've read the same reports I have. They bicker like brother and sisters. Would you be happy to let your sister or brother share your mind, if you were them?"

Ishabal sighed.

"You're being cautious for me — good. That's what I want," Berenene said lightly as she walked through the door to her dressing room. She called back over her shoulder, "But don't let caution produce monsters who don't exist. They aren't great mages, not yet, and you and Quen are."

Isha shook her head. I am not as certain of that as you are, she wanted to tell her empress. I can get no sensible reports of what Briar and Trisana did while they were gone so far from home. I do know that Daja Kisubo put out a fire by pulling in a vein of the Syth, and that she walked through three burning buildings, each bigger than the last. I also know that Vedris of Emelan, a wise and careful ruler, counts your pretty little cousin as his chief lieutenant. Without magic she is more clever than the average eighteen-year-old, and she is a powerful mage.

Isha gathered up her sheaf of reports. In all the years that she had served the empress, she had learned one thing: When Berenene wanted something, she could be relentless. She wanted these four young mages to stay in Namorn. Isha sighed and thought, It never occurs to her there are some people — they are rare, but they exist — who aren't particularly interested in money, position, or fame. I hope these four are not like that. Trisana Chandler could be wealthy anytime she wishes, if she chose to do war magic. Well, perhaps it's war magic — not a dislike of money — that has kept her from accepting a position. If we offer her wealth to do magic as she wishes it, perhaps she will choose to stay. It is worth a try.

Sandry was stitching an embroidered band for Ealaga when she realized the hair at the nape of her neck tickled lightly. A moment later she heard Daja's voice in her mind.

You'd best dress nicely and come downstairs, Daja told her. *We have company.*

What sort of company? Sandry wanted to know.

Daja showed her friend rather than told her. Through her eyes Sandry saw the empress and her court climbing the steps to the great hall of the Landregs. Daja stood there, watching, as Rizu, Caidy, Fin, and Jak rushed forward to greet Berenene and their friends.

Sandry also noticed that the man standing at the empress's right hand was Pershan fer Roth. She replied, *I'm coming.*

Wait a moment, said Daja. *Isn't that the fellow you were talking to, that day in the imperial gardens? Shan? Why are you interested in him?*

Never you mind, retorted Sandry as she flung her wardrobe open. She had forgotten that Daja might notice who she looked at. Closing off her tie with her sister, she called, "Gudruny!"

Her new maid rushed in. For the first time in three days, she was not accompanied by her children.

"Where are the little ones?" asked Sandry, stripping off her plain overgown. Her crisp white linen undergown would do for a meeting in a country setting, but not the light blue wool gown she wore on top. She inspected her clothes. Blue silk, blue silk, blue satin, she thought, her fingers walking through the better clothes. Don't I have any other colors than blue? Ah.

She had found a crinkled silk overgown in a delicate blush pink. Carefully she drew it out and undid the top buttons so she could slide it on over her head.

"The children are with Cook," replied Gudruny, gathering up the discarded overgown. She put it on the bed and began to tug the pink silk into place. "They are afraid the empress will force me to return to their father."

"She can't," Sandry replied, trying to stand still. It's just that I haven't gone beyond the village in three days, she told herself, trying to excuse her sudden attack of the fidgets. I want to see new faces, that's all. "I got Ambros to explain it all to me while you were getting your things, and he gave me the law books to read. No liege lord may interfere in her vassal's dealings with her own people. My vassals, my commoners, answer only to me. Her Imperial Majesty would have to get my consent to make any ruling with regard to you, and I won't give it. That's my right, under the Namornese charter of noble privileges."

Gudruny shrugged. "I'm afraid my children won't grasp the ins and outs of lawyers' talk," she explained, guiding Sandry over to the stool before the dressing table. "I shall have to think of a simpler way to explain it to them."

Something in what she had said distracted Sandry from her own appearance. "Were *you* worried she could make you go back?" Sandry asked as Gudruny bustled around the room, finding a veil to match the gown, then taking up a comb.

"A little," the maid admitted with a rueful smile. "Her lack of sympathy is so very well known, *Clehame* Sandry. She is one of those who cannot believe that not everyone has her strength of mind. There is a reason people will say a thing is as unbreakable as the will of the empress." She bit her lip and added, "I also think those who kidnapped Her Imperial Majesty were far more gentle with her, more careful of doing her harm, than are those who steal women who are not imperial heiresses. I think perhaps she had more opportunity to escape, so she believes we *all* have such opportunities to escape."

"Oh, dear," whispered Sandry. Horrified, she thought, That has the dreadful ring of the truth. No one would want to bruise a wife-to-be who might be empress one day, but it's a different kettle of fish for a poor girl who has no interest in the local miller. I'll bet Halmar tied Gudruny a lot tighter than anyone ever tied Berenene.

She watched Gudruny in the mirror as the woman briskly neatened Sandry's hair, then pinned the veil on her gleaming brown locks. She's certainly grown in confidence since our first meeting, Sandry told herself. It's a good thing I hired her, telling that husband that he had no more rights over her.

Once Gudruny was done, Sandry leaned forward and patted her cheeks to get a little color into them, then bit her lips gently until they were more red.

"I have face paint," Gudruny offered. "Lash blackener, lip color, something to make your cheeks glow."

Sandry got to her feet hurriedly. "I don't want anyone thinking that I, well, that I wanted to attract attention," she said, nearly stumbling over her own tongue to make her reply sound innocent. "I just thought my cheeks were a little rough, that's all." She turned and fled from the room.

Gudruny's right, thought Sandry as she prepared to descend the stairs to the main hall. I must have looked as if I were primping for . . . someone whose attention I'm trying to get. And I'm not. I'm glad Shan — I'm glad my cousin is here, after all. I want to get to know *all* of my family, even if Cousin Berenene refuses to see that I don't intend to stay.

From the shadows in the hall, Chime glided over to Sandry and perched on the girl's shoulder. "Very well, you," Sandry murmured, tugging her veil out from under the dragon's hindquarters and straightening it. "But behave. No screeching."

Chime wrapped her tail gently around Sandry's slender throat. It felt as if someone had placed a ring of cool ice around Sandry's neck.

"*Now* we'll make an impression," Sandry told Chime. Slowly she descended the stairs as if she had not hurried in the least. She sailed out the doors in Ambros's wake. Everyone stood aside so that Sandry, as the highest in rank of the household, might go first. She pattered down the steps, knowing that the empress would not like her to remain higher than she was for long.

"Cousin!" she cried, settling into a deep curtsy in front of Berenene. "What brings you all this way?"

Berenene raised her up and kissed Sandry on each cheek as Sandry kissed her. "It was not so very far, my dear. I took it into my head to shift my household to the royal residence at Sablaliz, just twenty miles northeast of here, on the Syth. It's an agreeable summer residence — so much cooler than the palace! And it makes it easier for me to get to know my young cousin better while she attends to her home estates." She turned and looked at Rizu, Caidy, Jak, and Fin. "Have my four wicked ones kept you tolerably well-entertained?"

"They've been wonderful company, Your Imperial Majesty," Sandry replied. "I don't know how you could manage without them to amuse you."

"It was a sacrifice, I admit," said Berenene.

She looked at Ealaga, who promptly curtsied. "We have

refreshments in the summer room," Ealaga said. "Rougher fare than you're accustomed to, Imperial Majesty, but I think I can safely say that our wines are good."

As the empress and her companions entered the great hall, Daja found that Rizu had somehow slipped out of the gathering around her patron and come to stand with her. "I suppose you'll be happy to get back to the round of court entertainment," Daja suggested, feeling a little depressed. It's just that the place was fairly quiet, and now it'll be all noisy, she told herself.

"I was enjoying myself here," said Rizu. "I manage to enjoy myself wherever I land. A good thing, too, when you're in the empress's service."

"Did she send you along with us to spy?" Daja asked, not looking at Rizu.

The young woman chuckled. "She doesn't need me to spy. The people she has for that are very good at it." She hesitated for a moment, then said, "You four are an odd crew."

Daja looked at her, confused by the remark. "What do you mean?"

"Well, anyone at court and quite a few people *not* at court would kill for the chance to join Her Imperial Majesty's circle. And yet you all stand aloof. Is Emelan so much more filled with diversions and interesting people, compared with here?"

Diversions? thought Daja, confused. "Our work is in

Emelan. I have a house, with a forge, of my own. The Trader caravans know to find me there. My teacher Frostpine is nearby, and the temple libraries, for when I want to tackle something magically complicated. Sandry is her uncle's assistant, and he needs her. I don't know about Briar, but Tris means to go to Lightsbridge to learn academic magic. I suppose you could say we're not really the 'diversions' sort."

"But there are forges here in Namorn," Rizu pointed out. "Sandry could advise the empress, I suppose, if she cared to." She looked down. "I know I would like you to stay."

Daja's heart thudded in her chest. A fizzing sensation filled her body, while her mouth went dry. "Me?" she asked, her voice cracking. She cleared her throat. "We'll be here most of the summer," she replied, trying to sound relaxed. "You'll be more than tired of us all by then. We're a difficult lot, and we usually only get on with difficult people."

Rizu raised her eyebrows. "Usually the difficult need people who aren't in the least difficult around them. I try to be very *un*-difficult. Daja. . . ." She put her hand on Daja's arm.

"Rizu! Daja!" Caidy stood in the open doorway. "She's looking for you!" When she spoke that way, "She" meant only one person. To Daja, Caidy said, "Have you any idea where Briar got to? She's asking for him, too, and she's got that wrinkle between her brows."

"The one that means she's deciding whether to be

offended or not," said Rizu. "*Do* you know where your brother is?"

Daja quested out with her power. She found Sandry and Tris instantly. Her connection to Sandry was reopened all the way, so that Sandry blazed bright in Daja's magical vision. Tris had not thawed, but the lightning in her was clear to the fire in Daja's magic. Briar was still completely invisible.

But maybe not to everyone, she thought. Looking at Caidy, Daja said, "I can't find him, but Tris might. She usually keeps an eye on Briar."

Tris shook her head when Caidy, Rizu, and Daja asked her where Briar was — but she had an idea. She felt the finest cobweb of a bond between her and Briar. Perhaps it was there because after everything else was said and done, Tris had taught Briar to read, and they could still talk about books together. Neither Sandry nor Daja read as much as they did, or shared books with them. Shared reading made for solid friendships, like her relationship with Duke Vedris, Tris had found.

She excused herself politely to the courtiers and wandered away with relief. How many times in one day can a person curtsy or bow without tripping over their own feet? she asked herself. It gives me a headache, and I don't have to live at court.

She wandered down the back halls of the castle, pretending to ignore the servants who edged away from her. Word about the river repairs at Pofkim had spread in the last three days.

Forget it, Tris ordered herself as she passed through the kitchen, a cook stepping away from her. When I have my Lightsbridge credential, I'll be able to work in a way that won't make people nervous. Nobody shrinks from the village healer or the woman who sells charms in the marketplace. I'll be able to keep to small magics, and people will stop looking at me as if I had two heads.

Her steps carried her down a corridor where the storerooms were located. A stair at the end led her down into the cellars. There she found a light shining through the open door of the room nearest the stairs. She poked her head inside. This was a cold room, spelled to hold winter temperatures all year long. Here the castle stored things that would spoil. In the outer room, they stored meat, butter, eggs, urns of milk and cream, and large cheeses. In the room off the main one, Tris saw the silver bloom of magic. Briar was working with household medicines.

She sent a pulse down their hair-thin magical connection so she wouldn't startle him, then entered the smaller room. Briar had a series of small bottles in front of him, each holding a seed of magical fire. Three, off to one side, held more than a seed. Standing with his hands around one bottle, Briar was waking up the green power of the plants that had gone into its contents.

"You'll freeze down here in that dress," he said without looking up. He wore heavy woolen clothes. "Why are you bothering me, anyway? I thought you had Zhegorz to teach meditation to, and Gudruny's kids for their letters."

"Zhegorz is hiding in the wardrobe in your room," Tris said calmly. She was starting to shiver.

"Now why in the Green Man's name is he doing that?" Briar inquired absently. The magic in the bottle flowered into bright strength.

"He's afraid your friend the empress will realize all he has overheard and decide to execute him for the realm's safety," Tris continued, her voice even. "He's convinced she knows every scrap he's ever picked up."

"What a bleat-brain," Briar replied. "Even if she could do such a thing, and she can't, she's never laid eyes on him."

"He's convinced he might, what with her being in the summer room right now," said Tris. "That's an aid to digestion you're fixing, isn't it?"

Briar's head snapped up. He stared at Tris. "Here? She's here?"

"I thought that would get your attention," murmured Tris. "She's here and she's asking for you. Perhaps you should change shirts."

Briar raced out of the room. Shaking her head, Tris went to the medicine he'd just finished working on and marked the label so the castle staff would know it had been strengthened. She took her time about leaving, making sure the other medicines he'd handled were also marked, and returning the neglected medicines to their proper shelves. Despite the cold, she was in no hurry to rejoin the hustle and bustle upstairs. The drafts upstairs had been filling her ears with the courtiers' babble since their arrival.

Too bad I can't hide in a wardrobe like Zhegorz, she thought as she casually renewed the cold spells on the rooms. But no, she added with a sigh, I'm a mage. Mages are supposed to take such things in stride.

Briar hardly noticed Zhegorz when he yanked his wardrobe open and grabbed the first decent-looking shirt and breeches he saw. He closed the wardrobe, then remembered he'd need an over robe. This time when he opened the doors he noticed Zhegorz huddled in the farthest corner.

"She's no mage," he told the man. "She can't see what you've heard, even if you could sort out anything she wanted kept secret from the whole mess of things she doesn't care about." He left the wardrobe open as he stripped off his work clothes.

"Easy for you to say," snapped Zhegorz. "You don't hear all the bits and pieces that make a single damning whole."

Pulling on his breeches, Briar asked, "And have you patched one together? A single damning whole that makes sense?"

"I could," Zhegorz insisted, "if I put my mind to it."

Briar did up the buttons on his long shirt cuffs. "Old man, your mind is in a thousand places. You lost it in a swamp of words and visions," he said, not unkindly. "Nobody can use them to harm you until you put them together and *tell* someone. Do you even want to do that?"

Zhegorz straightened slightly. "No," he replied slowly. "There's too much, and it's all a mess." He rubbed his bony nose. "You don't think someone could torture me to speak it all and put it together out of that?"

"They'd be as overwhelmed as you," Briar said, tugging on his boots. "Lakik's teeth, Zhegorz, you've been like this for thirty years. It's all swirled together inside your poor cracked head. Only another madman would *want* to fish for something real in there." He took out his handkerchief and gave the boots an extra wipe, shining the dull spots. "If you think *she's* so powerful, just leave Namorn."

"Just leave Namorn?" Zhegorz repeated, straightening even more.

Briar looked up, saw the peril to his clothes, and moved them away from the madman. While his mind knew that Sandry had made his garments to withstand all common wrinkles, his heart worried for his beautiful things. "Just leave Namorn," he said. "No Namorn, no empress. No empress, no torturers with painful spikes and tweezers and spells with your name on them. You haven't heard enough in any other country to make it worth their while, only here." He shrugged into his over robe and glanced into his mirror. One of the good things about very short hair was that it never required combing. "Do you think I should grow a mustache?"

When no answer came, he looked around. Zhegorz sat, his long legs half-in, half-out of the wardrobe, with tears running down his cheeks.

Briar found his handkerchiefs. He took one over to Zhegorz. "You have to relax," he told Zhegorz sternly. "You'll rattle yourself to pieces at this rate. What's wrong now? Or is it the thought of me in a mustache that made you get all weepy?"

"So simple," the man replied in a voice that cracked. He blew his nose with a loud honk. "You, you and Daja and Tris, you take the knot that has built up for so long, and you just . . . cut through it. I've tried for years to untie it, and you chop it to pieces in a matter of days. Why didn't I see that? I have the years of a man, while you're just children yet —"

"Watch the 'children' stuff," Briar advised. "It's taken me all my life to shed that name. I'll thank you to keep it in mind."

Zhegorz gave his nose a second blow. "You've shed half a dozen names," he said, his voice muffled by the handkerchief. "But there's one you'll never lose, and that's 'friend.'"

"That's it," Briar said, checking his cuffs. He was always embarrassed by emotional talk. "I'm going to go pay compliments to the empress. You can stay here, but you'll be a lot more comfortable in a chair, or on the bed."

Without looking back, he left the room, closing the door gently behind him. He'll do better once he's out of Namorn, Briar thought as he trotted down the stairs. Maybe better enough to salvage a decent life for himself with the years he's got left.

As he reached the ground floor he thought, Someone's got to do a better job of finding us peculiar ones, *before* they end up like Zhegorz.

He found the empress and her courtiers in the summer room of the castle, the one that caught the most light, and on the terrace outside it. Berenene sat on a chair placed against the terrace rail, where she could enjoy the scent of the roses that twined around the stone rail from the garden just below. Briar approached her and bowed deep, summoning a rose with an as-yet-unopened bud to him. The empress moved aside as the vine thrust its thorny arm out to Briar. The bud swelled, then bloomed as it came closer to him, revealing a heart as crimson as blood. He used his belt knife to carefully cut the blossom free, trimming its thorns and healing the cut on the main vine before he sent it back to the others.

The mage Quenaill leaned against the stone rail beside the empress. He'd twitched when the vine crept past her, the silver fire of his protective magic collecting around his hands and eyes. When he realized it was Briar's work and not a threat to Berenene, Quenaill held the fire close but did not allow it to sink back under his skin until the vine had returned to its proper location.

"It's forbidden to practice magic in the imperial presence without permission," Quenaill said drily, as if it were no great matter. "Though I don't suppose she'll scold you as she ought." When Berenene looked up at him, Quenaill bowed. "Your Imperial Majesty," he said, to take the sting off his hinted-at rebuke.

She smiled impishly up at her guardian mage. "*Viynain* Briar has my permission to work any plant magic he feels is necessary in my presence, and has had it since I showed him my greenhouses," she informed Quenaill. "Now stop sulking, Quen, there's a dear."

When she looked at Briar again, he presented her with the crimson rose. "It pales beside your lips, Your Imperial Majesty," he said boldly. "But it was the best I could do on such short notice."

"Hmm." Berenene drew the rose down from her chin over her bosom. "Short notice to whom? *I've* been waiting here forever. I supposed you'd gone off to look at the Landreg fields rather than make your bow to an old woman like me."

Briar grinned. "The Landreg fields need no attention from me. *Saghad* Ambros's people are good farmers. No, I was in one of the cold rooms down below, working on medicines. I came as soon as I knew I could admire Your Imperial Majesty."

"You, my dear young man, are a flatterer," Berenene told him flirtatiously, tapping his cheek with the rose. "You mean to tell me that Rizu and my dear little Caidy held no charms for you? One of them hasn't stolen your heart?"

"Caidy has stolen my arm, perhaps, or maybe my breath, but my heart could only belong to you, great lady," Briar said, enjoying the flirtation. He knew better than to take it seriously.

"Then she has made more progress with you than my young men have made with Sandrilene," Berenene observed, gazing darkly at Jak and Fin. If they noticed, they showed no sign of it. Instead, Jak fanned Sandry gently while Fin offered her a plate of delicacies.

"She's not much of a player when it comes to games of the heart," Briar said. "If you sent them to engage her in such a game, Imperial Majesty, they were doomed to failure."

"Does she favor girls, then?" Berenene asked. She smiled up at Briar. "You see I will introduce her to anyone who might persuade her to make her home with us."

Briar scratched his head, then remembered it was vulgar to do so in normal company. "I don't know," he replied frankly. "But Sandry won't stay for a pretty face, whoever it belongs to. Some plants grow where they will, Your Majesty. You know that. Coax them, water them, light them, repot them, do as you like, they will only grow where they have decided to. The only way you can make them do as you bid is to kill them, which seems like a waste, if you ask me." He smiled cheerfully at her. "But there, I'm just a scruffy gardener, dirt under my nails and in my ears. I do better with what plants grow best next to which vegetables than I do with matches between people."

Berenene took a breath. Is she going to scorch me for my uppitiness? wondered Briar. Turn her mage boy on me? Or take it from one gardener to another?

The empress released her breath and reached out to slap Briar's arm with her free hand. "You are a vexatious youth, and an honest one. You have my leave to bring me some fresh berries from the food table."

It took a polite, blushing excuse that hinted of a need to use the privy to free Sandry of the courtiers who had swirled around her since Berenene's arrival. The moment she was out of everyone's view, she ran down two connecting hallways and out into the garden for some quiet.

What is *wrong* with them? she wondered, thinking mostly of Jak and Fin. They're sweet and funny and perfectly decent companions, except for wanting to flirt. Then my cousin arrives. Suddenly they act like every word from my lips is struck in solid gold! Green Man snarl them in vines if they cluster around me like that again! It's that or I'll set their breeches to dropping. See if they fawn over me while they hold their pants up.

Scowling, she found a bench in the herb garden and sat, letting the smells of rosemary and basil soothe her rattled nerves. With her eyes closed, she could pretend she was back on the step of Discipline cottage, bathing in the scents that came from Rosethorn's herbs.

She opened her eyes at last. My problems aren't at Discipline. They're here, and they have to be faced. I can handle Jak and Fin — I've been doing it since we got here. If they were the only ones bothering me, I'd send them about their business! The problem is, they aren't the only ones. At least three other of Berenene's . . . *lapdogs* have been sticking to me like burrs! How do I get her to call them off?

"I'm sorry — I didn't know anyone was out here," a man's voice said. "Forgive me."

Sandry turned and ignored the treacherous bump of her heart at the sight of Pershan fer Roth. Green is a very good color for him, she thought, and smiled. "No, it's all right," she replied. "Unless you wanted privacy?"

He returned the smile, his brown eyes dancing. "I was just going for a walk. You're the one who looks as if she would enjoy some privacy. Or perhaps enjoy murdering someone."

Sandry put her hands to her forehead. "I don't like to be crowded," she explained. "I was being dreadfully crowded back there."

Someone had built a bench around a very old apple

tree. Shan sat there, his long legs crossed before him, and leaned back. "How's this? I'm not crowding you in the least."

Sandry giggled. "Thank you," she told him. "But wouldn't you have more fun with the rest of the court?"

"Maybe sometimes I feel crowded, too," he replied. "You should see my family's lands. They're a bit like Landreg, only at the feet of the mountains. On a good day you can gallop for miles without seeing another living soul." He smiled, his eyes closed. "I used to shove bread and cheese into my saddlebags, maybe some apples, and just . . . ride." He opened his eyes to grin at her. "Fin and Jak finally remembered to be attentive to you."

"I almost had them broken of the habit before today," Sandry replied tartly.

"Poor little caged bird," drawled Shan. "Look at it this way: If you marry one of them, they'll leave you alone afterward."

Sandry glowered at him. "There's more to marriage than being left alone when you like it. And all this scrambling for my attention — having all these *boys* thrown at my head, it's just so . . . *undignified.* Frankly, my cousin doesn't strike me as the crude type."

Shan grinned. "Ah, but you see, she's the victim of her own success. Since she took power, she's been slowly reducing the great estates of the realm, through taxes, and marriages, other stratagems. She offered one not-very-bright fellow a dukedom over thousands of acres near the

Sea of Grass if he signed over his extremely wealthy *Saghadat* on the western shore of the Syth. Now he finds himself building castles and trying to create wealth from grass and nomads. . . ." He realized he'd come to a full stop and chuckled. "Sorry, I still find it funny. Anyway, the last untouched great holding, apart from the Ocmore lands, is —"

"Landreg," said Sandry.

"Landreg," replied Shan with a nod. "The man who weds you not only has a delightful lady for his wife —" Sandry glared at him, making Shan laugh. He continued: "He also has a very, very deep purse, as well as any alliances *you* may form with the Mages' Council. Since Ambros has saved you from losing lands to pay taxes, Her Imperial Majesty now has to scramble to keep you from the courtship of a man who is more seasoned and experienced. Someone who *isn't* under her thumb. She is putting you in the way of the young men she is sure of, men she can control even after they're married to you."

Sandry picked up a pebble and threw it into the garden. "Well, she's wasting her time. They're wasting *their* time. I don't want to be married at *all.*" She stood, shaking out her skirts. "Shan, why don't we go for a ride?" she asked impulsively. "Down to the village and back? Just a quick gallop —" She stopped herself. He was shaking his head.

"The empress will have my guts for garters," he said plainly. "To her it would look as if I were trying to cut out the others. That would make her unhappy. It is *such* a bad idea to make Berenene unhappy."

"Don't you want to go for a ride with me?" asked Sandry, puzzled.

"I also want to keep my intestines right where they are," Shan informed her. "A man at the imperial court serves the empress first. We don't form ties of affection to anyone but her, no matter how hard it is. Take my word for it, the only reason those eager suitors are so eager? She's let them know they have her permission. Once one of them snags you, they'll be back at court, paying attention to *her*." Seeing that Sandry was wide-eyed with fury, Shan added, "She nearly had one of her maids of honor executed for marrying a nobleman behind her back. The priestesses of Qunoc had to intercede. Now the couple is forbidden to ever show their faces at court again."

"But that's *silly*!" cried Sandry.

"No," Shan replied. "It's the disadvantage of having a great, unmarried ruler who has always been exquisite. She can order us to dance to her tune, and we do it. There is always the chance that one day she'll fall madly in love with one of us and make that man emperor. Even if she falls in love and doesn't marry, she showers her lover with titles, lands, and income. Hers is the hand filled with gold. If she were ugly as a boot, we would still worship at her altar, and she's not ugly."

Sandry shuddered. "I would never live that way. People ought to be free to love and marry as they wish."

"In an ideal empire, they would," Shan agreed. "But we don't live there. Don't look so upset. She likes you. If she likes you enough, she'll make you one of her attendants even if you are married. Life at court can be amusing."

Leaning over, Sandry plucked a sprig of mint and held it under her nose, enjoying its fresh scent. "And if I lived only to be amused, I might even like it, who knows?" she asked with a shrug. "But I'm a mage. I live to work. I *love* my work. The court will have to amuse itself without me after Wort Moon." She named the last month of summer.

Shan got to his feet. "I'd better put myself back under her nose before she suspects me of courting you. I haven't been disciplined by Her Imperial Majesty in four months. I'd like to keep the winning streak going. If you'll excuse me?"

It was the first time all day that a young man had left her and not the other way around. "Don't you want to court me?" Sandry heard herself ask, her mouth seeming to have a will of its own. Although her tone was one of mild curiosity, she could feel a beet red blush creep up from her neck to cover her face. Stupid! she scolded herself. Stupid, stupid! Now he'll think you're throwing yourself at his head, when you just wanted to know why he wasn't grazing with the herd!

Shan laughed, which made her blush burn all the hotter. "I like you, Sandry, but I'm not on the permitted list," he said, grinning. "Besides, friendship is always better than courtship — that's what my grandmother used to say. I'd like for us to be friends."

"Oh," she said, struggling to keep her voice disinterested, even if her blush still lingered on her cheeks. "I'd like that, too."

"Good," he said, offering his hand. Sandry took it and discovered that his hand engulfed hers. "Friends it is," Shan said, giving her hand a single, firm shake before he let it go. He grinned and walked back to the castle.

Sandry could still feel his warm fingers against hers. She looked at her hand, wonderingly. There was a green streak there, and the scent of mint.

She smiled. He had stolen her mint sprig.

When Sandry returned to the empress, she was once more surrounded by nobles. Daja couldn't help noticing the look Sandry traded with the man who now lounged at the empress's elbow. That was Shan, who had talked to her that day in the imperial gardens, Daja remembered. I hope Sandry isn't hoping for something there. He and Berenene seem really, *really* friendly, and that Quenaill, who I thought was really friendly with the empress, too, he took himself off to a corner when Shan arrived. He's been there ever since, glaring at Shan.

Daja nudged Rizu, who sat on the bench next to her with Chime in her lap. When Rizu looked at her, Daja ignored that fizzing sensation inside her skin and whispered, "Her Imperial Majesty seems very friendly with Shan."

Rizu chuckled, a sound that raised goose bumps on Daja's arms. Am I coming down with some sickness? Daja wondered.

Leaning over to whisper in Daja's ear, Rizu said, "I should hope they're friendly, since he shares her bed."

Daja flinched, almost bumping Rizu's nose with her own. Rizu giggled and brushed Daja's nose with her fingers. Daja gulped and turned to whisper in Rizu's ear, "He's her *lover*?"

Rizu slid a little closer. "He is, Quen was and may well be again, and there are two other fellows you may have seen glaring at them, who might just bounce to the front of the line if Berenene gets bored."

Daja rocked back, startled. Plenty of people had lovers if they weren't married, but it seemed greedy to have more than one.

"How do you think a nobody like Pershan fer Roth got an important position like Master of the Hunt?" Rizu wanted to know. "He couldn't have afforded the fifty gold argib fee to get the post. Her Imperial Majesty paid it." Rizu lowered her long lashes. "He's been the imperial favorite for about five weeks. Do you like him?"

"No," Daja said, bewildered that Rizu should even ask. "Oh, he's pretty enough. With those shoulders he could be a smith, but no. I was just curious."

"Sandrilene," called the empress.

Sandry looked at Berenene with yearning. She silently asked Daja, *Is she going to pull my suitors off me now? Before they smother me?*

Daja snorted.

"What?" Rizu wanted to know, but Daja just shook her head.

"We are of a mind to go hunting tomorrow, in the Kristinmur Forest," Berenene explained. "We invite you and your friends." Her tone made it not a request, but a statement.

Sandry frowned, then got to her feet, shooing the young men who sat in front of her out of her way as a farmwife might shoo chickens. "Your Imperial Majesty is gracious," Sandry replied slowly. Daja could tell she was groping for words that would not offend. Sandry went on: "The truth is that my friends and I do not hunt."

Briar sauntered into the clear space before the empress. "Well, I've hunted, when I had to," he said with a polite bow. "But not as Your Imperial Majesty means it, with horses and the birds and the dogs."

"And beaters," added Tris, coming into view from a pocket of shadow where she'd been talking with Ishabal. "Frightening helpless animals."

"A boar or an elk is hardly helpless," the empress said drily. She found Daja immediately. "Do you also object to hunting?" she asked mildly.

Daja shrugged and got to her feet to bow. "I never

learned, Your Imperial Majesty. I ride well enough, but the only weapon I'm good with is a staff, and that's for bashing human heads, not animal ones."

The courtiers laughed as Berenene smiled. "Delightfully frank," she told Daja with a smile. "You must forgive us northerners. We all learned to hunt as children on our first ponies. Very well, since hunting does not appeal, what do you say to a visit to Dragonstone? *Saghad* Ambros knows where that is, between here and Sablaliz. It's a fortress from the old Haidheltac empire, very lovely. I've been remaking it as a kind of stone garden, in and around what remains of the buildings, with ponds and places to picnic."

Sandry curtsied. Tris followed suit, as Briar and Daja bowed. "It sounds wonderful, Cousin," replied Sandry. "We would love to join you."

12

The 4th and 5th days of Rose Moon, 1043 K.F.
Clehamat Landreg to
Dragonstone, Namorn

Supper that night seemed lonely without Rizu, Caidy, Jak, and Fin to tell stories and make jokes over the table. They had returned to Sablaliz with the empress, who had declared herself helpless without their companionship. Jak and Fin had seemed genuinely sad to leave Sandry. And Daja was definitely sad that they had lost Rizu and Caidy.

Over supper, Ambros announced, "Her Imperial Majesty has invited Ealaga and me to join you tomorrow. In addition, I'm detaching five men-at-arms to guard us. There's no need to bring more. The presence of the empress in the district should discourage kidnappers. Besides" — he began.

Sandry and Tris chorused with him, "There's the plowing to be done." It was why they had taken so few guards to Pofkim.

Ambros gave his crackling laugh. His wife and daughters fell victim to the giggles. Daja fixed it in mind to share with Rizu, who probably would have joined their chorus. They'd all had plenty of time to learn that Ambros's first priority, apart from acquainting Sandry with her estates, was to make sure every acre that could grow a crop was plowed and sown. Despite Sandry's visit, the yearly round of the castle continued.

"And I will stay here," Zhegorz said firmly.

Sandry gave him her warmest smile. "You'll stay here," she reassured him. "No empresses for you."

At dawn their small party left, along with their guards and two donkeys who carried picnic delicacies from the Landreg kitchens. The four mages rode silently, saving their conversational skills for the day ahead. When they reached Dragonstone, they were rewarded for their early ride. Berenene, as wide-awake as she had been the day before, took them on a tour of the fortress ruins.

Every inch of the crumbling great hall and the inner bailey had received attention by gardeners. In pockets between stones Briar found tiny, ground-hugging flowers with spiky white petals, rockroses, and pinks. Trickles of water ran over mossy stones, or formed small waterfalls that dropped into pools set in what must have been the dungeon level of the castle. Small willows and dwarf maple trees grew on the grounds, shading ponds and benches. Everything fit the ruins but did not obscure them.

It's a pity Berenene loves orchids so, Briar thought, trailing loving fingers over the happiest jasmine vine he'd ever met. She could create the perfect *shakkan* garden.

"Do you like it?" Berenene asked, coming up next to

him. "This was the garden I had as a girl — the only thing my father would let me tend. I lived in the gatekeeper's lodge and studied with the Sisterhood of Qunoc in the temple on the shore, until my older brother died and I became the heir. I built on this place for years. Now I have gardeners to tend it, but any changes are done to my request."

"I think you're wasted as an empress," Briar said without thinking. He winced, then grinned at her when her only reaction was laughter.

"Spoken like my gardeners," she said. "I'm honored. And if you see anything that requires attention, please let me know. I'll be in your debt."

Briar, who knew what privilege she had just given him, bowed low. I'll make her a *shakkan* garden for the palace, he thought. A miniature of this one. It will take work, but she's worth it.

Looking at him from beneath lowered lashes, Berenene asked, "Could you do better, with your potions and spells?"

Briar gaped at her, genuinely shocked. He quickly recovered and asked, "Why would I want to tamper with perfection? All this is yours, with your shaping on it. I'd no more change it than I would change you."

Berenene looked down. Finally she said softly, "A mage who does not think magic betters everything. I am not certain I can bear the shock." She took his hand and ran a finger along the lines in his palm. "I could make you the greatest gardener in the world, you know. I could place the resources of the empire at your disposal." She placed her finger against his lips. "Don't say anything now. I don't want an answer now. But think about it — think what being my chief gardener could mean. I will ask again this summer, I assure you." She stepped away. "I'll see you at midday, Briar."

Dazed, Briar watched her as she made her way back to Sandry, who was taking a drink of water from a well. Today Berenene was dressed for spring in a leaf green undergown and a cream-colored overgown embroidered with gold flowers. She's the most beautiful thing *in* this garden, he thought wistfully. But she's not for the likes of me. I know what the girls think — that I'd bed her if I could. But she's too grand. Too glorious. I would rather leave her be than get all disillusioned when I find out she's human.

A sharp elbow caught him in the ribs. He turned. Caidy glared at him, her hazel eyes fiery. "I'm away one night and you forget all about me?" she asked dangerously, roses of temper blooming on her ivory cheeks. "You're setting up to storm the palace when the castle was half-won."

"I got discouraged," he told her, trying to look penitent. "You defend your castle so well. Besides, aren't you used to everyone being in love with her?"

"Everyone better not be thinking of kissing me, then," she warned. "Because I'm fresh out of kisses. I'll go see if Jak has any."

She marched away, chin in the air.

Briar grinned. I do like a girl with some thorns to her.

Better still, a real girl, one I *can* kiss instead of worship. Worship's all well and good, but it doesn't keep a fellow warm when the night turns cold. I'll have to think of something to make Caidy happy again.

Thinking about what he might create to draw a smile from her, he carefully descended the stairs that led through the long-vanished floors down to the water pools.

After the tour of the garden, the company broke up into various groups. To Daja's surprise, Berenene went off to confer with secretaries at midmorning. It seemed that the empress's secretaries followed her everywhere and conducted business from horseback, if necessary. Fortunately for them, she thought, they don't have to work in the saddle while there's a lodgekeeper's house on the grounds.

Ambros, Ealaga, and some of the older nobles had gone off to sun themselves on a ruined terrace circled by lilacs and bitter orange bushes in full bloom. Up on the rim of the same terrace, Daja could see Tris and Ishabal in animated conversation.

Probably about something that comes only in words of ten syllables, Daja thought with amusement. It looks like that kind of talk.

Daja herself stood on the edge of a cropped grass circle. All around its rim lazed younger nobles on drop cloths. At the circle's heart were Rizu and some other young ladies who played a ball-tossing game. Daja was happy just to watch, leaning on her Trader staff. She had brought it to make her way over uneven ground, to poke under stones to ensure that no early rising snakes lurked in wait, and to show to Rizu. When she had discovered that each marking on a Trader's staff stood for part of the person's life, Rizu had made Daja promise to tell some of the stories about her markings. Now Daja watched her catch the ball gracefully and toss it high, enjoying her new friend's joy in the beauty of the day and the setting.

Movement drew her eye past the ring of laughing noblewomen. Three men had turned to listen to a fourth. Something about that fourth man's excitement, the way he spoke with one hand raised to cover the movements of his mouth, and the slyly eager looks exchanged by his companions, told Daja there was trouble afoot. When they all ran off around the ruins of a wall, she was certain of it. As a Trader and as a mage she knew the look of overgrown boys up to wickedness.

As Berenene had led the tour, she had kept Briar at her side. Some of the courtiers — including three of the ones who had just left — had been displeased by the attention the empress gave Briar. Many of those courtiers had also grumbled when Berenene took Briar into her greenhouses, where they were forbidden to go. Traders were taught from the cradle to notice who complained and when: Often those were the people who led the attacks on Traders. Now the empress was occupied, and Briar was nowhere within view.

Briar? Daja called down the withered thread that remained of their old bond. She heard and felt nothing. *You'd think you* want *people to know you were all right*, she added tartly. There was still no reply.

Daja sent a pulse of magic along their connection to see where the bond led. Walking slowly, sending magic along the tie in waves, she followed it into the garden. She didn't realize it, but she was twirling her staff in a circle, hand over hand, loosening her muscles in preparation for a fight.

She had to climb over four walls, apologizing to flowers as she stepped on them. I hope the empress doesn't learn this was me, she thought as she fluffed a patch of moss she had crushed. I'll have Briar fix these when I find him.

Down two sets of ruined stairs she went, then along an open inner gallery now used as a rose trellis. The thread led her up another set of stairs, or rather, it went through the stairs; Daja had to climb them and jump down from a six-foot wall. She walked among some trees into a clearing by a stream. Young noblemen stood there in a half circle. They watched Briar, who faced one of the men who so often watched the empress.

Olfeon fer . . . something, Daja remembered. Master of the Armory. The one who gets the cream from Namorn's armorers when it's time to buy weapons for the imperial guards. Is he one of the empress's ex-lovers, the jealous sort Rizu mentioned?

"— as I thought," Olfeon said, contempt in his voice.

"You mages are all cowards. If you have to take on a real man, you can only do it with your stinking magic."

Briar's six inches shorter than this *kaq,* thought Daja as she moved into a space in the half-circle. The men next to her were too interested in the brewing fight to do more than glance at her. But they're muscled about the same, Daja thought as she continued to measure Briar against Olfeon. He may be a warrior sort — that scar on his cheek isn't some lady's kiss.

Briar raised his eyebrows. "Of course, if you think so, how could I possibly disagree?" he asked politely. He'd shifted his weight so he was balanced properly. "Look, are you trying to challenge me to a duel or something? Because if you are, could you get it over with? And if you aren't, would you go away? There's blight in that patch of speedwell over there, and I'd like to get rid of it before Her Imperial Majesty sees it and gets upset."

"Duel?" snapped Olfeon. "With *you,* guttersnipe?"

Stinking kaq, thought Daja in disgust.

Olfeon continued: "I'd no more duel with a peasant like you than I'd duel with dog dung on my boot. Duels are for *noblemen.* I'll just have my lackeys whip you. And if you go whining to Her Imperial Majesty about it, you won't live to make it to the border."

The men who watched laughed. Daja wrinkled her nose in disgust. Civilized Namornese my eye, she thought with disdain. They treat their women like property and outsiders like idiots. They deserve a lesson or two. She leaned on her staff with a smile and waited.

Briar looked over at her. "I can handle this myself," he said, eyes glittering in anger. "I don't need imperial protection — *or* yours."

Even a former street rat has his pride, Daja told herself. To Briar, she said, "I'm just here to take wagers, if he'll actually deign to trade blows with you." She looked at the other noblemen. "I'll bet gold that my friend hurts this *kaq* if it comes to a fistfight."

"You'll lose your money. We don't wager with Trader mage spawn," said one of the nobles.

The two closest to her kept their mouths shut as the others laughed. My neighbors fear my magic, not my staff, but it's still rather sweet of them to be scared, Daja thought. Aloud she said, "Oh — too bad, because I'm giving five-to-one odds on a fistfight between my friend and yours. You know Traders don't wager money they don't have." She looked at Olfeon and sighed. "I forgot. You won't fight a commoner, even bare-handed."

"You both need a lesson!" snapped Olfeon. He glared at the other men. "Bet, rot your eyes!" To Briar, he said, "When I leave you as jelly, get your friend here to pack you in a basket and send you home. Have we a bargain?"

Briar spat on his palm and offered it with an evil grin. It was a way for street rats to conclude a deal.

It was not the way Namornese noblemen sealed their

oaths. Olfeon produced a handkerchief and let one end of it hang. "You may grab that," he said impatiently. "Wipe your hand, while you're at it." He pointed to Daja. "No magic from you, either. These two?" He pointed to two men. "They see that nonsense. The fight will be forfeit in my favor if they catch either of you trying it."

"Don't think much of mages, do they?" Briar asked. He gave the handkerchief a sharp yank, then retreated to take off his boots and stockings.

"Apparently not. Let me know if you want me to ignore the rules. For you I'll bash a couple of heads," Daja offered. Olfeon sat on a rock to take off his own boots and stockings.

"You were always the most commonsensical of my sisters," Briar said with a grunt as he worked a boot free. "If they kill me, just break their knees. They're not worth a death sentence." His second boot was off. Next he began to remove his knives, starting with the two he reached through the pockets of his breeches, and ending with the flat one that lay just below the nape of his neck under his shirt. There were eight in the pile when he finished, not including the pair he'd left in his boots. The nobles stared at the blades in shock. Briar continued, "Though, if you smack 'em on the head, the skull will cave in because there's nothing to hold it up, and then you can sell 'em to Her Imperial Majesty as planters."

Daja eyed the noblemen, who looked as if they would be glad to leap on Briar at this very moment. "Wagers, gentlemen?" she asked coolly.

She carried a small tablet and a stick of charcoal in a holder in an inner pocket of her tunic, in case she got the urge to design something. She used them now to record wagers, making sure each man wrote his name down clearly.

They were almost ready when she heard a familiar voice snap, "What is going on here?"

She looked up. It was that fellow Shan, the one who was the empress's current lover.

Olfeon, who had stripped off his coat and was rolling up his sleeves, glared at the newcomer. "Not your affair, fer Roth."

"Do you think she'll be gratified if you kill her pet gardener?" Shan demanded. "She'll be livid."

"For all I know, she'll be vexed with *me* if I dent one of her playtoys," Briar said.

"Silence, clodhopper!" snapped Olfeon.

Briar looked at Daja and sniffed. "He's so mean," he said plaintively.

Daja tucked her tablet and the charcoal holder away. "I noticed that. You should be very offended and hit him first."

As they had meant it to — it was how they'd have played it in the old days, when they were bonded — this exchange brought Olfeon hurtling at Briar, hands outstretched. Briar let him get almost close enough to touch, then twisted to the side and smashed his knee into Olfeon's belly.

Daja watched with interest as the fight continued. He learned a lot while he was away, she thought as Briar used new throws and twists to slam Olfeon to the ground time after time.

He knew better than to let the bigger man get both hands on him. Then Olfeon would use his superior weight and height to drag Briar down. Instead, Briar aimed for nerve points he had studied for medicine, added to his old street fighter's arsenal of tricks. At the end of the fight, Briar's foot rested on Olfeon's neck, pressing the right side of his face into the grass as Olfeon flailed wildly. When he tried to grab Briar's leg, Briar pressed harder. The Namornese collapsed at last, starved for air. Daja made the final tally. Briar had a black eye, several cuts, a split lip, ripped clothes, bruises, and perhaps a sprained knee. Olfeon had facial cuts, a sprained wrist, a broken nose, ripped clothes, and his own collection of bruises.

"Pay me by the end of today," Daja called to the losing bettors. "I won't take signatures in place of real coin, and I'm cross when people think to cheat me." She looked around, about to call for Sandry to fix the clothes, when she saw her sister being handed down the stairs by Shan. Quenaill followed Sandry, a scowl on his long face.

As they approached, Shan said to Briar and Olfeon, "Did you think I'd leave you both to face Her Imperial

Majesty in *this* condition? *Clehame* Sandry will see to your clothes, Quen to your wounds."

You just did it for an excuse to have Sandry hold you by the arm, Daja thought cynically. I bet you couldn't care less for Briar or the other fellow.

Sandry glared at the two battered young men. "What was this about?"

Briar glared back. "Namornese sheep," he retorted. "He claimed Namorn breeds sheep that think for themselves."

"We fought over his right to wear that medallion," said Olfeon. "Right, lads?"

The young men nodded. Through their magical connection Daja told Sandry, *It was over the empress. I suppose she would be vexed with Olfeon if she knew.*

Sandry shook her head. *As if I would believe they would have a fistfight over Briar's right to wear the mage medallion. They must think I drink stupid potion for my morning pick-me-up.*

She walked briskly over to Briar. "I didn't make those clothes for brawls," she told him irritably. "I didn't think even *you* could find a fight at the court of Namorn." She set her hand on the ripped seam that had once joined sleeve to shirt. A rough tear over Briar's knee was already starting to weave itself back together as grass and dirt stains trickled off his clothes.

"Well, you're forever underestimating me," Briar told her. "If there's a fight about, it's nearly guaranteed I'll be in it."

Sandry looked over at Olfeon. "You were lucky," she said sharply. "He could have ripped you to pieces with thorns if he wanted."

"No, no," protested Briar, his eyes warning Sandry to be silent. "Blood's horrible for grass, and there's always some thorns left after. Don't mind her," he told Olfeon. "Girls have no appreciation for the rules of combat."

Olfeon spat on the ground in disgust, then winced as Quenaill set to work healing his wounds. "Hold still and be silent," Quenaill said, frowning. "The quicker this is done the better, unless you *want* to spend the winter in a log cabin on the Sea of Grass."

"She says if we have that much spirit we can use it to fight the Yanjing emperor," Shan explained to Sandry. No one doubted that "she" was the empress. "Where did you learn to fight like that?" he asked Briar.

"Everywhere," Briar replied, grinning at the tall huntsman. "And isn't it a good thing for me?"

A tap on the back made Daja turn. Some of the men who had bet against her waited to pay their wagers.

They spent the rest of that week riding between Sablaliz and Landreg, attending social occasions with the imperial court. Finally, one night after a late supper at Landreg, Sandry looked at Ambros and Ealaga, then at her exhausted companions and guards, who wearily picked through their meals.

"I'm sorry," she told her cousin and his wife. "But she's

going to kill us at this rate, or our horses, at the very least. The court is returning to the palace in Dancruan. We must go with them, I think. Her Imperial Majesty has invited us to stay at the palace. I don't believe I can refuse politely."

"No," Ambros replied, shaking his head. "She would be much offended if you did."

"Gudruny will require maid's clothes fit for the palace," Ealaga said. "I'll make certain she has some."

Sandry drummed her fingers on the table. "If I only had *time,* between estate matters and the empress keeping me hopping, I could make her clothes myself!"

Gudruny looked up from her spot at the table, next to Tris. "My children?" she asked, her voice strained.

"They can stay at Landreg House in town," Ambros said. "Along with Zhegorz. Your cousin Wenoura is our chief cook there, remember?"

"Truthfully, you won't have to wait on me," Sandry told Gudruny. "You can stay with the children —" She halted abruptly. There was a decidedly militant look in Gudruny's eye.

"And have them say you don't know how to get on as a proper noble?" the maid asked. "Their servants already turn up their noses because you have only one maid, and your friends have no servants at all. I heard them gossiping when they were here, spiteful creatures. I wouldn't *think* of leaving you in the palace to be talked about! I'm waiting on you, and that's that!"

Ambros's mouth twitched in a smile. Briar looked from Gudruny to Sandry. "Who works for who?" he asked, his eyes twinkling.

Tris excused herself quietly. When the other three went upstairs to bed, Briar found her in his room, talking quietly to Zhegorz as she hung onto the man's bony hands. She looked up at Briar. "He's afraid to go so close to court."

Briar sighed. "It's terrible, when a man has no faith. Did you tell him what you did, that first day at the palace? What you did to the pirate fleet?"

"Pirates?" Zhegorz asked with a wild start that jerked his hands from Tris's hold. His eyes were so wide with terror that the white showed all the way around. "There are pirates coming?"

Now look what you did, Tris thought at Briar, forgetting his mind was closed to her. *I'd just gotten him calmed down.*

"Here you go, old man," Briar said, pouring out a tiny cupful of the soothing cordial he gave Zhegorz for his bad moments. "These pirates were seven years ago, and they are most seriously dead. *She* did it."

"You helped," snapped Tris. "And Sandry, and Daja, and our teachers, and every mage in Winding Circle. And you *know* I don't like that story repeated."

Briar ignored her. "She did it with lightning," he told his guest, putting the cork back in the bottle. "And when we first got to Dancruan? Some fishing boats were in danger of a storm on the Syth, but Coppercurls here sent a wind to blow them home and another to eat the storm. She likes rescuing folk. So don't you get yourself all worked up. You'll hurt her feelings, letting her think she can't protect you."

"She didn't protect you, wherever you were, in the bad place you dream about," Zhegorz pointed out. He had bolted the cordial as if it were a glass of very nasty tea.

And here I thought I made that stuff taste nice! thought Briar in disgust, trying to ignore what their madman had said. I should've given him nasty tea instead of something I worked cursed hard over.

"You dream about it all the time," Zhegorz insisted. "You toss and turn and yell about blood and Rosethorn and Evvy and Luvo."

Tris raised her pale brows at him.

Briar was about to tell them both that his dreams were no cider of theirs, but there was something about the way Tris looked at him. He'd forgotten that side of her, that he had always been able to tell her the most horrific things, and she would never laugh, be shocked, or withdraw from him.

Briar slumped to the floor, leaning back against the stone that framed the hearth. The stone was warm, the fire a comforting crackle in his ear. "The emperor of Yanjing tried to conquer Gyongxe," he muttered at last. "We were at the emperor's court when we heard, and then we ran for it, Rosethorn and Evvy and me. That's when we met Luvo, on our way to warn Gyongxe. Luvo's this . . . creature, Zhegorz. He lives with Evvy now."

"The Mother Temple of the Living Circle," breathed Tris. "It's in Gyongxe. The one all the other Circle temples look to. Their first and oldest Circle temple."

Briar nodded. Zhegorz slid down the side of the bed so he, too, could sit on the floor and lean against the bed. It seemed to be his way to comfort Briar. Chime, who had spent suppertime around Tris's neck, now glided over and settled into Briar's lap. He stroked the little creature, feeling her cool surfaces against his palms.

"So we fought our way into Gyongxe, and then we fought the emperor, and then we came home," Briar whispered, closing his eyes. "The pirates was nothin' to it, Coppercurls." In his distress he had slipped back into the language of the streets he had left seven years before. "The whole countryside was afire, or so it seemed. The dead . . . everywhere. The emperor's army filled the roads for *miles,* and they didn't care what they did to folk in the lands they marched through. So sure, I dream about it all the time. I'll be fine."

"You'll be seeing a mind healer when we get home," Tris said firmly. "I've heard of this. People who have been through some terrible thing, it leaves scars where no one can see. The scars hurt, so they dream, and they snap at people for doing things that seem silly compared to the horrors. Sometimes they see and smell the thing all over again."

"So I'm just some boohoo bleater, looking for a mama because I have bad dreams?" Briar asked rudely, though he didn't open his eyes. "Looking for a handkerchief everywhere I go so folk will think I'm tragic and interesting?"

"If the scars were on your flesh, would you even ask me those things?" retorted Tris.

There was a long pause. At last Zhegorz said hesitantly, "She's right."

"She 'most always is, when it comes to other folk," replied Briar softly. "I got off lucky. She's being nice right now." Inside the magic they shared, he said, *I missed you, Coppercurls. With you there,* we *might've conquered Yanjing.*

She looked down, her thin swinging braids not quite hiding her tiny smile. She waved a hand in awkward dismissal.

Briar waited until he was sure of his command over himself before he looked at Zhegorz. "So don't you worry about being at Landreg House, you hear? It's just for six more weeks or so, and then we take the road home."

"But the city," whispered Zhegorz, his eyes haunted. "The roads. The chatter, and the visions. The headaches, the gossip, the lies, the weeping —"

"Stop that," Tris said sharply. "We've talked about you working yourself into swivets."

Briar rubbed his chin in thought. "He's right, though," he remarked slowly. "He's going to be out in the wind, with all the talk it brings. I remember you, as jumpy as a mouse on a griddle for days, when you started getting a grip on what you were hearing. And it's worse for the old man, here, because he's crazy to begin with. You were just a little daft."

"Well, we certainly can't leave you here," Tris drawled, looking at Zhegorz. "And Green Man knows potions or oils won't work for long. And you can't wear my spectacles for the scraps of things you see, because my spectacles are specially ground for my bad eyes. It's too bad it isn't a matter of a living metal leg, or living metal gloves . . . living metal spectacles?"

"Maybe like nets?" suggested Briar. "To catch visions in?"

"Or sounds. No, that's mad. Perhaps. Let's go see Daja," Tris said.

"Daja will do something mad?" asked Zhegorz, now thoroughly confused.

Tris sighed. "Daja can make spell nets of wire, and she can make a leg that works like a real one. She was even crafting a living metal eye, once. Maybe she can think of something in living metal to help you."

Briar and Tris were both dozing on Daja's bed as the smith finished the pieces they had decided might serve their crazy man best. Zhegorz himself sat on the floor by the hearth, watching Daja work.

For Zhegorz's ears, Daja had fashioned a pair of small, living metal pieces that looked like plump beads pierced by small holes. Once they were done, she wrote a series of magical signs on them under a magnifying lens, using a steel tool with a razor-sharp tip.

"You understand, this will take adjustments," she told Zhegorz softly. "Depending on what you want them to do, just speak the name for each sign. Then the pieces should let that much more sound into your ears." She knelt beside Zhegorz and gently fit one of the living metal pieces into his left ear. Watching as it shaped itself to fill the opening precisely, Daja asked, "How is that? Comfortable?"

"It's warm," whispered Zhegorz, looking up at her.

"I'm not going to put cold metal in your ears," Daja said, a little miffed that he would suspect that of her. Once she checked the fit of the first piece, she gently turned Zhegorz's head and inserted the second. "There," she whispered, deliberately speaking more quietly to test the ability of the pieces to pick up everyday sound. She recited the first lines of her favorite story. "In the long ago, Trader Koma and his bride, Bookkeeper Oti, saw that they had no savings in their accounts books, no warm memories laid up for the cold times."

"That's a Trader tale," Zhegorz said. "It's about how the Trader and the Bookkeeper created the *Tsaw'ha* and wrote their names in the great books."

Daja sat back on her heels. "On the way to Dancruan you can tell me how you learned Trader stories," she told him with a smile. "Not now. I *would* like to get some sleep tonight." She reached over to her worktable and carefully picked up her second creation. Tris had sacrificed a pair of spectacles for this piece. Daja had replaced the lenses with circles of living metal hammered as thin as tissue. Once they were fixed over the wire frames, she used her sharp-pointed tool to write in signs to fix the metal in place and cause it to work as she wished it to.

Gingerly she settled the bridge on Zhegorz's bony nose and hooked the earpieces in place. I really don't know about this, she thought, nibbling her lower lip. I've made plenty of odd things, that's certain, but eyeglass lenses that let someone see normally and not magically? Only Tris would even come up with the idea.

"Can you see me?" she asked.

Zhegorz nodded.

"He'd have to be wrapped in steel not to see you, Daja," said a grumpy and drowsy Tris from the bed. "You're a big girl and you're right in front of him. Chime, will you fly around? Zhegorz, can you see Chime?"

Daja watched Zhegorz follow the glass dragon's flight as Chime dove and soared around the wood carvings of the ceiling. She began to grin, elated. "I begin to think I can cure dry rot with this stuff," she said, proudly stroking the living metal on the back of her hand.

"Rosethorn would say pride will trip you on the stairs," Briar said with a yawn. "Come on, Zhegorz. We'll give those things a *real* trial in the morning."

Daja got to her feet, wincing as her back complained after hours bent over her work. She was stretching when Zhegorz patted her shoulder. "I'll tell you what they do in the morning. I'm sorry I ever said no one could see through metal spectacles." He scuttled out of the room as Daja shook her head over him.

Tris caught her by surprise, swooping in to press a rare kiss on Daja's cheek. "I know they'll work," she said. "Thank you, for him."

"He's my crazy man, too," Daja said as Tris hurried from the room.

13

The 6th – 8th days of Rose Moon, 1043 K.F.
Clehamat Landreg to
Dancruan, Namorn

They traveled the next day with Ambros, his family and personal servants, their own servants, and ten men-at-arms for company, plowing or no. Even in the short time they had stayed at Landreg, Sandry noticed plenty of changes. The fields now flourished with assorted grain crops, made heartier and more immune to blight by Briar. He had done the same work in the orchards. Workers labored on the restoration of the bridge on the road to Dancruan. "By the time we return, it will be fixed," Ambros said as Sandry waved to yet another knot of farmers who bowed to her from the fields.

It's good to see all this progress being made, Sandry thought as they passed two wagonloads of mortar and slates destined for the repairs at Pofkim. Back at the castle, jewels that had belonged to her mother alone and were not part of the Landreg estate now lay in a locked box in Ambros's study. In that same box were three copies of Sandry's handwritten orders to her cousin. He was to sell the gems for any future work required to keep the estate thriving.

As they passed through the estate's boundary walls, Tris scowled at her sister.

"What?" Sandry demanded, flushing slightly.

Tris drew even with her. "Will you just leave things like that?" she asked quietly. "The estate paying out to you and vulnerable to the empress's taxes? They're still in danger from those."

"I'm going to see an advocate in Dancruan," Sandry replied, keeping her voice soft. Ambros didn't know her plans. "I'll get a letter drawn up reducing my share and allowing Ambros to default on it entirely if taxes and estate work are high that year." When Tris's frown deepened, Sandry felt her temper start to boil. She stuck out her chin. "They're *my* lands, left to *me* by *my mother*," she whispered hotly. "I'm in the *direct* line of descent. As long as I have breath in my body, I will *preserve* that line of descent and inheritance, all fourteen generations of it! Those lands are mine — no one else's! Don't you *dare* lecture me about it, Tris. You don't know the least thing about being nobleborn. About our ties to our lands and our names. My younger children will have Landreg to ensure their place in the world and the continuance of the Landreg name and bloodlines."

Tris clenched and unclenched her hands on the reins.

Heat bloomed under her breastbone as her face turned red in fury over the rebuke. She did not see the guards on her far side or the people who rode behind her check and move away as sparks raced over her coiled braids. Sandry got even angrier. Now they know we're quarreling! she thought. Why can't Tris ever keep her feelings to herself? Why does the world *always* have to know when she's vexed?

Chime wasn't afraid of lightning. It was the blood through which her magic flowed. She glided up to Tris from her seat on Daja's saddle and landed on Tris's head. Slowly, gently, the glass dragon sank her claws into Tris's scalp.

"Ow!" Tris winced: Her concentration broke, and the lightning began to die. With no more new sparks being spawned, Chime began to lick up those that remained.

"No, I'm not noble," Tris finally told Sandry in a voice that trembled. "And given that you're turning into one just like the rest of those at court, I'm *glad* I'm not." She turned her mount and rode back to Zhegorz, Gudruny, and her children, who rode in a luggage cart behind the others.

"Is something wrong?" Ealaga asked Sandry after Tris rode out of earshot.

Sandry shook her head, keeping it down so no one could see the tears of anger that sparkled in her eyes. Tris doesn't know what being a noble means! Sandry thought. You can't go about ignoring your family's long history or the things all your ancestors did to build your name and your lands. It's like telling them they never counted, if I lose my holdings as a Landreg, or worse, if I give them up. If I let Berenene take them for some reason. I owe my parents — my ancestors — the continuation of our line, and our name. Mama didn't surrender the title when she married Papa. What excuse do *I* have?

Once they started to pass other people on the highway, Briar kept an eye on Zhegorz. It took some effort to do it without laughing, at least at first. Zhegorz was a sight, perched atop one of Sandry's traveling trunks, a well-dressed scarecrow in a good clerk's sensible gray coat and breeches, wearing what looked like shiny amber spectacles on his eyes. Sandry had even tied his hair back in a horsetail with a ribbon that was the same color as his spectacles. At first passersby got no chance to appreciate his new eyewear. As they came within view, Zhegorz pulled his broad-brimmed hat low over his face and bent down, trying to hide in plain sight. Later, he got more bold as parties over-took and passed them, or parties rode by. He flinched less and watched more.

Finally Briar could no longer bear the suspense. He rode over to the cart. "Zhegorz! The ear things, and the spectacles. Are they working?"

Zhegorz beamed. "I hear only our people's talk, and only from close by. I see only what is in front of my nose. No flying pictures, no conversations popping into my ears! It's wonderful — I'm cured! I don't need the lessons anymore. I'm sane, sane as a bird, sane as a sheep, sane as a — ow!"

While he had been babbling, Tris had ridden up on his other side. She had leaned over and flicked him on the ear with her finger, producing his cry of pain. When he turned to glare at her, Tris asked drily, "And if you lose the spectacles?"

"Or if the ear beads fall out?" Briar wanted to know. "The magic's still there, old man." To Gudruny's children, who had listened to this exchange with open mouths, he explained, "The magic's *always* still there."

"The lessons continue," said Tris. "Take out one of the beads, and practice managing what you hear in just one ear."

Zhegorz sighed; his shoulders drooped. He looked at Gudruny and shrugged. "It was lovely to dream about, anyway."

"Dream all you like," Briar suggested cheerfully. "Just keep practicing."

The roads were drier than they had been the first time the four mages had come that way. With better footing they made better time, reaching the Landreg town house by midafternoon. That night was spent settling Ambros and his family in for the palace social season, and introducing Gudruny's children and Zhegorz to Wenoura.

They woke the next morning to learn that the imperial party had arrived at the same time they did and was still settling in. Sandry declared that they couldn't interrupt the court while it unpacked. Instead, she went out to confer with an advocate and to shop with Gudruny. Briar, too, went shopping, for *shakkans* and potting soil, placing an order for a very large pottery dish made specifically for several *shakkans.* It was part of the gift he had planned for the empress. Tris remained to work with Zhegorz on meditation and on limiting the number of things he heard and saw. Daja thought to shop as well. When she realized that the only things she wished to buy were expensive gifts for Rizu, who was not related to her in any way, she returned home to do whatever metalwork was in the house.

The next day the four and Gudruny moved to the imperial palace. Footmen raced ahead of them to let the palace staff know they had arrived. More footmen took charge of their horses and their belongings, vanishing down a side road with them. Briar was prepared to fight over the handling of his own *shakkan* and the ones he'd bought for the empress, but when two of the footmen showed themselves adept at handling both plants and crockery, he had let them take over.

A very superior footman led them to the first story in the northwest wing. He bowed Sandry into one suite near the intersection with the palace's north wing, and Tris into the other. With a sugary smile he led Daja to a suite halfway down the same hall. Briar he showed to rooms at the very end that looked out over the formal flower gardens.

Tris, Daja, and Briar soon discovered they had also been assigned maids to look after them. "At least they don't *sleep* in our rooms," Tris grumbled when they met at mid-hall to compare situations.

"You don't have to worry about her snooping in your mage kit, unless you want her to brush your hair," retorted Briar.

Tris grimaced. "Please! I can brush my own hair, thank you all the same!" She smiled. "And it would be a fatal exercise if anyone else tried," she admitted slyly. "I need special brushes and combs to manage it, myself."

"I just told mine that she'd best tell me know where her family is, so if she meddles with my kit, I know where to send the body," remarked Daja. "She squeaked. I think my kit's safe."

Sandry would have argued at the imposition of two more maids and two footmen to wait upon her, but Gudruny gently urged her young mistress to see the dresses she'd laid out for the welcoming party that night. Once Sandry was in the bedroom inspecting the clothes, Gudruny closed the door.

"Please, my lady, they're already sneering at me and saying I can't be very good, if I haven't taught you what's due to your station," she explained. "With more servants to direct, I grow more important in the servants' areas. Then they'll *all* serve us as they should. It may sound like little things to you, but one of those little things is your bath water. We'd both like it to be hot when it gets here. Servants are far more snobbish than nobles."

Sandry gazed at her sidelong. Gudruny got nervous if

Sandry looked her in the eyes: It was yet another of the many things that meant trouble between nobles and commoners in Namorn. "This isn't a story you're telling me?"

Gudruny shook her head. "I tried to warn you back home, but it was all I could do to get you to take *my* service," she reminded Sandry. "You're going back south soon enough. Surely you can afford to play by their rules until then."

Sandry slumped. "Very well, Gudruny. They can stay. Happy?" She was trying to decide between a blush pink overgown or a pale blue one when she realized that Gudruny looked uncomfortable. "What?" Sandry wanted to know.

"Well, begging my lady's pardon, but there's the matter of the hairdresser," Gudruny explained. "He's agreed to fit you in after midday. He dresses most of the ladies-in-waiting's hair, and we were lucky that he agreed to see you. I believe the empress herself had a word with him."

With a loud groan, Sandry collapsed onto a chair.

Tris waited until after her new maid had taken away the remains of her midday to explore her new chambers thoroughly. Much to her surprise, Tris noticed the history of Namorn she had found that first day in the palace was placed beside her bed. In fact, someone had taken the small blue-and-gold dressing room that Tris would never use and turned it into a library, stuffed with books on Namornese history, wildlife, crafts, religions, magic, and languages. Fascinated, Tris plopped into an armchair and began to read as Chime soared around the much-carved and painted chambers, exploring moldings and hanging lamps. She had just returned to curl up on Tris's lap when someone knocked on the door.

Tris opened it to find Ishabal there. "I thought we might talk," the older mage said. "May I enter?"

Tris let the imperial mage in. Closing the door, she asked, "Were you the one who picked out the books?"

"I directed one of the imperial librarians to select what might interest a learned stranger," Ishabal replied. "I take it she chose well?"

"Please be seated," Tris replied instead of answering the question. She returned to her own chair as Ishabal took the seat.

"What was found for you in no way represents the total of books on those subjects," Ishabal pointed out. "The imperial libraries are vast. If you were to choose to serve Her Imperial Majesty, you would have the key to such libraries. Moreover, you would have the wealth to create a proper library of your own."

If Tris was greedy for anything, it was books. Her sisters and brother had learned early on that her personal books were not to be touched without permission, and handled carefully with it. For a moment she had a vision of a two-story room with books on shelves that reached to the ceiling, all filled with volumes on anything that did or might interest her. *It's certainly possible,* she mused. *I doubt*

Berenene is stingy with her mages — not the way Quenaill and Ishabal dress. Simple, but elegant, and costly.

"Her Imperial Majesty wishes to employ me as a war mage." Tris said it flatly. She had been approached with offers of work before, all of them with the same price attached. Why do they always assume a lightning mage wants to kill people? she wondered tiredly.

"Actually, she would like to offer you employment as anything you choose," replied Ishabal smoothly. "On the Syth, the ability to banish storms is always in great demand. Moreover, we have reports that you have been able to create rain —"

"Not create it," Tris interrupted. "I don't *create* weather. I draw it from someplace else."

"Very well. The empire is vast, as your books will tell you. It is always raining somewhere," Ishabal said evenly. "You could draw rain to those places who need it. You could give winds to becalmed ships here and on our coast on the Endless Sea. Your value to the imperial crown is endless, Tris. Her Imperial Majesty is a gracious employer who rewards good service, and she does not overwork her mages. You would have time for your own projects."

Tris removed her spectacles and rubbed the dent they always left in the top of her long nose. Even if they don't say they want war magic, they usually do, she thought. If they know you can do it, they always end up wanting it. I certainly got asked for it often enough, traveling with Niko. Even when they start out nicely, it always comes down to "Kill people for me."

"I am flattered, of course," she replied, her voice quiet and polite. Three years earlier she might have been cruder, but she had learned a few things. Nowadays she always thought before she spoke in these situations. "Deeply flattered. Might I have time to consider this?"

Ishabal inspected her nails. When she looked up, she met Tris's eyes and said in a business-like tone, "Five hundred gold argibs the first year. Your own rooms here in the palace, your own horses and maid. Your health is tended by imperial healers without charge. Materials for your magic and research are supplied free of cost, within reason. I determine what is reasonable, not a Privy Purse clerk who doesn't understand mage work."

Mila bless me, thought Tris, rattled despite her resolve. The offer was ferociously generous.

Her practical self gripped her greedy self by the ear. It always comes back to war magic, and I want to go to Lightsbridge! she told herself firmly.

No need to rush or offend anyone, not if I'm stuck here for at least another month, Tris told herself. "I must think it over, please," she said. "You must understand how overwhelming this is, for someone like me."

"Of course," Ishabal replied, getting to her feet. "You are wise to think about it. But Her Imperial Majesty also wishes you to know she sees your worth. She values it."

Tris got up and nodded. "I am greatly honored. Please thank her for me."

She saw Ishabal to the door and let her out, then closed it behind her. I am not going to think about the money, or the funds, or the healers, she told herself, biting her lip. I want to go to Lightsbridge. She turned the key in the lock. And I won't do battle magic. *Ever.*

She was settling into her chair when someone rapped hard on the door. She had locked out the maid.

They all gathered in Sandry's rooms before the welcoming party so that Sandry could inspect them. Briar wore his favorite deep green tunic and breeches with a perfect white shirt, Tris a vivid blue undergown and sheer black overgown in the Namornese style. Daja was glorious in a bronze silk tunic that hung to her knees, and leggings of the same color, the tunic heavy with intricate gold embroideries. Sandry had chosen an undergown of pale blue and a white lace overgown, with blue topazes winking at her ears and around her neck. She smiled at her family.

Gudruny sighed, looking at them. "If clothes were armor, you would be defended against all your enemies," she said. "And you've your wits, too — that's something."

"Splendid," said Briar drily. "I now feel suitably armed for a swim in a tub of molasses."

"She's just being cautious — that's Gudruny's way," Sandry told him. "And you *do* look fine." She smoothed away a wrinkle in Tris's overgown. "Definitely a match for all these Bags."

Briar grinned at her use of slang. Bowing, he offered her his arm. "May I?" he asked gallantly. "At least, until one of those Bag boys tears you away from me?"

Sandry laughed. "There isn't a man here who could do that for more than an hour."

"Are you sure?" asked Briar, raising an eyebrow. "Nobody?"

Sandry blushed slightly, but said firmly, "Nobody."

One of Sandry's new footmen led them to the Moonlight Hall, where the party was being held. As they entered the room, Briar said, "Well, I mean to tear myself away from you a bit tonight. That Caidy just might get herself kissed, if she's lucky."

"And more if she's unlucky?" Daja asked.

"No girl who draws my eye is ever unlucky," Briar assured her solemnly. "How could she be?"

"It's a good thing we know you're not really this conceited, or we'd have to take you down a peg or twelve," murmured Tris. "Shurri bless me, this room is *packed*."

"Don't run away too soon," Sandry pleaded, looking over her shoulder at Tris. "I know you hate parties, but please stay with me. You can glare all the idiots away, since Briar's leaving me forlorn on the sidelines."

Though Tris consented to keep her company, Sandry did not remain on the sidelines for long. Fin was the first to claim a dance when the musicians began to play, followed by Jak, Ambros, and Quen.

After Quen handed Sandry off to Shan, he chose to sink into a chair beside Tris. "Hello, Red. You'd like Imperial Service," Quen said abruptly, his eyes smiling at her. "Her Imperial Majesty understands the value of research."

"Does *everyone* know she's asked me?" Tris inquired. "Let me think about it!"

"Just Isha and I know. Very well, I won't pester you. Do you know why Shan waited till now to ask *Clehame* Sandry to dance? Berenene left the room to attend to some reports." When Tris glanced at the empty throne, then looked at him, Quen shrugged. "She wouldn't be at all happy to see her current lover paying court to Sandry."

Tris fingered one of her free braids. "So that's how things stand," she murmured.

"For now," Quen replied. He reached out a long arm and snagged a glass of wine for himself and a cup of cherry juice for Tris. He handed her the juice, saying, "I noticed that you four are the kind of mages who don't drink spirits. As for Shan — Berenene's moods change. Her lovers change."

"And I suppose you'll tell her, to help her mood change?" Tris asked, sipping her juice.

Quen chuckled. "No. She doesn't like tattletales, either." He grimaced and drained his glass. "She *really* doesn't like them. But she's no fool. She'll learn about Shan's little game soon enough." He handed his glass to another servant. "So tell me, what's Niklaren Goldeye like outside a classroom? I took one of his courses when I was at Lightsbridge. Every day I came out of one of his lectures, I felt like my brain was overstuffed."

Tris cackled with glee. "That's Niko, all right," she told him. "I thought my brain would explode for that first year."

As Tris and Quen talked about Niko, and then Lightsbridge, Daja watched the dancing from a seat next to Rizu. Sooner or later all of the younger courtiers came to sit around them, leaving and returning to dance or to nibble and drink as servants loaded the tables at the far end of the silver-gilded room. Daja relaxed, feeling more comfortable in this gathering than she had expected to. She wasn't hungry, and limited her drinking to the fruit juice that was served along with the wine.

Finally Rizu patted her face with a lace-edged handkerchief. "I am suffocating," she whispered to Daja. "Let's go cool off."

Daja was happy to go. The room was full of people who danced and sweated, while the many candles that lit the room made it even hotter. Though heat didn't bother her, she would welcome a breath of fresher air. She followed Rizu out, winding through clusters of courtiers, until they passed through one of the double doors to the terrace. There they leaned against a broad stone rail in the shadows. Daja lifted her heavy weight of beaded braids to let the cool night breeze flow across her neck.

"Are all the parties here so, so populated?" she asked Rizu.

Her companion laughed. "This is an intimate gathering," she informed Daja. "Wait till two weeks from now, with the banquet and ball for the ambassador from Lairan. Then all the *old* nobility will totter in, and the people who don't really approve of the way Her Imperial Majesty lives her life, though they do approve of the peace and prosperity she brings. And then there will be all the other ambassadors . . ." Her full mouth widened in a brilliant smile. "Except perhaps the Yanjing ambassador, who may be feeling ill by then."

Daja smiled, briefly remembering Sandry's first maneuver before the empress. At the same time, seeing the way the light struck Rizu's curly lashes, casting their shadow over her eyes, she thought, She's so beautiful. The question burst out of her before she realized it: "Why aren't you dancing? You haven't danced all night. And nobody's asked you, even though you're almost as beautiful as the empress."

Rizu smiled. "You think so, truly?"

Daja opened her lips to say that of course she thought so, but she didn't get to speak. Instead, Rizu leaned over and kissed her softly, gently, on the mouth.

After a moment, she pulled away. There was a look of worry in her eyes. Her hands were fisted in her skirts.

"Oh," said Daja when she remembered how to talk. She felt as if the sun had just catapulted into her mind. Dazzled with what it showed her, she realized also, Rizu's afraid. She's had enough people tell her no that she's not sure. . . .

Strictly to make Rizu feel better, certainly not because she wanted more of that sunlight spilling into her heart and mind, Daja leaned over and kissed Rizu's mouth all on her own. Then, rather than ruin the quiet between them, Rizu took Daja's hand and led her into the palace by a door that did not open into the Moonlight Hall.

"I'm serious — stop laughing!" murmured Fin as he twirled Sandry around in the dance figure called "the Rose." "Just the two of us, with your maid for chaperone, tomorrow or the next day. There's a cove down on the Syth where the pools are inlaid with semiprecious stone. It's exquisite. You'll be enchanted."

"But I don't know you well enough, Fin," Sandry replied in her lightest tone. "What if a strong fellow like you were to kidnap me and try to make me sign that marriage contract I keep hearing about?" She batted her eyelashes at him, as if she didn't really believe he might try that. The truth was that once she knew it was possible, she suspected the men that Berenene had assigned to court her most of all. As far as Sandry knew, they could have orders to marry her by summer's end, one way or another.

"But you're a mage," he coaxed, leading her in a circle with the other dancers. "And kin to Her Imperial Majesty. You —"

A surge of emotion — tenderness, shock, heat that flooded her veins and made her muscles loose — struck Sandry like a wave, making her sway. At a distance, as if she were someone else, she felt lips touch hers in a kiss, and she kissed back.

Oh my, she thought, very severely rattled. Daja and, and Rizu.

She grabbed Fin by both arms, partly to steady herself, partly to make her story convincing. "I'm sorry," she said. She flashed a smile at her fellow dancers and spoke a little more loudly. "It's very warm in here, isn't it?" Hurriedly she threw up a barrier on her connection to Daja, who was following Rizu giddily. "I'm sorry, I really must sit down."

A lady's wish was a command at a dance. Fin guided Sandry to a chair. "May I get you something cool?" he asked, concerned, as she located her fan.

"Shaved ice would be wonderful, thank you," she said. She waved the fan hurriedly, trying to cool the scarlet blush she felt rising on her cheeks. Once he was gone and she didn't have to work to talk to him, she put up more blocks on her connection to her sister, trying to keep it open without knowing anything of what Daja was up to now. Only when she had reduced it to the merest thread did she lean back in her chair and close her eyes.

I don't think she knew, thought Sandry. Or if she did, she thought she was more like Rosethorn, interested in women and men. I know she's mentioned boys, once or twice, but never girls. Thinking of Rizu, Sandry added, Or women.

A hand rested on her shoulder, making Sandry jump. She turned as Shan bent down and whispered in her ear, "It's cooler outside."

And it's dark, so nobody can see my face till I get myself under control, Sandry added silently. She bounced out of her chair and followed Shan onto a terrace, thankfully a different terrace from the one Daja and Rizu had just left. She wasn't completely sure that the other terrace wasn't aglow from that sudden flare of passion in Daja.

"Oh dear," she whispered, hesitating. "Fin will think I've deserted him."

"Tell me he doesn't deserve it for hounding you," Shan replied quietly, tugging her away from the windows. "I saw the look on your face when you were dancing with him. He'll recover."

Sandry shook her head, but she didn't resist the tug on her hand any longer. Shan was right. She *was* uncomfortably warm. I'll tell Fin I was going to faint unless I got fresh air. I'll make it up to him somehow. Maybe he'll take the hint and stop trying to get me alone.

Out here, the wind cooled Sandry's hot face. She let Shan guide her to a shadowed bench, where she sat with relief. "Sometimes there are things you just don't want to know the details of," she murmured.

Shan took a seat next to her. "Was that aimed at me?" he asked.

"Goodness, no," Sandry replied. "Oh, dear, Tris is up there again." She pointed up to the curtain wall.

Shan was a large source of warmth against Sandry's left side. "The Master of Ceremonies should just build her a room up there," he remarked, his voice soft music over her shoulder. "Has she always liked high places?"

Hearing his male rumble, Sandry felt better, less giddy. "Well, she *is* a weather mage," she pointed out. "It's the best place to reach for weather. If we weren't sure where to find her, back at Discipline, the wall was the first place we started. We —"

Fingers touched her chin and turned her head. Shan bent down to kiss Sandry gently.

She jumped away as if stung. The sensation was too close to Daja, what Daja had felt. Sandry couldn't tell the difference between her reaction to Shan and Daja's to Rizu. "Please don't be offended," she said, even more rattled now. "I . . . I'm just, all the light and the dancing — I really must get back to it!"

She fled back into the Moonlight Hall, this time almost flinging herself into Jak's arms. "I promised you a dance, didn't I? Isn't this a lovely time for a dance? I think so!"

Jak frowned at her, his open face worried. "Are you all right, Sandry?" he asked. "Has someone insulted you?" He looked up and glared at Shan, who had followed Sandry inside. "If fer Roth upset you in any way —"

Sandry covered Jak's mouth with her hand. "I'm *fine*," she told him, catching her breath. "Let's dance, please."

As Jak guided her out onto the floor, Sandry gave herself a good talking-to. You've been kissed before, she scolded silently. Now you act like a girl who put on her first veil just a day ago. Get hold of yourself and stop acting like a ninnyhammer! Try some of the complicated dances you keep refusing to do. Concentrating on your feet could keep your silly imagination from, well, imagining.

She danced often and, despite her fears about the complex dances, very well. She danced until her garments were soaked with perspiration and she couldn't catch her breath. Only when her feet began to hurt did she excuse herself and retire to her rooms.

She took a quick bath first, while Gudruny took care of her damp clothes. Once she had slithered into her nightgown and robe, she let Gudruny brush her hair. As soon as her maid was gone, Sandry threw herself onto her bed with disgust.

Now Shan will think I don't like him, and I do! I don't suppose there's a way a lady can apologize and say, I wish you'd kiss me again, now that I'm not so distracted. I have to let him know somehow that it wasn't anything to do with him.

Well, nothing much, she amended honestly. I just got kissing and love all confused.

That thought made her sit up. Daja's in love, she thought, feeling woebegone. After all this time. It's wonderful, but . . . she'll want to stay, won't she? She'll want to stay with Rizu. She won't want to go home.

A single large teardrop rolled down her cheek. Sandry dashed it away impatiently. Of all times to turn into a big bubble of jumpiness, this is the worst, she told herself, getting out of bed. I need to calm down.

There was only one thing she could do. She took out her night light, placed it on a small table, then got her workbasket. Embroidery, she said firmly. Just what the healer advised.

Finlach fer Hurich slammed into the miserable two rooms that were his lot in the imperial palace and kicked a footstool into the wall. A laughingstock, he thought, grinding his teeth until they ached. She made me a laughingstock before the entire court, getting rid of me on a pretext — oh, Fin, I'm so hot, I simply must sit down and have some ice! And the minute my back is turned, she's dancing with that brainless chunk of muscle Jak!

He paced in the little space he had, considering his options. They're saying Shan courts her behind the empress's back, he thought, running a restless palm over the dagger on his belt. I know the man's ambitious, but surely he's no fool. Even the Landreg moneybags can't protect him from imperial disfavor — can they?

He waved the idea away. Only a fool would try to deceive Berenene, Fin decided. But Jak. Sandry's favored Jak since we got to Landreg. Tonight she openly snubbed me for him. So I've lost that race. Well, I'm not going to wait for her and Jak to start billing and cooing, for me to become the laughingstock of the empire. Her Imperial Majesty admires bold men who take what they want — well, at least, bold men who don't try to take her. Maybe, if I'm bold enough to snag her precious cousin, *I* could be her next favorite, and Sythuthan take Shan and Quen and her other pets!

My uncle said I was to call on him if I need help.

I don't dare wait. Summer goes quick as the wind in Dancruan, and Jak's a fast worker.

His mind made up, Fin sat down at his desk, found his ink bottle, paper, and pen, and began to write.

14

The 8th – 22nd days of Rose Moon, 1043 K.F.
The Imperial Palace
Dancruan, Namorn

The party was not going the way Briar had expected it to. He'd certainly come with the intention of luring Caidy into a shadowed corner of the garden for a bit of fun, but Caidy had chosen to torment him first. She snubbed him three times as he approached to ask her to dance, walking off with someone else as he approached. The first two times he simply grinned and asked another girl to dance. The third time, when Caidy smirked at him over Fin's shoulder as he whirled her away, Briar stopped to reconsider.

This is stupid, he thought. All these people with their jewels on, watching to see who envies them and who doesn't, who favors who, it's all a waste of time. What do they accomplish by it? Why do I waste my time on this silly game?

An image of the dead of Gyonxe blotted out the gaudy dancers. Briar could smell rotting flesh. For a moment he heard not music and laughter, but the whistle of the wind blowing over rock. He shook his head to banish the image and pinched his nose to drive out the stench. I left all that back *there,* he thought fiercely. All I wanted to do was go home and remember what fun is like!

Weary, sweating, Briar looked at the thronged room. All these nice clothes, all these jokes and drinks and food, what good does it do? he wondered tiredly. Tomorrow, folk will be poor and starving and dying with a soldier's pike in them, and these people will have another celebration, more nice clothes, more jokes, more gems. The suffering is forgotten, or ignored — why sorrow? The war victims aren't *our* people. And the wheel turns and suddenly they *are* our people.

I have better things to do with my time, he realized. *Important* things.

He eased himself out onto the terrace, ignored by the couples who had picked a strip of shadow in which to kiss, and trotted down the stairs to the gardens. He instantly felt better on the Rhododendron Walk, surrounded by the dark-leaved plants. Even the blossoms looked shadowy in the scant moonlight that reached them. He walked past them, mending a damaged leaf here, making another unpleasant for the insects who tried to gnaw on it.

Somewhere nearby he sensed Tris. He didn't even bother to check their reformed bond. He didn't have to. If Tris was close, she was at the highest point close by. There she stood, atop the outer palace wall. The wind off the Syth made her skirts flap. What does she hear up there? wondered

Briar. If what I suspect is so, what does she *see*? How did she learn to see it? And that's got to be how she knows Zhegorz is seeing things, right? She knew to get Daj' to make him spectacles. So why won't she just tell us she can do it?

He grinned. Shoulda known she wouldn't stay in the ballroom any longer than it would be polite. He hesitated, then silently called up to her, *Want to come see the empress's* shakkans? *She won't mind I took you there. She gave me a note saying I had an open pass to the greenhouses.*

Tris didn't even seem surprised to hear from him. *Too much up here,* she replied. *Shaggy white bears, lights in the sky . . . Not tonight, Briar.*

He was about to walk on when she added, *It is a waste of time and money. The dancing and the expensive foods.*

Briar flinched. *How'd you know?* he demanded sharply. *How can you eavesdrop and me not know it?*

I didn't eavesdrop, she replied. *You've just gotten a little more like me since you went away.*

I'm not sure that's a compliment, he grumbled.

Neither am I, replied Tris. *Oh, look! An old ship trapped in ice!*

Shaking his head, Briar ambled on down the path.

At first he returned to his chambers, where he put his feet up and read for a while. When the palace sounds had died down to the rhythms of sleep, and the plants said that most of the walking flowers — their idea of gaudily dressed humans — had gone into their sheds, he realized he wasn't a bit sleepy.

He changed to plain clothes, slung his mage's kit over his shoulders, and left for the greenhouses. He was surprised to find no guard posted. As protective as Berenene was, he'd have thought guards would be everywhere around the costly glass buildings. Then he put his hand on the latch of the door into the greenhouse where the *shakkans* and orchids were kept. Fire blazed, giving him just enough of a burn to make him pay attention.

Briar scratched his head. Her Imperial Majesty never mentioned warding spells, he thought. Maybe she wanted it to be a surprise.

He let his power flow up to that magical barrier. It was thorough. The workmanship screamed of Ishabal to his senses. About to give up, Briar remembered the pass Berenene had given him. He took the paper out and unfolded it, then laid it against the barrier.

He stumbled as it gave way, leaving enough room for him to open the door and walk through. Behind him he felt the magic close. I hope it lets me out, he thought as he surveyed the miniature trees.

The *shakkans* clamored for his attention. Pine and miniature forest, fruit-bearing and flowering, they all wanted him to handle each of them, feeling their leaves and trunks and telling them what fine trees they were. Briar did his best to oblige. He never felt he wasted his time with *shakkans*, whether they stored magic or not. They were their own reason for being, lovely without causing harm to anyone else. Their scent of moss and dirt blotted the ghosts of Gyongxe in his mind. The whisper of their leaves covered the sounds of screams that he kept thinking he'd just heard. When his eyelids finally grew heavy, he lay on the ground under a table with his mage kit for a pillow. He slept deep, and he did not dream.

A much amused Berenene woke him around dawn. Briar grinned as he apologized, and excused himself to go clean up. Before he left, he asked her, "Would you object if I did more than just trimming and freshening these *shakkans*? Some of them need a shape that's better matched with their natures."

"As long as I may keep them later," the empress replied, her eyes on the door to her orchid room.

Briar had his hand on the door latch when Berenene called, "Do you understand that we could arrange things so that you would have authority here second only to mine? You would be the imperial gardener. I meant what I said to you at Dragonstone. You would be a treasure of the empire, famed for your skill. I would pay you richly for it. I would make you a noble, with estates of your own, and a *Giathat* — what you would call a dukedom. Neither you nor your heirs would ever want for anything." She waved, and vanished among her orchids.

Bemused by her offer, wondering if her nobles would

appreciate having a street rat duke, Briar returned to his room. His manservant was up and nervous that Briar wasn't in his bed: His face brightened when Briar came in. "*Viynain,* what is your pleasure?" he asked, bowing.

"Food, lots of it. A hot bath," replied Briar absently. "And the least smelly soap you can find. My *shakkan* hated that sandalwood-scented glop I used yesterday. No point in making it jealous."

The servant blinked. *"Viynain?"* he asked at last, confused.

Briar sighed. His sisters would have understood. "Just . . . soap with as little scent as possible, if you please."

The servant snapped to his tasks. As if he's afraid if he stays near me anymore, I'll turn him into something, Briar thought disdainfully.

After breakfast he read for a while. Normally he'd expect his sisters to be awake not long after dawn — their lives had made all of them into early risers — but after a gathering like last night, he couldn't blame them for sleeping in. When the ornamented clock in his sitting room chimed the hour before midday, he put his book aside and went in search of Daja.

At first, when he knocked on her door and there was no response right away, he thought she might have gone out. Then he heard female voices, muffled ones.

Maybe the maid will know where she got to, Briar thought, and pounded harder. At last he heard fumbling at the latch. The door opened to reveal Daja wearing only last night's rumpled tunic. "Sorry," she mumbled, letting him in. "I couldn't find a robe."

Briar smiled at her knowingly and glanced at the open bedroom door. Rizu stood there, wrapping a sheet around herself. Her long curls were free of their pins and dangled to her waist. The sheet only enhanced her buxom figure.

Briar raised his eyebrows at Rizu, then looked at Daja, who scratched at the floor with a bare toe. "Well, that explains more than it doesn't," Briar remarked. He told himself, Now I know why I was sure Rizu was never interested in me, or any man. "Daja, why didn't you say you're a *nisamohi*?" he asked, using the Tradertalk word for a woman who loved other women. "What with Lark and Rosethorn, did you think we cared?"

"I didn't know that I was a *nisamohi*," Daja whispered, still not looking at him. She shrugged. "I've been too busy, and there was never anyone . . ." She looked back at Rizu, who smiled at her with a beautiful light in her eyes.

"I'll go away in a hurry if you've got some of that heavy copper wire," Briar said. "The stuff you can just manage to bend around your wrist."

Daja went over to her mage's kit and hunted until she produced the coil of heavy copper wire. "It's not spelled, so it should act as you want," she said, handing the wire to Briar with one hand as she pushed him to the door with the other. "Don't tell Sandry or Tris yet, please," she added as she let him out. "It's just . . . so new."

"I wouldn't dream of it," Briar said, but she had already shut and locked the door. Grinning and shaking his head, he headed down the hall to the garden door, tossing and catching the copper wire as he went. So that only leaves one of us who isn't human, the way Sandry keeps tracking Shan when she thinks no one is looking, he thought cheerfully. And I tremble to think what kind of person Tris might like. They'd have to be all dressed in lightning and rain for her even to look at them, that's for certain!

Whistling a tune that their adopted mother Lark had forbidden him to whistle under her roof, Briar opened the hall door and passed out into the spring day.

After the upheavals of the party, Sandry was grateful for a quieter day after. The empress took chosen members of her court for a sail on her private ship. It meant that none of Sandry's suitors could corner her, though it amazed her how, on such a small vessel, she never found herself next to Shan. She gave up trying and stayed close to Daja and Rizu, enjoying the safety of the number of their friends as well as the bright glances and touches they exchanged.

The ship carried them to a cove on the eastern coast where they dropped anchor and went ashore for an excellent midday. On the way back, everyone cajoled until Tris released a breeze that filled their sails. While it carried them along, Tris turned aside the prevailing winds so they could make headway, earning many strange looks from captain and crew. Chime entertained nobles and crew alike. Tris had brought glass-coloring agents along. Chime ate them with glee, then spat glass flames in different colors so that everyone had a flame-shaped memento for the day. She then flew around the ship in loops and spirals, the sun glancing off her wings in flashes of rainbow light. As most of the court watched her, Sandry noticed that Ishabal had drawn Tris over to sit between her and Quen.

Those two certainly have a lot to say to Tris, Sandry thought, watching them. And why does Tris have that polite look on her face? It's the one most good courtiers learn so they never offend anyone in case they're bored or angry at what's being said.

She turned her head and saw Briar leaning against the rail near Berenene. She was laughing. Looking more closely, Sandry saw why: He'd brought a dozen tiny sprigs to life from a plank just under the rail, creating a tiny forest there. Briar looked up and caught Sandry's eye. He winked, and the sprigs shrank, retreating back into the wood.

"There. How can you possibly say no to my offer?" Sandry heard Berenene ask.

Sandry grimaced and turned her head. It's not just me she wants to stay, Sandry thought. It's Briar and Tris. She glanced at Daja and Rizu. Rizu was whispering into Daja's ear, making Daja laugh. And maybe even Daja Berenene wants to keep here. Why not? Even among ambient mages, they've done unusual things, brilliant things. *Shakkans* and living metal creations have made Briar and Daja rich and famous. Tris *could* be, if she were willing to do battle magic. Even as a weather mage she would make people think.

Sandry looked down, tracing the brocade pattern of her overgown so she could hide her face from those around her. If my cousin has her way, I might just have to stay here to keep seeing my sisters and brother. What will I do? What will I do if I have to choose between them and Uncle Vedris?

A tear dropped onto the brocade.

With the court dazed after a day in the sun, they were given the evening to themselves. Sandry invited her sisters and brother to supper in the elegant small dining room that was part of her suite. She would have asked Rizu as well, but Rizu had gone with Berenene to a meeting. Sandry wasn't sure if Briar and Tris knew what was going on, or if they would appreciate Rizu's presence at a dinner that was confined to their small family.

Gudruny was still setting the table when Briar arrived. He carried his mage kit and a *shakkan* from the imperial greenhouse. "I thought I'd work on it later," he told Sandry, placing the *shakkan* on a side table. "Hullo, Gudruny. Did you see your kids and Zhegorz?"

The maid nodded. "Zhegorz asked me to tell you and *Viymese* Tris, he followed one single conversation all the way to the green market today. He says to say it was real, bargaining between a cherry seller and a potter. He said he did it after he took out just one ear bead — whatever that means. And I think Wenoura is spoiling my children."

Briar chuckled. "Good cooks do that. If you worry about this sort of thing, once we get to Summersea, keep them away from Gorse at Winding Circle. Otherwise you'll have kids that roll, not walk."

Sandry had inspected his miniature willow while Briar talked to her maid. "What's wrong with it?" she asked when she had the chance.

Briar grimaced. "See how it's shaped so it's bent almost clean out to the side? The bleater that shaped this beauty actually thought the tree ought to be trained up in the full Cascade style. She properly needs the Windblown style, with the trunk more upright. Anyone can see that. The empress had the eye to see it, even if she hadn't had the time to get to work on her yet." He caressed the tree's slim branches, which twined gently around his hand. "Nobody ever asks the tree, do they, Beauty?"

Sandry shook her head. "If only you found a human being you loved enough to talk that way to."

"Isn't one of us in love bad enough?" Briar asked.

Sandry knit her brows. "You know, then. About Daja. And Rizu."

"Couldn't hardly miss it," Briar replied, pinching off tiny new leaves. He glanced up at Sandry. "How'd you know?"

Sandry blushed and looked down. "Daja and I reopened our bonds with each other a little while ago."

"Interesting way to find out," Briar murmured, his concentration on the tree again. "Don't hold your breath for me to throw myself down in a heap of contriteness and beg you two to include me in all this joy."

"I wasn't going to," retorted Sandry, her eyes flashing. "Of all the selfish, rude, impertinent boys —"

Briar grinned at her. "Well, I *am* family."

Sandry couldn't help it. She had to laugh as Gudruny admitted Tris and Chime.

"Good to see you two getting on," the redhead remarked. She came over to look at the miniature willow. "Reshaping her?" she asked Briar. Chime stretched out from Tris's shoulder, her head at the same angle as Tris's as they eyed the tree.

Briar nodded. "No willow tree bends over on itself. That was pretty decent of you today, taking some of the load from the sailors."

"Too bad it only made them uncomfortable," Tris replied drily.

"It's just that weather magic and anyone who can do more than control a wind here and there are so uncommon," explained Sandry. "If you'd brought up a big wave that just rolled us toward shore, they might not even have noticed."

"But the shore would," Tris said. "Besides, Her Imperial Majesty and her pet puppy dogs wanted a wind. Can you imagine how His Grace your uncle would react if every time he asked for something, everyone around him asked for the same thing?"

Sandry winced. Uncle Vedris had expressed his opinions of such fawning behavior very forcibly in the past. "They wouldn't do so more than once," she said as Gudruny responded to a knock on the door.

Daja came in, looking oddly uncertain. Rizu stood by her shoulder. "I — I told Rizu it would be all right if she joined us."

Sandry beamed at the pair. "Of course you may," she told Rizu, glancing back to make sure neither Briar nor Tris was about to make a liar out of her. Briar's eyebrows were slightly knit; Tris had that same politely interested expression she had worn that afternoon while talking with Quen and Ishabal, but neither one said anything. Sandry continued, "You never asked permission to join us at Landreg Castle, Rizu — why start now? Gudruny?"

The maid was already rearranging chairs and settings for a fifth person at the table. As soon as she finished, they all sat down to eat.

To Sandry's relief, everyone relaxed once they were eating. They talked about the ball for the Lairan ambassador in two weeks' time and that day's sail. Now that they knew more people at court, Rizu could tell stories about them that the others would understand. She and Daja remained for a while after the footmen cleared away the plates, then excused themselves and left.

There was a long silence once Gudruny had retreated to her own room. Briar concentrated on the willow *shakkan*. Gently he urged it up from its ugly, bent-over stance, raising it to the limit the trunk could handle even with his magic to make it more flexible. Once it was as straight as he could make it for the time being, he fashioned a sleeve of heavy wire to help it keep from folding down again. Tris petted Chime as the glass dragon gave off her singing purr. Sandry peered at her embroidery and waited for one of the others to say something.

At last, Briar sat up. "Just because she has a partner now doesn't mean the partner is one of us," he grumbled. "You don't see me dragging a girl everywhere."

Tris looked at him steadily. "Have you cared enough about a girl to want us to accept her?" she asked.

Briar couldn't meet her level gaze. "Well, Evvy," he mumbled.

"Evvy is your student," Tris replied quietly. "Face it, Briar, you don't like any of your bits of entertainment enough to worry if we know who they are."

"At least I don't pretend Caidy ought to belong to our circle," protested Briar.

His words were like a needle's jab. Sandry looked up.

"We're not a circle," she said tartly. "Daja and I reopened our bond. You two don't even care, so why does it matter if Daja brings Rizu?" Her mouth trembled. "They're in love. You should be happy for them."

"In love enough for Rizu not to tell everything she's heard if the empress asks it?" Briar demanded hotly. "I think not. Rizu's all right, but I think she belongs to Berenene first and anyone else second." He looked down at his hands. All the flowers on both had sprouted tiny black roses. "Face it, Daj' won't be coming home with us," he went on. "For that matter, will either of you? I've seen that Shan look at you when Berenene isn't around, Sandry. And you can't tell me they didn't offer you good coin to stay on, Tris."

Sandry glared at him. "The empress isn't offering you the moon to stay?"

"The whole palace is talking about how you alone have her permission to enter the greenhouses at any time," added Tris. "The gardeners say she's never let anyone but herself recommend pruning, but they have orders to take such direction from you. And I've heard she's offered you a bottomless purse and the post of imperial gardener if you stay."

"You hear too festering much," complained Briar. "How would you know, when you always hide?"

Tris looked at him over the rim of her spectacles, and tapped one ear.

"Oh." Briar grimaced.

"These halls are chimneys for drafts and chatter, dolt,"

Tris informed him firmly. "Leave Daja and Rizu be. They'll do as they need to."

"Daja won't thank you for saying anything against Rizu," Sandry reminded him.

"It's not against her," protested Briar.

"Is that how Daja will see it?" Sandry wanted to know.

Suddenly she felt the touch of Tris within her magic. *Calm down,* she said. Sandry could feel that Briar heard Tris as well, though his bond to Sandry herself was still closed. *We four will always be one, whether we live together in Emelan or not,* Tris told them both. *You ought to have more faith.*

The next two weeks were a whirlwind for all four mages, not just Sandry. The empress seemed determined to woo them with entertainment and splendor. They were caught up in a myriad of hunts — for unusual flowers and tucked-away picnics, since Lady Sandrilene did not like to hunt game — card parties, rides, breakfasts, and voyages on the Syth. Sandry noticed that even Tris could not evade them all, though she was better than the other three at vanishing. Daja and Rizu were glued together. They hardly seemed to care what they did as long as they did it in each other's company, as Briar pointed out more than once. Occasionally they joined Sandry, Briar, and Tris for a private midday or supper. Sandry noticed that, despite his grumbles, Briar voiced no objections to Rizu's company when Daja was present.

To Sandry's relief, Fin said nothing about her desertion of him that night at the welcoming party. Knowing his tendency toward passion and uproar, Sandry was sure that he would kick up a fuss. She was surprised instead to find he seemed to have forgotten all about it. He continued to court her along with Jak, without making any particular effort to get her alone.

I suppose I'm inconsistent to be miffed that he doesn't much care, she thought ruefully. Really, it would be a pain if he did get all offended, but he could at least pout a little.

She carefully did not think about Pershan fer Roth at all. It wasn't that she didn't see plenty of Shan — she did. He was always at Berenene's side, or at her back, bringing her delicacies, carrying her falcon until she chose to fly it to hunt, helping her to dismount. Sandry tried not to begrudge her cousin the feel of Shan's big hands on her waist as she slid down from the saddle, or the way he bent over the empress to feed her a cherry, but the bile of envy was very hard to ignore. If Shan remembered that he had kissed Sandry, he did not show it. The smile he gave her when she caught his eye was the polite one of one noble to another.

Serves me right, she told herself one night, punching her pillows into a more agreeable shape. Whenever she closed her eyes, she saw Shan and Berenene practicing Lairanese dance figures that day, particularly the one in which Shan lifted the empress high in the air. The man *kisses* me — punch, punch — and I run like a scared kitten. I bet the *empress* doesn't run!

Sandry growled and stuffed her coverlet in her mouth. Now I'll have to think of a good lie for Gudruny, she told herself. And it has to be really good, because I think Gudruny suspects far too much as is. Not that she would say anything, but she'll just tell me some bit of woman's wisdom about how some men are just out of a person's reach. I don't want to hear woman's wisdom, or any wisdom. I just want Shan to kiss me again so I can tell if I got all wobble-kneed was because I knew about Daja and Rizu or if it was the way he kisses!

The day of the Lairan ambassador's ball, the entire palace was in chaos. Dodging servants with their arms full of burdens, Sandry and Gudruny fled the palace. Landreg House was far more peaceful. Sandry could take her midday with Ambros, Ealaga, and their girls while Gudruny visited her children.

Before she left, Sandry went in search of Zhegorz. She found him seated on the balcony outside Tris's window, facing into the breeze that came over the walls. He had one of his metal ear beads in his hand and his strange metal spectacles on his face. "Don't trouble yourself about me," he said with a cheerful smile. "*Viymese* Tris visits once a day for my lessons."

"That's good to know," Sandry told him. "Are they going well?" He seems so much calmer now.

Zhegorz, who had been sitting on a tall stool, was getting to his feet. He was frowning as he turned this way and that, the ear with no bead in it facing into the wind. "I don't know," he murmured. "Why would sailors be prepared for a midnight getaway?"

Sandry had to smile. "For as many reasons as there are sailors, I should think," she replied. "I shouldn't worry, Zhegorz. Unless you know the name of the ship or her captain, there's nothing you can do."

Returning to the palace, she napped, then ate a light supper. There would be a larger banquet that night, but Sandry knew she would collapse before then without something in her belly. Afterward, she bathed, then let Gudruny dress her and arrange her hair. After that, she sat down to read. Berenene had said a courtier would bring her to the Imperial Hall, where the ball was to be held.

A rap on the door announced Sandry's escort. Gudruny opened it to reveal Fin, gloriously handsome in navy velvet and silver. He might have chosen his clothes to complement Sandry's own pale blue and silver. He grinned at Sandry. "I hope you appreciate all the begging and pleading I did to get Her Imperial Majesty to agree I could escort you to the ball," he said. "You look glorious, Lady Sandry."

She smiled and let him kiss her hand. "Careful," she warned.

Fin raised his brows. He knew what she meant. "Flattery?" He looked at Gudruny. "Do I flatter? Is she not beautiful?"

Gudruny blushed and curtsied. "You do look so lovely, *Clehame.*" She curtsied again, and opened the door for them.

Fin placed her hand on his arm and guided her down the hall.

They turned inside the lobby that connected the three wings of the palace and walked until Fin led her through a door into a back corridor.

"But the Imperial Hall is that way," Sandry protested, stopping.

Fin smiled down at her. "We've had a change of plans. Her Imperial Majesty has asked me to take you by a side route to the entrance she uses — she wants you beside her when she greets the ambassador."

"But isn't that properly where her heir should stand?" asked Sandry, letting him pull her along.

Fin nodded. "Except Princess Maedryan lives in the eastern empire," Fin explained. "You will act as her stand-in tonight."

Sandry frowned. "I hope the princess understands I'm only holding her place," she said, troubled.

"It's common," Fin explained. "You see, after two kidnap attempts, Her Imperial Majesty sent her to live in secrecy. Others have served in her place before, but no one is silly enough to believe that anyone but the princess holds that place in reality. This way." Fin steered Sandry around a corner.

Sandry turned with him and walked into a damp cloth. Whatever was on it swamped her mind, letting her sink into black sleep.

Somewhere nearby was the living world.

I fell asleep . . . when? I did it sitting, with my knees drawn up? Why in Mila's name would I do that? And when did it get dark?

My head aches so! I must be dreaming yet, because I think my eyes are open, but it's still pitch-black.

Everything above my chin is throbbing.

Sandry tried to press her hands to her eyes — the throbbing was at its worst there — only to find she had little room to move her arms. When she did touch her eyes, she could feel her eyelids move. The brush of lashes against the inside of her fingers told her that her eyes were wide open . . . and it was still dark.

She searched for light, her breath coming faster. I cannot, *cannot* be in the dark, she told herself. Everyone knows. Gudruny, Briar, Daja — *everyone* knows I must not be left in the dark, alone. Not ever. Just breathe, Sandry. Slowly. This is all easy to explain if you collect your wits and don't panic.

There — a faint glimmer: magical signs, written just inches away, over her head, to either side, and on what she could see underneath her. Sandry put her hands out and explored her surroundings. There was a solid barrier some inches before her knees and under her. Her back pressed it. It was inches from her sides and above her head. The silver gleam came from spells that covered it. As she squinted at them, forcing herself to think, to see what they were, she began to recognize them. These were signs to unravel and undo. They had been written in combinations and materials to keep a stitch witch's power weak and confined. They cast no light. They did nothing to dispel the darkness.

The dark. She was trapped in pitch darkness with no light and no crystal lamp.

With complete understanding came real, uncontrolled panic. She gasped, unable to breathe. Suddenly she was ten years old and trapped below a palace, the dead strewn through the building above her. The only person who knew where Sandry was, who had locked her in this cellar, had been murdered within earshot.

Now Sandry was alone again, and she had no light.

Sandry screamed. She shoved all of her magic outside her skin, fighting to call light to the very fabric of her clothes, only to have her power dissolve. She screamed again, begging for someone to let her out, to light a lamp, to find her. Shrieking till her voice cracked, she hammered at the wooden trap her with feet and fists, ripping her delicate dancing slippers, bruising her hands, banging the back of her head against the unforgiving wood. Again and again, ignoring the pain that shot through her muscles and veins, she dragged at her power, trying to thrust it through her pores. Silk, silk had worked before, it had held light for her before, she was wearing all kinds of silk, but the magic would not come. She finally stopped screaming and wept, shuddering in terror.

She had not been silent for long when someone outside said, "My bride-to-be awakes."

I know that voice, she thought slowly. I know it . . . Fin. Remembering his name started a slow flare of rage in her chest. Finlach fer Hurich. My escort. That "special entrance" he guided me to.

"Come, Lady Sandry," he said, his voice very close to her prison. "You were lively enough a moment ago."

He had heard her crying — *screaming*, like a child lost in the dark. "Tell me —" She stopped. Her voice had been a low croak. She cleared her torn and scraped throat and tried again. "Does my cousin know about this?"

"Why would I trouble her with details?" he asked. "Your imperial cousin appreciates deeds, not promises. Once you've signed a marriage contract — with all the constraints required of a mage wife, of course, to ensure you never turn your power on me — I will accept Her Imperial Majesty's congratulations and praise for my boldness."

His smug reply set not the frightened child, but Vedris of Emelan's favorite niece, to blazing. "Maggot-riddled festering dung-footed imp-blest mammering *pavao*!" she growled, scrambling again for her power and feeling it trickle away. "Bat-fouling dung-sucking base-born churlish milk-livered *kaq! Naliz! Amdain*!"

"Endearments," he replied. "You'll find better ones when we're married. Once you've put your signature to the contract, and your kiss, too, marked in blood for surety, I will even let my uncle give you control of your magic again. Not until then, of course. Not until you know that if you *ever* defy me, I will turn the marriage spells on you until you will crawl to beg for my forgiveness. The men of Namorn know how to handle mage wives."

"If you think my cousin will congratulate you for kidnapping me in her own palace, you don't know her," Sandry retorted. "She'll free me of your precious contract and your precious uncle!"

"Not if she wants your moneybags to stay in Namorn, which she does," Fin reminded Sandry. "And my uncle is head of the Mages' Society for all Namorn. I think even Her Imperial Majesty will have to swallow any vexation with me, once I have the mages' backing *and* your wealth at my command. What?" He was answering a question from someone outside Sandry's trap. "No, she will be well enough. I must show myself at the ball, so no one believes I had anything to do with her disappearance." The sound of his voice came closer to her prison. "Don't fret, my dear," he told her. "Later you may write to your friends from our honeymoon nest. Oh — if you're hoping for rescue? You're belowground. No wind will carry word of you to that red-headed terror. You're in a room without plants, so the green lad can't find you. And if you're waiting on the handsome and clever Pershan, even if he *could* find you, he wouldn't dare. Her Imperial Majesty knows her lover's attention has been straying."

Despite her fear, Sandry gulped. Shan and Berenene? She could be his mother!

Fin continued: "She's watching him. He hasn't been allowed to leave her side for two days without her knowing exactly where he goes. Poor Quen was getting all excited, thinking she would get rid of Shan and turn to him again. Instead, she's clutching Shan tight. It shows how much she wants to keep you here — normally she just dismisses the girl from court."

"You're disgusting," Sandry croaked. "Making up such foul lies about people."

"Oh, I've made you unhappy, ruining your pretty little dreams. Get used to *our* marriage, if you please," retorted Fin. "Once you present me with an heir, I'll be happy to leave you to your own devices. Until later, my dear."

Then he was gone. Without Fin to hate, her fear of the dark swamped her again. Sandry screamed until she had no voice. When that was gone, she slid down and slammed her feet against the side of her prison over and over, until her back was bruised and her knees and ankles were on fire. Only when she could no longer kick did she curl up into a tiny ball, shuddering. The dark overwhelmed her for a while.

The sound of people banging around outside brought her to herself again. It seemed Fin's helpers were settling down to a game of cards nearby. Oddly, their voices gave Sandry's mind something to latch on to. She wasn't *quite* lost, not if she could hear rough men cursing each other's bets and cards.

What am I without magic? she asked herself dully, forcing herself to sit upright. Just a game piece, like Zhegorz said. Just a pretty . . . Zhegorz. Daja. Briar, Tris.

Wait. Wait. I have bits of *Briar*'s magic in me, from when we were kids. And Tris's, and Daja's. I spun us into one magic, but then I had to weave us into four separate people again. Still, we each kept some of one another's power so we could go on seeing magic, and hearing conversations. What's around me are spells only for thread magic, not green or weather or metal magic.

It was hard to ignore her terror and her very real pain. First she had to rip pieces from her linen shift to bind up her bleeding hands and feet. Her throbbing head was hard to ignore, too. Somehow she forced herself inward, thrusting her awareness of the dark from her mind. She even made herself forget those voices outside her trap. Slowly she sank down into herself, into the core of her power.

She was shocked to find it in disarray. When did I tend it last? she wondered, seeing a mess of threads and connections where she was accustomed to finding a spindle of fiery thread. Oh, cat dirt — not since we reached Dancruan, I think. I never used to be this sloppy, she thought as she poked through the tangle. I shouldn't get so distracted that I don't straighten things up. For one thing, here at least I can see light.

She found the crimson thread that was her bond to Daja. She gave it a few sharp tugs. She waited, but no response came. She bit her lip to keep from wailing as her grip on her power started to melt. Daja was blocked off, which meant that she must be with Rizu. There would be no help from her.

For a moment, darkness surged back into Sandry's mind. She kicked the wall again, then cradled her throbbing foot, tears streaming from her eyes. She had forgotten her bruised and bloody feet.

Enough, she ordered herself as the pain ebbed. *Enough.* I have one tiny setback and I go to pieces. Gudruny held on for ten years. Zhegorz survived for fifty. Daja floated in the sea five days thinking she was lost forever, and she let a forest fire go through her, and walked through burning buildings. From what Rosethorn said, she and Briar were in a *war.* I get locked up by one silk-breeches noble and I just collapse? *Enough.*

Forcing herself to be calm once again, she sank down into her power to find her connection with Tris. It wasn't as strong as the bond with Daja, probably because they'd only used it once, and that recently. Sandry shoved herself through the thin strand, questing for the redhead.

A monstrous jolt shocked her clean out of her concentration. She leaned her head back carefully, tasting blood where she'd bitten her lip.

"Of all times for her to play with lightning," she croaked, feeling for her handkerchief. Not many people would rather shroud themselves in storms than attend a brilliant party, she added silently, so she wouldn't hurt her lip or her agonized throat.

What is the time? When will Fin come back? She had no idea of the hour. She wasn't sure that much time had passed, but it was impossible to tell with her magic loose and floppy, and Tris and Daja both unavailable. He could be on his way back here now. Sandry wasn't sure how much longer she could endure this tiny, dark space and be sane. If she was going to be in any condition to rip him to shreds when she was free, she had to escape.

That left Briar, who had not allowed her back into his mind. Her tie to him was dull gray. Too bad, Sandry told herself. This is no time for niceties.

She reached into the pouch at her neck and took out her precious thread circle. She found Briar's lump in it easily. It blazed green in her magic, with filaments of Sandry's, Tris's, and Daja's powers mixed in. Plunging through it, Sandry shrieked silently, *BRIAR!*

Images shot through her mind: lace-trimmed skirts, Caidy's wild eyes, a thud on the floor, Briar helping a livid Caidy to her feet.

I told you to keep OUT! he roared at her down their connection. *Oh, cowpox,* he said, recognizing the thread circle as it blazed in her mind and her hand. *You're using the string. I thought you said you'd* never *make us do this. "Your own free will," that's what you said. So just shut . . .* He slowed, spreading himself through her mind. *Say, what's all this? You're in a box with magic in it.*

No, do you think so? demanded Sandry, fighting to keep her mental voice from shaking. *Here I was thinking it was the empress's chambers. No wonder I feel so cramped.*

Don't bite my nose off, he said absently. *How did you get into this thing? Where's your night lamp?*

I jumped in. For good measure, I pulled the top on and put locks on the outside. I decided I needed a challenge!

What's the matter with you? Briar asked, so caught up with Sandry that he barely felt it when Caidy slapped his face. *It's Tris who's the grouch, remember?* "Good-bye," he called absently as Caidy walked away from him.

Sandry made herself take a breath. *If I'm grouchy, it's because I need rescuing*, she said reasonably. Losing her temper, she cried, *And I* hate *needing rescue!*

I guess so, Briar replied, walking outside into the gardens. Rain soaked him instantly. He ignored it. *Now, where are you?*

He said the room was plantless so you couldn't find me, Sandry replied, fighting not to sound forlorn. *He left men to guard me, or help him smuggle me out of here, wherever "here" is.*

I don't need plants — I can follow our tie. Who's "he," anyway? Briar set off down a promenade through the rose garden, keeping an eye on the thread that shone silver through the dark and the pouring rain.

Fin. He was supposed to be my escort, and he lured me into a very well-laid trap. He was ready for this, Briar. He had drugs to put me to sleep and there are binding signs for my thread magic on this box as good as anything we could make. His mage uncle helped. Fin said he's got a house that's the same. A tear dripped from one of her eyes; Sandry ignored it. At least talking to Briar helped her keep the dark from overwhelming her, barely. *He said Berenene didn't know, but that she admires boldness in a man.*

The Sandry-thread led Briar back inside, through a side door with freshly oiled hinges. He found himself in an older wing of the palace, where the thread took him to a small back hallway. *The good news is that you're still in the palace, I think*, he told her. There were signs of neglect everywhere. Human footprints marked the dust on the floor tiles, leading him to a small door. *You said you're guarded? I'd better get reinforcements.*

They're blocked off, Sandry replied glumly. *Probably Daja and Rizu are together. Tris was playing with lightning. I think I have a scorch mark on my power.*

Briar grinned at the thought. *Well, the stormy part's over.* He reached out along his newly strengthened connection with Tris.

What? the weather mage demanded. Briar got the impression she was back in her chambers, changing into her nightclothes. *I was busy —*

Briar opened his mind, trusting her to know what to look at and what to leave alone. It took Tris only a glimpse of what lay before his eyes, then Sandry's eyes. The redhead put her book aside. *I'm coming*, she told them.

15

Briar slumped to the base of the wall, taking out two of his knives in case someone arrived who felt he did not belong there. *We have a bit of a wait*, he told Sandry. He felt their connection shudder, and knew that her fear of the dark was returning. It had always been a marvel to Briar. Sandry was the least fearful girl he knew, and yet the dousing of a lantern could leave her trembling if no other light was available. It was the reason that he, Daja, and Tris had made Sandry's night-light crystal in the first place.

I never really talked to you about Yanjing, did I? he asked, pretending not to notice her fear. *They call it the Empire of Silk for a reason, you know. They have this cloth they call the Rain God's Veil, just a hair thick, almost. They dye it colors they call by names like Green Tea, Almond Milk, and Lotus Pollen. If you don't pin it down, it just drifts away, like invisible creatures are carrying it. The imperial concubines wear it for veils, and they all have a little girl servant whose only job is to catch the veils if they slide away.*

He could feel Sandry take a deep, shuddering breath and lick her lips. Briar promised himself that Fin would pay for frightening her so badly. He couldn't have scared her more if he had planned it deliberately. Only terror of the unknown could have made Sandry as strident as she had been when she called for him.

You know that penchi silk you were so curious about? They get it from silk made by worms they find in wild trees, not ones on farms. The country people make it, so its threads aren't so smooth, but the thing is, they could *be. One old thread mage told me her family has made penchi silk for ten generations and could do as fine a thread as the fancy houses. But the little imperfections, the "slubs," you called them? Every family that does it does them in a pattern. Back home in my notes I copied down some of them for you. She says it's how they used to send messages under the emperor's nose, and sometimes they still do.*

Sandry's mind filled with wonder and excitement. *Lark and I thought so, but Vetiver told us that was silly,* she replied, her mind on silk now and not her captivity. *She said who would be desperate enough to send messages in tiny slubs like that!*

Well, it's the slubs and *the weave,* Briar explained, delighted to have her attention. *And they don't always do it, so it's not every piece of cloth.*

He had exhausted penchi silk and was describing the butter sculptures of Gyongxe when he felt a roiling storm of power approach. He got to his feet. "That would be Tris."

Down the hall, he heard a door slam. It was indeed Tris who came down the hall. She had put on a gown again, though it was hard to see it under the lightning that crawled over her head and dress. It glittered on the onyx buttons of her shoes and sparked on the rims of her spectacles. Chime stood on her shoulder, one tiny forepaw gripping a braid, lightning sparking from her eyes, claws, and wingtips.

Briar opened the door and bowed. "After you, *Viymese*," he said. It's not that I mind a good fight, he told himself as he followed her down the long, curved stairwell that lay beyond the door. Still, why wear myself out when she can wind things up in a hurry?

A draft blew into his face as he descended. She's pulling the air up past us, so they may not hear us coming, he realized. *You're wasted, not being a thief*, he told her.

So funny, I forgot to laugh. Her retort fizzed in his mind. She was *very* angry.

He was impressed. *Back at Discipline, you got this mad, you'd scorch the top off the thatch*, he reminded her. *Or at least, you did before me and Rosethorn protected it.*

I won't lose control, if that's what worries you!

Worry? No. I'm hoping for it, he replied.

The round shoulders ahead of him slumped briefly. *I'm not.* Her reply was much less crackly. Then it surged again. *Though I'll probably change my mind when I see Fin next!*

The stair seemed to descend forever. The walls around them were carved stone, cut from the living rock under the palace. They were also old. The two mages passed through sections that had been braced with heavy wooden beams to keep the passage from collapsing. *Fin must have had fun carrying a knocked-out girl down here*, Briar told both Sandry and Tris.

Too bad he didn't fall and break his neck! Sandry retorted.

Well, then he might have also broken yours, Briar pointed out. *Excuse me for saying as much, but I wouldn't dare show my face to your uncle if I'd let that idiot kill you* and *himself. The only way His Grace wouldn't keelhaul* me *is if I could give him Fin.*

At last they reached the bottom and a door. Tris listened at the keyhole for a moment, tugged at an unraveling braid she had pulled from its net, and flung a fistful of hard air at the door as she thrust it open. The air exploded into the room, knocking over the table that stood between two men, scattering cards, mugs, their unsheathed swords, and a bottle on the floor.

As Tris and Briar came in, the men jumped to their feet, cursing, and grabbed for their fallen weapons. Tris loosed hair-thin bolts of lightning at the blades, forcing their owners to drop them with a yelp. Briar went over to collect the swords and strip the guards of their daggers and any other weapons. Once he was done, Tris set a ring of lightning around the throats of each guard. They dared not move a hair for fear of touching those fiery collars.

"Please, *Viymese*, don't kill us," babbled one rogue. "He's our master, we had to obey!"

"Shut up," Tris ordered softly as her fistful of wind dropped a coil of rope in her outstretched hand. "You annoy me."

Briar opened the other closed door in the room. The scent of salt and drops of spray struck his face. He looked back at Tris. "It's a cove tucked under the cliff."

Tris set about binding one guard's hands. "So that was the plan? Escape with her by boat?" When he said nothing, she gave the rope a hard yank. "We don't need both of you," she pointed out.

Would you really? Sandry asked. She could see all this through her friends' eyes. *Would you really kill one, when it's Fin who's to blame?*

They don't know that, snapped Tris. She took away his lightning collar and shoved the man onto a chair. As she tied his legs, Chime flew to his shoulder. To make sure he didn't kick, the dragon gripped his shirt collar with her hind paws and his nose with her forepaws. She leaned into his face and silently hissed, her curved glass fangs within an inch of his eye.

"Yes — by boat," said the talkative man. He stood perfectly still, sweat dotting his forehead in large beads. "Up the coast to a place where my lord has a cart and household troops waiting."

"They've got a long wait, then," Briar said, shutting the door to the cove. "Now, let's see about this box." He went over to it, running his hands over the iron straps that held the top in place.

"You can't open it," said the talkative guard as Tris tied his arms, then removed the lightning collar. "*Bidis* Finlach has the key!"

"Locks are for the unimaginative," said Briar, placing his hands on the wood of the box. "Unless they're artists, of course. Normally I'm all for art. . . ." He fed himself into the wooden boards. They were new, as they had to be to take the magic that had been placed inside them, all relatively young and plump boards, not long off the tree. Briar called that green life to him, yanking it from the wood, leaving them dry, wizened, and shrunken. The box fell to pieces. Briar caught the iron straps to keep them from hitting Sandry. Once they were safely put aside, Briar helped her to her feet.

She stood, her eyes watering in the sudden light. Once her vision cleared, she lunged for the open stairway door and nearly toppled. Briar held her as her legs cramped and her wounded feet refused to take her weight. He looked around for more linen to use as bandages. Not finding any, he took off his belt knife and swiftly cut off the surly guard's coat. Raising his knife, he was about to remove the man's shirt when it simply dropped off his body in pieces, the seams unraveling in the blink of an eye. Briar looked at Sandry, whose eyes blazed with fury.

"Thanks," he said casually. He smiled pleasantly at the guard, who was now shirtless in the chilly room. "Hope you don't catch cold." He gathered up the pieces of shirt and began to tend to Sandry's feet.

Tris was calmly undoing two thick braids. "I am not climbing those stairs back up. None of us are."

Briar looked at her, astounded. "What did you think we'd do, Coppercurls, fly?"

She smiled evilly at him as the sea door blew open. "It's a trick I learned in Tharios. And it's *much* quicker than climbing."

Sandry hugged herself. She was a tangled, rumpled mess, but now that she was in the light, she was ready to do battle. "What if I don't want to go back to my room like a good little *clehame*?" she demanded, her voice shaking with her rage. "What if I would rather talk to my dear cousin Berenene about the behavior of one of her male subjects?"

Tris nodded. "I can take us to the imperial wing easily enough. It's like standing on a moving platform, the way I shape the winds, only you can't see the platform."

"Do it." Sandry stumbled out through the sea door. Tris looked at Briar as Chime flew over to her shoulder. "You two have to hold on to me, and promise not to squeak."

Briar shook his head. "The things I do for my sisters," he said with a sigh. He waved at the two captives. "We'll try and remember to send someone for you boys, don't you worry!"

Berenene looked out at her court, deeply dissatisfied with this night. True, her lumpish cousin from Lairan had been suitably awed by her splendor, and would report to his king that Namorn was, as ever, glorious and overpowering in its generosity. He was disappointed not to meet *Clehame* Sandrilene fa Toren, but understood that even the best healers in the empire could not erase the damage of a fever in an afternoon. Berenene had assured him that she would invite him to a private dinner: "just our family," she had told him, "when *Clehame* Sandry is herself again." It was beautifully done, with Isha to confirm the lie. No one but Ishabal, Fin, and the servants who had gone to find the girl knew the truth, that she had vanished. Fin had said, with a casualness that made Berenene want to slap his handsome face, that he assumed Sandry had gone to the ball with other friends.

"You are very casual about the fate of a woman who could make you rich and powerful," she had accused. He had begged her pardon, with such polished innocence that she had half-wondered if he had not arranged to kidnap Sandry tonight. She immediately dismissed the idea. Fin was not fool enough to stage such a thing within the walls of the palace, which was sacrosanct. No one would risk that.

At least Sandry was not with Shan. Berenene had seen to that, and had kept him at her right hand all night. He's spent too much time out of my view lately, and too much of it has been in Sandry's company, she told herself now, eying his muscled body sidelong as he watched the dancers. I like a man with spirit, as long as it isn't too *much* spirit. Quen never gave me so much trouble when he was my official lover.

She glanced at Quen, who had taken Isha's place on her right. The older mage had insisted that Sandry would turn up — the ball was large enough that she might be in one of the other rooms, or in the gardens, being romanced. No real inquiry could be made until morning without causing the kind of gossip Her Imperial Majesty wanted to avoid, so Isha was going to bed. Many of the older, more staid courtiers were also making their farewells. The younger members of the court were known to dance until dawn, with the empress joining them.

Sipping a goblet of wine, Berenene inspected the crowd. If Daja knew Sandry was missing, she showed no sign of concern. She and Rizu were surrounded by Rizu's friends. They made a lively group, and Daja and Rizu practically glowed as they smiled at each other. That worked out quite well, thought Berenene with satisfaction. My Rizu is happier than I have seen her in months, something I had not anticipated. And I shall have a strong smith mage to serve me by the time autumn closes the mountain passes to the south.

The empress looked for Tris, but the redhead was nowhere in view. I hadn't expected to see her, Berenene reminded herself. I will leave Tris to Ishabal. Oh, my. It looks as if Briar and Caidy have had a tiff. He is nowhere to be seen, and Caidy is flirting with every personable young man at court.

Berenene was about to ask Shan to fetch her a glass of wine when she saw that Ishabal had returned. The mage still wore her ball gown, and she carried a folded document in her hand. What business is so urgent that it could not wait until morning? the empress wondered.

Quen and Shan stepped aside as Ishabal approached the dais. The mage took his spot, offered the document to Berenene and whispered, "They wait in your personal audience chamber."

Berenene raised an eyebrow and opened the note. It read:

I beg the favor of an immediate audience with Your Imperial Majesty. I have been insulted tonight in the most vile fashion and wish to inform you immediately of what was done to me under your roof.

The signature was that of her missing guest: *Sandrilene, Clehame fa Landreg, Saghad fa Toren.*

Berenene looked up. Something had gone amiss, it seemed. "Isha, I think I will need both you and Quen. You should be prepared for any . . . mishaps. Who is with her?"

"Briar and Tris," replied Ishabal softly. "Majesty, Sandry looks battered. Her hands and feet are bandaged, her clothing torn. Trisana is throwing off sparks."

The empress bit her lip. This could be even worse than the note had implied. "Then I suggest you and Quen arm yourselves with defensive magics before we enter that room." Berenene beckoned to the captain of the guard as Isha whispered to Quen. When her guard approached and knelt beside her chair, she bent down to murmur, "Get one of your mages and a couple of guards to watch over *Viymese* Kisubo, subtly. Do not let her go anywhere but to her own rooms or to Rizu's."

The man nodded. Berenene got to her feet. As the dancers stopped and the conversation came to a halt, she smiled. "Amuse yourselves, friends. Imperial business calls me away, but there is no reason for you to interrupt your evening." She left by the rear entrance rather than have her departure slowed by farewells. "Did you read this?" she asked Ishabal as she strode along, the older woman at her side and Quen rushing to keep up.

"I would not presume," Ishabal replied stiffly.

Berenene slowed down and handed over Sandry's note. Ishabal read it, twice, closed her eyes briefly as if in prayer, then passed it to Quen. "Who would be fool enough to assault a noblewoman in the imperial palace?" Quen wanted to know. "And how would such an idiot think he could do it and escape?"

"We'll learn soon enough," retorted Berenene, stopping to collect herself. "After which I shall decide what to do with that fool, and with anyone idiot enough to assist him. But first, I would like the two of you to be ready. I would hate to learn the hard way that their teachers had underestimated our guests' control over themselves when they granted them their medallions so young."

Taking a breath, Berenene smoothed her gold skirts.

Then, as leisurely as if she walked in her gardens, she led her mages to her private audience chamber.

A guardsman stood outside. Years of service kept his face blank, though confusion showed in his eyes: Most visitors to the private audience chamber arrived during the day. When the empress stopped in front of him, he bowed and held the door open for her and her companions.

The three young mages seated there got to their feet as Berenene came in. All three, including Sandry, wore their medallions outside their clothes. Tris looked disheveled, two fat, kinked hanks of hair hanging loose from her usual netted bundle. Her face was pale and glistening with sweat, but her gray eyes were ice cold. The glass dragon sat on her shoulder with one paw in her hair, like a guardian statue.

Briar, too, was sweating. His face was unreadable as he looked at the empress.

Ishabal's description of Sandrilene's looks was about right. Sandry's hair was a tumbled mess, tangled and knotted. Her clothes at least were unrumpled, a testament to her power over thread, but her hands and feet were masses of rag bandages. Her face was dust-streaked and bruised. The look in her cornflower blue eyes was pure steel.

"My dearest Sandrilene," the empress said, striding toward her with her hands out. "Whatever happened to you?"

Sandry's eyes caught and held hers. "Finlach fer Hurich happened to me," she said, her voice an alien croak. "Fin, and that disgusting kidnap custom you let thrive in this country." She began to cough, wincing as she did. Tears of pain streamed down her face. She dashed them away angrily.

Berenene halted and blinked at the girl. "What?" she asked, baffled. "Fin — Finlach — is in the ballroom at this moment." Her brain worked swiftly, as it always did in a crisis. As she had trained it to. "What happened to your voice?"

"Screaming does that to a person," Briar said coldly. "May I go to my quarters to get something for her throat?"

"Quen, see to it, please," Berenene ordered.

As Quenaill walked over to Sandry, the girl backed away. Briar went to stand next to him. "Be very careful with what you do," Briar said quietly. "Our patience is just about gone."

"Understood," Quen replied. "It's just a mild healing spell, *Clehame.*" He leaned forward to place one broad palm on Sandry's grimy throat. She flinched, then closed her eyes. After a moment, Quen drew away from her.

Am I to understand Finlach did this *in my own palace*? Berenene wondered, ice closing around her heart. How? Not alone, surely. And how did he think he might escape?

She selected a chair, rather than the throne, and settled onto it. "I think I will understand your meaning so much better if you explain, Sandrilene," she said coolly. "Sit, everyone, please. If you have a grievance, I am certain it can be resolved."

"As I am certain," repeated Sandry, taking a chair. Her

voice was rough, but understandable. "Tris, please, sit before you fall down."

"I'm not some dainty flower, worn out by my own magic," retorted Tris. "I could lower us to the foot of the cliffs again right now, if you like. Though speaking of the cliffs . . ." She took a chair and drew a long braid from its place in the coil.

Berenene saw that Ishabal's attention was locked on the redhead. From a belt pouch the older woman drew a rope of silk twined with an assortment of powerful charms, each keyed to different protective spells. Her fingers were twined around one charm that the empress knew would throw a magical prison around Tris.

That's good, Berenene thought. Someone needs to watch *Viymese* Chandler. "Won't you sit, *Viynain* Moss?" Berenene asked with a smile.

His expression didn't change. "I'll stand, thank you, Your Imperial Majesty," he replied politely. He stayed where he was, legs planted, hands clasped before him, his eyes somber. For a moment Berenene feared that she had lost this young man's regard, or even worse, his friendship. She brushed the idea aside. Of far more importance was learning who had possessed the effrontery to attempt to kidnap her kinswoman in her palace.

"Finlach fer Hurich came to escort me to the ball," Sandry told the three Namornese, her voice cold and steady. "Instead, he led me down a back passage, claiming I was to stand beside Your Imperial Majesty as you entered the room from the rear."

"Did anyone see you with Fin?" asked Quenaill.

Berenene shot him a glare for interrupting, but Sandry was shaking her head. "Not after we turned away from the main corridors. I didn't see anyone else. When we turned a corner back there, someone placed a cloth over my face. It was soaked in a potion that made me unconscious. I woke up in a *box*." Her voice trembled slightly. She got it under control. "The inside was filled with spells to cripple a thread mage. Fin was outside. He said his uncle had helped him. He said he was taking me out to a house with the same spells on it. And he said I would leave only when I signed the marriage contract and put my lip print on it in blood, so a mage could use it against me if I tried to break it. He seemed to think you would let him get away with it, Cousin, since you admire bold young men so. Everyone knows you want me to stay in Namorn. And you expect women to escape like you did. Of course, I doubt that you were put in a box." The huskiness in her voice thickened. "I doubt that the head of the Namornese Mages' Society put spells on you and guaranteed to keep them there until you signed the contract. It would have been harder to escape under those circumstances, don't you think?"

"Then how did you escape?" Berenene asked coolly. The beginnings of a headache pounded in her temples.

"I found her," Briar said flatly.

"But how?" insisted Berenene. What she really wanted to know was, Did you use that magical connection my spies told me was closed? She could not ask that, of course. They trusted her little as it was. Adults understood that people spied on one another, but these young people were idealists, not realists. She doubted that they would understand that everyone spied on everyone who might be important.

"I . . . forget," Briar said coldly. "I have a terrible memory when it comes to secrets I don't wish to tell."

Berenene glanced at Tris. The redhead had undone a third of the braid she had pulled from her hairstyle. Now Tris ran her fingers through the loose hairs over and over, her attention locked on them.

"She's working magic," Ishabal said. "I cannot tell what kind, but she is cloaked in power."

"Then stop her," ordered Berenene.

Tris looked up, gray eyes glinting through her loose tresses. "I wouldn't do that."

"Tris, you'll never be a success as a diplomat," announced Briar. "You may as well put that right out of your mind." He turned his own bright green eyes on Ishabal and Berenene. "We all swear on our medallions, this isn't something that would affect Your Imperial Majesty in any way," he said, his voice as bland as cream. "In fact, Tris here is actually doing you and your devoted servants a favor."

"And if they stop me now, I can't promise the cliff under the palace wall won't drop into the Syth," muttered Tris.

"Pay her no mind," Briar continued as Sandry glared at Tris. "It's not a threat she's making, just a warning. You know how it is with mages and interruptions. Anyway, I suppose you didn't know it, or you'd have seen for yourself, but your palace has rats. Big ones. Doesn't it, *Clehame* fa Landreg?"

"Big ones," Sandry replied. "I don't know how she missed them, but anything is possible."

"She's an empress," Briar told her, his tone pure conciliation. "You can't expect her to know every rathole that opens up." To the empress and her mages, he explained: "This one is a real beauty. It opens in a northeast wing of the palace — I don't think anyone's dusted in there in months. And it tunnels all the way down through the cliff. Through solid stone, even under the curtain wall, can you believe it? Down at the bottom, it opens onto a cove of the Syth."

Berenene's veins filled with ice. The Julih Tunnel, she realized, horrified. How in Vrohain's name did Fin — his uncle. Notalos dung-grubbing fer Hurich. The Mages' Society is said to have the plans of the palace from its first construction — and I shall have his skin.

Briar continued, "Energetic little *nalizes*, rats, aren't they? To dig all that way. We stumbled on their hole purely by chance. Well, Sandry didn't stumble *entirely* by chance. So Tris here got all alarmed, because she hates rats, so she's stopping up that hole at the foot of the cliff. She's getting the lake to help. Some of the stones she's using are pretty big."

Tris looked up, her face relaxed and at ease. "It really is in your interest, Your Imperial Majesty. Who could sleep, knowing rats could get in at will? With that rathole closed, Your Imperial Majesty may sleep easily."

Berenene clenched her hands against her skirts. If the wench is doing what she claimed to do, she is trying to close the secret exit that saved my life in that assassination attempt years ago. Of course, it's no good to me now if *Viynain* fer Hurich has decided he need not obey his vow to keep those plans secret. "Can she do it?" she asked Ishabal. There were magical wards on the tunnel.

Ishabal watched Tris for a long moment. Finally, she nodded. "She *is* doing it." She asked Tris, "What if anyone is in the chamber at the base of the cliff?"

"I won't weep a tear if they drown," Sandry snapped, her voice rough. "But they could always climb. Tris is just stopping up the exit. You ought to put maids with brooms at the other end of the hole, to beat the rats when they come out."

The skin at the back of Berenene's neck crawled. She sighed lightly, as if she'd asked for a glass of wine only to be told there was no more. One of the hardest parts of being imperial was learning when to back off from a fight. "Quen, be a dear and send a message to the captain of my guard. Harm no one who comes out, please. I wish to have anyone who appears questioned." Quen bowed and went to give the message to the guard at the door. As he did so, the empress said, "Please continue, Trisana. Ishabal will watch all that you do." Berenene looked at Sandry once more. "So. Briar found you in a way he does not remember."

"Tris joined us," said Briar, his eyes cold. "We got Sandry out of the crate."

Berenene shook her head as Quen returned to them. "Cousin, what can I say?" she asked helplessly. "Finlach has committed a serious offense against you, without my knowledge or approval." Her voice hardened despite her struggle for an appearance of calm. "He forgot his duty to me. I assure you, he will be arrested and punished. You will see how quickly justice is done here."

"Cousin, justice should be done *very* quickly," Sandry replied, her face hard. "We are returning to Emelan as soon as we can pack."

Isha flinched despite her years at court. Quen halted rather than come closer. Slowly, Berenene replied, trying to think, "But the summer is only half done."

"I don't want to see how I will feel after an entire summer," Sandry retorted. "That a *custom* that permits such things against the women in this realm continues under a monarch who is female herself —"

"I am not the empress of weaklings," said Berenene. "A strong woman would find a way to escape, as I did. As you have. They have families to help them, if their families are strong."

Sandry shook her head. Her hands trembled as they lay folded in her lap. "Not all women or families are strong in the same way. They are entitled to your protection. I will not remain in a country that withholds that protection. And it's been made clear to me that I cannot even count myself safe in your own palace, Cousin."

Berenene felt as if the chit had slapped her. "You dare . . . ," she began to say, furious, then met Sandry's eyes. Of course she dares, thought Berenene. And she is right. I was so secure in my power that I did not realize spirited young animals, like my courtiers, are forever testing the leash and the rein. I relaxed my vigilance and she was offered an intolerable insult. The custom is supposed to apply only to women taken in the open, not when they are under the protection of their liege lords. In shattering my protection, Fin destroyed my credit with every parent who entrusts an unmarried daughter to my care.

She smoothed her skirts. "You are hurt and recovering from a bad fright," she said in her most soothing voice. "In the morning, you will feel differently. Would you really turn your back on all Namorn has to offer?" She met Briar's eyes when she said this.

It was Briar who answered. "If this is what Namorn offers, yes. It is only as a courtesy to you that I don't address Fin myself. It's *my* sister he tried to kidnap, and our magic is plenty thicker than blood. Or maybe I should just give him to Sandry when he *doesn't* have drugs and spells to make him the big man." His voice was heavy with contempt. "You think a strong woman can always beat this? I call it rape, in any country."

Berenene did not want to meet his eyes any longer. Something in them made her feel an emotion she had not faced in years: guilt. She didn't like it. Instead, she turned her gaze to Sandry. "And so like your mother, you abandon your lands and your duty to your people."

Sandry's chin thrust forward like a mule's. "My people are very well cared for by someone who knows them," she snapped. "How dare you speak to me that way, as if I'd gone roistering and left my tenants to beg? Instead, I am to remain here, where I am nothing more than money bags and acreage? Where I am a *thing,* to occupy a niche in some household shrine, except when my lord husband wants to polish me up a little?"

She doesn't even realize she's crying, the empress thought, feeling a quiver of pity which she dismissed right away. *I* managed well enough, she thought irritably, escaping two oafs who thought they had the better of me. Namorn is a hard country. It requires strong women, strong men, and strong children to survive and make it prosper. I learned that from my father, even as he signed my second kidnapper's execution papers.

Sandry shook her head and dashed her tears away. "I'm going home. I've made arrangements so Cousin Ambros will never be strapped for money again. My friends may stay or go as they will, but I'm going back to Emelan, where I am a person, not an *heiress*." She spat the world as if it were a curse, stood, curtsied briefly, and limped from the chamber. When Quen raised a hand to stop her with one spell or another, Berenene shook her head. There are other ways to bring a haughty young *clehame* to see things reasonably, she told herself.

She looked at the other two and realized they watched her, eyes intent.

What would they have done if I hadn't stopped Quen? Berenene wondered. For a moment, she was almost afraid. Those bright pairs of eyes, one gray-green, one gray, were fixed on her with the same unblinking attention with which her falcons watched prey.

You may have power, she silently told them, but I am older and far more experienced. I have true great mages at my side, not accomplished children. She held their eyes for a moment, before she looked at Briar alone. "You may stay," she told him, thickening the honey in her voice. "I still offer you the empire for your garden. Imagine it, Briar, spice trees from Qidao and Aliput, medicine ferns from Mbau, incense bushes from Gyonxe . . ."

His head snapped back as if she had slapped him. "And turn a blind eye to this? Wonder what woman scuttling by is with her husband of her free will? Here I was thinking only street rats got treated like roach dung. I'm honored you think so well of me, Imperial Majesty, but I'm leaving with Sandry." He bowed to the empress briefly and looked at Tris.

"Coming," she said, getting to her feet. "The rat hole's plugged," she informed Berenene. She fought a yawn. When it passed, she added, "Thank you for the offer of a position, but I'm with Briar and Sandry." She bobbed a curtsy, took the arm Briar offered, and walked out with him.

The door closed silently.

Berenene sat back in her chair and closed her eyes. She could feel her two great mages waiting for her to speak. In my own palace, she thought, furious. My own *palace*! When dozens of nobles trust their daughters to me, to serve as ornaments to my household!

"Quen," she said, forcing her voice to be calm. "Send orders down. I want Finlach fer Hurich arrested immediately. Put him in the dampest pit we have. In chains. Throw his servants in with him, also in chains. Check the end of the tunnel Tris blocked, in case any of them are hiding there. I will deal with them tomorrow. Then take a contingent of mages as well as a company of guards and arrest *Viynain* Notalos fer Hurich on the charge of high treason."

"The head of the Mages' Society?" murmured Quen nervously.

Berenene opened her eyes to glare at him. "Do you mean to tell me you can't take a sniveling political games-player like Notalos?" she snapped. "Have you let your skills and those of your people go slack?"

"He means no such thing, Imperial Majesty," Isha announced smoothly. "It is easily done, my boy. And he has betrayed a trust. Use the jar of ghosts spell." Isha rested a hand on Berenene's shoulder. "It will be done as you require."

The empress closed her eyes. "Then go do it, Quen. I want him in the mage's cells here by sunset. If the Society whines, send them to Isha." She listened as Quen's footsteps receded, and waited for the sound of the door as it opened and shut behind him. Only when he was gone did she say, "Do something about Trisana Chandler, Isha. They will be so much less cocky — *Sandrilene* will be far less cocky — without their little weather mage to safeguard them."

Ishabal nodded. "I will see to it," she replied softly. "It is easy enough."

"Subtly." Berenene knew it was insulting to imply that Isha did not know how to wield a proper curse, but she no longer cared. "I want her for our service even more now. When she swears to us, *you* will bind her so she knows who is her mistress, Isha."

It took a while to treat Sandry's hands and feet — she was in such a fury that it was hard to make her sit quietly. Briar had sent Gudruny for mint tea to calm Sandry down, but Sandry threw the cup into the hearth.

Gudruny looked at the mess, her mouth twisted to one side. "You don't need me if you mean to have a child's tantrum, my lady," she said, sounding like the experienced mother that she was. "Wake me when you come to bed and I'll help you with your nightgown. I'll clean up whatever else you throw in the morning."

Briar hid a smile and went back to wrapping clean linen around one of Sandry's feet.

"I am *not* a child," Sandry muttered.

From long experience with his sisters, Rosethorn, and Evvy, Briar knew when to keep silent. Instead, he tried to remember if he had ever known Sandry to be in such a towering rage. Even her anger when pirates had attacked Winding Circle was not the same as this. A lot of it's fear, he thought, drinking the other cup of tea that Gudruny had poured for him. But she's just not used to being treated like she's of no account. I only wish she could see that she's treating her Landreg people the same way, but I can tell it's not worth talking to her about it right now.

Tris had left when Gudruny fixed the tea, but Chime stayed behind, chinking at Sandry with worry. It was Chime who finally calmed Sandry down. The dragon simply curled up in Sandry's lap, chiming in a low, clear tone that penetrated the young noble's rage. The more Chime sang, the slower Sandry's hands petted the dragon, until Sandry finally smiled ruefully.

"I'll be fine," she assured Chime. "Truly." Sandry looked up at Briar. "I don't need nursemaids."

"Then it's me for bed," said Briar with a shrug. "You know

Her Imperial Majesty will put obstacles in the way, right? Neither you nor she knows how to leave well enough alone."

Sandry blew out a windy sigh. "Did I ask you?"

Briar propped a fist on one hip. "Since when do I ever need you or anybody to ask?"

That actually got a thin smile from her. "You're Rosethorn's boy, all right. You sound just like her." She kissed the top of Chime's head. "I really will be fine," she whispered.

Chime voiced one last sweet note, then took flight, shooting through an open window. They didn't have to worry about where she would go: Tris had developed a disconcerting habit of sleeping with all of her windows open.

"Then I'm off, too," Briar told Sandry. "I hope you know what you're doing."

Sandry's voice stopped him with his hand on the latch. "You don't have to come. I can't offer you an empire to garden. And you're still my brother, even if you choose to stay here."

"For your information, *Countess*," he retorted without turning around, "I ain't going 'cause of you." As always when he was truly angry, Briar lapsed into the thieves' cant that was his original language. "I've a mind of my own and I can make it up without you sticking *your* neb in. In case you didn't notice, if someone of rank like you don't have safety here, nobody does. Nobody, from the biggest noble to the smallest street rat. If *you* ain't safe, where does that leave folk like Gudruny, and Zhegorz? I'll tell you where — crated up in a secret chamber somewhere. Or just dumped off a cliff." He slammed the door behind him when he left.

He used the familiar routine of meditation to calm down after he had brushed the dust and dirt from his magic-woven party clothes. Finally he clambered into bed and blew out his candle. Beds on the road won't be so soft as this, but they'll be an ocean's worth of safer, he thought. The night's weariness swamped him, and he slid into sleep.

Armies moved in his dark dreams, killing and burning. The flames of the towns they had set alight formed bright spots on the mountain horizon. This was the rocky hidden road into the heart of Gyongxe. The villages that burned were as much Yanjingyi as Gyongxian.

They're burning out their own people! the dreaming Briar thought in panic. He was small and rabbit-like, fleeing the army as if it were a pack of wild dogs, growling and snapping at his heels. With him stumbled Rosethorn and Evvy and Evvy's friend Luvo, snug in Evvy's arms.

Trumpets blared. In his dreams the armies were always right over the next ridge, moving rapidly. Briar and his companions always seemed to crawl along the ground. Awake he knew they had made better time, but in sleep they were on the army's heels, doomed to warn the inland temples too late. The trumpets blared, the hunter dogs of the armies howled, and Briar tried to run.

He stumbled on the bottom of a heap. One hand pressed against a face, another against a naked leg. Now there was light enough to see what he had found: people, grandparents to babies, all stripped naked, all flung together like discarded dolls. There was blood on his hands.

He screamed and woke at the same time, gasping for breath. As always, he had sweated through his sheets. Sweat stung in his eyes. He got up and wiped away the worst of it with a water-soaked sponge, then changed to casual clothes.

No point in going back to sleep, not when I'll just dream again, he thought as he fumbled with his shirt buttons. Guess I'll gather up all the stuff and the *shakkans* I took from her imperial majesty's greenhouse and carry them back. I don't want her thinking I'd take so much as a pair of shears.

It was hard to open the imperial greenhouse with a miniature willow in one hand and a basket full of tools and seedlings in the other, but Briar managed it. Once inside, he pocketed the paper that acted as a magical key and returned each item to its proper location. On each of the seedlings he set a good word for growth and immunity to plant problems. He also left the copper wire wrapped around the willow's new shape.

I don't have to punish the plants because my mate's cross with her cousin, he told the willow, which he had spelled for health and proper growth when he'd first taken it into his care. Even if I feel curst irritable with the empress myself, I won't let you return to the world without all the protection I can give you.

The willow clung until he coaxed it to release him. You've all kinds of mates here, he scolded gently. You don't need one human who's just going to vanish, anyway. Aren't I right? he asked the others, the pines and the maples, the fruit trees and the flowering ones. The greenhouse sounded as if a breeze had blown through as they shook their branches in reply.

His good-byes said, Briar took the paper key from his pocket and crossed into the orchid half of the greenhouse. He meant to place his key by that door to the outside, so Berenene would see it. Instead, he found the empress herself, wearing a simple, loose brown linen gown over her blouse, slumbering with her head pillowed on her arms as she sat at an orchid table. She blinked and stirred as Briar came in. His heart twisted in his chest. She was beautiful even with her unveiled coppery hair falling from its pins and a sleeve wrinkle pressed into her cheek. She smiled at him.

It's like being smiled at by the sun, Briar thought. Being warmed and a little burned at the same time. No. No, she's Namorn itself, the land folk inhabit. She values the rest of us because we'll water her, plow and plant her, keep the bugs and the funguses off her, harvest . . . but in the end we are as important to her as ants.

She stretched out a hand. "I cannot persuade you?" she asked, her voice husky with sleep. "You know that you would be happy in my service, Briar."

Briar sighed and rubbed his head. Sandry would argue, trying to convince her to change the way she did things. Daja would put on her Trader face, say polite nothings, and mention schedules where she's needed someplace else. Tris would refuse in some tactless way and apologize without pretending she meant it. And me? he asked himself. What can I say? I escaped one emperor that wanted to put me in an iron cage, and from where I sit, her gold one looks no better?

He stepped forward and placed the paper key in her beckoning hand, bowed, and walked away.

16

Daja was tying her braids into a tail when Rizu came back from dressing the empress. Usually Rizu had some witty imperial remarks to share, but not today. This morning she was silent.

"Is something wrong?" Daja asked as she straightened her tunic. "You look, I don't know, concerned." She ran a finger down Rizu's forehead, still amazed at the good luck that had brought her to the point at which she could touch this vivid woman. "You'll get wrinkles," she teased gently.

"It's Her Imperial Majesty," Rizu explained softly. "Something's happened, something that's made her angry. She treated me all right, so it wasn't anything to do with me, but when I asked her what was going on, she said that I ought to ask *your* friends." She looked at Daja in confusion. "What do you suppose she meant?"

Daja shrugged. "Let's go to breakfast and see — if they are even out of bed."

As Rizu led the way out of Daja's rooms, she looked back over her shoulder to say, "I did talk to the servants. Finlach fer Hurich was arrested sometime after we left the ball, and some men he had hired with him."

Daja, who had been admiring the sway of Rizu's hips, halted. "Fin, arrested? Whatever for?"

A footman hurried past overheard. He paused, then came over to them. "There's more, Lady Rizu," he said quietly. "Word just came: *Bidis* Finlach's uncle, *Viynain* Natalos, was just arrested by Quenaill Shieldsman and a crew of mage takers. No law-court papers, only by imperial order."

"Does anyone know *why*?" asked Rizu.

"Only that the charge was high treason," whispered the footman. He bowed and scurried on his way.

"It must be serious," Rizu murmured. "To arrest the head of the Mages' Society for the entire empire? It has to be high treason, indeed." She and Daja and Rizu hurried to Sandry's rooms.

Gudruny let them in, but there was no meal set out on the table. "What's going on?" Daja wanted to know. "Where are Briar and Tris?"

For a moment Gudruny looked shocked. "You don't know? Oh, gods — you must ask my lady. She's in her bedchamber, if you'll follow me."

They obeyed, to find Sandry busily folding clothes. Trunks stood open on the floor.

"Sandry?" Daja asked, confused. "I feel like you started a forging without me."

Sandry looked up. Her face was dead white under its gold spring tan; her blue eyes were hot. "Ask her," she replied in a husky voice, jerking her chin at Rizu, who stood behind Daja. "Or were you two so wrapped up in each other that neither of you has heard yet? It should be all over the palace right now."

Daja sighed. "If she knew, why would we be talking to you?" she inquired reasonably. "Where were you last night? You didn't even come to say hello to us. And now there's a story going around the palace that Fin's been arrested." She kept her voice soft. She knew this look of Sandry's, though she had only ever seen it a handful of times. Whatever had brought Sandry to her boiling point, she required careful handling, or she would explode.

Sandry threw a gauzy overgown to the bed. "Fin crated me up for shipment last night. Crated me up like a, a *cabbage*, only you don't need unraveling spells to keep a cabbage from misbehavior. I got this" — she rubbed her throat — "from screaming for someone to let me out. She had him arrested? I thought she would applaud his boldness. He certainly thought she would, or he never would have dared try."

"Not in her palace!" cried Rizu, shocked. "Not when there are so many women who look to her to keep them safe inside her walls. Sandry, how could you even say such a thing?"

"Because Fin kidnapped me inside these curst walls!"

cried Sandry. She turned on Daja. "I tried to call *you* for help, but you were occupied." There was a cruel tone in Sandry's voice that cut Daja like a whip. "Luckily there are others who don't shut me out of their new lives."

"That's not fair," retorted Daja, her eyes stinging.

"Isn't it?" demanded Sandry, hugging herself around the waist. Her eyes dripped tears onto the discarded overgown. "Maybe not, but it's true all the same. Well, I'm not staying in this oversized cage one night longer. I'm not staying in this festering *kaq* cesspool of a country for so much more as a week. We're going back to Landreg House today. Briar, Tris, and I are going back to Emelan as soon as we can pack up. You do as you like." She glanced at Rizu and looked away. "You may come with us, Daja, and anyone who chooses to accompany you is welcome, but you had best decide fast." She wiped her eyes on her sleeve. "You'll always be my sister-*saati*," she added more softly. "You'll always be welcome in my home, wherever the trade winds take us both. But just remember: They won't care if you prefer women to men if they can still isolate you and force you to sign a marriage contract written to bind a mage." She glared at Rizu. "And since you're a foreigner, Daja, I suppose you wouldn't even have a liege lord to appeal to. You'd be trapped until the end of your days."

Daja heard the door slam. Rizu had left the room.

"She didn't know," Daja said, defending her lover. "You didn't have to be nasty."

"Then I'll apologize later," Sandry replied. "If she comes."

"Of course she will. I suppose she'll take forever to pack," Daja whispered, hoping that if she said it, it would be true. She looked at Sandry. "Would you *please* tell me what happened?" she asked, taking a load of folded scarves from a chair so she could sit down. "And don't insult me anymore, Sandry. I didn't turn Namornese just because I fell in love."

An hour later, Daja slowly walked to Rizu's rooms. She felt as if she had aged a hundred years. Suddenly all of the elegance around her looked like a mask for some cruel beast. She had to eye every man who passed her, asking herself if he had ever kidnapped a woman — or if he would, given the chance. Were all men like this?

No, she told herself firmly. Never Briar. Or Frostpine. Or Tris's teacher Niko, or our sometimes teacher Crane, or Duke Vedris, or Dedicate Gorse, the temple cook. She doubted Ambros or Zhegorz would consider it, either. No, Daja, don't be a fool. You know plenty of men who would never even think of pulling such a vile trick.

But here, well, I can't be surprised at Fin. He's always had the air of a horse fighting the rein. Some of the others I've met might do the same, if they dared to kidnap a mage. But they wouldn't do it in the palace, for fear of the empress. Though somehow Fin thought she might actually turn a blind eye to it, if he succeeded. Who is a bigger idiot than the man who believes the lies he tells himself?

Quen might try such a kidnapping. He'd succeed if he did, but I don't think we have to worry, because he's obviously in love with Berenene. Jak, maybe? No, Jak's too good-hearted at bottom. What a heap of ash this court is, and most of it clinkers at that. I guess Rizu's too close to the empress to have ever looked over her shoulder for kidnappers.

Her heart thudded in her chest. It's trying to drown out that question in my mind. I thought I'd have all summer to work on her before having to ask. I thought we could build something solid in that time, when all we have is something new. I wish we'd had more time to fuse together!

Wishes are toys your mind plays with while pirates sneak up behind. That had been one of her aunt Hulweme's favorite sayings, ghost words from an aunt seven years dead.

Daja shook her head to clear it. I never liked Aunt Hulweme, she thought as she rapped on Rizu's door.

"It's open," she heard her lover call.

Daja bit her lip and entered Rizu's room.

As Mistress of the Wardrobe, Rizu had two of the tiny rooms set aside for those in the empress's service. Only imperial guests actually have room to breathe, she had joked on the ten-odd nights she'd spent in Daja's suite. Now Rizu sat at the desk that took up a corner of the sitting room, writing something. She looked at Daja and tried to greet her with her usual sunny smile. Her lush mouth quivered at the attempt.

Daja looked into the bedroom. It was neatly made up. There were no signs of packing. She went in and sat on the bed, smoothing wrinkles out of the airy coverlet with fingers that shook as much as Rizu's mouth had.

"You could stay." Rizu had come to stand in the doorway. "Stay here, with me. Be a jewel in the imperial crown. All your work with living metal would earn you a place among the great mages. I want you to stay. I *need* you to stay."

"Why won't you come with me?" Daja asked, her voice cracking. For the first time in her life, she understood all the love poetry, all the passion that described a lover's kiss and a lover's touch. I always thought magic had burned that kind of excitement right out of my veins, she thought as she traced an embroidered rose with a fingertip. I always thought that was why boys' kisses left me feeling odd, not faint, and boys' hands didn't make me feel anything but distant. Now I know I wasn't looking at the right people. Now I've found someone who's right for me, and that's her. "How can you feel this way and not want to come with me?" she asked. "Don't you love me?"

"I do," whispered Rizu. "You're so strong, and sweet. You make beautiful things, you sing me songs from distant places. . . . I do love you."

Daja looked up and saw the rest of the answer in her friend's averted eyes and pale lips. "You love the empress more."

"Not the way you mean," Rizu protested. "Not in bed. I would never feel that way about her. But don't you see? She is all that is bright and beautiful in Namorn. She saved me from a marriage I didn't want. She made me a gift of lands and income of my own, so I didn't have to rely on my family — or obey my family's wishes for me." Rizu sat next to Daja and took her metal-gloved hand in both of hers. "I have power in her household. I'm part of something splendid. She builds bridges, hospitals, libraries, dams, you name it and she has built it, for the glory of the empire. How can you not want to belong to that?"

"She does all these things, and yet she lets the empire's women be preyed upon," Daja replied, yanking her hand free.

"I'm not preyed upon," Rizu said. "Not me, not Caidy, not Isha, not any of the women of her household. You would be safe, too, Daja. And we'd be together." She leaned forward and kissed Daja, promising love with the kiss.

Daja got to her feet. "Do you know, I even believe I'd be safe in her household," she told Rizu. "But Sandry isn't. She won't ever be, as long as the empress wants her bound to Namorn. And Sandry is my sister. We are closer than you can begin to imagine — Sandry, Briar, Tris, me. We are the same person in a way you have never heard of."

Rizu looked up, reaching a hand for Daja. "It doesn't have to be settled like this. Persuade Sandry to finish the summer, at least. Then we'll all understand one another better."

I understand well enough, thought Daja. I understand as much as I need to. So I should talk Sandry into staying — if I even could, which I doubt — so that other men may have a chance at binding her to a marriage contract? Biting her lip so she would not cry in front of the *kaqs* who walked the halls, she went back to her bedroom to pack.

The news that Sandry meant to leave for Emelan within the week made Landreg House buzz like an overturned beehive. The servants soon learned that when the normally kind Sandry was this angry, it was best simply to get out of her way. Ambros and Ealaga were made of sterner stuff. Their discussion with her ended in a shouting match that drove Briar out into the rose garden. He had little to pack now that his things from the palace were bundled up. He placed his personal *shakkan* on a stone bench so it could soak up sunlight while not moving and proceeded to give the garden a last inspection.

Ambros found him while he strengthened the roses against parasites. "I had thought she would finally see it is her duty to stay and represent her people," Ambros told Briar without preamble. "To represent them in the Noble Assembly. You must reason with her."

"She's in no mood for reason, or didn't you notice?" Briar asked, viewing one rose's leaves and stems from every angle. "Besides, she's got duties at home, too. Didn't she tell you? She's one of His Grace's two top people. She keeps his castle for him and advises him as he governs the country. If he goes out of Summersea, she stays there in his place. There's rumors he's going to make her his heir. She doesn't believe that one, but I do. His Grace's heir is bleat-brained."

Ambros sat hard next to the *shakkan*. "She never mentioned it."

Briar gently fed the rose a little extra power. "Probably because she doesn't think he'll disinherit Franzen to put her in his place. The rest of it she calls 'just helping Uncle out.' His own *seneschal* gets her signature for plenty of things, rather than pester his grace. But just because she talks it down doesn't mean she doesn't think it's important. She loves Emelan. Maybe she could've loved it here, but there's no chance of that now. Once Sandry hates something, she puts all she's got into it."

Covering his face with his hands, Ambros groaned. "The Landreg women all have this mulish streak," he said, his voice muffled.

"Do you think?" Briar asked a little too innocently. Moving to one of the trees, he called, "This is the last year you'll be getting apples from this old woman. She's tired." He stroked the tree's trunk. "But let her stand, will you? She's got plenty of good years as a tree left."

"I wouldn't dream of cutting her down," Ambros said, dropping his hands. "I've had plenty of good apples from her, and hid out from my relatives in her branches. I only wish you'd had time to go over all our fields at Landreg Castle."

Briar looked at him. "There's no saying I might not come back," he informed the man. "But on *my* terms. Without all this glitter and flash. I'm just a plain lad at heart."

Ambros's grin made him look like a boy for a moment. "Well, plain lad, you're always welcome in my home, wherever I make it."

As soon as they reached Landreg House, Tris abandoned her packed trunks and bags to the care of servants. Saying the briefest hellos to Sandry's cousins and to Zhegorz, she went to her room to lie down. She had expected that playing with storms would give her a sound night's sleep. That was always a treat for a light sleeper like her. Working with the Syth to block up that hidden entry to the palace would have been a guarantee not just of sound sleep, but of late sleep. Doing both, then waking at dawn to pack, left her feeling as if someone had put gravel in her joints and plaster in her skull. She needed to rest for a while, to ease her aching limbs. That took longer than she had expected. It was late afternoon when she opened her eyes.

"Oh, cat dirt," she muttered. She clambered down from the high bed, stripping off her overgown and undergown.

She traded them for a plain blue gown in the Capchen style, then washed her face and hands. At least her braids did not look tatty. The forces she kept in them made each hair cling to the others. It was a side effect that not only looked tidy, but it spared her the need to rebraid her hair every day. Tris hated repeat work.

After smoothing her stockings and putting her shoes back on, Tris went to see if Zhegorz needed help in his packing. There's no telling how far he's gotten, given how easily distracted he is, she thought as she knocked on his door.

There was no answer. Tris knocked again, then consulted with the draft that slid into the hall from his room. "You'd best not be naked," she called through the keyhole, and opened the door.

Zhegorz was fully clothed. He had jammed himself into the corner between his bed and the wall, where he had curled into a knot, his arms locked around his drawn-up knees. Chime clicked anxiously at him from the bed, her clear wings half-outstretched to keep her balanced. Tris looked around with a scowl. Zhegorz's scant belongings were still in the cupboard where he kept them.

"Were you planning to leave everything you own behind?" she asked, her voice tart. "Were you going to count on the wind to keep you warm in the mountains? They get *very* cold this time of year. You're going to need the woollens we got you."

"I'm not going." The man's voice came from inside the

tangle of arms and legs. "*Viymese* Daja told me to go away. If she's leaving and she wants me to go away then I can't come. And she's the one who speaks for me, because the fire is hers. If she goes away and tells me to go away, then I have to stay here."

Tris propped her hands on her hips. "In case you haven't noticed, and it seems you haven't, *I'm* the one who's been looking after you lately — well, Briar and I. *We're* the ones who said you were going to Winding Circle." With dreadful patience she continued: "To go there, you have to leave here. If I have to show you the kind of fire *I* handle, Asaia witness it, you'll be too scared to think. And since you're not doing so well at thinking right now, maybe that's for the best. You forget about Daja's fire and worry about *mine*."

Zhegorz looked up at her, his eyes haggard. "You're confusing me. I only know *Viymese* Daja says I can't be around her. She's going, so I can't."

Tris turned on her heel, ready to do battle. "Gods save me from madmen and their notions," she muttered. "As if my temper hasn't been tried enough lately." She stalked down the gallery to Daja's room and knocked, then turned the doorknob. The door was locked. "Daja!" she cried, letting a wind carry the call through the keyhole so she wouldn't startle the household.

"Go away!" a harsh voice shouted in reply. "I don't want to talk to *anyone*!"

You don't get off that easily, thought Tris.

She went to the bay at the end of the gallery and opened the windows. As far as she could tell, no one on this floor had taken advantage of the narrow terrace that wrapped around the building on this level. Tris knew it was there because she had looked down on it during her time in the house. Now it gave her a second way to get to Daja, one that Tris was irritable enough to use. Whatever mood she's in, she had no right to upset Zhegorz, thought Tris angrily. Daja of all people should know how fragile our crazy man is!

Walking past the long sets of windows that formed doors into the rooms beyond, Tris reached the pair that would open into Daja's room. They were unlocked. She yanked one open and walked into Daja's sitting room. "Daja, I want a word with you!"

A silver goblet flew at her head from the shadows. Tris ducked out of the way. She knew a warning shot when she saw one. Preparing for a flying piece of metal that *would* hit her, she twirled on one foot. The still breezes that were as much a part of her clothing as her shift twirled hard around her and continued to twirl. They made an airy shield that would knock the next missile aside.

Daja's power shone from the bedroom. Determined, Tris went to the door. "If you were just going to be a brute to me, I would have stood for it, because when itch comes right down to scratch, you Traders don't know how to act," she said cruelly. Tris knew from early experience that sharpness spurred Daja harder than kindness. "But you had no right to frighten poor old Zhegorz out of what wits he's got. You're some kind of talisman for him, and when you tell him to go away, he thinks it means he can't travel with us. Now you get off your behind and go tell him you wouldn't *think* of leaving him!"

"Later!" Daja cried. She lay in bed on her belly, raising her face from her pillows to talk. "I'll talk to him later, Tris, and I won't talk to you at all right now, so go away! And insulting my Trader blood won't work, either, you rat-nosed, pinch-coin, gold-grubbing *merchant*."

Tris was about to blister the other girl when she caught the ragged tones in Daja's voice. With a frown she walked over and plumped herself on the bed, reining in her whirling breezes until they were still again. Daja turned her face away from Tris too slowly.

"Oh, dear," Tris said, understanding. Daja's eyes were puffy and wet. Her nose ran. Tris dug out a handkerchief and stuffed it into Daja's hand. When Daja tried to pull the hand away, Tris grabbed her wrist.

Did you really *think she would come?* Tris asked through their magic. *Give up her own place at court, at the empress's side, to live on your generosity? Rizu's proud, Daja. She has every right to be. As Mistress of the Wardrobe she decides what every guardsman and servant in the palace wears. She chooses the imperial wardrobe. What would she have in Summersea compared to all that?*

But I love *her!* cried Daja, accepting the renewed connection between them without a struggle. *I thought she loved me!*

Tris sighed and patted Daja's heaving back. *At least she didn't laugh at you when she found out how you felt,* she remarked. *At least she didn't turn you into a joke for her friends. And she told you something about yourself you really ought to know: that you're beautiful, and worth loving. Even for just a summer.*

All the boys I went with in Summersea after we came back from Kugisko said I was cold, Daja replied wearily. *I didn't like kissing them. It was nothing special, like all the books say love is. Then, when I liked kissing Rizu . . . it was such a blessing. I'm not cold. I was just kissing the wrong people. Even living with Lark and Rosethorn,* I *never thought that maybe I should try kissing girls. None of them drew me. Have you ever . . . ?*

Tris shook her head. *No interest,* she explained. *And the boys don't want to kiss a fat girl like me. They're also scared of me. That doesn't help.*

They sat in silence for a long time, Tris simply rubbing Daja's shoulders. Finally Daja pushed herself up and turned over to sit on the bed. "They made a *joke* of you?" she asked roughly, and blew her nose.

"Twice," Tris answered softly. "After that, I tried not to let boys know when I liked them. One time the boy set up a meeting in a garden. Then he and his friends dumped honey on me. They told me even a gallon of honey wasn't enough sweets to satisfy a tub like me."

"Miserable dung-grubbing *pavao*," whispered Daja. "Did you . . . lose control?"

"I called the rain," replied Tris. "To get the honey off me. All right. To run them off, too. But I've been trying to be good about it. About the weather."

"And the other boy?" asked Daja, getting up to splash water on her face.

"They made fun of him until he came to hate me," Tris said with a shrug. "At least both times we left the towns, eventually." She could feel the heat in her face. If there had been light in here, Daja would have seen her humiliated blush. "I dove into my studies after that and tried not to notice any boys. Most of them just aren't like Briar, you know. He'll drive you to commit murder, but the only part of him that's hidden is the good part. And he isn't nasty to any female, have you noticed? Not to the little farm children or the old grannies who want to tell him how beautiful *they* were in their prime."

"That's because he knows Rosethorn would pull him out by the roots and throw him on the compost heap if he was," Daja said. Both girls looked at each other and giggled softly at the image of Briar thrown out with the rotten leaves of cabbage and the heaps of dead weeds.

When they had quieted, Daja suddenly kissed Tris on the cheek. "I had forgotten that Sandry wasn't my only *saati*," she whispered. "Thank you."

"Don't go telling people," Tris fussed. "I have a reputation to protect." She slid off the bed. "I am sorry about Rizu, Daja."

Daja sniffled, and blew her nose again. "I think it will probably hurt for a while," she said. "I felt so free when I was with her." She shook the wrinkles from her clothes. Obedient as always to Sandry's wishes, the garments went as smooth as if Daja had never lain on them. "I'll talk to Zhegorz. I wish he wouldn't take things so literally, but then, he *is* mad. Isn't he?"

"I think he'll always be somewhat mad, yes," Tris replied, following her down the gallery. "But he's somewhat on the mend."

They were all sitting down to a strained dinner when Zhegorz sat bolt upright. "A man with a blade," he said, eyes wide. "In the house!"

Briar and the girls scrambled to their feet as a footman darted in from the kitchen, panic in his eyes. "My lady, my lord, he came through the servants' gate," he cried. "Forgive me, but the guard just stepped away!" There was a sword at his back, with Jak gripping the hilt. Briar readied his magic, as did his sisters; from the corner of his eye Briar saw Zhegorz grab a silver pitcher for use as a weapon.

"You *dare*," cried Sandry. "You —"

Jak sheathed the sword and raised his hands. "I'm sorry,

but I had to see you, and it's not like you're opening the door to callers," he said, his eyes on Sandry. "I just wanted you to know I had no part in what Fin did. I'll have no part in anything else of the kind. I swear it by Vrohain the Judge, may he cut off my hands if I lie."

They all watched him for a moment. Then the tension in the room eased. Briar sat down and applied himself to his meal once more. If Jak wasn't a threat, Briar wasn't about to let his food get cold.

"Why?" Sandry demanded, quivering as if she might yet flee him. "Why do *you* have such a distaste for it, when so many other men do not?"

Ambros cleared his throat. "You judge us all by the actions of a few, Cousin."

Sandry made a face. "I'm sorry, Ambros," she apologized, her voice still raspy. "I'm overwrought, I suppose."

Ealaga sighed. "Really, my dear husband, for a man who is so clever, you can be so shortsighted," she said with unhappy patience. "What else is she supposed to do, when any unmarried woman of western Namorn must live her life and judge all men by those few who have successfully stolen women away? Each time a man succeeds, we place our daughters and our sisters under new safeguards. We put their lives under new restrictions. We give them new signs that a man in whose company they find themselves *might* plan to kidnap them. Don't we teach our women to view all men according to the actions of a few?"

Ambros stared at his wife, speechless.

Ouch, thought Briar, finishing his sturgeon. That's got him where he sits. I wonder if it will make him a little more angry about this precious custom he's lived with?

Ealaga beckoned to a maid and the footman who had announced Jak, and murmured instructions. The maid hurried from the room; the footman brought a chair from against the wall and set it at the table between Ambros and Daja. "And I'm one of the ones who gets to live with what those few have done." Jak looked at Ealaga. "You remember, don't you? My mother's best friend?"

Briar saw a shadow cross Ealaga's face. "I certainly do. She killed herself rather than live with the man who stole her."

Jak looked at Sandry and shrugged. "My mother told me the story all my life. She made me swear never to insult a good woman in such a way, and to protect any women in my care who were trapped in that situation. You're a lovely girl, Sandry, even if you *aren't* exactly broken to bridle —"

Briar choked on a mouthful, thinking, Someone else isn't falling all over her *Clehame*ness! Sandry glared at him.

"But I won't break my vow to my mother," Jak continued, "not for all the fortune in the world. You can't judge all Namorn by the imperial court, Sandry. I feel like you haven't given us a chance."

Sandry looked down at her lap. For a very long moment she said nothing. Finally she replied softly, "Probably I haven't. But as long as I am who I am, I don't think your court will give me a chance, either."

Makes sense, Briar thought. And she's got a point. They all wanted to be her friend without even knowing who she is.

Daja inched her chair over, leaving room for Jak to take the empty seat as the maid returned with place settings so he could join them for their meal. As the footman filled Jak's wine glass, the young nobleman looked at Sandry. "This is also me saying good-bye for a while. I'm in disgrace with Her Imperial Majesty, so I'm on my way back to my family's lands."

Ealaga gasped. Briar grinned. Somehow, he wasn't surprised. I bet he was supposed to try grabbing Sandry if she wouldn't say yes to a normal proposal, he thought. "You've been a bad lad?" he asked.

Jak grinned. "Until one of her hunting dogs takes sick again, or one of her old great-aunts descends on the palace for a visit. *Then* she'll remember I have my uses." He winked at Sandry. "I'm very good with crotchety ladies, old and young."

Sandry sat bolt upright, glaring at him, then seemed to remember where she had left her sense of humor. She began to giggle.

"Oh, good," said Jak, applying himself with gusto to his veal with caviar. "I was afraid that pinecone you've been sitting on so righteously was dug in permanently."

"Jak!" cried Ealaga, shocked. Ambros and Daja groaned. Tris shook her head over this unexpected side to the nobleman, while Briar cackled wickedly. Glancing at Sandry, he thought to her, *Nice to see someone who will say what he thinks straight out.*

She made a rude gesture in reply.

You never learned that from the duke, Briar told her. *You learned that one from* me. "I'll have to remember that pinecone," he said to Jak. "Every time she loses it, you think life is safe, and then she finds it again."

Sandry threw a roll at him and looked at Jak. "You've never been like this before," she accused.

Jak cut another bite of veal. "See, I'm off my leash. I don't have to worry about pleasing you *or* the empress."

"So why don't you leave?" asked Briar, curious. "If it's that much of a pain?"

"Because I like being useful," Jak replied. "Don't you?"

The evening took a lighter turn after that. They lingered at the table, talking long after the last crumbs of their fruit and cheese were gone. Then they went to the sitting room to play games, tell stories, and nibble on cakes for tea. Even Daja stayed and seemed at least to be happy for something to take her mind off Rizu. At last Jak said good-bye in the front hallway and went on his way.

Sandry sighed as the door closed behind him. "I'm sorry I didn't get to know him better now," she told the rest of them. "Maybe I would have liked him enough to stay — but

I couldn't. Not and leave Uncle without someone to look after him properly."

"We're hardly going to talk you out of that," Briar said. "We all like the old man. And he doesn't play games with his people."

"It sounds wonderful," Ealaga told them wistfully. "But Her Imperial Majesty really has done so much good for the empire."

"And she's done it without me," Sandry replied. "As soon as I'm gone, she can get back to her real work. She'll hardly know I'm gone."

Tris thought that Berenene would remember Sandry for quite some time, but she also thought that another yawn like the one that had just overtaken her might split her jaws apart. "I'm for bed," she said drowsily. "Good night, everyone."

She climbed up the staircase, Chime flying in loose circles over her head. It was time for the nightly battle she always fought when she shared sleeping quarters with Chime. Who knew so much space could be taken up by a small glass dragon? she asked herself for the thousandth time. She just sprawls somehow, and manages to fill any bed or bedroll I want to sleep in. . . .

Just before she reached the top step, Tris felt something, though she could not be sure what it was. A cold pocket of air? she wondered. *Slimy* cold air, if there's such a thing?

It was her last coherent thought before her foot slipped.

Tris fought to turn and fall the way her teachers in hand-to-hand combat had taught her, but some other force yanked both of her feet high in the air. She did not simply fall. With Chime's screams like scraped crystal in her ears, Tris cartwheeled and bounced down the long stair, hitting every hard step with what felt like a different part of her body.

17

While servants ran for the best healer in the district, Sandry requested, and got, a heavy sheet of canvas. She spread it out next to Tris, struggling not to look at her sister's contorted body. *I'll just cry if I do, and if I cry, I'm no good to anyone,* she told herself, smoothing the canvas over and over. She looked around. "Briar?" she asked, her voice still rasping.

"Right here." He had come to stand on Tris's other side, knowing without asking what she needed from him. Together, using their power as carefully as they had ever done, Sandry and Briar worked with the hemp cloth, wriggling it very carefully under the unconscious Tris. All of their concentration was on getting the cloth in place without causing her more pain. By the time it was under her, the healer and her two assistants had come. The woman nodded in approval of their work, then stepped back. The assistants let their magic flow out to grip the makeshift stretcher. Gently they raised it and floated Tris upstairs.

Sandry trotted after them. "She's a mage, she's a mage with weather, her hair is her mage kit," she explained breathlessly, frightened for Tris. "Chime, go to Briar, you can't help her. Chime, I mean it! Don't make me use magic on you!" When Chime reluctantly changed course and flew back downstairs to Briar, Sandry babbled on: "Please, whatever you do, *Viymeses, Viynain*, don't undo Tris's braids or you'll release something. I think they're spelled so only she can untie them —"

They had gone into Tris's room. Now the healer turned back, her finger to her lips. "We will tend to her. Thank you for the information about her power, and her braids. Now let us do our work." She closed the door in Sandry's face.

Briar and Daja came up the stairs at a slower pace, Briar with Chime on his shoulder. Once the door was closed, the only signs of life inside came when the assistants popped in and out with requests for hot water, cloths, tea, and the like. Sandry, Daja, and Briar sat on the floor out of the assistants' way, Sandry with Chime in her lap, Daja and Briar leaning against each other.

Ambros and Ealaga had stayed below to settle the household and to bring in a mage to see what had made Tris fall so spectacularly. When they finally came upstairs, Ealaga ordered a footman to bring chairs for everyone. She and Ambros took their own seats, waiting for news, while the three young mages lurched to their feet to sit in a more dignified way.

After half an hour's silence, Briar announced, "We can see magic, you know. There was no need to call an outsider in. There wasn't a spell on the steps."

"Have you studied curses?" Ambros asked quietly.

"Just the usual stuff, no specialization," whispered Daja. "They're disgusting."

"Yes, but some people here use them." Ealaga said. "A very few are so good that they can place a curse in a hidden place, where even those who see magic won't see it. There it remains until it's called to life. Then it will seek out its target." She looked at her hands. "Ishabal Ladyhammer is said — in whispers, you understand — to be able to wield curses without detection. Subtle curses. Ones that seem like accidents."

"But then every time there is a household accident, people could well think they had drawn the wrath of the empress," protested Sandry. "You would follow that road to madness!"

"Or to very well-behaved citizens," Daja murmured.

"It was an *accident*," Sandry insisted, her face white. Did I bring this on Tris? she asked herself. Is she hurt now because I couldn't be a good girl and simply wait out the summer to go home?

"When I fall on stairs, I land on my knees or my back or my side," Briar said hesitantly. "If I'm on my side: I roll, if I'm on my back, I slide. On my knees sometimes, I slide down a little." Briar traced a vine on the back of one hand, his voice muffled. "I never cartwheeled. I never bounced. She couldn't even grab hold of the rails — did you see? But she was taught how to fall, same as the rest of us. She can twirl a mean staff, she can kick a fellow's" — he looked at Ealaga and changed what he was about to say — "teeth up between his ears, and she can fall properly, so she doesn't hit anything important. So she can stop herself and get back on her feet. Except here she just kept going."

"They hope if she stays behind, they can persuade her that her interests are better served in Namorn?" suggested Ambros. "What she can do — it is so very overwhelming. To manipulate the weather itself . . ."

"But if this is a curse from Ishabal, and Tris finds out, I wouldn't want to be in her shoes," pointed out Daja. "Trader log it, I wouldn't want to be *near* her. Tris certainly won't be hoping to work for the crown!"

Sandry nibbled her thumbnail, considering what Ambros had said. "She's the most fearsome of us, on the surface of things," she commented slowly. "What if they just didn't want her going with us?"

Briar shrugged. "Easiest solved. We don't leave without her."

Sandry agreed, but her skin crept at the same time. Tris's injuries weren't as simple as a broken leg. Even with a good healer, she would need time — weeks — to recover. How many things could go wrong if they stayed on here for weeks?

The clock had struck two and Daja was drowsing when the bedroom door opened. The healer emerged. She was sweaty and shaky. Her hair straggled out from under the cloth scarf that covered her head. One of her assistants had to help her to stay on her feet; the other carried her medicines.

The healer looks like she battled Hakkoi the Smith God and lost, thought Sandry, rising to her feet. Everyone else stood to see what the woman had to say.

"The last time I treated anyone so badly off, he'd fallen thirty feet down a cliff, and he died." The healer's voice was an exhausted croak. "Your friend won't die. Miraculously, she has five broken ribs, and none of them punctured her lungs. None of the broken bones cut through the skin, a blessing I never looked to get."

"A very well-crafted curse," muttered Ambros.

Ealaga glared at him. "How bad is Tris?" she asked.

The healer had looked at Ambros when he said "curse." "Ah," she murmured. "Things become clearer. It explains much." She sighed.

Sandry beckoned to the assistant who held the woman upright and pointed to her chair. Getting the hint, the young man carefully lowered the healer to the seat. Ealaga whispered to the maid who had stayed up in case anyone needed anything. The girl scampered off.

"Your girl has no punctured organs or skin. She has a broken collarbone, a dislocated shoulder, two small cracks in her skull, a broken cheekbone, one arm broken in two places, a broken wrist, five broken ribs, a dislocated hip, three breaks in her right leg, and a broken ankle on the left. She also has several broken fingers and toes," the healer said once she'd caught her breath. "It is a miracle, or, if it is a curse, as you say, then it was deliberately constructed to save the girl's life. There is only one curse-weaver in the empire with that level of skill, and that is all I will say on that topic."

Sandry, Briar, and Daja exchanged horrified looks. They had all seen their fair share of injuries and healing. Never had they seen anyone who had endured the mauling Tris had.

I'm going to be sick, thought Sandry. She bit the inside of her cheek and forbade her stomach to misbehave.

"I did what I could tonight," the healer continued. "She has been very well taught — I was able to work inside her power and around it with very little difficulty indeed. It's always delightful to handle a mage who has been trained by good healers in the art of keeping power controlled. The hip and shoulder are back in their sockets. I was able to heal the ribs and skull completely — they are the most dangerous breaks. She is fortunate that she had no blood collecting inside her skull. I started the healing of the collarbone and jaw, and braced the broken limbs. I have safeguarded her for infection and shock. Tomorrow, when I come, I will bring two colleagues who will help to undo what healing has been done tonight on those breaks I was unable to look after, and begin clean healing for the rest of the broken bones."

"Begin?" Ambros asked with a frown. Briar was nodding.

"This is not as simple a matter as a single broken arm or leg, good *Saghad*," the healer's male assistant replied at his most polite. "The more injuries the victim endures, the more time is needed for healing. If the healers do not take care, the repair will be weak and the bone will break again. Or scarring will take place and will put the patient's entire body at risk."

The senior healer nodded.

"But we were planning to leave for Emelan soon," Sandry heard herself say.

"My dear *Viymese*, forgive me," said Ambros as the maid arrived with tea for everyone. She served the healer first as Ambros continued, "This is my cousin, Sandrilene, *Clehame* fa Landreg, who is also *Saghada* fa Toren in Emelan. These are *Viymese* Daja Kisubo and *Viynain* Briar Moss. Your patient in there is *Viymese* Trisana Chandler."

"Clehame." The healer bowed her head, but did not try to get to her feet. She impatiently waved away an offer of cakes from the maid. "The girl — Tris? — she tried to tell me she was leaving soon as well. I let her know she won't be leaving that bed for at least a week — more, if she tasks herself."

Sandry firmed her lips, which tried to tremble and make her look like a pouting child. "As my sister, she will have the finest care money can buy," she informed the healer.

"Hmph," replied the woman. "Not much family resemblance. But it is as I have told you. She asks to see the three of you. She will not take the sleeping medicine until she sees you, so please, attend to her immediately, so she will sleep."

Chastened, the three young mages filed into Tris's room, Chime riding on Daja's shoulder. Once inside, they all stopped to stare. One of Tris's arms and one of her legs was bound to slats and covered in tightly wrapped bandages. Splintered fingers and toes had their own wooden supports secured with white linen. All of her braids hung loose. The lingering tracks of the healer's magic were evident on Tris's skull and body. None of them had ever seen anyone so badly hurt that they weren't on their feet in a few days, given a good healer.

Tris looked naked without her spectacles, which had been smashed in her fall. Sandry went to Tris's writing box and took out one of the spare pairs of spectacles that lay with the pens and ink sticks. Carefully she settled them on Tris's nose, taking care to touch none of the bruises on Tris's face. "At least your nose wasn't broken," she whispered.

Tris raised the unbroken arm and laid her splinted hand on Sandry's. Her magical voice, while exhausted, was not as faint as her battered form might lead them to expect. *Don't put off leaving for me,* she told them, her magical voice reaching Briar and Daja as well. *You meant to go day after tomorrow — go. Don't risk getting stuck here.*

We're not leaving you, Sandry retorted, her chin sticking out. *Don't be ridiculous.*

Don't you *be ridiculous!* Tris snapped in reply, her thought-voice as stern and forceful as pain and drugs would allow. *I can catch up once I'm able to ride. I move faster alone than you will in a group. And when I go, I'll have cooked up a shield that will return any ill wishes and curses to the sender, whether I see them coming or not. But the longer you put off going, the more they'll be able to put in your way. Right now they seem to think* I'm *the biggest threat. They have no idea how dangerous you all are. That will help you. Take Zhegorz and Gudruny and the children and go, now.*

"I don't want to say it," Briar said aloud, "but she makes sense."

"I hate it when she does that," added Daja.

Sandry glared at them. Apparently Daja and Briar had yet to reopen their connection to each other, though obviously they had renewed their ties to Tris and Sandry.

This is no time for jokes! she shouted.

"Oh, there's *always* time for jokes," Briar replied with his sweetest smile.

The healer's male assistant opened the door. "She says to come out." He walked over to the bed and picked up a cup of dark liquid. "And she says *you* will drink this."

"Go home," croaked Tris. "I'll catch up as soon as I can."

"We'll do it," Briar assured Tris. He leaned down and

kissed her unbruised forehead. "You've got a good plan there. Get better."

"I'll be happy to leave as soon as possible, Rizu or no," Daja added, kissing the top of Tris's head carefully. "Don't mind Sandry. She only goes on Her Nobleness when she's frightened." She followed Briar out of the room.

Tris looked at Sandry. The healer cleared his throat.

"I feel like I'm deserting you," Sandry explained, looking at the floor.

"Try feeling like you're using common sense," Tris suggested quietly. "That's what I do when I'm doing what I think is right." She swallowed the medicine. The healer set the cup aside and steered Sandry out of the room, closing the door behind them. A last look at Tris showed Sandry that her eyelids were shut. She was already asleep.

The 23rd – 26th days of Rose Moon, 1043 K.F.
Landreg House
Dancruan, Namorn

Sandry lowered the lid on her last trunk and locked it, then nodded permission for the footman to take it away. She wondered if she ought to look in on Tris one last time. Tris had barely woken for two days, steeped in the spells of three healers. Sandry, Briar, and Daja had already said their good-byes to her around midday. Somehow Sandry doubted Tris would be up at dawn to wave good-bye to their small caravan of three mages, Gudruny and her children, Zhegorz, and the ten men-at-arms Ambros had detailed to escort her to the border.

Sandry looked at Ambros, who sat in her window seat reading an account book. "I wish you wouldn't send those ten guards with me," she told her cousin. "You need them back home and we'll move faster without them."

"It would look shabby if we sent you off without," Ambros said in his dry way. "I will not let it be said that I failed in my duty to you."

Sandry shook her head and took a folio of advocate's papers from the bed. She gave it to Ambros. "They're properly witnessed and sealed. The advocate filed copies with the clerks of the Court of Law here and for Landreg district. It's what I said I'd do. You'll never have to send me a set allowance every year again. Before you send a coin to me, you'll see to any repairs and improvements on the estate."

"The empress will still tax me. I'm not the landholder, so I cannot contest the taxation in court. And I won't be able to free other brides like Gudruny, because I am not her liege lord," Ambros pointed out.

"Do as the advocate suggests in there" — Sandry pointed to the folio — "and double-list all the unmarried women of my estates on your own lands, so *you* can declare yourself their liege lord. He says it should withstand a challenge in a court of law. It's expensive, but you can take the money from what you would send to me for that purpose, with my blessing." Sandry twisted her handkerchief. "Cousin, if I put off my escape, sooner or later the empress will find a way to keep me here. I can't allow that. I have duties in Emelan, as she well knows. I've told her I will not stay. I will not give way to that famous imperial will. Uncle needs me, and you are a far better landlord than I could be. Can't we just leave it at that?"

Ambros was about to reply when a maid rapped on the open door. "Forgive me, *Clehame, Saghad*, but a man has come to call on the *clehame.* He says to tell her only that it is Shan."

"*He* plays a risky game," Ambros murmured as he stood to go.

Sandry got to her feet, shaking out her skirt. "I will see him in the small sitting room," she ordered. As the maid went off to do as she was told, Sandry went into the dressing room to inspect her appearance. Her gowns were an arrangement of two shades of blue that made her eyes brighter. She tucked a strand of hair away and pinned a sheer white veil over her head, then bit her lips gently to make them look redder.

I don't know why I'm doing this, she thought. After the way he's lied to me. Making me think . . . well! I'll at least give him a piece of my mind!

Shan stood by the window when she came in at a

bustling pace, her chin up, her hands folded in front of her. When he turned and bowed she caught herself admiring his broad shoulders and warming to his kind smile. Stop that! she ordered herself. He's played you like a fish on the line — start acting less, less *damp*!

"Sandry, they told me you're leaving." Two steps brought Shan up to her. Before she realized his intentions, he wrapped his strong arms around her and kissed her, slowly and sweetly. When she tried to pull away, he simply deepened his kiss. Finally, when they were both breathless, he drew back to whisper, "Don't go. Stay here. Marry me. You like me, you know you do. I think I would make a wonderfully amusing husband."

That brought her to her senses. When he moved in for another kiss, she got her hands up to his broad chest and shoved. It was like trying to push a marble statue.

The bang of wood on wood outside reminded her that servants were stowing their luggage for their departure tomorrow. Shan held her tighter and ran his lips over her ear. Sandry gasped, her treacherous knees going weak, then ordered his clothes to move away from her.

Shan could hardly fight his own clothing as it dragged him back. He clung to Sandry until she summoned a cushioned chair. Since the cushions were firmly nailed to the seat, the entire chair slammed into Shan's knees. He yelped and let go of her. His clothes yanked him down onto the chair and wove themselves into the cushions.

"Don't try to get up," she warned, her voice trembling. "If you do, I swear it by Shurri, you will go home with a chair as part of your breeches. You'll be the laughingstock of all Dancruan, *and* your precious court."

He stared at her as if she had lost her wits. "What is going on?" he wanted to know. "You like me!" He smirked. "And I know you like kissing me."

"Kissing isn't all there is to life," Sandry retorted, repeating something her uncle's mistress had once said. "I *did* like you — before I found out what a two-faced liar you are! You sneak around to see me because you have all you can handle at night, in Berenene's chambers!"

Shan shook his head. "That has nothing to do with you and me, Sandry. Yes, I'm her lover, but it's not like I really have a choice. She holds my purse strings."

"I'd say that's not all she holds," Sandry snapped, blushing for her own vulgarity.

"And I repeat, that has nothing to do with you or me, or our getting married. Once we're married, I'll be yours completely. I'll be a faithful husband, and a good father," he said, reaching out to her. "We can make a wonderful life together."

"You'll have more than that," said Ambros. The door was open a crack. Now Ambros opened it all the way to come in. Meticulous as always, he closed it behind him. "Did Pershan ever mention that the Roths were the second most powerful family in the empire, until his father and uncles gambled most of the estate away?" Ambros inquired, testing the cushion of a chair as if to make sure it would not attack him. "They have fifty acres where once they had twenty thousand. From twenty seats in the Noble Assembly, they have one." He sat gingerly and continued: "I think Pershan came to court thinking that he could woo the empress into marrying him. It might even have worked — his family is so reduced, he presents no threat to the lords who might reject a more powerful man as Imperial Consort. If she had set that marriage before them, they might well have approved it." Ambros looked at the captive, ice in his pale blue eyes. "But he knows Her Imperial Majesty better now, don't you, Shan? She means it when she says she will not share power. When she tires of him, he returns to being nothing, instead of a man who wields influence over her. And she will tire of him. Quenaill can vouch for that."

Ambros turned his gaze to Sandry as she sank down in a chair. "But you come along. If you cared to, you could wield real power in the empire. You are a kinswoman of the imperial house, vastly wealthy in your own right, with plenty of rich farmland, tenants, mines, fishing grounds, and forests as your inheritance. Married to you, Pershan fer Roth would be a great noble. He would no longer fear the day when the imperial smile vanishes. Even Berenene would have to treat him with respect."

"Sandry, why do you even listen to this dried-up bookkeeper?" Shan begged. "Love isn't a requirement for marriages in our class, but I know we would come to love each other. You're so beautiful, you're charming, you're intelligent, you have a sense of humor — how could I not love you? I would treat you with the respect and affection you deserve. And any man who offended you would be my enemy. Moreover, I'll wager your mage friends would stay if you did. Rizu would be overjoyed if Daja changed her mind —"

Sandry held up a hand to stem the flood of persuasion. When he shut up, she asked, "Did you tell her?"

"What?" asked Shan, baffled.

"Did you tell Berenene you were going to ask me to marry you?"

"Her Imperial Majesty? No. I didn't want to come back to her in shame if you refused me."

"Did you tell anyone?" Sandry asked. "Any of your friends at court?"

"Of course not. You know how they laugh at failure —"

"Is it their laughter you fear? Or the chance they might tell Berenene what you're up to?" Sandry got to her feet, unweaving his bonds to the chair under him. "You're so afraid of her, you sneak behind her back to even talk to me. I bet the next thing on your list was suggesting a nice, *private* wedding. Intimate, just a few friends, no fuss — maybe out in the country?"

"Assuredly out in the country," murmured Ambros.

"And then we get to the business of baby-making, and return once I'd begun to show. Because you'd want to come back to Berenene only after there's absolutely no way she can break the marriage without looking foolish. This is about her, not me. You want to throw it in her face that you could be politically powerful without her."

"Sandry, you're taking this all wrong," protested Shan.

"Get out," she said coolly. "Go on, stand up." Carefully Shan stood, and dusted his backside. Sandry continued in an even tone, "When and if I marry, it will be to an honest man. Please go now, before I lose my temper."

"My dear, think this over," Shan said. "We could truly be happy together."

"My temper is fraying, and so are your clothes," she replied evenly. "Good-bye, Pershan fer Roth."

Ambros opened the door. Shan risked a last look at Sandry, then fled. Ambros closed the door. "Will his clothes really come off?" he asked. He saw that Sandry was silently weeping. Walking over, he held her as he would one of his daughters. "He was unworthy of you, Cousin."

"I just hate being made a fool of," she explained.

"Love makes fools of us all, and desire does far worse," Ambros explained. "Forget him. You deserve better, and you will find it."

Sandry hugged him tightly, then pulled away, searching for her handkerchief. She blew her nose and said mournfully, "But he probably won't be as handsome."

Ambros chuckled. "He will be if you love him. Come along to supper. You'll feel better for some beet soup."

* * *

Tris stirred. It was near midnight. She remembered saying farewells to her friends earlier, though the spells and drugs the healers used to keep her still made her memory a bit fuzzy on exactly when. She knew she was not alone. There was a maid stitching by lamplight in one corner. From the way she jerked her thread through the cloth, she was angry. From the frequent glares she cast at the corner to the left, the cause was the person who huddled there.

"Zhegorz," croaked Tris.

The man sat up. The maid put her sewing down and came to Tris's side. "*Viymese,* I'm sorry, but he wouldn't go away. *Viymese* Daja said to leave him be, but he's been here for an hour at least —"

"Thank you," Tris said, her voice still rough. "I needed to talk to him. I would like some cold water, if you don't mind."

The maid leaned down and whispered, "Are you certain? He is so very *odd.*"

A smile struggled on Tris's battered face. "So am I. It's all right."

The maid left them, muttering. Zhegorz inched closer to the bed. "I was thinking," he explained. "I ought to stay here. I'll travel with you. They don't need me, not even *Viymese* Daja —"

"*Pavao,*" Tris said rudely if softly. "They're *going* to need you, heading south."

"Need me." For a moment, Zhegorz's voice was so dry

that he might well have been completely sane. "They need *me*? *Viymese* Tris, it's clear the healers must take the magic off you. You're starting to imagine things."

"They need someone who can see and hear things on the wind," Tris said. "I won't be there to do that for them. That leaves you. You can warn them of danger they don't expect."

"But I can't control it," Zhegorz protested. "It comes and it goes!"

"You can control it more than you did," Tris reminded him. "You have your ear beads and your spectacles. Any little bit of warning will help them. Please, Zhegorz."

He shook his head.

Tris sighed. "Zhegorz, you're a mage. What's the point of being a mage if you don't do something useful with your magic? Something most people can't do for themselves?"

He stared at her, nonplussed. Tris met his eyes firmly.

Finally he mumbled, "I'm fit to work as a mage?"

Tris smiled and winced. "More fit than I am," she reminded him. "Come on, old man. It's time to go to work. Keep doing your exercises, mind. If you have questions, Daja or Briar or Sandry can send them on to me. May I count on you?"

He hung his head, trembling. "No one's ever counted on me before, except to be crazy."

Tris's eyelids were fluttering. "Then this will be a new

experience. That's a good thing." Her eyes closed. From her slow, deep breathing, she was asleep already.

Zhegorz gently patted her unsplinted arm. "I hope I don't let you down," he whispered.

Sandry, Briar, and Daja said their good-byes in the predawn light, though not to Tris, who was still sleeping under the healer's spells. They had seen her during one of her brief waking periods before they had gone to bed, and they could always speak with her from the road. They would be close enough still. Only separations of thousands of miles, as in previous years, could cut their ability to speak together.

As they rode through the city gates, Sandry straightened in the saddle. Watching her, Briar thought, It's like having thick walls between her and the empress sets her free. Through their bond he said, *She's got a thousand tricks, and she hasn't played one of them yet. Don't get to feeling* too *comfortable.*

She turned and wrinkled her nose as if she had smelled something bad. "As if I would!"

The sergeant in command of the Landreg men-at-arms looked at her. "*Clehame*, at the hostel near the inn where we stop tonight, there will be merchant caravans. Some of them will be going south. If we might join one . . . ?"

Sandry shook her head. "A caravan is slower. Stop fussing, please. We can move faster and take care of ourselves as a small party. And we number three mages among us. Four, if you count poor old Zhegorz."

"'Poor old Zhegorz' sure isn't himself today," murmured Briar. Zhegorz, to everyone's surprise, had requested a horse. It wasn't hard to see exactly how much experience as a rider he possessed. His mount insisted on wandering sidelong over the road each time he tugged the reins. Now he rode up beside Briar, a scarecrow in strange, brass-lensed spectacles, on a blue roan gelding that could tell his rider was uncertain. The madman's insistence on riding in the front was also unusual, particularly when Briar could see it made Zhegorz nervous.

"Are you sure you wouldn't prefer keeping to the rear?" asked Briar, jerking his head toward the luggage cart, where Gudruny talked to the driver and her children hung out the sides. "That way you're not all out in the open."

Zhegorz gulped visibly. "I promised *Viymese* Tris I would look out for you. That's what I'm going to do. I'm working as a mage."

Briar rolled his eyes at Daja, who smothered a giggle. Chime makes as good a mage, and she isn't half-cracked besides, thought Briar. Oh, well. Zhegorz will get tired of this soon enough. He's jumpier 'n a flea on a hot griddle.

What was Tris thinking, anyway? he asked Sandry, who was close enough to hear Zhegorz. *What does he mean, "working as a mage"?*

Maybe she just told him that so he'd have something to do,

Sandry replied. *Remember yesterday he wasn't going to come at all? I'll wager he talked to her. She must have known he'd come along if he thought he could help out.*

Remind me to thank her, Briar said wryly.

Zhegorz turned his face into the wind. "Sheep up ahead," he said to no one and everyone. "Lots of them. And rain tonight."

18

The 27th day of Rose Moon—the 2nd day of Mead, 1043 K.F.
The Imperial Palace
Dancruan, Namorn

The next morning Ishabal Ladyhammer woke before dawn, as was her long habit. She rose and dressed, then went to see if anything important had come to her desk during the night. Entering the rooms where she did her work as the empire's chief mage, she was pleased to find that no one was there. Even Quen, who had been keeping long hours since Berenene had set him aside, was absent.

A rare gift, this silence, she thought, passing through the waiting room to her personal office. *A chance to create a plan for the control of Trisana Chandler, before I see Berenene.*

A folded and sealed letter was on her desk. She picked it up: the seal was Quen's. She cracked it open and read.

> *Dearest Isha, when I got to my room last night, I found a letter from my mother. My father is ill and is asking for me. Please forgive me. Make my apologies to her imperial majesty. I hope to return within a couple of weeks. — Q*

Ishabal folded the letter with a frown. It is unlike Quen to abandon Berenene without saying his own good-byes, she thought. And it is doubly so now. He has to have heard the rumors that Berenene is vexed with Shan. Even if his father's illness is real, Quen would want to take leave of Berenene himself, to impress her with his devotion to her and to his family.

She stared at a branch of candles without seeing it. Quen, dear boy, please do nothing you will regret.

Berenene was irritable as she ate breakfast that same morning. She had been irritable ever since Fin's attempted kidnapping revealed a severe flaw in her control over her courtiers. In the stack of notes beside her plate were a number of politely worded expressions of concern from the parents of many young women who feared for their daughters. The brave ones actually spoke to me, annoying leeches, she thought irritably. Vexing me. *Doubting* me.

She glanced at another stack of notes. These were more serious. They had come from Dancruan's mages, who wished to know why their leader had been arrested. It won't be long before the Mages' Societies throughout Namorn start writing to ask the same questions, she thought. They'll be harder to placate than parents who wish their daughters to make good marriages. No matter. These mages will learn better than to question my will. Ishabal has put quite a few tricks away against a time they might think they can defy me. If necessary, they'll all find themselves sharing cage space with *Viynain* Natalos, and they can rot with him as far as I'm concerned. They'll learn to respect the crown if I have to repopulate every Mage Society in the empire!

And I blame Sandrilene, unfair though that is. If the girl had simply done her duty, none of these annoyances would be on my plate now. She must be brought to an understanding of her place in my scheme of things. Thus far I've shown her the orchids, thought Berenene, throwing down her napkin. It's time she found the thorns.

She stood abruptly, startling her attendants. "Hunting will settle me," she announced. "Send for Shan. Tell the huntsmen I'll look for hares for supper."

She was half-dressed in riding gear when one of her ladies came in from the outer rooms. The girl had that timid look that Berenene loathed. I'll be so glad when Rizu feels she is her old cheerful self and can take up her tasks again, Berenene told herself mournfully. Rizu knows how to keep these silly girls from annoying me. If I could get her Daja back, I would have her company in the mornings again sooner, rather than later.

"Imperial Majesty," the young lady began, half-shrinking.

Berenene glared at her. "Stand up straight. I want ladies-in-waiting, not mice!" she snapped. "What is it?"

The lady shrank even more. "The, the huntsmen say Pershan fer Roth got word of a white stag seen in the Hobin

Forest. He left this morning at dawn to confirm its existence before your Imperial Majesty went to the expense of a hunt for it. Huntsmaster Pershan left word that his assistant would take your orders."

Berenene gripped a handkerchief and twisted it. Shan didn't ask my permission, she thought angrily. If he thinks he may punish me for not welcoming him to my chamber lately, he will soon learn otherwise. But what if this report of a white stag is true? Perhaps Shan believes finding it is the way to return to my good graces.

A week ago, would he still have dared leave without permission?

Berenene flapped a hand at the shrinking lady. "Fetch the assistant to me, then, and stand up straight!"

The gates of Roth House, near the Landreg estates, were closing behind Shan and his companions when he saw Quen Shieldsman. Shan reined up next to his rival, certain this meeting was no accident. "What do you want?" he demanded, his fair skin flushed with rage. "If you're here to bring me back to heel, I have mages of my own." He signalled a man and a woman who rode with his men-at-arms. They came forward, watching Quen anxiously.

"And very effective, too, I'm sure," Quen said easily, leaning on his saddlehorn. "Vrohain's witness, Shan, you may as well put candles against those three young people.

Did you think they wear medallions because they like the effect? No offense," he said to Shan's mages. "They got their medallions at thirteen."

"We may not be great mages, but that does not mean we will fail," the woman retorted. "We lesser mages often work under the sight of you powerful ones. The powerful mages do not know of their danger until mages like us trap them."

"That would sound better if you weren't sweating, *Viymese*," retorted Quen. "Shan, you mule, I've come to help. She doesn't know I'm here." There could be only one "she" when these two men spoke: the empress. "I found you in my scrying-glass."

"*You're* here to help *me* wed the richest marriage-prize in memory?" Shan asked, frowning. Then his face brightened. "I see it now. If I snag Sandry, I'll be in disgrace with her imperial majesty. Since she's still fond of *you* . . ."

"Exactly," replied Quen. "I hope you know side roads, if we are to get ahead of the *clehame*."

"I've left nothing to chance," Shan said grimly. "I'd hoped it wouldn't come to this. If Berenene hadn't put Sandry's back up —"

Quen interrupted with a raised hand. "Spare me the tale of woe," he said, reining his horse in next to Shan's. "I'm not interested."

"So sure in your magic," Shan said with a glare. "Whatever

else, *you'll* never be poor like me. *You'll* never sleep with holes in your sheets. . . ."

Quen sent out a spark that stung Shan's mount on the rump. She broke into a gallop. By the time Shan got the mare under control, he'd lost all interest in talk. He led them on, up through the hills and fields that paralleled the Southern Imperial Highway, where Sandry and her companions would ride. With less traffic on the side roads than on the main route, they made good time. Experienced at long rides, Shan was careful to see that they paced their horses and switched to their remounts, resting often. Rather than deal with inns, they bought space in farmers' barns on the way.

"The trick," Shan explained to Quen over their fourth night's supper, "is to catch her when she believes no one is going to give chase. She's looking for an ambush near Dancruan, or the border. She'll be ready. But in the middle of the journey, between the two? They'll figure they're safe enough. They'll be relaxed. That's when I'll take her. I have spelled charms to distract her, if you can hold Briar and Daja. My people can handle the servants and the men-at-arms."

"Of course," Quen replied, his face unreadable. The firelight made his face look like a mask. "I *did* come prepared."

"They may not even be that much of a problem." Shan cut pieces from a sausage and ate them from his knife. "Plant magic and metal magic — they're not much good in a fight, are they? And we are talking about child mages, pretty much. They're young to be wearing medallions." There was a wicked glint in his eyes. "That must scrape your paint, to know they got them before you did. Perhaps Sandry bought the medallions for them, so they'd feel accomplished."

Quen raised his eyebrows. "If you're looking for a fight with me, stop it. Worry about your own problems," he drawled. "Even once she's signed the contract and marked it with her blood, she may be hard to handle. You can't keep her bespelled all the time. What do you think will happen when you let the spells lapse? There's plenty a wife can do to a husband short of killing him, and mage wives are known to be inventive."

Shan leaned back on his elbows. "I'm not worried. You didn't see her with me, Quen. I had the girl. She would have said yes to my proposal, if some damned busybody hadn't told her I was Berenene's lover. I can win Sandry back. Once she's realized this really is what she wanted all along, I think she'll be very happy to make ours the second house in the empire. I'll ensure that she's happy. It's to my advantage, too, after all."

Quen raised his brows. "I had no idea you were so ambitious. Or so foolish. Her Imperial Majesty is not going to let you off easily, you know. You'll be in disgrace. Her memory is long —"

Shan smiled. "But her pockets are not. She can't afford to keep Sandry and me in disgrace for long — not if she means to keep squabbling with the emperor in Yanjing. I plan to spend my time in exile making alliances in the Noble Assembly and in the Mages' Society. Berenene helped me there, arresting Fin's uncle. Once we have enough of the people Her Imperial Majesty has vexed on our side, she will have to accept us. Me."

Quen rubbed his nose. "She *is* practical, it's true. Who knows? You may have the right of it. Now, where is this perfect plucking spot you told me you mean to use? You said it's just two more days' ride."

"It's perfect," Shan said, pulling a map from the saddlebag beside him. "Canyon Inn. The main inn on the highway, the Blendroad Inn, will be full to bursting. There's a horse fair in that village at this time every year. My nurse's cousin, who runs Blendroad, will be sure to tell *Clehame* Sandrilene that Canyon Inn is more suited to her gentle nature." He laid the map flat and indicated each location. "And the Canyon Inn is all set as a trap for my pretty bird and her little flock. With your spells, and those of my mage friends, to help me escape, I'll be long gone with Sandry by the time Daja and Briar can track us. My mother's prepared a place where I can keep Sandry till she's signed the contract and married me."

"You've thought of everything, it seems," murmured Quen.

"I've planned since I knew she liked me," replied Shan. "I'd have preferred her to accept when I proposed, but . . . women." He shrugged. "She'll come around."

* * *

Shan, Quen, and their companions arrived at the Canyon Inn well in advance of Sandry's party. A check of his scrying-glass told Quen it would take her another five days to reach them, moving at a slower place on the main highway. Armed with that news, Shan paid a visit to his allies at the Blendroad Inn, where preparations for the horse fair were underway, and finished his arrangements at the Canyon Inn.

The money for all this, Quen discovered, came from one of Berenene's gifts to Shan. He really knows no shame, Quen thought, watching Shan spar with his guardsmen once he returned. I wish I could share the joke with Isha. Thinking of Shan's intentions with regard to the Noble Assembly and the Mages' Society, he wondered, Should I arrange for Shan to fail in his kidnapping? Sandry is a sweet girl, and I like her. No, I have to follow through. If Shan doesn't succeed, Berenene might forgive him in time. If he does, she will never forgive him, even though she wanted to keep Sandry in Namorn.

Briar and Daja should be easy to handle. Plant mages and smith mages are generally limited to their direct workings. Once I have them bound, the hard part will be over. All I have to do is hold them until the kidnapping party is safely gone. Sandry will be Shan's problem.

With his own battle plan worked out, Quen relaxed, ambling along the gorge that was meant to be Shan's escape route, cooling his feet in the small river outside the Canyon Inn, and gathering plants in the surrounding forest. He also made certain to regularly check his scrying-glass for signs of Lady Sandrilene's progress.

The spies' reports reached Berenene two days before Sandry and her companions reached the Blendroad crossing. The empress read the reports twice, the enraged flush on her cheeks deepening. Finally she slammed a hematite ring she never took off against the desk. It would bring Ishabal to her as quickly as the woman could run.

Berenene wasted no time on pleasantries when her chief mage arrived. Instead, she threw the reports at Isha's head. "*Both* of them!" she snapped, shoving her chair back from her desk. "*Both* of those arrogant young pups! Vrohain witness, they will pay for this! For defiance, and for thinking I would be so foolish — so besotted! — as to let them get away with it!"

Ishabal pretended to read the reports. Copies had already reached her that morning. "You like proud, hotheaded young men," she said carefully, watching the empress as she stood to pace. "Such men do as they wish, always thinking there is a way to make it right." Despite her apparent calm, she, too, was seething. Quen had lied to her. She did not like that. She waited until the empress looked her way, then shrugged. "They may well succeed. They are intelligent and talented. Lady Sandrilene's gold will stay in Namorn. They may even have been foolish enough to think you would be practical, as you always are. That you will settle for the solution to the more expensive problem — the loss of Sandrilene's income to Emelan."

"I will not be made a laughingstock," Berenene said. "Not by them, and not by that girl. The entire world will say the chit snagged my lover, and my former lover helped them! Enough. I have been too kind, this summer. You see where my generosity has gotten me. Send orders to my household and to my men-at-arms, to those we trust without reservation. You and I ride south, today. The word for my court is that I am bound for the Carakathy hunting lodge for relaxation. No one must know my true intent. I want all of them to feel my hand on them. If we must raise the magical border to stop them, I will keep all three of those young people in Namorn. Pershan and Quenaill will remember who is the ruler in this empire."

Isha curtsied. "Very well, Your Imperial Majesty."

"Put a guard on Trisana," Berenene snapped. "Have her watched. Place your best people on alert. *She* is not to leave Dancruan, should she be in any condition to try."

That same day, Tris got out of bed. She ached from head to toe and had to be helped into a bathtub, but she was on her feet. Grimly she made herself walk the circuit of her room twice that day, five times the next. The healers ordered her not to test the healing, ignoring her glare. On the third morning, as she stood on the landing and contemplated the stairs to the next story down, Ealaga came up to her.

"Are you supposed to do that?" the lady asked.

"I'm *supposed* to be with my family," Tris replied. She gripped the banister and took one step down. "It's a very nice bed, Ealaga, and you've been wonderful about sharing books, but I do them no good here. None of us believes Sandry will be allowed to dance out of Namorn."

Ambros's wife steadied Tris. "Dressed yourself, I see," she remarked, redoing the topmost button on Tris's gown. "Come to my room and tell my maid how to pin your braids."

"I'd appreciate that," Tris said. For once she did not thrust away the offer of help. I don't want to admit I can't walk down on my own, she thought. "I want to visit the palace tomorrow, but when I try to tuck up my braids, I get dizzy lifting my arms." Tris paused to catch her breath, thinking, Five more steps and then I'll sit down. I'm in splendid condition for a fight, I am!

"The palace?" Ealaga asked, puzzled. "You aren't fit to visit anywhere, let alone the palace. Who did you wish to call on? We can invite that person here."

"I'd rather have my chat with *Viymese* Ladyhammer somewhere else, if you don't mind," replied Tris, taking the next step with trembling legs. "It may not go well."

"That chat seems like a very bad idea to me." Ealaga

was as full of practicality as her husband. "Surely your business with her is best left *un*done."

"It is not," the redhead answered. "I've had plenty of time to pick apart that whiff of magic I smelled before I decided to do bad tumbling tricks on the stair. It was her work. I don't know what I did to Ishabal to deserve that, and I don't care. I just want to express my unhappiness in the clearest possible way." They had reached the second floor. Tris leaned against the banister, her face beaded with sweat from exhaustion as much as pain.

Ealaga helped Tris into her own dressing room. "Well, then, if you're foolish enough to want to quarrel with a great mage, I can't be sorry to tell you that your luck is out. *Viymese* Ladyhammer is not at the palace. She and her imperial majesty left some days ago, to do some hunting." She guided Tris onto a chair and rang the bell for the maid.

Tris watched Ealaga's face in the looking-glass. "Do you know where?"

Ealaga met her gaze with sober eyes. "She has a residence in the Carakathy Hills, near Lake Glaise and the Olart border."

"Where the Imperial Highway crosses the Olart border," Tris said.

"Yes." Ealaga beckoned to her maid. "The empress often goes there, Tris. It doesn't mean anything."

Tris shifted in the chair so she could meet Ealaga's eyes. "You don't believe that."

Ealaga sighed and took a seat of her own. "It's said she was in a rage when she left, and Pershan fer Roth was missing. The gossips believe he may have gone to try to persuade Sandry to marry him after all."

Tris took a moment to explain to the maid how each braid was tucked and the mass of braids coiled before the silk net Tris offered her was pinned in place over them. As the woman got to work, Tris bit her lip, her brain racing. Shan is the empress's toy, thought the redhead. Her lover. If he went after Sandry — if he was fool enough to do it! — Her Imperial Majesty would feel he'd shown her disrespect. If there's one thing rulers hate, it's disrespect. That and the possibility that people might think they're weak if it looks like someone has defied their will. So now the empress is angry. She's worried people might say Shan, Sandry, Daja, and Briar are getting away with saying no to her. She'll want to stop them from leaving, to prove they aren't defying her.

Tris had spent much of the last three years entering and leaving countries. One thing most had in common was magical walls at the borders, walls that could be relied on to slow an invader and stop an individual. They could not remain up all of the time. It was too costly to do so: Such walls demanded immense amounts of magical power. They were shaped to be raised on command. The mage who did the raising had to be a great one, a mage with the power to raise a shield that held other mages back.

Berenene has lost patience, thought Tris. She means to keep all four of us as a lesson to others. Ishabal has gone with the empress to raise the border against my sisters and brother. Namorn means to hold us like caged birds.

Tris didn't notice when Ealaga left her alone. When the maid finished, Tris thanked her and tipped her a coin for her labor. Then she left the room and began her slow, weary, aching climb back up the stair.

It took her the rest of the day to pack, including stops to rest and to nap. She worked steadily with shaking hands. She had to make sure that she carried all she would need. Chime looked on. She had been in and out during Tris's recovery, and she did not care for the way Tris was acting.

At sunset, Tris opened her window and turned her face into the cool wind that blew south off the Syth. She gathered its strength and put it behind her call to her friends: *I think they mean to raise the borders against you. Can you find a way around? The empress and Ishabal will be there, I think. Maybe Quenaill, too. Can you hear me? Can you take strength from me?*

There was no reply. It could be a few things, Tris thought, lurching back to the hated bed. It could be they've gone too far, and there's too much ambient magic between us that blocks my voice. More likely, I'm worn out. If they knew I was calling and reached back, I could speak easily then, but they don't know. They're walking into the empress's arms with no one to warn them except Zhegorz.

She lay down and slept, rising in the pale gray hour before dawn. Once dressed, she freed a wind to take her saddlebags out through her window and down to the ground. That was all she dared to take with her if she wanted to move fast. It cost her a pang to turn her back on the wardrobe Sandry had made her for court, but perhaps Ambros and Ealaga would ship the trunks to Emelan. She placed her letter to them on her bed, gathered Chime up in her arms, and slowly made her way down the stairs and out of the house. While she had enough control over her magic and her winds to lower saddlebags, she didn't feel confident enough to lower herself. She would need all of her strength to get through the day.

Once outside, her wind met and followed her to the stable, where it left her saddlebags. Tris thanked it and set it free.

The stables were dark. Tris didn't care: She could see perfectly well. Her mare, an easygoing creature that was accustomed to Tris's peculiarities, stood quietly as another wind from that same braid lifted blanket, saddle, and saddlebags to her back. Slowly Tris did up buckles and settled bits of tack, checking it all twice. Finally she placed Chime on the saddlebags and dragged a stool over to the mare. When she tried to pull herself into the saddle, her strength failed her partway. She lay there, half-on and half-off, wondering if this would be how she departed Landreg House.

"If I had any sense, I would leave you there," Ambros said,

pushing open the stable door to admit the early morning light. "You're in no condition to attempt anything like this."

"I have to get closer to them," Tris mumbled. "Close enough at least to warn them. The healers said I was mended."

"If they had known you meant to attempt a three-hundred-mile ride when you'd been out of bed less than a week, they would have revised their diagnosis," replied Ambros at his driest. "They might even have determined that you took a harder blow to the head than they had originally thought."

Tris considered telling him "You can't stop me," but it was hard to do while hanging crosswise over a horse's back. "I'm going," she said, gripping the saddle horn. She shoved from the foot that was in the stirrup.

A firm pair of hands gripped her ankle and pushed, helping her slide the rest of her weight onto her horse. Ambros went around to tug the free leg down and place that foot in its stirrup. Then he went to saddle his own horse.

Tris watched him as Chime climbed up the back of her gown and onto her shoulder. "What do you think you're doing?" she asked Ambros.

"Since I have an idea I'll face lightning or something worse if I try to keep you, I had best go along," he replied calmly. "That way, when you fall off sometime around noon, I will have the very great pleasure of saying, 'I told you so.' Should you remain in the saddle, you will need me to pay innkeepers." He hesitated as he checked the placement of his bridle, then asked quietly, "Do you honestly believe the four of you can overcome border protections raised and held by a great mage? Perhaps more great mages, if Ishabal sends for them?"

Tris leaned down to rest her forehead against her mare's mane. "I don't know," she said honestly. "If I tell them they aren't going to be allowed to leave, they'll be angry enough to try. It may be we have a few tricks to us that no one knows of yet."

They were riding out the house gate when Ambros drew up. "I had forgotten we were being watched," he admitted.

Tris squinted to see what he meant. Across the street, two mages stood on either side of a smaller town house. They were coming forward now, the silver fire of their power flickering around their hands. Chime darted forward, uttering her nails-on-glass screech, forcing them to watch her as she flashed close to their faces.

Tris took advantage of their distraction to undo a quarter of another fat wind braid gleaned from a tornado. As the watchdog mages tried to strike at Chime with their power, Tris released her wind. It blasted down the street, whipping up dust, making the manes and tails of the horses stream. It yanked the female mage's veil off her hair. Chime instantly flew upward, out of the wind's reach.

Tris called the gale-force wind back to circle the watchdogs. It grabbed them, scrabbling in their clothes with greedy fingers. Tris did up the braid again, then gave the small gale another spin. It picked up speed, whirling around the watchdogs like a cyclone. Inside it they were blind and captive, unable to move or see. Tris gave the wind a last, hard spin, then freed it into the open air over Dancruan. It fled, leaving the pair behind. Briefly they wavered, then fell.

It took Ambros a moment to shake off what he had just seen. "You killed them," he said nervously as Chime dropped down to land on Tris's saddle horn.

"Nonsense." Tris glared at Ambros. "I knocked them out. They'll come around. I don't go around killing people, you know. Not unless I have to."

Ambros dismounted and checked for himself. He had to yank at the watchdogs' disheveled clothing to uncover their faces and find if they were still breathing. They were. Ambros shook his head, covered their faces again, and mounted his gelding. "Let's go, before they wake up," he said, still shaking his head.

"I *told* you I don't go around killing people," Tris said fiercely. "It's not exactly something I'd want to lie about."

Normally Gudruny's children were patient travelers, helping with chores and gleefully striking up conversations with passersby. But the closer their company came to the Blendroad crossing and its horse fair, the unhappier the children got. Sandry could understand their basic disgust at the slowness of their travel, the dust, the lack of consideration from others on the road, and the noise, but more than once she considered cocooning the children to silence them.

Zhegorz did not help. He still insisted on riding beside Sandry, his bony nose in the wind, whatever its direction. His declarations — "I hear the palace" — got to be maddening. The problem was that the empire maintained fortresses along the highway to preserve the peace. Could his palace sounds simply be the conversation of servants of the empire? He couldn't say. From time to time he would go silent, but he always started up again. The only rest Sandry got from his declarations was if she chose to ride at the back of their group, when she got dust in her teeth. By the time they finally crawled into the overstuffed courtyard of the Blendroad Inn, Zhegorz was shouting his news, drawing stares from everyone who heard them, and Sandry had a headache.

"Zhegorz, will you please be quiet!" cried Gudruny as Sandry rode forward to talk to the innkeeper. "The children are bad enough" — she glared at her crying youngsters in the cart — "and I mean to paddle them if they do not stop it, *right now*! I will paddle you as well if you cannot act like an adult!"

Briar, too, was covered with dust and headachy with sun, but Gudruny made him smile. "Here I thought she was a mouse," he remarked to Daja as Sandry passed them. "Seemingly she's not."

"I don't think mothers are supposed to be mice,"

murmured Daja. "Maybe that's what Zhegorz needs — a mother."

"I hear the palace," Zhegorz called back to Gudruny. "Plots and betrayal and intrigue."

"Hear them *quietly,*" Gudruny insisted. She gave her children one last glare. They at least had heard the tone of their mother at the end of her rope, and fallen silent.

"*Clehame,* I'm sorry, but we have not a single room. You see how it is — every house in Blendroad is full up for the horse fair," the innkeeper stammered. He had to talk between two of Sandry's guards. They would not let him get any closer to her horse. "All who travel the highway this time of year know of the fair. I will turn folk out of their rooms, being as you're a *clehame*, but it will cost me guests I depend on every year."

Sandry rubbed her temples. "No, please don't do that on my account," she told him, hating herself for caring about such things when she just wanted a bath. Why can't I be like other nobles, and demand he look after me and mine right *now*? she asked herself petulantly. I can't see Berenene caring if he loses customers or not, as long as she gets a bath.

"Just like a man, to not to offer a solution!" scolded a woman — obviously the innkeeper's wife — as she thrust her way through the crowd. Reaching Sandry's fence of guards, she curtsied. "*Clehame*, forgive my silly clunch of a husband. He's forgot the Canyon Inn. It's just ten miles down Deepdene Road." She pointed to a road that led west. "Truly, it's far better for a refined young lady and her household. 'Tis small, quiet, not well-known, but well-kept. My sister-in-law owns it. They've some guests now, but not enough to fill the house. My sister-in-law is not so good a cook as I am, but no one grumbles about her fare."

Daja leaned on her staff and looked the woman over. "If this place is such a gem, why isn't it full?"

"It's ten miles off, for one," said the innkeeper, clearly relieved his wife had stepped in. "And it's more to the noble style and hunters' style. They're full when hunt season begins, sure enough, and with the fur traders in the winter, but less so this time of year."

Sandry had borne enough. Her head was killing her. "Let's go," she ordered her companions. "The sooner I lie down, the better."

One of the guards flipped coins to the innkeeper and his wife. Briar and half the guards followed Sandry, while Daja muttered for Zhegorz to be silent. He obeyed only briefly. Sandry was barely a mile down the smaller road when he cried, "Silks, brocades, swords — I see them on the wind!"

"Because Sandry and her guards are upwind of you, Zhegorz," Daja told him. "Are you going to behave, or will I have to make you take your drops?"

"I said I'd watch over you," Zhegorz informed her with dignity. "You should listen when I'm watching over you."

Daja looked at Gudruny. "Is this what having children is like?"

The maid sighed. "Very like."

"Hush, or take drops," Daja ordered Zhegorz. "I don't care which."

Zhegorz hushed, falling back to the rear where he could ride with the more sympathetic Briar.

When they reached the Canyon Inn, Daja was relieved to find a very different situation from the last inn. The only other guests were four soldiers on leave from the army, which meant there were rooms for everyone but Sandry's guards in the main house. Her guards were happy to make camp outside, on the nearby riverbank. The innkeeper immediately took their party over, escorting Sandry to a cool room, clean sheets, water to wash herself with, and quiet. As the others relaxed, Daja lingered in the common room to talk to their fellow guests.

"It's not as expensive as it is later in the year," one of the men explained. "And honestly, *Ravvikki,* my friends and I are glad for the quiet."

One of the others nodded. "We're here to fish, explore the river, and forget there ever was a place called the Sea of Grass. That was our last posting. We're on leave, thank the gods."

"You've come a long way, then," Daja remarked.

"Thousands of miles, as fast as possible," one man said reverently, to the rueful laughter of his companions. "And now we're done. That Yanjingyi emperor is a cruel, hard fellow. We're hoping our next post is a safe little soldier box in maybe Dancruan."

"Talk to my brother Briar when he comes down from his nap," Daja suggested as she got to her feet. "You can trade curses on the emperor's name. He just got back from Gyongxe this spring."

The men traded looks. "Saw some fighting there, did he?" the first one to speak asked. "He's a busy fellow, that emperor. But we may not be around this afternoon." He coughed into his fist. "We were thinking of riding off to the horse fair this evening for a spot of entertainment."

"It's odd," Daja told Briar later, when he came downstairs. By then, the men were long gone. "They didn't seem like they were going much of anywhere." She stretched. "I'm going to practice my staff. Care to swap a few blows?"

Briar grimaced. "When there's a river and greenery practically on our doorstep, and the little ones sound asleep, so they won't trail me everywhere? Thanks, no. Go see if one of our guards wants to get his fingers cracked."

Briar's wish for solitude was meant to go unfulfilled. He was inspecting a small patch of ferns, wondering if he could get them home if he used one of the small pots in his packs, when Zhegorz found him. The older man knelt abruptly, missing the ferns by an inch.

"You almost killed a plant, Zhegorz. Lakik's teeth, you got to use your eyes for something other than visions," Briar said patiently, making sure the moss under Zhegorz's bony knees was not damaged. "If you won't watch where you're stepping or kneeling or whatever, you can't be following me around."

"I promised Tris I would look after everyone, but no one will listen," Zhegorz muttered. "How can I make you listen when the air is full of plots and the wind hung with sights of plotters?"

"Because you keep saying the same thing, and you say it about everyone, old man," Briar told him. Dealing with Zhegorz required the same kind of patience that dealing with acorns on the ground demanded. All of them clamored to sprout and put down roots, and they didn't understand that not all of them could. It always took time to get through to them. "You've got to concentrate harder and give us more details. And you've got to learn to tell what's a real danger from what's always there. Imperial soldiers are always there — the empire's lousy with them, like the fellows Daja was talking to."

"They don't talk imperial," Zhegorz mumbled.

"*Belbun* dung," Briar said, half-listening. "Green Man bless us, *you're* a long way from home." The tree beside the one that sheltered the ferns was stocky for a tree, with leaves marked by distinctively silvery undersides. "Zhegorz, have a look. This is a Gyongxe sorbus. Someone had to plant this here. It's not natural to Namorn, though I suppose it would do all right. Soil's a little rich for you, though, girl."

"They don't talk imperial," Zhegorz insisted.

"They're trees, they don't talk at all," Briar replied. "Well, not so *you'd* hear. . . ."

"Those men. They talked about 'my lord,' and rabbits in traps, and 'beats catching a flogging for tarnished brass.'"

"They're imperial soldiers on leave, and their troops are commanded by nobles," Briar insisted, sending his power into the sorbus to fortify it against any hazards that might plague a foreigner in Namorn. "And they're here to hunt. I wouldn't talk imperial, either, if I was on leave after fighting Yanjing. Stop fussing."

"They talked about *weddings*," Zhegorz insisted.

"Men on leave get married. If you don't have anything more serious, go soak your head in the river," Briar snapped. "I mean it, Zhegorz. Tris just told you to come with us so you wouldn't lurk about Landreg House giving her the fidgets. Once they've fixed you up at Winding Circle, you'll be able to manage better. Now scat! And put your spectacles and both ear beads back on!"

Without a word, Zhegorz got to his feet and returned to the inn. Watching him go, Briar felt a rare twinge of conscience. He kicked that out, too. I'll make it up to him later, he promised himself. But truthfully, sometimes a fellow needs time alone with green things. They won't talk me half to death.

Tired of people, he returned to the inn for his *shakkan.* With it in his hands, he went out onto the riverbank and settled between the roots of an immense willow. There he spent the afternoon, the *shakkan* at his side, soaking in the feel of all that green life around him.

While Briar relaxed, Daja offered to take Gudruny's children off her hands for a while. Gudruny accepted with gratitude. Once they were awake, Daja took them on a hike along the canyon that opened to the rear of the inn, where she could sense some metal veins in the rock walls. Sandry and Gudruny dozed and read. Zhegorz sulked in the stable, then paced outside the inn, restless under the threat of his calming drops from Sandry.

Everyone ate a quiet supper. Briar's impulse to apologize to Zhegorz died under the older man's glare during supper. He was happy to watch Zhegorz climb the stairs to go to bed early. Briar wasn't sure he could keep his temper if Zhegorz continued to stare at him as if Briar had just murdered his firstborn. Instead, Briar listened to Sandry tell Gudruny's children a bedtime story. Once they had gone upstairs, he helped Sandry straighten her embroidery silks. Despite the naps nearly everyone had taken, all of them were yawning not long after twilight had faded. They soon went to bed. Even the staff vanished. When Briar got up to close the front door, he saw that the guards were asleep around their fire. He had planned to set his *shakkan* back with the packs before he turned in, but something made him change his mind. After trying to think, and nearly splitting his jaws as he yawned, Briar had simply carried the old pine upstairs.

Zhegorz was already sound asleep in the other bed, a mild buzz of a snore issuing from his lips. Grateful not to have to have to talk to him, Briar set the *shakkan* on the floor and took off his clothes. Clad only in his loincloth, he crawled under the covers.

Given all the yawning he had done, he had thought he would be asleep the moment he put his head down. Instead, he felt imprisoned by his clean cotton sheets. His brain felt as if it were weighed down by clouds; his nose was stuffy. The feeling was one he knew, one his tired brain associated with blood and weapons in the night. Briar half-heard the roar of Yanjingyi rockets overhead and the shriek of dying people all around. He fought the clouds, turning his fingers to brambles to claw his way out of them. The clouds thickened. Desperate, he made his fingers into hooked thorns and slashed through layers of heavy mist.

The clouds parted slightly. Briar thrust a vine of power out through the opening, groping blindly for help with the weight that made it hard for him to breathe or move. He fumbled and reached — and touched his *shakkan.* White fire blazed, burning the clouds away in a heartbeat. Briar took deep breaths of clean air and woke up.

For a moment he thought he lay in a Gyongxe temple. The scent of sandalwood and patchouli was heavy in his nose; the ghosts of warning gongs thudded in his ears. When he put his feet on the floor, however, they met thin carpet, not stone. The smells faded in his nose; straining, he heard no war gongs. He wasn't in Gyongxe. He was in a Namornese room. The two had only one thing in common: Someone very powerful was trying to keep him asleep.

He used the water pitcher to fill his washbasin — tricky work when his hands shook so badly. Then he ducked his face in the basin and splashed water on the back of his head, cleaning off some of the nightmare sweat. They're powerful, whoever they are, but they ain't the Yanjingyi emperor's mages, he thought grimly. He checked the bond that linked him with Sandry. She was missing.

Not again! he thought angrily. Don't these clod-headed bleaters ever give up?

He looked over at Zhegorz. Normally their scarecrow, less of a scarecrow after some weeks of decent meals, would have been up after the noise Briar had made. He slept very lightly, but not tonight. Briar shook him with no result.

Sorry, old man, he silently told the sleeping mage. You were right all along.

Briar grabbed his mage kit, yanked open the door, and raced down the hall to Sandry's room. Gudruny and the children were sound asleep on pallets on the floor. Sandry was not in the empty bed. Instead, he saw a complex sign, written in pure magic, on his friend's mattress. Briar had never seen anything like it. He tried to inspect the curls and twists inside the thing, only to find he was swaying on his feet, sleep already blurring his mind.

This sign felt different, more powerful, from the fog of sleep that had wrapped him around beginning in the common room. Briar dug in his kit until he produced the slender vial whose contents he had labeled *wake the dead.* Once he removed the cork, he quickly stuck the vial under his nose and took a breath. For a moment his nose and brain felt as if they might well be on fire. He yanked the bottle away and recorked it, then wiped his streaming eyes and took a second look at the design. It tugged at him, urging sleep, so he hung on to the bottle of scent. Bending down to risk a closer look, he saw the design was done in oil. Moreover, it bled along the threads of the sheet, uncontained.

Done like that, it wouldn't last very long, he realized. Which means I'm not looking at the original spell. He stripped away the sheets to reveal the mattress. There, too, the design had bled up and through. Briar shoved the mattress aside. On the slats that kept it up he found the original spell. It was done on parchment in oils, and kept within the bounds of the parchment by a circle drawn in ink. Briar turned the parchment over: The mage who had made it had glued spelled silk onto the back and had written signs to enclose on that, to keep the spell from leaking down.

Musta been under the mattress for hours, to bleed up

through everything, Briar decided. The energy in the oils had to move somewhere. The only way the mage that made the spell left it to go was up.

He couldn't say how he knew the mage was a man, but he did. Moreover, the fiery brightness of the original spell and its complexity, even if he didn't know how it was made, told him that they faced a very powerful mage, even a great mage. It was as bright as any work done by the four's teachers.

To keep her asleep longer and deeper than the spell on us, I bet, thought Briar, recognizing some of the signs written into the original spell. To keep her out for days, not a day. And it woulda seeped into her power slow, so she'd never feel it coming over her. She'd be halfway across Namorn before she'd wake.

As soon as we get the rest of the household up and on her trail, we'll destroy this and wake her up. Won't that be a fine surprise for whoever's got her? He smiled thinly and placed the parchment on the frame of the bed. Mage kit in hand, he went to Daja's room. She slept as soundly as the others. Once more, Briar uncorked his wake-up potion and put the vial under her nose. She gasped, choked, and opened her eyes. Coughing, she swung a fist out to clip Briar's head. Expecting it — the potion had that effect on many people — he dodged the blow.

"Kill me later," Briar told her as she scrambled to get at him. "Some *belbun* nicked Sandry, and he's got a serious mage in his pocket. If he isn't the mage himself."

Daja rubbed her eyes. "What's in that poison?"

"Just the biggest wake-up weeds I know, spelled to crunch through any sleep spell. That's how they got us in Gyongxe, sleep spells."

Daja pulled a sack out of her mage kit and began to put items in it. She wore only her medallion, a breast band secured with a tie looped around her neck, and a loincloth. Her lack of clothing didn't seem to concern her. "One of these days you're going to have to tell me about what happened in Gyongxe," she said, turning a spool of fine wire over in her hand before she stuffed it into the bag. "And not that 'It was just a war' *pavao*." She straightened. "Let's go smelt this down and see what floats."

19

Briar suddenly realized he was *very* glad it was Daja with him. She was solid in spirit and heart — he'd forgotten that. She didn't have Tris's temper, vexing even with its most dangerous aspects held under rigid control, and she wasn't inclined to the kind of noble arrogance that Sandry kept displaying. Of course he wouldn't tell Daja that, but it was good to be reminded.

They trotted downstairs. The inn's staff was asleep in a private parlor. It looked as if they'd told themselves they'd just put their heads down for a moment, then fallen asleep at one table. The four other guests had not returned from the horse fair.

I bet Zhegorz was right. Maybe they were soldiers, but now they're in the pay of whichever imperial favorite tricked us this time, thought Briar. Maybe they had charms to hold off the sleep spell, but old Zhegorz scared them into the woods to wait till we were snoring, instead of being all nice and snug in here. Briar spat on the tiles in disgust. Tris was right to send him, and I was a bleater.

Daja went outside and quickly came back. "Asleep, all of them."

"Stables are through the kitchen," Briar said, pointing. "They'll have needed horses to take Sandry."

Daja nodded grimly. They walked through the kitchen door together into a force that felt like hard jelly. It wrapped around them in an eyeblink, then pulled them apart, leaving a yard of space between them.

One man was still awake. Quen lounged at the cook's big table, fiddling with pieces of chopped turnips and carrots obviously meant for soup tomorrow. "I'll wager you've never walked into anything like that before, have you?" he asked casually, his brown eyes gleaming in triumph. "Don't worry, you can breathe. In fact, inside that working, you can stay alive for weeks. I tested it on a criminal scheduled for execution. After three months, Her Imperial Majesty lost patience and had him executed anyway." He yawned. "I can't leave this inn and still hold you two like this, but I've had worse situations. I wish you could tell me how you broke my sleep spell. No one was supposed to wake from that for three days. And I shaped it so that it couldn't *be* broken once you were asleep." He scratched the side of his mouth. "You'll tell me when I free you, perhaps. Or I could let the glove of air down enough to free your mouths, if you swear to behave. Or not. I suppose you're a little more powerful than I expected." He smirked. "So, what shall I talk about?"

Daja and Briar reached out at the same moment along their magical connection, withered as it was. It sprang to life as Daja said, *He'll bore us to death if he keeps talking.*

It seems like that, Briar answered. *While he natters, we still don't know about Sandry.*

Sandry! cried Daja, grabbing for their bond. *Sandry!*

I couldn't reach her before, Briar said. At the same time, he added his call to hers. They still found no trace of their friend.

"I suppose you're running through all the spell-breaking charms you know," Quen observed. "But that's the beauty of it, don't you see? They're layered shield spells, but some of them are reversed. My own design. No single charm possessed by any mage will work on this glove spell. Well, Isha broke out, but she's even more powerful than I am. She just blasted it. She said I need to stay humble. She even thought she might not be the only one who could do it, but really, outside noble courts, or the universities and the Living Circle schools, you're not likely to find that many great mages. People tend to dislike us. They think we're conceited and high-handed. They never think that perhaps we just spend so much time trying to wrestle our magic into behaving that it makes us short-tempered with the everyday world. So we hide."

Quen ate a chunk of carrot, his eyes alert as he watched

them. "Frustrating, isn't it? I had to spend plenty of time at Lightsbridge breaking out of trap spells as part of my specialization. Maybe you could do a double working that would get you out eventually, but that's why I pulled you apart." He studied his nails. "You really should consider employment with Berenene. She takes good care of her people. I'll even teach you some tricks once Shan and Sandry are wed. Not this one, of course. But you'll see I'm a decent enough fellow after that."

He is starting to annoy me, complained Daja.

Let's shut him up, then. Briar and Daja thrust at the spells with their own spells for destruction, Briar's for decay and the destruction of parasites, Daja's for rust. Nothing worked. Each suggested charms and tricks they had learned in the last three years, creating variations within their own specialties. These, too, failed. The glove spells slid around them, jelly-like, making Daja's knees weak with distaste. Quen took a fiddle from the bench and played it, which made Briar crazy. He hated being laughed at.

Should we yell for Tris? Briar finally asked.

There's a way we can do this, Daja said stubbornly. *On our own, without Tris and her book learning. Besides, she's probably still weak as a kitten.*

Something caught Briar's attention then. *Tris. Book learning.*

Daja waited to hear his thought.

When Briar worked it out, he was both jubilant and

ashamed for not seeing it sooner. The solution lay in his own experience and his own teacher. Rosethorn had engaged in a constant battle with university-trained mages, over the difference between academic magic and ambient magic.

Stop playing his game and start playing ours! he said. He tapped into his *shakkan* and the plants around him, drawing their power through himself and turning it into vines. These he sent through the spells of the glove. Like all vines, they found each and every chink and opening, spaces no human being used, weaving their tendrils through to break into open air. Reaching Daja's prison, they did the same thing all over again, finding the openings between the spells. At last they broke through to twine themselves around her, growing until they cupped her entire body.

Daja called to the metal on her hand and in her mage kit, the strange living metal that was always growing and absorbing new metal. She drew on the strength of the kitchen's metal and fires as well, adding it to the liquid metal until she could spin wires of power out of herself. They twined with Briar's vines, following the paths the magical plants had taken through the openings in Quen's spells. Busily they worked themselves into Briar's prison, encasing him as his vines had encased Daja.

Slowly, the spells that enclosed Daja and Briar began to melt, like thick ice under boiling water.

Quen dropped fiddle and bow and stretched a hand out to them, his lips moving as he tried to renew the spells. The mess around Briar and Daja struggled to rebuild, and collapsed completely.

Quen gestured. A fresh shield billowed toward them like a giant, thick bubble. Daja leaned forward and blew like a bellows, hard and long, forcing the heavy thing back toward Quen. He fought to hold it off. While he was occupied, Briar reached into an outer pocket of his mage kit and pulled out a small cloth ball. Deftly, he tossed it on the floor. It rolled to Quen's feet.

Briar filled the seeds in the ball with green magic and called them to wakefulness. Weaving the shoots as they thrust up, he gripped them in an iron hold and kept them from sinking roots. All of their strength had to go into growing up, not down. He needed this cage to move.

The plants shot through the cloth of the ball that held them, weaving. They were as high as Quen's knees before he saw the danger. He turned his shield on them, but Briar was ready. The vines, thick with thorns, spread out and over the shield, still growing.

Watching Quen's sweaty face, Daja pulled a spool of fine wire out of her sack. She sent the wire's end snaking toward the base of the vine cage, where it began to weave itself in among the vines. As it climbed she called light to it, making Quen blink and shield his eyes. It was a distraction, something he could not afford. While he tried to shield his vision, vines and wire finished a globe of a cage.

Briar had prepared the seed ball to withstand the magic

of mages and hill shamans alike, both hazards of the road to Gyongxe. It was why he had brought it downstairs. Daja had made this spool of wire to handle and contain power, her own or that of others. Bearing down with their wills — Briar's forged in the streets, in epidemics, and in war; Daja's, in forges and mammoth blazes — they tightened their cage on Quenaill, crushing his last shield.

Briar and Daja joined hands and fed their cage a last surge of power. The gaps between wire and vines blazed, sealed against magic from within. The pair let go.

For a moment they could hardly see Quen inside the cage. Magical workings rayed out from the man like sunlight, connecting him to every spell he still had in place — those on the inn, and those that served Sandry's kidnappers. They blazed with silver fire in Briar's and Daja's vision.

"Once more," Daja said, panting. "Drain him, so his other spells break." Her knees wobbled; her thighs felt loose. They touched fingers this time and hammered the cage with the last of their strength. At first they saw no difference. Then the first fiery strand vanished. Another followed, then three, then more. All winked out inside the cage. At last Quen stood inside, naked of power.

All around them, the inn stirred. Briar could hear the inn's staff moving in the private room. He sat down on the kitchen table and began to eat chunks of carrot. Daja took a seat on a stool and leaned against the wall.

Will it be enough? she asked him wearily. Their bond to

one another remained even when their power was as weak and floppy as a dead fish.

We cut off all he had. Sandry was at the end of some of it. We'll hear her soon enough. "Can we get some food in here?" Briar yelled. "I'm *starving*!"

Sandry was moving. That was the first thing she noticed. The second was that a man sat with her in his arms, one easy tan hand holding a horse's reins. She saw the reins, and the hand, when she opened her eyes just a crack. Little weights struck her lightly all over her body, clinking when they hit one another. All around her she heard men talking and joking. Someone asked if he could actually bring himself to wait three days, and the man who held her laughed.

"I want her in my little love nest, all nice and cozy, where I won't need all these charms Quen put on her to keep her tame," a too-familiar voice said.

Charms, Sandry thought. That's what the little weights are, and the clinking noises. Someone has tied a basket full of charms all over me, as if I were some nomad's bride to be protected from spirits.

"With the potions I have for her to drink, and the spell patterns he gave me, she won't be able to lift a finger against me once we're inside." Lips kissed the back of her neck, making Sandry's skin crawl. Shan added, "She'll get accustomed. She was half in love with me before some idiot gossiped to her. I just have to convince her that Her Imperial

Majesty was a relationship of convenience, while she is my own true love. Trust me, you tell a woman things like that, and she's putty in your hands."

"Her Imperial Majesty won't kill you when she learns?" someone inquired.

"She needs every copper this lady's lands provides. All that adventuring along the Yanjing border has stretched the imperial treasury *very* thin," Shan explained. "If I make a big enough present to Her Imperial Majesty, she'll let me be." The confidence in Shan's voice made Sandry want to scream. Instead, she continued to flop in front of him, limp and supposedly well asleep.

It's morning, if not afternoon, she realized, hearing birdsong and feeling the sun's heat on them as they rode. There's a river nearby, and lots of echoes. We're in the canyon people spoke of, I think.

They rode on for some time. Shan had just called for a break to rest and water the horses when a thin magical voice filtered through the spell that still lay on Sandry's skin like a film. *Can you hear?* Daja asked. *It's taken hours for the workings to wear off enough for me to find you. We've been trying since dawn. Why do those charms even have magic still?*

Maybe he bought them from someone else, Briar put in. *We undid all his spells to keep us all under wraps, but it didn't touch the extra charms he used.*

I'm waking up, Sandry replied. *Yes, there's still a bit of power in these charms.*

Shan let Sandry drop into another man's arms. This captor placed her gently on a patch of grass. *Don't worry about me*, she told Daja. *The charms are on my outside, but I've all my magic still, and the pig-swiving bleat-brain tied the charms to me with ribbons. I suppose it didn't occur to him ribbons are made of cloth. I'll come to you when I'm done. Quen did all this magic?*

Our little friend Quenaill, Briar said with contempt. *He spelled us asleep. If I hadn't been wary, thanks to Zhegorz . . . We owe old Zhegorz a big apology. He tried to warn us, and just because he talked crazy, we didn't listen.* He paused for a moment, then asked gruffly, *Do you need our help? We know you like Shan —*

Used to, Sandry interrupted. *I* used *to like him.* She sank into her magic, and spoke a word of command. The knots that tied those carved-stone charms to her clothes and body came undone at once. They slid to the ground with a soft series of clinks.

She waited for a moment until she knew that she had the strength to stand, then did so, lashing out with her power. The six men and one woman lingering on the riverbank dropped whatever they held as their sleeves flew together and fused, binding their arms from wrist to elbows. Before they could do more than blink, their riding breeches did the same thing, the thread of each leg weaving itself with the opposite from knee to lower calf. They fell forward helplessly.

The woman and one of the men began to mutter. Silvery tendrils rose from their bodies.

Magic, Sandry thought disdainfully. Try *mine.*

Threads shot from the mages' collars and jackets, darting into their wearers' open mouths. Their upper garments continued to unravel into their mouths until they couldn't even close their jaws. Sandry relented at the last minute, making sure that the thread inside their mouths simply wove itself into a tight ball rather than choke them. It then attached itself to a strap wound around the mages' heads. She didn't want to kill them. She just wanted them silent and out of her way. A hard gag would do the task.

Sandry heard a thud. Shan was fighting to get to the knife in his belt. A twist of her will sent his sleeves down over his hands and into the fabric of his breeches, weaving them together.

Sandry gathered up a blanket of her power and flung it over them all. It separated as it draped over each person, trickling down into that man's or that woman's clothes. Threads in their garments broke free and linked themselves together. With her magic to shape them, the fibers sped as garments unraveled and rewove. She was so angry that her will did not falter once, even when the people on the ground began to spin in place. Seeing that her cocoons were coming along nicely, Sandry looked for appropriate places to display them.

I have to be careful with the trees, she reminded herself.

I don't want a bough to drop someone on the head. And Briar would never forgive me if I hurt a tree. But I do want to make them the laughingstock of the empire when I'm done.

She chose her trees, and her display place for Shan, then checked the progress of her spinning. The two mages were done first, their shoulders and heads bare, the rest of them completely embraced in thread. Sandry called the man's cocoon to her first, holding out her hand for the rope that trailed below his feet. Once she had it in her grip, she threw it at a solid oak's branch. It whirled up and over the bough, drawing its human burden up until the man dangled several feet above the ground. She directed the rope to wind itself around the branch five times. Then she rewove the loose end into the human cocoon. The weavings and the cocoon itself were more than strong enough to hold the gagged mage until help should come. She appraised her work, hands on hips, testing it to make sure there were no fatal weaknesses in her work. Satisfied, she turned to do the same with Shan's remaining companions. All along they tried to fight, as Shan did, but their efforts were useless. She had practiced her craft hard and long: They were gagged before they even knew to make a sound, secured before they understood she was awake. By the time Shan and his followers understood they were cocooned so tightly they could neither squeak nor move.

Shan himself she placed on a large, table-like rock near

the spot where the horses were picketed. Using her power, she commanded the rope that ended in his cocoon to drag him onto the rock. As he bumped across the grass, she rewove three saddle blankets to make a second rope. Gently she placed one end on Shan's chest as he cursed her to Blaze-Ice Bay and back — she had left his mouth and head uncovered — then gave both ropes their orders. They wove themselves together and went flying, as if they ran on invisible shuttles around the rock.

When she finished, Sandry patted Shan's chest. "You can tell all Namorn this is what happens when I'm vexed," she informed him softly.

"Little *bitch,*" he snapped.

Sandry looked him over soberly. "If you had understood that earlier, we could have avoided this unpleasantness," she replied.

Ignoring his curses, she helped herself to apples, bread, and water from someone's supplies. *I'm coming back*, she told Daja and Briar, who sent her a wave of relief in answer. She took Shan's horse. The gelding was a fine animal that deserved a better master than Shan. Mounting it, she realized she was still wearing her nightgown. Cursing Shan for the indignity, she hauled the thin garment up around her thighs to get her feet in the stirrups and her behind, where it should be.

It's not how *I* envisioned the kidnapped woman's return after triumphing over her would-be captors, she thought angrily. Why is the real thing always so much more ordinary than the vision?

She had no fear she would be lost. The tie that bound her to Briar and Daja stretched, thickly silver, down the road. There was one last thing to do before she followed it, however.

She urged the gelding over to Shan, whose face was purple with rage and helplessness. "Now you know," she said hotly. "When I say I don't like you, it *really* means *I don't like you*!"

The 4th–11th days of Mead, 1043 K.F.
The imperial hunting lodge, the Carakathy Mountains to the Olart border crossing, the Imperial Highway South, Namorn

The empress of Namorn and her escort were always given the right-of-way on the roads. They passed Deepdene Road not long after Sandry and her party turned down it in search of the Canyon Inn. By the time Sandry had escaped Shan's trap, recovered, and returned to the road for two days, Berenene had taken up residence in the imperial hunting lodge near the Olart border.

With the empress came imperial business, including her spies' reports. Reading them, Ishabal learned that Quen had been left in a cage of wire and thorns, while the imperial

Master of the Hunt had been found, with his companions, trapped in thread cocoons. She took these reports to Berenene, who had been a difficult companion since they had left Dancruan.

"So the children have power," the empress snapped, tossing the papers to the floor. "We knew that. Do you know what the gossips will make of this? The wench spurned *two* of my favorites — never mind that Quen is no longer a favorite and he wasn't trying to marry her. That's what they'll say. Two! And they'll whisper that perhaps my favorites are not so devoted to the old woman as they pretend to be!"

"Imperial Majesty, *I* am old," replied Isha gently. "*You* are in your prime."

"I'm sure the Yanjingyi emperor will see it just that way!" retorted Berenene. "No, Isha. I cannot afford even the *appearance* of weakness. You of all people know that. When they get to the border, I want you to raise its defenses against them."

Isha gathered up the reports, trying to think of a tactful way to speak her thoughts. She could think of none. "Imperial Majesty, what if the borders fail?"

Berenene's eyes bulged. "*What?*"

"We must consider the possibility," Isha went on. "Two of these children bested Quen, who has spent six years defending Your Imperial Majesty with his power. He has been tested by great mages and succeeded, but a girl and a boy wrapped him up in a neat bundle. Lady Sandrilene did the same with *seven people*, two of them mages. Not great mages, but good ones. The possibility of failure must be considered."

"If you approach it with that attitude, you open the door to failure," snapped the empress.

Ishabal sighed. "All of our work in recent years has gone to the barriers in the southeast and the east, where our greatest enemies are. We have had neither the funds nor the mages to reinforce everything. I know that, given time and preparation, Quen and I could walk through the protection wall at Olart. We must ask ourselves if these three young people might now manage it as well. Majesty, *Quen could not break out of the cage Briar and Daja made without a mage's help*." Isha watched nervously as Berenene took a chair and sat in it. Calmly she continued: "You are angry because you fear you'll be seen as weak, Majesty, but it need not be so. All we need do is announce that your cousin and her friends are returning home. It is earlier than planned, to be sure, but stories can be spread that our court is far too sophisticated for them! There are still ways to make it seem as if they fled with their tails between their legs." She took a deep breath. "But if you raise the border against them, and they break through, that will be far worse than stories that say they fled our men. All of your neighbors will know you tried to keep them, and failed. You will have exposed a weakness."

"I do not believe the border will fail," Berenene said flatly, her mouth a hard, tight line.

Isha shrugged. "Nor do I, but I must examine possibilities and damage if you will not. The chance of failure *must be considered.* I beg you, let them go."

"I will not be defied." The refusal was a quick one, but she had not ordered Isha out of her sight. There was an opening in the empress's thinking.

Isha rushed through it. "Then let me go, alone, to do it," she said. "You remain here. If they fail to hold the wall against them, I shall bring them here to you. If I fail to hold the wall against them, you can say I am weary from travel and the wall needs work. It has gone neglected and now it will be seen to. No one will know this was in any way a matter in which you were involved. They will speculate, no doubt, but they will not prove."

Berenene looked down in thought at her perfectly cared for hands.

Isha pressed. "You have always said it is far better to appear innocent while others take the blame."

Berenene rubbed her temples. "You ask me to surrender my pride."

Isha bowed her head. "Only when it is a liability, Imperial Majesty."

"You are willing to take the blame if the border fails."

"If *this* traditionally safe border fails," corrected Isha. "If this seldom renewed border fails. If older, weary me fails against three powerful young things who just tied my best assistant in a knot."

Isha knew that remote look on Berenene's face as the empress smoothed her fingers over her sleeve. She was always glad to see it, because it meant that her mistress was turning a thousand thoughts over in her mind, seeing a multitude of outcomes and weighing them all. Few people glimpsed this cold calculation on the empress's beautiful features. She didn't want them to. It suited her that people thought of her as a passionate creature delighting in love and money. Few realized that Berenene cooled off far sooner than she let on, and that she did nothing that would not enhance her standing in the eyes of her people and the world.

Finally Berenene shook out her cuffs and got to her feet. "Very well, Isha. Do what you must. And I'm going to change. I've a mind to ride along the lake today."

Sandry refused to stay a second night in the Canyon Inn. *I don't trust them,* she told Daja and Briar. *If Shan had their help, I don't want to punish them. I know how hard it is to refuse a noble. But I don't want to stay here, either.*

I have potions. I could find out, offered Briar.

They've had enough magic, said Daja, who had watched the staff skitter around the caged Quen. *Let's just go. If you're feeling so energetic, grovel to Zhegorz some more.*

Briar winced. All three of them were doing some serious apologizing to Zhegorz. Sandry even invited him to ride beside her as they left the Canyon Inn. Strangely, the whole mess seemed to have calmed Zhegorz down. Even when they passed the next imperial fort, he kept warnings about palace matters to himself. He was learning to sift images and his words more.

Since they were only two riders, Ambros and Tris had an easier time on the road in some ways, despite Tris's weakness. When Tris felt she could stay in the saddle not another moment, she wove ropes of wind to bind her to it and her mare, and trapped two more pads of air to keep her upright. If she grew vexed at traffic, she sent winds ahead to drive those in the road to its sides until she and Ambros passed by. When those attending the horse fair did not respond to wind, she reddened and began to play with balls of lightning. The people scattered. She, Ambros, and Chime passed through the meeting of the highway and Deepdene Road far more quickly than had Sandry and her companions.

By then, Tris was able to sense Briar and Daja. Her strength returned with each day she rode, though her hips ached fiercely when she dismounted for the night. She said nothing about it. She also said nothing when Ambros paid for a private room for each of them at the inns when they halted. By the time they passed the fort beyond the Blendroad Inn, Tris had begun to ride part of the time at the trot. Briar, Daja, and Sandry were telling her that Zhegorz was in a bad state, babbling about walls of glass. Tris knew what he meant, just as her brother and sisters knew: There were magical walls ahead. Tris fidgeted when they rested the horses, and she slept badly, always wanting to get on the road at dawn. It was one thing to talk to her friends, another to shift power to them. She needed to be closer.

Ten days after they'd left Quen and Shan, Sandry, Briar, Daja, Gudruny, her children, and Zhegorz topped a rise in the Imperial Highway. Before them lay a great green plain dotted with villages, and a massive blue lake. The border fortress was on the far side of the gleaming water. To the east lay the smoky foothills of the Carakathy Mountains, where the empress was said to have a hunting lodge. According to Tris, Berenene and Ishabal Ladyhammer were there now.

"Out in the open," muttered Zhegorz, staring at that broad emerald expanse. "No place to hide from watchers, no place to hide from the wind."

"As long as my imperial cousin and her pawns do nothing but watch," retorted Sandry. "As long as they keep out of the way." She urged their company forward, down the slope to the plain.

It took them two days to cross it and skirt the lake. On the third day, Briar woke to find Zhegorz gone from his bed and his saddlebags missing. He was also missing from breakfast. "Now that's a worry," Briar told Sandry. "Zhegorz has lived hungry too long to miss any meals."

Gudruny's children searched the inn and its outbuildings, but there was no sign of their crazy man. They did find his saddlebags in the stable with his horse, but there was no trace of the man himself.

Sandry paced in the courtyard, working steadily more intricate cats' cradles in her fingers. "I don't want to leave him, and I don't like not knowing where he is," she complained. She had yet to give the order to saddle the horses or to hitch up Gudruny's cart. "I didn't know I'd need to put a leash on him. Who can scry among us?"

"Tris," chorused Briar and Daja. They looked at each other and grinned. That was when knowledge struck Briar like one of Tris's own lightning bolts.

"That's what she's been dancing around," he told his sisters. "That's why she took old Zhegorz aside. It's not just sounds she's hearing on the winds. She knows how to scry on them, too. She learned somehow."

"She didn't want you to know for silly reasons," Zhegorz said reasonably. He had walked in the gate to the inn's courtyard, his lean face glowing with sweat. "She said you'll think she's conceited if you knew she can do it."

All three young mages traded exasperated looks. "Have you ever known such an annoying girl?" demanded Sandry.

"But she couldn't do it before," Daja said. "She learned? While she was away? But people go mad, trying to see things on the wind! No offense," she told Zhegorz.

He shrugged. "I was born with it."

"Yell at Tris later," said Briar. "Yell at Zhegorz now. Where *were* you, Zhegorz? You had us all fretting."

"I went to see," Zhegorz said, wiping his face on his sleeve. "They look for *Clehame* Sandrilene and her escort, so I went to the border crossing to see who is looking. A white-haired mage who blazes like the sun waits on a platform by the arch. Three mages like stars and soldiers with the gold braid of the palace soldiers guard her on the platform." He held up one of his ear beads. "The white-haired mage will raise the border magic to stop you three. Only you three. She is in charge. She tells her guards that, and she tells the border guards that. She is to deal with you and only you, and all others may pass." Zhegorz rubbed the back of his neck. "She is not happy with her work. Why is she not happy?"

Daja shrugged. "Your guess is as good as ours. Was there anything else?"

Zhegorz reported the gossip of merchants headed south, and of merchants on the far side of the border who waited for the gates to open so they could head north. When she realized that he had told everything he knew of their situation, Sandry kissed his stubbled cheek. "Go eat a good breakfast," she told him affectionately. "And thank you." She watched him walk into the inn, then looked for Gudruny.

"Gudruny, would you come with me, please?" she asked. She led her maid over to the cart and opened one of the trunks. The first thing she pulled out of it was a heavy canvas tarp with shifting patterns on it. Underneath it were four hooded cloaks, two large and two small. "You and Zhegorz each get one, and the children each get one," she told the maid, handing the cloaks to her. "I thought we might need them. With these on, and the cart covered with the tarp, you won't look like the people who traveled with me. Tell them you're joining a merchant caravan in Leen, traveling south."

"*Clehame*, this is silly," protested Gudruny.

Sandry put her hand on the woman's arm. "It's going to be a mage fight at the border," she explained gently. "If you leave right away, you can pass through long before we get there. We'll meet you at Ratey's Inn on the other side, once we've . . . worked things out." When Gudruny opened her mouth to argue again, Sandry shook her head. "Get the little ones and Zhegorz safely out of this, please," she said firmly. "That's Ishabal Ladyhammer who waits for us, Gudruny. You have our purse with you. If we fail, choose what you will do. I'd *like* you to take Zhegorz to Winding Circle temple in Emelan. They'll be able to help him, and my great-uncle Vedris will look after you and the children. Or you can return to me in Namorn, if I can't escape. I can't choose for you, though I hope you'll regard my wishes."

Gudruny curtsied, a troubled look on her face. "I hope I'll see you on the other side of the border, *Clehame*," she murmured. "Then neither of us will have to choose."

Sandry patted Gudruny's arm, then went to see how

successful Briar had been in explaining their plan to Zhegorz.

"I can't," Zhegorz protested when Sandry found them. "Tris said I must watch and listen for you."

"And you have," Sandry told him. "While we slept, you did. Now I need you to safeguard Gudruny and the children. Please, Zhegorz."

He nodded, without meeting her eyes. Can I ask for anyone braver? she wondered. He's terrified, and yet he has spied on the might of the empire that's here for me. For us. Maybe it takes a coward more courage — not less — to do and not do things. Perhaps cowards understand the world so much better than brave folk.

Once Gudruny, Zhegorz, and the children had left with the cart, Sandry, Briar, and Daja settled into the common room to give them a couple of hours' head start. As Briar drew strength from his *shakkan* and Daja mended a piece of tack, Sandry asked the sergeant who commanded their guards to come see her. When he arrived, he did not look at all comfortable.

"Forgive me, *Clehame*," he said, "but word gets around. There's imperial mages waiting at the border. I hear they mean to stop you. What does that mean for my lads and me?"

Sandry smiled at him. "You were only supposed to bring me to the border," she told the man. "I would no more ask you to defy your empress than I would ask you to cook your own children. Please tell Cousin Ambros you guarded me well. And my thanks to you and your men." She drew out the pouch of coins she had kept for this moment. "To buy some . . . comforts . . . on your way home." She gave it to him with a wink.

The sergeant bowed and accepted the pouch. "You are always gracious, *Clehame*," he said. "We thank you and ask Qunoc's blessing on your journey home."

"You'd be better off asking Sythuthan's," Briar muttered.

The sergeant grinned at the suggestion that they should appeal to the notorious trickster god. "Your gods bless and hold you evermore, *Clehame* Sandrilene," he told Sandry. "We wish you and *Viymese* Daja and *Viynain* Briar a long life and much happiness."

Watching through the common room door as the Landreg men-at-arms rode away, Sandry felt a weight fall from her shoulders. "It's just us now," she murmured. "We don't have to be responsible for anyone else. What a relief."

20

The 11th day of Mead, 1043 K.F.
The Olart border crossing, the Imperial Highway South, Namorn to Ratey's Inn, Olart

Two hours before noon, the three young mages approached the border crossing. By then, all those who had bunched up to pass through at dawn had gone on their way. Gudruny and Zhegorz and the children had passed through hours before, disguised as a common family. Sandry, Daja, and Briar now rode with a few remaining packhorses since they had not wanted to let their mage kits go in the cart. Briar in particular did not trust Gudruny's rowdy son to not sit on his *shakkan*.

As they approached the great stone arch that marked the crossing, Sandry said abruptly, "Ishabal sad? Zhegorz said she's unhappy. Why on earth would she be unhappy? Could it be she doesn't want a fight?"

Briar shrugged. "That's a bit of a reach, don't you think? Maybe she just wasn't awake. Maybe she had mush for breakfast instead of bliny. That would depress *me*."

"Because your best love is your belly," Sandry told him, her voice dry. "Did they starve you in Gyongxe, too?"

His face turned somber. "They starved us all. Some they starved to death. I tell you, it was enough to put a fellow off emperors. Once they start thinking they're bigger than kings, they don't just ruin the lives of a couple dozen folk here and there. They ruin thousands of lives at a twitch."

Daja had been studying a miniature portrait of Rizu she carried in her belt purse. Hurriedly, she put it away. "It doesn't matter why Ishabal's unhappy," she said abruptly. "If she wants a fight with us or not. I heard plenty of stories about her in Kugisko, and from Rizu and her friends. They call Ishabal 'the imperial will.' What the empress wants, Ishabal gets done."

"Not this time," said Briar.

"People shouldn't always get what they want," Sandry replied grimly. "It's very bad for their character."

As the three approached the crossing, they could see the wooden platform built on the western side of the arch. There were the mages, just as Zhegorz had said. Their own suspicions were correct: The white-haired mage was Ishabal Ladyhammer. When they were about one hundred yards away, Ishabal sprinkled something on the platform. On the ground, a captain of the soldiers who manned the crossing stepped into the road. Twenty of his men trotted out to form a line at his back, leveling crossbows at the three.

"Halt!" cried the captain. "You will halt and submit yourselves for imperial inquiry!"

Briar lobbed a cloth-covered ball at the man. A mage who stood with Ishabal burned it from the air. He didn't see the cloth ball that Daja rolled forward until it stopped at the captain's feet. Once she had tossed it, she drew heat from the summer air, concentrating it in the crossbows. The metal fittings smoked, then got hot. The archers were disciplined; they fought to keep their grip on their weapons. Daja got cross, and dragged the heat from the stones around them into the metal of the bows and of the bowmen's armor. They shouted in pain and dropped their weapons.

Vines sprouted from the cloth ball at the captain's feet, slithering up and around his legs like snakes to hold him in place. He drew his sword and tried to hack at them, only to have the weapon suddenly grow hot in his hand. He dropped it. Daja summoned more heat to the men who faced her, running her fingers over the living metal on her hand as she tried to hold the line between too hot for comfort and hot enough to do permanent damage. The border guards yelped and shed belts, helms, swords, and daggers, any metal on their bodies as Daja called heat to it all.

"If you want a fight, have it with *us*," Briar called to Isha. "Leave these soldiers out of it. They'll get hurt."

He felt something like a shiver in his bones. It was a swell of power on the far side of the stone gate. With it rose plants, stones, even trees, all things that had been growing in the track where the spell anchors for the magical barrier had been set centuries before.

Sandry rode up to the gate and tried to go through. She met a force there like a solid, invisible wall. Her mount shied when it struck it, spooked by a barrier that it could not see. Sandry fought her mare to a stand, then dismounted. She walked up and found the barrier was every bit as solid as stone, for all that is was completely invisible. It was as if the air had gone hard.

She turned to look up at the people on the platform. "How does my cousin intend to keep me, *Viymese* Ladyhammer?" she demanded. "In a cage like this?" She struck the barrier with her fists. "Married off and locked up in some country estate, my name signed in blood and magic to a promise to be a good little sheep? Can you people *afford* to keep me long? All magic has limits. There is no way you can force me never to use my power again. You know power *must* be used, or it goes wrong. And when I have the chance to use my power . . . You *all* wear clothes. You *all* stitch things together." She tried to pinch some of the wall, to twirl it. If she could make thread of it, she could unravel the wall.

She could not even scratch it.

"You might well spend your life in a cage, if you will not sign a vow of obedience to the imperial throne," Ishabal said calmly. "You cannot be so foolish as to think the powers of the world might allow you to pursue your own selfish desires all your days. Wake up, children. It is time to learn to live in the real world. What the empire wants, the empire keeps."

Briar walked up next to Sandry, carrying his *shakkan* on one hip. "She doesn't know anything about us," he murmured in Sandry's ear. "Me and Daja wrapped up Quen like he was fish from the market. Her 'real world' is just more dead fish." He held out his hand.

Sandry hesitated, then put her hand in his. Daja dismounted and took her staff from its sling. With it in her grasp, she came over to join hands with Sandry.

They let their combined magics pull and tug at the barrier. Daja dragged more heat up from lava flowing far underground. Sandry borrowed part of it and a length of magical vine from Briar. Fixing the image of a drop spindle — like a top with a long stem and flat disk — in her mind's eye, she wrapped the heat-soaked magical vine around the spindle and twirled it back and forth like a handmade auger, trying to bore an opening through the wall. It made not a dent.

For an hour or more they struggled. They sought the top of the barrier and its roots, unable to crack it. Daja hammered. Briar spread himself as a vine, seeking even hair-thin cracks into which he could insert a tendril, as he had in Quen's glove spells. Sandry hunted for loose threads, with no luck.

"Are you quite finished?" called Ishabal from her platform. "I am impressed — most collapse long before this — but it changes nothing. Better mages than you have pitted themselves against our barriers and lost. You will not be permitted to leave the empire."

Briar glared up at Ishabal. "You think I'm scared of empires?" he yelled. "*Here's* what I think of empires!"

He drew on his *shakkan*, flinging that power at the wooden platform on which Isha and her companions stood. The mages who stood with Isha were there to guard against attacks on her. They were prepared for a mage to turn fire or wind against the platform. They were not prepared for the wooden boards to shift, and groan, and sprout branches. Whole new trees suddenly exploded from dead wood. The mages dropped to the ground, bruising themselves on knobby roots that dug into the earth around them. Sandry and Daja as well as Briar felt the *shakkan's* glee at creating so many new lives.

"Maul us all you like," cried Isha, staggering to her feet. "You will get not one whit closer to home! *This* is your home, and you will bend the knee to your new mistress!"

Why not name her? Daja wanted to know, exasperated. *Everyone knows who has commanded her to do this — why be so festering delicate with Berenene's name? The rude jokes told in the forges of the empire aren't so polite about keeping her name out of the conversation!*

Sandry wiped sweat from her cheeks with a handkerchief. *Normally I'd say it's because she wants to keep Berenene's name out of it if this fails, but it's not like we're succeeding.* She nibbled a lip in thought. *Unless it might still fail? What else can we do?*

Daja grabbed Sandry. "The thread! Our circle!"

Sandry reached into her neck pouch and produced the thread circle once more. "I don't know if it will work without Tris," she protested. "It's got some of our strength, but this is a nasty barrier."

I suppose it is, Tris said through their magic. *But while I may be a day's ride from you, I still can hold my part.*

Silver fire bloomed in the vague shape of a hand in the air. It wrapped itself around Tris's lump in the thread circle. Sandry grabbed hers. Daja did the same and smacked Briar on the back of the head. He whirled, then saw what they held.

"Keep growing," he muttered under his breath to the trees. Then he grabbed the knot that stood for him.

Sandry anchored herself in the thread with a feeling of stepping into her own skin. This was also her first leader thread, in part, the one on which she first spun wool. Over the years, she'd placed a great deal of strength in this symbol of the union between them. Now it was also a symbol of what had happened on this trip. At last they were one again. She still had them, and they still had her.

That never changed, Briar told her before he took the *shakkan*'s remaining magic and dove into a forest of roots underground, spreading out through the land to draw on some of the power of its plants and trees. He drew it from the algae on Lake Glaise, the forests on the mountains around it, and the vast plain of grass on which they stood. Brambles and pear trees fed him, as did wildflowers and ancient pines. With their green fire running through his veins he felt better than he had since the battles in Gyongxe. He blazed with it.

Daja sank into veins of metal ore below. She followed some to the mountains and others down through the dense part of the earth, until she found the immense hot soup in which they were born. The lava's heat bubbled through her, driving up to her body, seeking a way to break free into the world. She laughed at the strength of molten stone and metal, feeling it inhabit her skin, making her indifferent to the petty fire marshaled by Ishabal.

Tris swept up into the rapid winds high above the mountains, where birds couldn't even fly. She dove down to draw up the power in the movement of lava and the pressure of water channeled through cracks in the ground. Despite her physical distance from her sisters and brother, she saw them in her magical vision, their images carried to her by the warm air that raced from Daja's smoking body. They turned, the three of them, with Tris's insubstantial form just behind, and walked into the barrier.

Magic inside it, built up over centuries, flew at them. Daja and Tris burned it away. Briar and Sandry wove nets of green and thread magic that snared the lattices of power that made the barrier. Slowly they dragged at the nets, forcing the barrier open.

As they walked into the open air on the Olart side of the border, the magical barrier shattered for over a mile in each direction. It was gone, as if it had never existed.

"I feel like I just walked through a glacier," grumbled Daja, rubbing her arms. She bumped the palm that was not covered in metal and yelped. "*Now* what?"

"Good thing we didn't get frozen, if it was a glacier," Briar remarked with a shrug.

"Where's the circle?" Sandry wanted to know. "Did I lose it?" she asked, looking at the ground, then at the hand in which she'd held it. "Mila, what's this?"

There was a slight lump at the center of her palm, covered by shiny scar tissue. She pressed it and gasped at a sting of pain. Then the lump sank into her palm completely, leaving only the scar.

Briar also felt pain. He and Daja eyed the hands that had clasped the thread circle. Daja's creamy brown palm showed a scarred lump like Sandry's. When she tapped it, the lump also sank into her flesh, leaving only a round scar. Briar's had burned a circle among the plants that grew under his skin, but the lump itself was gone. The plants were blooming in extravagant reds, purples, and blues all around the newest scar. It had fitted itself right between the deep pockmarks where a protective briar had bitten into his hand years before.

Tris, miles away, watched as a tiny sun shone and faded where a lump sank into her palm. Instant warmth spread from it like wildfire, easing some of the aches in her newly healed bones. "Every time I think I understand magic, I learn that I don't understand anything at all," she murmured, and looked at Ambros with a broad smile. "I like that."

Sandry took a few steps back through the gate to look at Ishabal. "We did warn you it wouldn't go well." The empress's mage sat gray-faced at the foot of one of the trees that had sprouted from the platform. "What's the matter with you, *Viymese* Ladyhammer?" she asked.

"Backlash," muttered Ishabal. "I was still bound to the barrier from raising it. When you . . . did what you did . . . the barrier took much of me with it." She looked up, her dark eyes glinting. "I will recover," she said grimly. "In time."

Sandry saw only a feeble silver glow under the older woman's skin. "It's going to be a while before you make any magic, particularly any curses," she observed. "That can only be to the good. I only wish I were willing to incur the shadow on my heart I could get by arranging for you to practice tumbling on a long flight of stairs, like you did Tris. You really should be punished specially for that."

Ishabal met Sandry's cold eyes. "Go ahead," she said. "Do it."

"No," retorted Sandry. "I like to keep my magic clean."

Ishabal sighed. "So, young mage. What will you do now? Take the throne? You're powerful enough, you've shown us that." The mages and guards who had shared the platform with her had retreated up the road into Namorn, away from the three young people. Their faces were as ashen as Ishabal's.

Sandry took a step back. "Power? I'm going home." She looked at Daja and Briar. "*We're* going home. And Tris had better be coming home, too. We'll be back here tomorrow. If you don't let her through . . ."

"I cannot stop her," Ishabal said honestly. "In fact, I believe I shall contrive to be miles away."

You heard that? Sandry asked. *Do you want revenge?*

No, replied Tris. *It's too much time and bother.*

"Tris says she had best not see you," called Briar. He and Daja had heard the conversation. "She says if you cross her path again, she'll have to get strict with you." *No sense in letting her — letting* any *of them — relax,* he told the girls firmly. *We don't want them forgetting this day anytime soon.* He trotted back to collect his *shakkan* and the horses, and returned with them through the arch.

In the meantime, we are now out of Namorn and in Olart. Aloud, Daja said, "Here come Zhegorz and Gudruny. Isn't it past midday? I'm ravenous!"

Sandry mounted her horse. While Briar and Daja rode on, she stood before the gate, frowning.

Things undone, thought Sandry. What have I left undone? Tris is right: Revenge isn't worth the trouble.

She turned her mount away and followed the others. She came up in time to hear Briar say, "Now, if memory serves me, when we came here last, we ate at Ratey's. The Traders were having some fasting holy day. Ratey's had the best fish casserole I've ever eaten. I wonder if it's on the bill of fare today?"

Their reaction to the magic they had worked set in over midday. Suddenly it was all even Briar could do to keep putting food into his mouth. All three young mages soon apologized to the cook for not finishing their meal and retreated to the rooms that Gudruny had thought to hire for them.

When they woke, they had slept the night through noon. Ambros and Tris had arrived after sunset, though Tris, worn out by trying to catch up to them, woke as they were finishing their second midday. When she limped out to their garden table, Chime on her shoulder, Zhegorz rushed to help.

"I did as you said," he told her. "Did I tell you last night?" He helped her sit on the bench next to Briar. "They know you see things on the wind now. I don't think they believe you are conceited."

Tris sighed. "No doubt you're right. Zhegorz, thank you for helping them. I knew you could do it. Now, please, I would like to eat, if it's all right. I'm starved." She looked at

Briar's plate. "Is that cabbage rolls? I don't care if I never see another cabbage roll in my life."

A girl who had waited on them came to tell Tris the day's selections. Once Tris had chosen, a brief silence fell. It was broken by Zhegorz, who said, "I liked it."

Tris and the others turned to look at him. He had chosen a bench at the table next to theirs. From the tilt of his brass-lensed spectacles, he was staring into the distance. "Liked what, Zhegorz?" Sandry asked gently.

"Being attended to. Being heard. Being useful." There was wistfulness in his voice. "I was never any of those things before, only crazy. I don't want to go back to being the crazy man who hears all manner of things and sometimes sees them. I like being attended to." He got up and wandered off, his hands in his pockets.

"Zhegorz," called Tris. He stopped, though he didn't look back at her. "It *is* nice. I know," she told him.

He nodded, and left them alone in the garden.

Once he was gone, Ambros looked at Briar, Daja, and Sandry. "Your friend over there is very determined," he said with respect, nodding to Tris.

"Oh, all three girls are like that," Briar said carelessly. "Sometimes you need to hit them with a brick to get their attention. They get it from our mothers, I think."

"It occurs to me, that it's possible to be *too* determined," Daja remarked with a glance at Sandry. "Determined to the point of not doing right by people because we insist on only seeing things one way."

"Determined that what's good for you is just good," drawled Tris.

Sandry scowled, knowing they were trying to tell her something. "Hush. I have things on my mind," she informed them, picking at her berry pie.

"Not enough things," Briar grumbled.

The maid returned with Tris's food, while Ambros excused himself to buy supplies for his trip home in the morning. Sandry picked up her embroidery hoop after she finished her own meal. Something was still bothering her. Embroidery usually helped her to think clearly, but not that afternoon. She snipped off one color of thread. Chime was seated in her basket, holding up the next color she needed, when Sandry realized that Briar, Tris, and Daja were watching her.

"What?" she asked. Briar whistled silently. Tris drummed her fingers on the table. Daja leaned her head on her brass-mittened hand and watched Sandry calmly.

What?! Sandry demanded.

Maybe you *got what you wanted, but the empress still gets most of what* she *wants, too,* Daja told her. *She can tax Ambros until he calls for your help, and you'll have to come or leave him to flounder. And if you come, it will be this all over again —*

Except now they know what we can do, and they'll be ready, interrupted Briar. *They'll have more great mages waiting.*

And the women of Landreg will have no one to go to, added Tris. *Unless Ambros does that really expensive double registering thing you thought of, where he pays twice to enroll women as your subjects and his. He still won't have seats in the assembly to influence the other nobles to vote down new taxes. You saw how she treated him. She acts like he's a caretaker, and he is. The power's all yours.*

Sandry stared at them. "Stop nagging me," she snapped. "It's not your history. It's not *your* family."

No, said Daja. *But it's his. And frankly, he's put a great deal more work into it than you have.*

There's one way you can make sure Berenene doesn't win anything, Briar said. *After all you put us through there, you ought to be decent enough to admit it.*

It's mine, argued Sandry, though the remark felt watery and overused to her.

How much more rich than disgusting rich do you want to be? asked Briar.

Sometimes you owe your people a little less pride and a little more respect, Daja added.

"I refuse to listen!" cried Sandry. She tossed her embroidery into the basket, forgetting that Chime was in it. Her exit ruined by the dragon's unhappy scratching noises, she uncovered Chime and set her on the table. "I'm going for a walk!" She marched out of the inn, accompanied only by her own uncomfortable thoughts. She returned while their entire group was at supper in the common room, and ate alone in the room where she slept with Gudruny and the children. When they came up to bed, Sandry hired a private room where she could sew — and think — alone.

Very late that night, Briar, Tris, and Daja were jolted out of slumber by a silent call from Sandry. *Don't let Ambros leave in the morning,* she ordered. *Satisfied?* She did not wait to hear their reply, but cut them off and went to sleep.

Keeping Ambros there in the morning was a chore. He was determined to go. He might have actually left, had his horse not lost a shoe. Getting a farrier who was not already busy with a week's worth of other such chores to replace the shoe lasted well past midday, particularly since Ambros stumbled over Briar, Tris, Daja, Zhegorz, or Gudruny at every turn. The one person he didn't trip over was Sandry. She was strangely absent.

Once the horse was shod, it was so late in the day that Ambros gave up leaving until morning. He settled down to a game of draughts with Daja. They were nearly done when Sandry returned. With her she brought a trembling woman in the gray gown of an advocate.

"Cousin, may I speak with you?" asked Sandry. She indicated one of the inn's private chambers.

Briar, Tris, and Daja waited in the common room. They were content to wait in silence: Tris had a book, Daja some work for the farrier who had seen to Ambros's horse, Briar the potted herbs from the inn's kitchen. It was nearly suppertime when the door to the private room opened and the advocate lurched out.

"I've never heard of the like!" she babbled as the hostler fetched her horse. "Never. A, a count, just like that. Like . . . that!" She tried to snap her fingers but failed, due to her shaking. "Has she always been mad?" she asked Briar.

"No, usually she's sane enough," Briar said, grinning as he jammed his hands in his pockets. "Every now and then, though, she does the right thing."

"You're as mad as she is!" exclaimed the advocate. She ran out into the inn yard.

Ambros and Sandry emerged from the private room. Ambros looked overwhelmed. Sandry glared at her friends. "Are you happy now?" she demanded. "Meet *Cleham* fer Landreg, sole heir to the Landreg title and lands."

All three of the young mages rose. Briar and Daja bowed to Ambros; Tris curtsied. After a moment, Sandry curtsied as well.

"I never expected . . . ," Ambros began to say. His voice trailed off in confusion.

"That actually made it easier, that you didn't," admitted Sandry. "And they're right. I just had to, oh, catch my breath." She smiled. "And now the rest of us can go home. Back to Summersea, and back to Winding Circle."

Zhegorz cleared his throat. When they all looked at him, he said, "Do you know, *Viymese* Daja tells me it never snows in Emelan. Never. It seems unnatural to me. And they have no beet soup, or bacon and millet soup. I'm quite fond of that. Please understand, I'm certain that Winding Circle is a splendid place."

"Well, it produced us," Briar said with a grin. "Zhegorz, it's all right. Go ahead. Whatever it is, you can tell us."

Zhegorz smiled shyly. "I know, I know. Except that I want to tell *him*." He pointed a bony finger at Ambros, who blinked in confusion.

"Me? You hardly know me," he said. "I mean, we've seen each other, but . . ."

"I know you're a good man," Zhegorz said firmly. "A good *Namornese* man." He looked at Briar, at Daja, and at Tris. "Don't you think a *Cleham* who is not a favorite of Her Imperial Majesty could use someone in his service who can hear conversations on the winds? Who can see things on the winds?" He looked at Ambros. "I get better every day. I breathe, and I sort through what I hear and see. I practice every day. I will always be a little shaky. But I can be useful." He looked at the mages.

Briar nodded. "He could be useful, Ambros."

"He's wobbly, but I would trust him," said Daja.

"As would I," confirmed Sandry.

Tris glared at Ambros. "You'd be a fool not to take his service. Just treat him with kindness" — Briar snorted, and she ignored him — "treat him with kindness, and he'll help you navigate that snakepit Her Imperial Majesty calls a court," Tris continued.

Ambros looked at Zhegorz and took a deep breath. "Then we'll discuss salary and where you'll be living, your duties and so on, on the way home," he said. "Welcome to my household, Zhegorz."

Ambros was quiet through dinner. He picked at his food, which was very good. Briar took pity on the man and helped himself to bits when it was plain Ambros wouldn't eat it all. Even the sight of Chime discovering she did not like mushrooms failed to engage Ambros's quiet sense of humor. Finally, as the dishes were removed by wide-eyed servants — the advocate had told the hostlers what she had come there to do, and the hostlers had spread the word — Gudruny asked, "My lord *Cleham*, what occupies your thoughts? Repairs that you can now order done?"

Ambros looked at her. His face lit with a smile that he shared with them all, one that turned his eyes to pale blue diamonds. "Actually," he said, his voice cracking slightly, "I believe I will confer with my fellow members of the Noble Assembly. It is time, and past, that the forced marriage of unprotected women is banned in Namorn."

That night, Sandry lay awake, listening to Gudruny's soft breathing, her son's muffled snorts, and her daughter's occasional mutter. Others might find the company, and the close quarters, annoying, but she liked it. Here were three lives she had wrested from Namorn and that disgusting custom. And she had come to like Gudruny's steadiness and common sense. At first she'd meant to find Gudruny some other post when she got home, but not any longer. Unless Gudruny wanted to leave her service, Sandry would keep her as her maid. She liked having Gudruny — and the children — around.

Listening to them, she felt a tug in her magic, in a part of her that had not been active in far too long. She followed that magical tie and found herself emerging into the direct sunlight of a summer afternoon at Winding Circle. She stood on a familiar straw-thatched roof. It gave off the rich scent of sun-bleached hay as she sat down on it. When she looked around she saw Tris. Unlike their last time on the roof, this was not the child Tris, but Tris the adult, who wore her many braids tucked into a silk net. She lay flat on the straw close by, hands clasped behind her neck, staring dreamily at the clouds that moved overhead. Briar straddled the peak of the roof, a piece of straw sticking from his mouth. Daja, too, straddled the roof, leaning back against the stone chimney of Discipline cottage.

"How did you do this — create this so it actually feels real?" asked Sandry, delighted. "I can smell, I can hear . . . which of you did it?" Below, she could see Rosethorn's garden in full summer extravagance. Around them spread the temple. The spiral road was empty: Very few people cared to venture along its unshaded length during the postmidday rest period during the blast of Mead and Wort Moons. Yet the long hand on the Hub clock moved as it ticked off the minutes. The wind brushed Sandry's face as it carried the scents of lavender and herbs into her nostrils.

"I did," Briar admitted. "I was locked up for a while in Gyongxe. It was either go mad imagining what might happen to me, or . . . retreat, inside me. I made it, inside my power." He lay back on the peak, balancing easily. "After that — I did things I'm not proud of when I got out. It was a bloody mess. Thousands died who should have lived. I don't know why I'm here, and they aren't. I didn't want any of you knowing that. I didn't want you knowing I thought I should be dead. That's why I shut you out."

Silence stretched. It was all he could tell them for now.

"Mine is just silly," admitted Tris. "So many of the mages I met with Niko took it so personally that I learned to scry the winds that I forgot who you all were. Niko acted like it was something you had to expect — that when you learn a strange kind of magic, one that so many fail at, you have to expect jealousy. I don't want people to be jealous, I don't want them to be *anything.* I was afraid to find out you'd be like them." She hung her head. "I'm just too gaudy. That's why I want to go to Lightsbridge. So I can just do what I want and people won't stare at me."

Daja and Sandry exchanged shrugs, as if to say, That's Tris for you.

"I made something that helped Ben Ladradun kill a lot of people," Daja told them somberly. "So many. I thought catching him and seeing him get an arsonist's sentence would fix it in my heart, make it right, but it never did. I still liked him. So I helped kill him fast, so he wouldn't be in pain. I didn't want you to know something of mine — something of ours, because it was living metal, and we were all part of that — caused so many deaths. I can't forgive myself, some days. I didn't think you could." She closed her eyes, her full mouth quivering.

Sandry looked down at her knees. She wore pink, as she had that same day in the advocate's office. "I tore three people to pieces to save the life of my student," she said flatly. She heard Tris draw a deep breath. "Did you think I would be safe at home? They were murderers, they were being eaten alive by unmagic, with little humanity left in them. There was no other way, and yet." She put her face on her knees.

"So now we know the things we hid from each other," Tris said drily after a while. "Does it change anything?"

"How could it?" Briar wanted to know. "Fighting off those pirates didn't make us hate each other. We knew why we did it. Not being able to forgive *ourselves* isn't the same as understanding each other. We're a lot easier on each other than we are on ourselves. As for *you*, Coppercurls, you've always been fooling around with the weird magics."

"That's just you, Tris," said Daja.

Sandry lifted her head. "I wouldn't be you for a thousand gold majas, Tris. I see the way people twitch around you. But that doesn't change how *I* feel about you."

Tris looked at her. "So we're a circle again."

"Suits me," Briar said. "I never knew how much I missed it till we came back."

"Till we remade us," said Daja. "Till Berenene reforged us."

"You'll forgive me if I don't thank her," Sandry told them as she lay back on the thatch. "She may be related to me by blood, but I much prefer the family I chose."

"Briar, can we come back here?" Daja asked. "Will this be here?"

"I made it for us," he replied, surprised she hadn't realized it. Here, in this place, they could feel what he felt. "All right, I made it for me first, but it was us. It is us."

It's always us, the four said.

Cast List

Ambros fer Landreg	Saghad, steward of Sandry's lands as well as of his own, dependable, family man, married to Ealaga
Amiliane fa Landreg	Sandry's mother and Namornese heiress, deceased
Bancanor	goldsmith family in Kugisko, friends of Daja's and Frostpine's, their twin daughters are Daja's first students
Bennat Ladradun	widower, fire expert, deceased (COLD FIRE)
Berenene dor Ocmore	Sandry's cousin, empress of Namorn
Briar Moss	former thief and street rat from Sotat, Sandry's foster brother, plant mage, maker of medicines, gardener, expert in *shakkans* (miniature trees), Evvy's teacher
Caidlene fa Sarajane	pert, dark-eyed, flirtatious lady-in-waiting
Chime	living glass dragon made by Kethlun Warder (SHATTERGLASS), living with Tris

Comas	Lark's new weaving student, temple novice, lives in attic at Discipline cottage
Crane	Dedicate Initiate, First Dedicate of the Air Temple at Winding Circle, sometimes teacher of the four
Daja Kisubo	former Trader, Sandry's foster-sister and Frostpine's student in metal shaping magic; carries a Trader staff and is marked by a piece of living brass that is molded between the fingers and over the palm and back of one hand
Dymytur fer Holm	bidis, border bandit and would-be kidnapper
Ealaga fa Landreg	Ambros's good-humored wife
Erdogun fer Baigh	Duke Vedris of Emelan's seneschal
Evvy	a street girl who was Briar's student, a stone mage
Finlach fer Hurich	Fin, a handsome noble who is one of Berenene's choices as a suitor for Sandry's hand
Franzen fer Toren	Vedris of Emelan's third son and present heir
Frostpine	Dedicate Initiate at Winding Circle, great mage, specializing in metal and fire magic, Daja's mentor.

Glaki	orphan, academic mage, formerly Tris's student, now Lark's at Discipline cottage
Gospard	Vedris's middle son, admiral of Emelanese navy
Gudruny Iarun	wife of Halmar and mother of his children, living on the Landreg estates
Gurkoy	family who lost everything for crossing the empress
Halmar Iarun	Gudruny's husband, the miller
Holab	grain broker on the Landreg estates
Ishabal Ladyhammer	Berenene's archmage, specialist in curses, a great mage
Jakuben fer Pennun	saghad, one of Berenene's favorite young noblemen, chosen by her to court Sandry
Kethlun Warder	Tris's student, the one who made Chime (SHATTERGLASS)
Lark	Dedicate Initiate of Winding Circle, specializing in magic through spinning and weaving, a great mage, Sandry's mentor, foster mother to the four
Little Bear	once a puppy the four rescued, the dog traveled with Tris and Niko, now lives with Glaki at Winding Circle

Luvo	strange friend of Evvy's
Maedryan dor Ocmore	princess, Berenene's daughter and heir, living with her foster family in secrecy
Maghen	village girl on Landreg estates
Mattin fer Toren	Sandry's father and Vedris's nephew, deceased
Niklaren Goldeye	Niko, a great mage whose power is with all kinds of magic that involve sight, he found Daja, Briar, and Sandry; he is Tris's mentor
Notalos fer Hurich	Finlach's uncle and head of Namorn Mages' Society
Olfeon	Master of the Imperial Armory
Pasco Acalon	young dancemage who is Sandry's first student (MAGIC STEPS)
Pershan fer Roth	Shan, handsome, young and ambitious nobleman who is one of the empress's favorites
Quenaill Shieldsman	great mage specializing in protective magics, Ishabal's assistant and one of the empress's favorites
Rizuka fa Dalach	young and charming, Berenene's Mistress of Wardrobe

Rosethorn — Dedicate Initiate at Winding Circle, specializing in plant and garden magic, a great mage, Briar's mentor and foster mother to the four

Sandrilene fa Toren — Sandry, clehame and heiress to the Landreg holdings in Namorn, foster sister to Briar, Daja, and Tris, her magic is with thread, spinning and weaving; she is a favorite with her great-uncle Vedris

Third Caravan Saralan — Trader land caravan

Trisana Chandler — Tris, an irritable, shy weather mage and bookworm trying to master the new skill of seeing images carried on the wind, Sandry's foster-sister and Niko's student

Vedris IV — Sandry's great-uncle, ruling Duke of Emelan, a powerful and subtle man who has taken the four under his wing while they lived in Emelan; it's rumored he may change his will and make Sandry his heir instead of his third son Franzen

Vetiver — head weaver and First Dedicate of the Earth temple at Winding Circle (Lark and Rosethorn are Earth dedicates)

Voskajo	name of the head of the Smith's Guild in Namorn, Daja's and Frostpine's friend
Wenoura	head cook at Landreg House in Dancruan
Yeskoy fer Haugh	saghad of an impoverished noble house on the border of the Landreg estates, half-bandit
Zhegorz Fiavrus	a crazy man who met Daja in COLD FIRE when she rescued him from a burning hospital

Glossary

argib	basic coinage of the empire, silver argib is the basic regular coin of Namorn, copper argib basic change coin
amdain	"fool" or "fools" in Namornese
Asaia	Air goddess of the Living Circle, goddess of birds and messengers
Bag	Briar's slang, contraction for Moneybag, or rich person
belbun	term Briar learned in Chammur for rat
bidis, bidisa	literally "dagger" — first rank noble, baron, baroness
bleater	Briar's slang for someone stupid
bleatin', bleating	Briar's slang for crying, complaining
Capchen	Tris's native country, west of Emelan
Chammur	city in east Sotat, where Briar met Evvy
cleham, clehame	literally "sword" — third rank noble, count, countess
clehamat	a count's estate